The Song of Daniel

Other Books by Philip Lee Williams

The Heart of a Distant Forest
All the Western Stars
Slow Dance in Autumn

For Mike —
My best always!
Philip Lee Williams

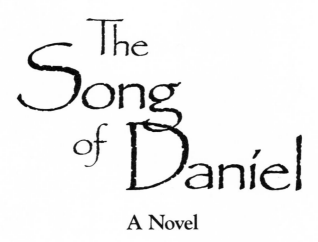

The Song of Daniel

A Novel

Philip Lee Williams

PEACHTREE PUBLISHERS
ATLANTA • MEMPHIS

Published by
Peachtree Publishers, Ltd.
494 Armour Circle, NE
Atlanta, Georgia 30324

Poem XLIV on page 282 from *The Marble Faun and A Green Bough* by William Faulkner.
Reprinted with permission from Random House. Copyright © 1933; renewed 1961 by William
Faulkner.

Manufactured in the United States of America

10 9 8 7 6 5 4 3 2 1

Cover by Studio Seven

Interior design by Patricia Joe; Interior illustrations by Jacelen Pete

Cover painting "Waterlilies" by Claude Monet. Reproduced with permission from The
Cleveland Museum of Art, John L. Severance Fund.

Library of Congress Catalog Card Number 88-61457

Library of Congress Cataloging-in-Publication Data

Williams, Philip Lee.
    The song of Daniel : a novel / Philip Lee Williams.
      p.   cm.
    ISBN 0-934601-75-5 : $17.95
    I. Title.
    PS3573.I45535S66   1989   89-3055
    813'.54—dc19   CIP

ISBN 0-934601-75-5

For Linda, with love

Author's Note

Certain places in this work of fiction actually do exist in Athens, Ga., where the book is set. Oconee Hill Cemetery is a real place, for example, as are some of the businesses and landmarks mentioned in the town. But characters I have created to work at the cemetery and in the University of Georgia Department of English are completely of my own invention and are not based on anyone, living or dead. I have also completely invented businesses and slightly altered a few geographic details in the town for my purposes. To anyone these liberties offend, my sincere apologies.

Little Lamb, who made thee?
Dost thou know who made thee?
Gave thee life, and bid thee feed,
By the stream and o'er the mead;
Gave thee clothing of delight,
Softest clothing, wooly, bright;
Gave thee such a tender voice,
Making all the vales rejoice?
Little Lamb who made thee?
Dost thou know who made thee?

Little Lamb, I'll tell thee,
Little Lamb, I'll tell thee;
He is called by thy name,
For he calls himself a Lamb,
He is meek, and he is mild;
He became a little child.
I a child, and thou a lamb,
We are called by his name.
Little Lamb, God bless thee!
Little Lamb, God bless thee!

— WILLIAM BLAKE

ONE

THE STONES LAY BEFORE HIM, dappled in the early morning sunfall, stretching far away down the slope and across the river. The aroma of gardenias, rich and pungent, drifted from the overgrown graves along the hill, and Daniel Mitchell knelt beneath a cool oak and pulled the vines back from a marker that had a single word: BABY. Once each week, Daniel would clean Baby's stone, but now that summer had come to Athens, honeysuckle embraced the grave too quickly for his clumsy hands.

"Good morning, Baby," Daniel said out loud. Whose baby could this have been, he wondered, and what had carried it into the waiting arms of God, and when? A hundred years before? Daniel tried to think of Baby as still beautiful in the deep, mossy earth, flowing in a white gown, peaceful as sleep. "It is a beautiful morning up here, Baby," he said.

Daniel's thick-soled shoes were worn, his clothes clean but shabby. All day, visitors would see him lumbering, heavy-footed, around the cemetery—mowing, pulling vines, revealing long-obscured names, some buried nearly two hundred years. If he stood here at the crest of Oconee Hill, he could see the university football stadium hulking to the west and hear the busy traffic of East Campus Road. The street was quieter now that summer had come. Daniel was twenty-eight, and this was the only job he had ever had, having grown up in Greenvale, a home for children near Augusta. He had done little more than this, than pulling weeds.

The cemetery was always threatening to close in upon itself, particularly in the old part where families no longer came to place flowers. The Oconee River, a turgid, muddy swell of water, bisected the cemetery, with the newer graves on the east, the older ones west nearer the campus. Daniel did not enjoy working in the newer section as much, because there were few trees and the stones seemed all alike. It had been a week now since he had checked on Baby, and already the honeysuckle was enfolding the lichen-coated marble in its tendrils.

Daniel was usually alone unless Frank Sutton, the sexton, saw him and waved from the house that squatted near the iron-gate entrance to Oconee Hill. Frank was fond of Daniel and often brought him water in a plastic milk jug, cold water from his refrigerator. Daniel tried hard to please Frank, but often when Frank came out to find his friend, Daniel would be sitting in the Gerdine-Cobb plot near the river, staring at the headless statue of a woman holding a lamb. Frank remembered one time he found Daniel lying there in a slow rain.

"Daniel, you should come inside," Frank said. Daniel was not startled; in fact, Frank could rarely remember anything startling Daniel.

"Was she pretty?" Daniel had asked.

Frank looked at the statue that cradled the lamb. "Her head's been gone for years," he said softly. "Long before I got here, Daniel."

"She was so pretty," Daniel said. "I wish I could tell her she was so pretty." He began to cry then, and Frank had helped him up and taken him through the steady rain back to the white frame house.

Frank was disturbed that Daniel seemed to know all the people lying beneath the soil of Oconee Hill, which got its name from the jutting mound of earth just east of Sanford Stadium where the cemetery had been started in the early 1800s. Once, when Frank was cleaning old flowers from graves in the new section, Daniel had suddenly appeared from behind him and said, "Henry May Long. THE STEPS OF A GOOD MAN ARE ORDAINED BY THE LORD." Frank knew the grave, which was back across the river, and at first such things unnerved him, but he slowly grew accustomed to Daniel's belief that everyone in Oconee Hill was alive and awaited his visits like lonely old people in a nursing home.

Now, Daniel finished breaking the honeysuckle from Baby's grave and rocked back on his heels. Down the sharp slope he saw a woman walking quietly among the headstones. He brushed the dark blond hair from his brown eyes and wondered if she were the same lady who had been coming here each day for a week now. Everyone came to Oconee Hill: mourners, lovers, students who wanted a peaceful place to cram for finals, riotous fraternity boys hunting ghosts. Daniel Mitchell did not believe in ghosts because to him everyone in the cemetery merely slept. The woman held a bouquet of day lilies in her hand and sometimes stopped, knelt and placed one gently in front of a grave. Yes, he thought, it is the same woman. She had long brown hair that draped, shining, over her shoulders, and eyes the color of a winter sky. The day before, he had stood nearby beneath an ancient cedar and watched her place a day lily on the grave of Howell B. Cobb, FIRST ATHENS BOY GIVING LIFE IN THE WORLD WAR. To Daniel, she seemed very sad. He watched as she kept walking around the hill and out of sight, and then he moved to the grave of Delphina Almeda Brown.

"SHE OPENETH HER MOUTH WITH WISDOM AND IN HER TONGUE IS THE LAW OF KINDNESS," Daniel said. He could read a little, and when Frank was around, he would ask him to sound the words he did not know. Daniel knelt and began to pull weeds out with his heavily gloved hands, but as he pulled, he could not stop thinking of the woman. So he stood and walked back across the crest of the hill, past the grave of Governor Wilson Lumpkin, and saw her, sitting on

3

a flat stone, her face buried in her hands.

Her brief sobs echoed past the song of a mockingbird that thrust from the pinnacle of a live oak, down the slope and over the regiments of the dead. Don't cry! Daniel wanted to say, even though he was always bursting into tears himself for no reason: a banking hawk, the smell of roses, which reminded him of Greenvale, the rain on the roof of his trailer, the sight of a boy's eyes so alone in the huddle around a grave. These were not reasons to cry, he tried to reason, but he could not stop the tears sometimes, and afterwards he always felt better, cleansed like the earth after rain. Daniel watched the woman, saw that she had smoothed her sundress under her hips as she sat on the flat stone, saw again that she was slender and that her hair seemed to gather all the light filtering through the trees.

Daniel smelled gardenias. He felt the warm wind stirring the dark green leaves high in the oaks, tasted the aroma of newly mowed grass that Frank had cut just after sunrise. Daniel inhaled the morning. He stood silently, leaning against the tree until the woman lifted her head and turned slightly back toward him. He felt sudden fear, and his shyness made him stumble back over the grave of Governor Wilson Lumpkin, back across the hill toward the stadium, back to the grave of Young B. Harris and its marble angel, the one holding an anchor and a cross. He looked up at the inscription: TRUSTING ALONE IN THE MERCY, THROUGH THE ATONING BLOOD OF JESUS CHRIST. He was breathing heavily, but when he caught a glimpse of the woman's light blue cotton dress, he crept safely toward her and then stopped and watched as she walked down the hill toward the old horse-watering trough, climbed in a small gray car and wheeled away.

He spent the rest of the day pulling honeysuckle not far from the grave of C.D. Barrett.

"June 13, 1852 to June 10, 1884," Daniel read slowly. "IN THE SILENT TOMB, REST FOR THE SHADOW AND THE GLOOM OF DEATH IS PASSED." Late that afternoon, he thought of the word "gloom" as he walked through the iron gates of Oconee Hill and headed along East Campus Road toward home. What did it mean? He waved at students as they passed in their shiny open cars. Although he could never remember the word for a car without a roof, he always liked it when one passed by him. The students were all so happy, laughing and even shouting, so he waved at them; sometimes, they waved back. Just as often they ignored the familiar sight lumbering along the road in his thick-soled black shoes.

Daniel turned right on Baldwin Street and walked under a railway bridge and then passed O'Malley's, a busy club, popular with students, which had an appealing deck cantilevered out over the edge of the river bank. Daniel could see it from the road, but he had never been there. He had not been to any restaurant during the three years he had lived in Athens. Each morning, he made his lunch and slid it into a brown paper bag to bring with him to work.

Daniel ate with his friends at Oconee Hill. He would talk to them beneath the soil as he ate, which led to several complaints from visitors who found him alone babbling as he stuffed a sandwich of thick bologna into his mouth. Frank sometimes wondered why Daniel did not eat more. He was thin, and not much taller than five-nine. In the afternoon, Daniel could only think about his small brown dog that stayed chained to the edge of his trailer. He had gotten the dog from two students at the end of school the year before. They had seen Daniel in the cemetery and, on a whim, asked if he wanted their dog since they were heading home for the summer.

"What is his name?" Daniel had asked.

"Aristotle," laughed the girl. So Daniel took the dog and, not understanding the name, called him Toggle. He had saved six dollars and bought Toggle a Cabbage Patch Kids swimming pool and kept it filled with cool water. Every evening, after supper, Daniel and Toggle would go for a walk.

Daniel passed O'Malley's and came to the Lexington Road and crossed the river on the sidewalk of an old bridge that pulled east and west Athens together. He walked past the Salvation Army Thrift Store and up Oconee Street, past the rows of old frame houses, until he came to the sign that seemed wonderful to him:

5

Oconee-By-The-River. He loved to tell people he lived in Oconee-By-The-River, not knowing it was the crudest kind of trailer park, with no grass and blowing clusters of litter everywhere.

A gravel road cut through the middle of the park, and over here was Bud Holt's place, an unpleasant plumber who lived alone. There, across the road was Daisy Saye, a widow lady who was nice to Daniel. Mike and Pam Gassner and their baby, Scottie, lived next to Daisy Saye. Somebody was always screaming or crying there, so Daniel stayed away from their place. Next to Daniel's was the trailer of two college students that he liked but who rarely said much to him. He knew the girl was Kelley and the boy was Rob, and some days they loved each other, and some days they sat on the front steps and stared down the hill toward the next level of the park. There were three levels in all, and Daniel was on the top level. Right across the road from Daniel lived Randi Ambrose, a young woman about his age who wore leather pants and sometimes had green hair.

Toggle began to bark, leaping in and out of his pool in delight as soon as he saw Daniel. Daniel called his name and clapped; when Daniel smiled, his face relaxed. When he got to Toggle, he released the chain from the dog's collar, and Toggle bounded up onto Daniel's legs, tail wagging, tongue out.

"Look at you," said Daniel. A door opened across the rough street, and Randi Ambrose came out, a cigarette dangling from her lips. Her makeup was heavy and purple around the eyes. She went to the New Music clubs early and stayed out late. Her hair was slightly pink this time and shot out of her head in thick spikes.

"Hi, Randi!"

She looked over at Daniel and nodded as she locked her door, her eyes squinting from the trailing smoke. "Daniel," she said around the cigarette. "How's it going?"

"You should not smoke, Randi," he said.

She came down the sagging wooden steps and stood in front of her old VW bug. "I know," she said harshly. "But I don't need you reminding me. Okay?" She seemed exotic to Daniel.

"Okey dokey," nodded Daniel. He barely heard her start the

car as he took from his pocket a single key attached to a rabbit's foot and unlocked his door. Inside, the trailer was neatly arranged, a sofa on one wall, a chair on another.

Daniel whistled as Toggle leaped onto the sofa and put his head between his paws, tail thumping the weak springs. Daniel loved the smells of his trailer, something reminiscent of cooked food and gas from the stove's pilot light. He loved the way sunlight filled the small rooms late in the afternoon. The first time he'd seen the room glowing with light, he stuck his tongue out, sure he could taste the rich beams. He did not have any books, but Daisy Saye often gave him magazines, and the coffee table was neatly arranged with copies of *Ladies' Home Journal* and *Redbook*. He never read them, but their stacked symmetry cheered him, made him feel that this was a home.

First, he would eat. Daniel turned on the radio next to the sink and listened to country music. Then he opened a can of pork and beans and dumped it into a dented sauce pan. He knelt and turned the burner on, loving the sight and smell of the burner leaping to life. He set the pan on the burner to warm, and soon the aroma began to fill the trailer. Next, he took two thick slices of bologna from the refrigerator and set them on the counter. Then he got a can of Crisco from the cabinet, put a small lump in a frying pan and watched it skate across the surface as the heat went up. When it was all melted he put the bologna in the pan and cut each piece on the side so it would cook flat. The bologna sizzled and popped, and Daniel loved the smell.

He took a third piece of bologna and carried it to Toggle, who was still lying on the couch. Daniel knelt and spoke softly to the dog and then gave it the meat. Then he got two slices of bread from the loaf, spread mustard on both sides and poured himself a glass of iced tea. They had taught him to prepare his own food at Greenvale. Each time he cooked, he thought of the people back there and how he was now out on his own with his own home. He turned the gas off and took the food to a table squeezed into the small alcove near the kitchen and he sat down to eat.

A window spread sunlight over the table. His eyes were clear as he looked out at the warm breeze playing among the pecan trees that lined the side of the road where Randi Ambrose lived. He stared at the trailer next to Randi's where Joe Dell and Irene Bailey lived, a black couple that often checked on him. You're my best friend, Daniel always said to Joe Dell, but lately, something had been wrong, and they did not come over very much. What could it be? Daniel thought of Joe Dell sitting in his house; perhaps he was crying or maybe Irene was sick and Joe Dell did not want him to know. He thought of Irene lying in bed shivering with fever, and he began to cry, and tears ran down his face. He stood, and his chair fell behind him as he stumbled for the door, with Toggle at his heels. He jerked open the door and lumbered across the street, blinded with tears, and knocked on Irene and Joe Dell's door.

Irene opened the door, and Daniel felt the blast of air conditioning. She was about fifty and heavy-set, and her face was kind and pleasant.

"Daniel?" she said. "Lord have mercy! Joe Dell!" She brought him into the trailer, and Daniel tried to stop crying and shaking as Joe Dell, an enormously fat man, came groggily from the bedroom with his pants unbuckled, barefooted. He worked nights at the DuPont Company as a janitor and was resting after supper before he went to work.

"Son, what's wrong with you?" asked Joe Dell over the din of a game show on TV. "You all right?"

Joe Dell brought Daniel to their sofa. Daniel looked around the small room, felt the air conditioner and smelled the lingering odor of turnip greens and fried fatback. Irene spoke his name and wiped his tears with a fresh Kleenex.

"Daniel, talk to Irene," she said. His tears slowly eased and his chest ceased to heave.

"I got it in my head you were sick," said Daniel. "I did not see you outside."

"Honey, we got this old air conditioner from my brother," Irene said, still wiping Daniel's face. "We been inside staying cool, and we didn't come see you. I'm so sorry. We fine, Daniel, just fine."

"My goodness," said Joe Dell. He looked at Irene and in that moment they exchanged something of pity and love, of fear that the man on their sofa was not like other men, that in many ways he was no different from the children who spent the summer trapping lightning bugs in Oconee-By-The-River.

"Well, my supper is waiting for me," Daniel said, sniffing. "I am sorry that I was scared for you."

"It's all right, Honey," said Irene, and she took his hand and squeezed it briefly.

When he got back home, Daniel tried to think about what had made him feel so sad. He sat at the table with Toggle thumping at his feet and ate the sandwich. He loved the tang of the mustard and the smell of the still-warm beans. Nothing came into his mind, and soon he was thinking of the walk that he and Toggle always took after supper.

They always went the same way. At a small house around the corner, there was a rose arbor. Everything around that house smelled of rose petals. At Greenvale, all the boys and girls wore roses on Mother's Day, a white one if their mother were dead, red if they were still alive.

Daniel was special and wore yellow because they did not know if his mother was still alive. The smell of roses always made Daniel Mitchell feel special.

TWO

IF REBECCA GENTRY HAD LOOKED OUT THE WINDOW of her apartment in downtown Athens, she would have seen Broad Street in its summer slumber. Only a few cars broke the hot twilight, and from the ninth floor, Rebecca could see it all: the green profusion of Bradford pear trees, the obelisk honoring Elijah Clarke, for whom the county was named, an Italian restaurant and, across the street, the elegant oaks on the University of Georgia's north campus. During spring quarter, the streets were clogged, but now Athens had shrunk to its small-town boundaries.

But Rebecca did not look out. Instead, sitting in the coming gloom and working on her third pack of Benson and Hedges that day, she listened to the Verdi *Requiem* on the town's National Public Radio station. One thing about living on the ninth floor, about as high as you could go in Athens, you could get great radio reception. As she had for weeks now, Rebecca felt trapped, confused.

At twenty-nine, she had been a rising star in the University's English Department. She had published her first book of poetry with Dutton, *Dead Lace*. It had even been reviewed in *The New York Times Book Review*. A second book of poetry came out the following year, but it was indifferently reviewed—when it was noticed at all. Since then, Rebecca had been laboring on an endless, disorganized book on the life of Lawrence Dale, a poet from the north Georgia mountains who had briefly attained fame in the Forties and Fifties before killing himself on top of Black Rock Mountain, in the far northeast corner of the state, the day before John F. Kennedy was assassinated. She had been to Lawrence Dale's home town, Newfield, and talked to his brother many times, had even tried to interview his aged mother, who could barely remember who Lawrence was. She had bought all his books, gained access to his correspondence with his agent and his publisher. She had talked to Dale's friends all over the country and had even been awarded a modest fellowship to work on the manuscript, but the more she worked, the more inchoate everything seemed. Lawrence Dale had become something always just out of reach.

Now, five years after the publication of *Dead Lace*, Rebecca was still an assistant professor, and the manuscript lay in shambles on the table in the living room of her stylish downtown apartment. The book had virtually no reference points, either starting or ending, and whenever she thought of it, Rebecca felt sick. She had not touched it for months now, and the mere idea of writing a poem filled her with a deep dread.

Rebecca finished the cigarette and went into the bathroom and turned on the light over the sink. The carpet was so deep you'd lose a quarter if you dropped one, she thought, enjoying how it felt on her feet. Strains of the "Dies Irae" from the *Requiem* drifted toward her from the kitchen. She stared at her face and sighed heavily. Her long, brown hair was as shiny and fresh as ever, thick and luxuriant around her cheeks. But lately, to Rebecca, her skin seemed pale and funereal, and her once-bright eyes appeared sunken, their color weak and indifferent. She was thinking of Charlie Dominic and the first time she met him when she realized that over the low drumming of Verdi, the phone was ringing. Her footfall was heavy, even though she was small, and she stared at the phone on the kitchen wall a full five seconds before she answered it.

"Rebecca," a woman's voice sounded. It was husky, almost hoarse, and full of unspilled tears.

"Annie, what's wrong?" asked Rebecca. Annie Phillips was her best friend and associate professor of Classics at the University. She and Annie had met just after Rebecca's first book had been published, and since then, Annie and her husband, Brad, often invited Rebecca out for dinner or to Atlanta for art shows and concerts. Annie had the kind of wholesome beauty men love and women think plain.

"It's my daddy," Annie said. "Mother called from Statesboro and said they just found out he's got liver cancer." The tears finally came.

"Oh, Annie," said Rebecca. "I'll be right over." Rebecca looked madly for a cigarette and saw an open pack of Benson and Hedges at the end of the kitchen counter, stretched the coiled cord as far as it would go and then grabbed it. Her lighter was in the pocket of her sundress.

"No, no," said Annie, driving the tears from her voice. "Brad's got his game here tonight."

"Then you come over here," said Rebecca.

"I don't want to go anyplace where it's quiet," Annie said.

"Then let's meet at Steak and Ale or somewhere," Rebecca said.

"Okay," said Annie. "Steak and Ale. About twenty minutes?"

"Fine."

"Can I pick you up?"

"No, it's just a few blocks away. I'll meet you there," said Rebecca.

"I really do appreciate it," said Annie.

"Listen, it's no big deal," Rebecca said. "I'm truly sorry about your daddy. Just stay calm. You'll be fine."

They sat at a dark corner table, and Rebecca could see the hurt in Annie's dark hazel eyes. Next to Rebecca, Annie looked almost chubby, with her round face. Once Rebecca had told her that she always looked like she was about to get into mischief. Where

Rebecca could be expansive, Annie was usually controlled, but both loved to laugh, and they often marveled how alike they were.

"I didn't think this would ever happen," Annie said. "He's always been strong as an ox, an outdoorsy kind of man. But he's nearly seventy now, and in the last year he has begun to look frail and old to me. I've never said as much, even to Brad."

"Did you tell him about your father?" asked Rebecca. A man at a nearby table was talking loudly about Amway.

"Yeah," Annie nodded. "He was wonderful. We're going down to visit them this weekend. I know I'm going to fall apart when I see him. I mean, what will I say, 'Hi Daddy, how's your liver cancer this week?' I feel like my heart weighs a million pounds. He was always my favorite. . . ." Annie looked into her whiskey sour and the tears poured out. Rebecca felt the tears at the edge of her own eyes, and she reached across the table and took Annie's hand. For a long time, neither of them spoke. "You ever feel like everything is coming to a close in your life, and you aren't sure if anything good is going to happen next?"

"Right now," whispered Rebecca, looking away and into the dining room. "All the time."

"Your father's passed away, hasn't he?" asked Annie. "You've never said much about him."

"My mother died about seven years ago," Rebecca said. She realized her hands were trembling, and she dug out another cigarette and lit it. Someone had put an old Carpenters' song on the jukebox. "My father left us when I was thirteen, and we never knew what happened to him. I heard he moved out West, but if Mama ever knew, she didn't say."

"I'm sorry," said Annie. "It's almost worse not knowing, somehow."

"You get over it," said Rebecca.

"You do?" asked Annie. "I don't think I'll ever get over it. I don't see how anybody ever gets over it."

"The world thrives on ideas," said Rebecca coldly. "You know that. Emotions just screw things up. I wish people didn't have any feelings at all."

"I don't believe that," Annie said. Another round of drinks came, and they were both feeling a little better.

"You of all people," Rebecca said. "Classics. All that pagan ritual of ideas."

For the first time all evening, Annie Phillips smiled briefly. "I don't want to talk about it," she said. "Where in the hell have you been lately? I haven't seen you around Park Hall. You aren't teaching at all this summer, are you?"

"Not teaching, no," said Rebecca. "I've been spending most of my time this past week visiting ghosts."

"Charlie?"

"Him and lots of others."

"You ever hear from him?"

"Not since Christmas." Rebecca shrugged. "He was living in Charleston and trying not to feel guilty about having a wonderful time."

"I'm sorry things didn't work out," Annie said. "I've always been sorry. Should I be sorry?"

The question shook Rebecca, but she tried not to show it. She and Charlie Dominic had been married for four years before their divorce last Christmas, an affair that was sad but not bitter.

"No," Rebecca finally sighed. "But he's just one of the ghosts. I am in mourning for everything I've lost in my life. I guess I'm trying to get it back undamaged."

"Like dreaming of when you were a little girl and then waking up and feeling sad," nodded Annie.

"I don't know if it's like that," said Rebecca. "I don't know what it's like at all. I just keep thinking I missed a turn somewhere."

They hugged when they finally left, both slightly woozy from the alcohol, Annie feeling a little better, but not much. Now, thinking that the exercise would help clear her head, Rebecca was glad she'd decided to walk to the restaurant from her apartment. She walked slowly up the still-warm sidewalk. Bugs buzzed around the street lamps, and Rebecca thought of trapped lightning bugs on the lawns of girlhood, how they bounced against the jar lids and turned to fire just for her. What did she feel, and why did she feel it? She wanted to dissect her emotions as a scientist cuts a frog, calmly and rationally. She wanted to make her name, have something to live for, some almost-but-not-quite attainable goal. But what was it? How could she make sure she should even be here at all?

She thought, for the first time all evening, of the thick shade of the cemetery. And she thought of Lawrence Dale, the late genius from the north Georgia mountains, wondered what was in his head those last moments before he climbed to the sheer face of Black Rock Mountain. Now the mountain was a state park, and you could put a quarter in a bifocal telescope and see the town of Clayton neatly huddled hundreds of feet below. It had happened on a cool November evening. Did Lawrence Dale see the coming of winter in the way trees bent? Did he feel an icy tremble, a mere whisper of the end? Or did he merely love himself and this world too well, so that the beauty had become too rich to bear?

Rebecca had gone to Black Rock often and sat all night on the jumbled boulders, staring at the fairy-tale lights of Clayton and the valley far below, reciting one of Lawrence Dale's poems over and over, the last poem he wrote before he died. She said the poem in her head now as she walked past the Phoenix Whole Foods store, alongside a new cluster of small restaurants tucked back from Broad Street and then up toward the bus station.

When she came to the bus station, she was aware that an old man, obviously drunk, saw her as he turned from a wall, still zipping up his pants. She walked faster, the Holiday Inn on her right across the street looking completely empty. The dim lights of its lobby were not powerful enough to brighten her dark path. Did she hear the sound of footsteps? She thought so. She walked faster and then broke into a small jogging step, afraid to turn around until she got to the corner at Campus North. Once there, she snapped around and saw that the street was empty. A hot wind was chasing an empty paper cup down the gutter.

She hurried inside the apartment building, her apprehension

slow to fade, and rode the elevator to her usual stop, grateful now for the ninth floor and the time to regain her composure. She opened the door to her apartment and surveyed the place for a moment in the light of the single lamp on the end table by the overstuffed white sofa. The entire apartment was decorated in shades of black, white and gray. Even the double-matted prints on the walls were non-objective doodlings with only the barest hint of color.

Rebecca turned the television on for the sound, ignoring what was showing. She settled on the couch, lit a cigarette, and thought of her father.

What she had told Annie had not been entirely true. She had thought of her father often, thought of him with love and bitterness, wondered where he had gone. Why did it have to end? When she had turned ten, he had bought her a *Compton's Pictured Encyclopedia*, and nothing could have excited her more. She understood the sacrifice, since he was only a cook at a small restaurant there in Raleigh, and her mother made a few dollars hemming trousers. She knew the scene, every smell and sound, felt it etched on her heart, and whenever she began to feel too good, she replayed it for equilibrium.

"Your daddy's left us," her mother had said. Rebecca had just come home from school. She was wearing a thin cotton dress and sandals. Her hair was long even then, and it was gathered into a neat pony tail with a rubber band. Her mother had said it even before Rebecca had set her book satchel on the peeling linoleum of the kitchen floor. The kitchen smelled of turnip greens, her father's favorite food, which her mother was cooking obsessively, as if the odor would bring her husband back.

"Left us? Rebecca had said. "What do you mean?" She remembered the way her heart drummed, the way she began to feel heavy inside and afraid. "Not coming back?"

"He said he wasn't," said her mother. Once, her mother had had brown hair, but by then it had gone gray, and she had gained weight. Rebecca loved her mother. She adored her father. "But things sometimes change."

"Why?" said Rebecca softly. Tears began to run from her eyes, but she did not sob. "Where will he go?"

"He's fell in love with somebody else," her mother groaned, her chest heaving. Mary Gentry had no education, and she knew her circumstances would soon be difficult at best. "I don't know where he's going to. Oh baby, I'm so sorry." She opened her arms, and Rebecca rushed into them, and they cried for a long time. Rebecca remembered the way her mother smelled. She remembered the muffled sounds of their twin sobbing.

Even though years had passed since her father left, she could still see the look of life draining from her mother's eyes that day. She thought about her father now. He was tall and good-looking in a country kind of way, always wearing a baseball cap tilted rakishly. He had deep dimples, which Rebecca had inherited, and he looked somehow devilish and out of control. Rebecca suddenly felt her body tremble. She stood up and went into the kitchen, took the bottle of Chablis from the refrigerator, and poured herself a glass. You bastard, she thought as she drank the wine. "Yes," she wanted to scream from her windows all over Athens, "I think of that son of a bitch. I think of him practically every day and wonder if he ever thinks of me."

She stood again, and walked to the window and tried to look out over Broad Street toward the University, but she only saw her own reflection. It made her uncomfortable. She was staring at herself when she realized that she did not know who she was, or where she was going, or why.

"Daddy," she whispered.

THREE

THE NEXT MORNING WAS HEAVY WITH UNSPILLED RAIN. Sullen clouds crowded in from the east, while Athens awoke and headed for work. Daniel had eaten his usual breakfast of Captain Crunch and toast and had tied Toggle near his swimming pool. As he walked under a bleak sky, he thought about the night before, how he had cried at Joe Dell and Irene's house. He tried to think of the fear that had consumed him, but it was as fleeting as a moth. Sometimes at Greenvale he would become afraid, and then he would run up the stone steps of Mr. Wilkins' house and find him, and Mr. Wilkins would hold him until the fear went away.

Even now, Daniel felt a sickness when he thought of Greenvale. He had lived there until he was twenty-five, three years before, when he had almost become a teacher himself—Mr. Wilkins' right-hand man. He would sit on the broad lawns inhaling the fragrance of tea olive bushes and tell newcomers the Greenvale motto: *You can do it!* The school was not for those with specific handicaps, never had been. Some were mildly retarded, but others were partially sighted or lame, and a few were victims of abuse with such severe psychological problems they had never been able to function normally at all.

Daniel stood on the Oconee River Bridge and stared at the water that flowed majestically twenty feet below. Where, he wondered, did it come from? He knew it wound past O'Malley's and then around Oconee Hill, but where did it go from there? The morning traffic was light, and by the time he reached the cemetery, the air was heavy, and an east wind was stirring the tops of the oldest oaks. He loved the tall stone walls that held iron gates which Frank swung back each morning. He gripped the brown paper sack tightly and was staring at the trees when he realized that Frank Sutton was standing right in front of him, not three feet away.

"Hello, Frank," Daniel said, stepping back and smiling broadly. "Where did you come from?"

"I told you to stop asking me that," said Frank wearily. "I've been walking toward you since you came through the gate. You don't notice things sometimes."

"I know," said Daniel, looking down.

"It's all right," Frank said. "We got a problem, Daniel."

"Okay," said Daniel.

"Up there," Frank said, pointing with his thumb to the crest of the cemetery's oldest part. "Somebody went nuts up there with a can of spray paint last night. Students out of school, I guess, letting off steam. If I ever catch one...." Frank shook his head. He was about fifty, short and red-faced, prone to bouts of excitability, but a decent man.

He is my best friend, Daniel thought. At Christmas, Frank had given him a new pair of white socks, and the gift had been so unexpected that Daniel had clutched the socks all night as though they were an ancient religious relic.

"Anyway, I need you to go get some mineral spirits. We've got a funeral across the river this morning."

"Who died?" asked Daniel.

"Lady named Gavoort," said Frank. "She was ninety-seven years old."

"SHE OPENETH HER MOUTH WITH WISDOM AND IN HER TONGUE

20

IS THE LAW OF KINDNESS," said Daniel haltingly. Frank stared at him and shook his head.

"Yeah. Well, anyway, I need you to walk up to Jones Hardware and get a couple of gallons of mineral spirits to clean the paint off those stones," Frank said.

"Who did they paint?" Daniel inquired intently.

"Just some of those damn stones up there." Frank sighed, taking a five out of his billfold and giving it to Daniel. "They're not people anymore, Daniel. It's just a rock farm."

"Okay, Frank," Daniel nodded. He looked down at the bill in his hand and suddenly felt his throat tighten. In the three years he'd worked here, Frank had never asked him to do anything like this. He had walked by the store uptown, but he had never been inside; he had hardly been inside any store except the Golden Pantry near his home where he bought food. He held the bill out toward Frank, and Frank could see Daniel's hand trembling.

"I don't know how."

"You can do it," Frank sighed. "Just ask a clerk for mineral spirits, get the change and bring it back to me. Go on. I've got to get over to that grave across the river." He turned and walked toward his old car and left Daniel standing there, still holding the bill out. "Put your lunch in the refrigerator, and then do what I told you, okay?" Frank looked at Daniel with sympathy. "Please?"

"Okay, Frank," Daniel said. He went inside the caretaker's house where Frank lived and down the dark hall toward the kitchen. He loved Frank's house, loved its colors and smells. The kitchen had a rich aroma of bacon and eggs. Daniel put his sack on the crowded top shelf of the refrigerator and walked back outside, still holding the bill tightly in his hand and saying over and over like a talisman: *mineral spirits, mineral spirits.* He knew what spirits were: they lived in cemeteries, like Oconee Hill, and they were the parts of people that did not die when their bodies did. He wondered if Mrs. Gavoort's spirit would be drifting around Oconee Hill later that afternoon. What was a mineral? Maybe it was rocks. Hadn't someone told him that at Greenvale one time, that minerals were rocks? Mineral spirits, something left from dead rocks. That satisfied Daniel, and so he walked back along East Campus Road, but instead of turning right on Baldwin street, going under the railroad bridge and heading toward O'Malley's, his habitual route, he went straight across Baldwin Street and up the hill toward downtown Athens.

Jones Hardware was in a new Butler building just east of a railroad track that was no longer used. Daniel came to a street crossing, and the light was green, so he started across, saying, over and over, his lips moving silently, *mineral spirits, mineral spirits.* Then the light changed, and a car screeched, its driver braking hard to avoid hitting Daniel.

"What in the hell is wrong with you?" a man screamed.

Daniel felt confused and turned to stare. The driver was a student with blond hair, and he wore a T-shirt that had strange letters on the left side of his chest.

"I am sorry," said Daniel.

"Shit," the boy said, shaking his head. He floored the Thunderbird and roared off. Cars were stopped in both lanes, blowing their horns, and Daniel lumbered on across the street, holding the bill out. He walked east along the sidewalk, feeling his chest heave. *I nearly got myself killed*, Daniel thought. *Lord have mercy.* Suddenly, he felt wonderful, as if he had been spared the eternal darkness the preacher at Greenvale always talked about. But if you went to heaven, there was eternal light. The preacher had said eternal meant forever, Daniel recalled. Baby was asleep in eternal light. I do not understand death, he thought.

He walked happily now, his arms swinging in the first drops of rain. He crossed the railroad tracks and walked up to the front door of Jones Hardware and went inside, taking off the Atlanta Braves baseball cap he always wore. Mrs. Wilkins had taught him to take off his hat indoors. The store was wonderful, but he was afraid and breathing deeply. He was dazzled by chains and hooks and bolts, boxes of nails and screws and nuts—thousands of intricate pieces of hardware. He did not know what any of it meant.

"Hep you?" a voice said.

Daniel turned and saw a middle-aged man with a huge stomach that hung out over his belt. Daniel held out the five-dollar bill and smiled, feeling wonderful. "What can I get you, son?"

"Get me?"

"What is it you want?" the man asked.

Daniel tried to remember. He thought of Mrs. Wilkins, and he thought of eternal light, and he even thought of Baby. He looked at the five-dollar bill and thought of Frank.

"Rocks of the dead," Daniel said, a little too loud.

"Rocks of the dead," the man repeated. He squinted his eyes and backed up a step. "Son, I don't have a clue what you're talking about. What's it for?"

"They spray-painted Baby, I guess it was Baby, and some other ones down at the cemetery, but Frank said it was a rock farm," Daniel spluttered. "I do not know what to say."

The man took Daniel by the arm and walked with him to the door. "Son, you go find out what it was you wanted and then come back," he said. Daniel nodded, and went outside into the rain. Looking back through the broad front window of the store, he could see the man talking to another man, then both of them laughing and shaking their heads. Daniel began to cry, but he tossed his head and the tears stopped. Things just didn't stay in his head. They never had. He could remember some things, like the names in Oconee Hill and the inscriptions, but others got erased as soon as they were written in his mind.

"I am so stupid," Daniel said as he walked up the street. "I am so stupid." This time he did remember to watch for traffic, and when the light went red, he ran across the intersection so fast that when he reached the other side he tripped over the curb, stumbled for nearly twenty feet and then fell heavily beneath a large ginkgo tree. He stood up and brushed himself off. The rain was not heavy, but it fell steadily. Daniel Mitchell headed back for the cemetery to find out the real name for rocks of the dead. He came through the gates and walked along the winding, tree-covered street that ran through the old section of the cemetery. He crossed an old metal bridge above the Oconee and walked into the newer part of Oconee Hill.

He could see the funeral long before he got there. Usually, people were buried in the afternoon, but they were already all huddled around a blue tent on this early morning. Once Frank had told Daniel they had to plant a man that day, and since then, Daniel had often thought of the cemetery as a farm, a growing place. He walked through the drizzle and came up on the funeral, which was being held on a gentle slope. No one was crying, and the preacher was droning. Daniel took off his baseball cap and stood there, looking at the coffin when someone touched his sleeve. It was Frank, who had been watching the funeral from a respectful distance.

"Hello, Frank," Daniel said, his voice much too loud. A few people turned to look and then glanced back at the preacher.

"Hush up, and get over here," Frank said. He tugged at Daniel's sleeve and pulled him down the hill away from the blue tent. "What in the hell are you doing over here? Did you get the mineral spirits?"

"Mineral spirits!" Daniel cried.

"Would you please shut up?" Frank said. His face was red and looked almost swollen to Daniel.

"I could not remember what it was," Daniel said. "I will remember now."

"Wait," sighed Frank. He took a small pad from his breast pocket and pulled a stub of a pencil from behind his left ear. On the top sheet he wrote "Two gallons of mineral spirits." He underlined it twice, almost tearing the paper. "Take this and just give it and the money to the clerk."

"Okay, Frank," said Daniel, smiling now.

"And get some rags out of the storage shed behind the house," said Frank. "Pour some of the mineral spirits on the rag, and then wipe it on the paint until the paint comes off. Think you can do that?"

"I sure can, Frank," said Daniel.

"Okay," said Frank. "Go on now." Daniel nodded and walked away back toward the bridge. When he was halfway across the metal span, he stopped and looked at the slick rocks far below. An elderly black man named Woodrow Faust, a retired house painter, came there to fish in the Oconee River with a limber, dipping cane pole and a box full of night crawlers. Daniel often took his sack and sat on the rocks and ate lunch with Woodrow.

"Hello, Woodrow!" cried Daniel.

Woodrow looked up and saw Daniel leaning over the rail, smiling broadly. "Good mornin', Daniel," He said. "How are things by you this day?"

"I am getting spirits of mineral for Frank today," Daniel said. He dug the bill from his pants and held it up. "I am walking to town now."

"That's good," said Woodrow. Daniel walked across the bridge and saw the column, a single shaft in the Gerdine-Cobb plot not far from the headless woman who held a lamb. The rain had stopped for a while but was now pattering the earth again. He knew Woodrow did not mind; when it rained, Woodrow snugged the hat over his eyes and slept beneath the trees by the riverside.

Birds sang. Daniel smelled flowers and newly mowed grass and felt the rain upon his skin, wet and cool. He thought of Toggle and wondered if he had gotten under the trailer and out of the rain. He came up the hill toward the old part of the cemetery and was not far from the gates when he saw the woman with the brown hair up on the top of the hill near the grave of Young B. Harris. Daniel stopped and looked up at her. She wore a pale blue dress, and even in the dull rainy light, her hair was beautiful. Daniel held the bill tightly and watched as she bent over and placed an orange day lily on a tombstone.

It was the same lady he had been seeing for a week now. He walked up the left side of the hill, careful to stay out of her sight, and watched as she moved slowly along, talking softly to herself and placing flowers on the narrow graves of men and women long dead.

The rain was slow and easy, and as Daniel watched her, drops fell from the bill of his cap. He stopped near the crest of the hill and stood behind the trunk of a spreading cedar tree. From here, he could see what Frank had been talking about. There were terrible streaks of green and orange paint on several of the stones, the lightning streaks of some fool's midnight wanderings. The woman sat on the iron rail surrounding the plot of Young B. Harris and stared at the oak leaves as they waved in the gentle rain.

Was she crying? Daniel could not say. She seems very sad, Daniel thought. He was thinking about how sad she was and did not even notice that she had moved from the rail and was walking straight toward him. Just then the rain suddenly started to come down hard, and the woman ran for the protection of the cedar tree. Daniel wanted to run, but he didn't know where to go, so he stepped from behind the tree trunk and took off his hat, just as Mrs. Wilkins had taught him at Greenvale.

Daniel did not know what to say, but he did not expect the woman to scream.

REBECCA HAD AWAKENED THAT MORNING thinking of Annie Phillips' father. Was it more terrible to face your father's death than merely to wonder what had happened to him? Why had she never learned how to love? She had lain in bed for a long time, smoking a Benson and Hedges and listening to the radio, laughing bitterly when she heard the news about Jim and Tammy Bakker. She had once told her friend, Kent Ziegler, a colleague in the English Department, that Tammy Bakker was the Aimeé Semple McPherson of the 1980s. All religion, Rebecca argued, was merely superstition induced from Roman times forward by power-mad monks. She had once written a satirical poem about Our Lady of Lourdes, which implied that *The Song of Bernadette* had performed more miracles for the career of Jennifer Jones than it had for Bernadette herself.

As she lay in bed, Rebecca decided this was the day she would make a new outline for her book on Lawrence Dale, the mountain poet. She got up, turned off the radio and then showered and dressed, slipping on a tank top and shorts. She ate a light breakfast and went into the study for the first time in two weeks. She flipped the switch on her desk top radio, and Dvořák's *Seventh Symphony* was on. She turned down the volume and lit a cigarette, took a sip of her steaming coffee and began to fall apart.

She stared at the screen of her IBM PC, watching the cursor blink until she thought its insistent pulse would drive her mad. Then she turned the radio off. Finally, after the coffee was gone, and she had smoked five cigarettes, she quietly turned the computer off. She went back to her bedroom and changed into a light blue sundress and took the elevator to the street. Athens was humid and sticky as it usually was in summer, and she could only think that the book would never be written, and she cursed Lawrence Dale.

Without thinking, she walked down the sidewalk on Broad Street and then went through the iron arches that mark the entrance to the University of Georgia campus. From there, she could stroll down the shaded walks of north campus, past buildings nearly two centuries old, past the history of a time and place long gone yet enduring. She loved that best about universities, their traditions of learning and exploring the riches of the past. She passed the Academic Building with its painted metal columns, Phi Kappa Hall, and then the Chapel, a quaint building which boasted a fine organ and which would be, she knew, the location for free concerts performed by Music Department faculty and students nearly every Thursday night during the summer quarter. She strolled past New College, which had been built in 1802 and around Old College, the most historic building on campus where Crawford W. Long, the first physician to use anesthetics in an operation, had lived as a student. Rebecca went past the law school and curved under the massive water oaks past the front of the Ilah Dunlap Little Memorial Library. Students seemed to move in slow motion toward classes, now that summer school had begun. A long-haired boy was throwing a Frisbee to a Dalmatian, and a heavy-set girl with thick glasses was picking up a messy pile of papers and books that she had apparently just dropped. Rebecca envied everyone, especially those who were just beginning their lives or their careers.

She walked down past Baldwin Hall and the Anthropology Department and then east down another hill to East Campus Road. Why was she still going to Oconee Hill? Maybe it was because there was no argument with death. It simply existed and was an inescapable fact, one with which Lawrence Dale had found an accommodation, but one that Rebecca could not bear. She was standing before the stone-girded gates before she realized that it was raining and that during the entire trip, she had been thinking of her father.

Rebecca did not mind the rain. When she was a little girl in Raleigh, her mother had often taken her along on walks in spring rains. Lois Gentry had wanted to be an opera singer, but her husband had ended that dream, and so Lois would sing arias softly to her daughter while they walked. Her favorite was "Un Bel Di" from *Madama Butterfly*. Lois would hold her hand as they walked slowly under the blue umbrella in the rains of spring and autumn and sing. That was the best time of her life, Rebecca thought, when she felt loved and sheltered, whole.

She stopped in a wild overgrown part of the cemetery, as she had every day, and picked a handful of day lilies. They will never miss them, she thought; after all, there must be thousands of them. Rebecca hardly glanced at the graves upon which she lavished the orange blooms. She did not read the names or dates. She wondered if her wandering father had a stone somewhere out West and if a cousin back home had lately pulled the weeds from her mother's small plot.

She was thinking again of her mother and the blue umbrella when rain once again darkened the sky.

REBECCA DID NOT SEE DANIEL until she was under the tree and only about five steps away from him. She gave a small cry of surprise and jumped backward out of the tree's protective canopy. Daniel tried to smile, but he only looked startled, just as Rebecca did. He moved back, slowly, and she came back under the tree; its branches broke the rain well. The hissing of the rain mingled with the wind in the trees. Daniel held his cap tightly to his chest, his eyes wide with wonder.

"You scared the devil out of me," said Rebecca. Her hair was wet now and hung straight down, glistening in the dark morning. "What are you doing standing here?"

"I work here at Oconee Hill," said Daniel. "I did not mean to scare you. Frank sent me for mineral spirits. Look what they did." He pointed to the stones, and she turned and saw the markings, swastikas, obscene words, huge angry blots all sprayed in green and orange paint.

"Good grief," she said. "Who did it?"

"Spirits," Daniel said, and then, realizing he had answered the wrong question, clamped his hand to his mouth. "I mean the students out of school," he explained.

Rebecca turned back to him and saw that he was blushing and looking down. She could see that even speaking took a great deal of effort for him, and his words sounded strange; she knew instinctively that something was wrong with him. But what? "I can't imagine somebody doing that to a gravestone," she said with disgust.

"Oh no!" cried Daniel. "They did paint Baby!"

He dashed out into the rain, and Rebecca watched his peculiar heavy-footed gait and catalogued his clothes: thick-soled black shoes, white socks, worn blue jeans and plain white T-shirt. She watched as he ran to a small jutting headstone and knelt before it, running his hand over the cut letters of one word: Baby. She did not move. In a moment, Daniel walked back, soaked with rain and stood not far away under the tree.

"Relative of yours?" she asked. Hell, she thought, nobody's been buried in this part of the cemetery in years.

"Baby," Daniel said, his voice wobbling a little. "Why would they paint a little baby?"

"I don't know," Rebecca said. They stood for a long time in the rain, silent. Finally, Rebecca said, "You work here, is that right?"

"Oh," he said, as if falling from a trance, "excuse me. I am rude. I am Daniel Mitchell." He came toward her, and she did not know whether to run or scream, but the look on his face was painfully innocent, so she did not move. He reached out for her hand, and she extended it warily. He took her small hand and pumped it three times and then stepped back.

"I'm Rebecca," she said, not wanting to tell this odd stranger her last name.

"Oh!" Daniel cried in delight. "We are both from the Bible, then." It was such a non sequitur that Rebecca felt in the presence of something sacred—or monstrous.

"Our names are from the Bible."

"I see," said Rebecca, relieved.

"You are the flower lady," Daniel said. "I have seen you put flowers on the graves."

"I have never seen you," she said. "You been working here long?" She took the pack of cigarettes from her shirt pocket and lit one. The smell of smoke drifted lazily through the rain.

"Three whole years," Daniel said proudly.

"Well, I wouldn't have seen you, anyway," she said. "I've been in Athens for years, but until a few days ago I'd never set foot over here."

"You bring flowers," he said. "You love the people down there." Rebecca was startled; she had never really thought of anyone being "down there" at all. "No," she said, "I just bring flowers. I don't know what in the world I'm doing here."

She tried to laugh, but it was dry and brittle. The rain slackened, and Daniel turned to her and put his hat back on. The sun suddenly burst through an opening in the clouds, and the trees and stones were filled with light.

"I have to go get mineral spirits to clean the stones," Daniel said proudly. "I have been glad to meet you, Rebecca."

She felt something strange clinging to her heart, something fragile and rare. "Goodbye, Daniel," she said.

He smiled at her and walked off down the road toward the iron gates of Oconee Hill. Rebecca watched until he was out of sight, and it was only then that she realized her cigarette had burned down to the filter and gone out.

FOUR

THE FOLLOWING MONDAY, REBECCA GENTRY SAT IN HER OFFICE on campus watching a nest of mockingbirds. The small cup of hatchlings was on the limb of a water oak just outside her third-floor window in Park Hall. She could not hear them, only the dull roar of the air conditioner and the sound of footsteps in the tile hall.

Summer quarter was always strange, few students milling around, no conferences, no grading papers, no excuses. The office was comfortably furnished, with ceiling-high bookcases that spilled paperbacks onto an expensive Oriental rug Charlie Dominic had given her when they were trying to save their marriage. On her desk here, just as in her condo, was the debris of Lawrence Dale's life, along with books colleagues had given her to read and two ashtrays full of cigarette butts. A ladderback chair, for students, was next to her desk.

Rebecca held a yellow notepad in her lap, and at the top of its first page had written the word "CHRONOLOGY" in block letters. So far, she had added only this:

Born—Rabun Gap, Georgia, February 14, 1917.

She had been at her office for nearly an hour, and that was all she had written. Now she looked at it with a rueful grin. That was the most basic thing about Lawrence Dale, the day he came into this world. What made him different? Was he marked from the beginning with the sweet introspection of a poet? Who in the hell read poetry anymore? Who, besides a few doddering ninnies and a fired-up promotions committee gave a shit about a dead writer from north Georgia anyway? She put her pen on the next line of the pad and held it there until her hand was trembling so badly that she did not notice the huge bent form of Kent Ziegler in her doorway.

"Hail to thee, blithe spirit," Kent said, and Rebecca looked up and smiled.

"Kent, how's it going?" she asked.

"I thought you wanted another line for the poem you were working on," he grinned. He was about forty, an amiable man with two critical books on contemporary American writers to his credit. Already an associate professor, he was rumored to be next in line for the Stevens Chair of American Literature, a post currently held by Stanton Decker, who at seventy-nine had started to look like a monument to himself. Kent was nearly six-five, prematurely gray and wore heavy black-framed glasses. He was plain, but when he smiled, his otherwise nondescript face lit up winningly.

"I want an angle for this interminable book I say I'm writing," she said. She picked up the pen and threw it and the yellow pad into the clutter of her desk.

"Well, your door was open, and I figured if you were creating you'd be bolted in a nunnery or something." He smiled expectantly.

"Come on in," she said, waving him into the chair.

"When are you going to get a visitor's chair worth sitting in?" he asked.

"When I no longer have to have conferences with students," she said. "What's up? How are Samantha and the kids?"

"Great," he said. "They've gone to her mother's in Panama City for a week and left me here to teach 202 to a gaggle of students with overactive glands."

"So you're a bachelor again," Rebecca said.

"Indeed," he said. "And to prove I can still boogie, I'm throwing a little wingding at our place Friday night. Free beer, free nachos and all the heady conversation you can stand. It's the first day of summer. It's also the birthdays of Reinhold Neibuhr, Jean-Paul Sartre and Mary McCarthy. What do you make out of that coincidence? I think I see a master's thesis brewing. We could write it together and sell it to one of the victims of the Master's Program. We'll call it 'The Influence of Birth Date on Fame,' or 'The Prophecy of the Days of Our Lives.' What do you think?"

Rebecca was staring at the books in the case behind Kent's left shoulder, barely listening to him at all. She held the cigarette as it burned down but did not draw on it. Kent stared at her, waiting for her to say something.

"Rebecca?" he finally said. "Are you okay?"

She looked back at him and tried to laugh. "I'm sorry," she said. "It's this damn book, Kent. I keep walking all around it and can't see this guy at all. He might as well be Jean-Paul Sartre, for all I care. The harder I try to grip him, the farther he moves away."

"Sounds Freudian to me," Kent said amiably.

"I'm serious," she said. "I mean, look at this." She stood and took a heavy manila envelope from a vertical file at the back of her desk, opened it and took out a tattered black-and-white photo. "What do you see?"

The photo showed a gaunt man who looked somewhat like Abe Lincoln—great, tired eyes, the body thin, all angles beneath the Fifties-style shirt with twin breast pockets and short sleeves.

"Lawrence Dale," Kent said. "You showed me that picture, or a smaller version, at Alban's party in April. He looks like a man falling in love with death."

"This was taken the month before he shot himself," said Rebecca. "In October 1963. It was going to be on the dust jacket of the novel he never finished."

"So?"

"So," she said, sure that he would understand, that everyone understood how unfinished she felt, how wayward her dreams had finally become. "So nothing. Forget it." She put the photograph back in the envelope and threw it on the desk with the legal pad.

"Don't be that way," he said softly. "I know you're having a tough time. Just hang in there. It'll come to you." Kent had often felt sorry that he was married, though he loved his wife and children, sorry because there were lovely women like Rebecca Gentry who were dying for the touch of something permanent and loving.

"Have you ever been to the cemetery?" she asked. She stubbed the cigarette out and did not light another. "Over there past the railroad tracks? To Oconee Hill?"

"I'm a critic," he said. "Critics don't wander in cemeteries. They wander in tea rooms where the women come and go, talking of Michelangelo."

"Is that a 'no'?" Rebecca asked.

"I went there once," he said. "When we first moved to Athens, we lived with a nice old lady. She died a few years ago. Went to her funeral. What's all this with death and funerals?"

"Oh," she said, shaking her hair, "it's not death and funerals. It's just...hell, I don't know what it is. Something about permanence maybe, about wanting things to last."

"Jesus, this is getting really deep." Kent smiled.

"Oh great," Rebecca said.

"Oh, I'm just kidding," Kent said. "I'm sorry. You just seem awfully gloomy. Hey—you know your literary history. You know creative people are all like this and always have been."

Rebecca stared out the window. The mother mockingbird was perched on the edge of the nest feeding the babies, which already seemed too large for the small circle of twigs.

"There's a young boy who works over there," she said. "Actually, he's a man, but he seems like a boy. I think he's feeble-minded or something. I met him over there last week and talked to him. I just wondered if anybody knew anything about him."

"Sorry," Kent said. "I could tell you about Dante's influence on Thomas Pynchon, though. Get past the printed page, and I start floundering."

"You're no help at all," said Rebecca.

Kent looked at his watch. "And I've got to go teach some testosterone-crazed coeds now," he said. He unfolded himself from the chair and walked into the hall with his hands in the hip pockets of his khakis. "And speaking of testosterone-crazed, I have the honor of introducing Dr. Annie Phillips." He bowed deeply and extended his arm, and Rebecca looked up to see Annie, looking tiny beside Kent, rolling her eyes.

"I don't want to know what that's all about," she said. "Ziegler, that's sexual harassment."

"An d'you jus' love eet," Kent said, narrowing his eyes and affecting a Charles Boyer accent. Annie laughed and shook her head as Kent went down the hall whistling "The Girl from Ipanema."

"He surely is full of himself," said Annie in her south Georgia drawl that Rebecca loved so much.

"He's just trying to cheer me up," said Rebecca. She looked at Annie and remembered her father and wondered if the bond between them had already begun to strengthen with each day. Then she thought of her own father.

"Have you eaten lunch?" asked Annie.

"I might as well," sighed Rebecca. "This book isn't going to write itself, and it doesn't look like I'm going to write it."

"I brought a sandwich," said Annie.

"I'm not hungry, anyway," said Rebecca. "Is it too hot to eat outside?"

"You got to eat."

"Mother?"

"All right," Annie said. "How about on the tables out back?"

They sat in the shade as Annie slowly unwrapped waxed paper from a tuna sandwich on thick dark bread, setting it next to a Classic Coke and a Red Delicious apple that almost seemed to glow in the light. A student with an armload of books and a worried expression came hustling past them and went in the back door of Park Hall, heading for class.

"Remember when you were that age?" asked Rebecca. "Everything seemed within reach."

"Everything was within reach because we didn't know what in the hell we were reaching for," laughed Annie.

Rebecca nodded. "How was it?" she finally asked.

"I never cried in front of him," Annie said. "I talked with Mama about it, and she was like Mother Theresa. She and Daddy almost glowed the entire weekend. We made peach ice cream and sat out until the backyard was full of lightning bugs just like it was so long ago. They told stories about me when I was a little girl and said how I was the smartest thing they'd ever seen, and Daddy did his imitations of Rudy Vallee and Jerry Colonna. We sat up until after midnight, and Mama and Daddy sat close to each other in the old metal glider out in the yard. They acted like they'd just met and fallen in love. Nobody cried, and the next morning we had a huge old breakfast with country-fried ham and eggs and grits and hot coffee, and Mama made biscuits with real butter. When I left they were standing on the front porch, smiling and waving. I got nearly to Macon before I started crying. I cried all the way back to Athens."

"Oh, Annie," Rebecca said. She reached out and touched Annie's hand gently.

"I'm okay now," said Annie. "It's just hard for me to believe he's going to die."

"It's hard to believe anything dies," said Rebecca.

After lunch, Rebecca sat in the whisper-quiet office and watched the mockingbird babies for a long time. She tried to see her own father's face, but it was elusive, out of focus. Instead, she thought of the young man in the cemetery. Who was he and where had he come from? She had not been to Oconee Hill since that rainy day, and she wondered if he had managed to scrub all the spray paint from the stones. She wondered if he was, perhaps, a secret poet like Lawrence Dale, spinning masterpieces at night after working all day among the shadows of the dead.

She wondered if he were happy.

DANIEL HAD SPENT THREE DAYS SCRUBBING the paint from the stones, and now the last vulgar stains were beginning to disappear beneath his insistent hand. The smell of the mineral spirits reminded him of something terrible, and he could not place it, so he hummed as he worked on the last sullied stone. Whenever he would feel the sickness come over him, he would stumble down the hill into the overgrown parts and press his face into a cluster of gardenias, planted there many years ago and now gone wild, profuse.

The day was very hot, and Daniel ate his lunch in the deep shade of the Billups-Phinizy headstones, resting long enough for a brief nap. He spent the humid afternoon finishing that last stone, walking around it, checking it from different angles until he was satisfied. Just then Frank Sutton, seeing him from back near the house, called his name. It was past quitting time, and Frank knew Daniel sometimes lost track of time when he looked at the graves. Daniel didn't move. To Frank, it seemed as if he had somehow become one of the statues, another sentinel of marble. He walked up the hill and found Daniel staring at the grave of Francina Thomas Singleton, dead since the winter of 1901.

"Daniel," Frank said gently. He didn't want to startle him, but Daniel did not seem to hear. "Daniel."

This time, he looked up, and a kind of radiance swept his face. Frank had seen this before, and it reminded him of the way sun rushed along the ground when a storm had blown past.

"A GODLY MOTHER," Daniel said, turning to look down at the grave.

Frank looked around him at the stones. He had presumed Daniel could clean the paint away, but this went beyond that; such thoroughgoing work seemed almost a form of devotion.

"Good Lord," Frank said. "Daniel this is real good. I can't believe you did such a good job."

"A DEVOTED WIFE IN AN...IT...ITER..." Daniel tried to read it.

"...I...TIN...ER...ANT PREACHER'S HOME," said Frank.

"What does that mean?" Daniel asked.

"Somebody who wanders around, who don't really have a home, I think," Frank said.

"A JOY TO HER NOBLE HUSBAND," read Daniel, halting between every word, "AND A BLESSING TO THE CHURCH OF GOD."

Frank thought it would take him a full minute. "I said you did a great job with this."

"Thank you." Daniel smiled. "They are all happier now."

Frank shook his head and took the rags and what was left of the last gallon can. "Come on down, and I'll get you a bar of soap to wash off," he said.

"Okay, Frank."

They walked with unmatched steps down to the house, and Daniel stayed outside while Frank brought him a new, heavy bar of Lava soap. Daniel washed his arms, rubbing hard to get the paint stains off. He finished, clapped his hands together as if ready for some grand beginning, and walked through the gate and up the long slope of East Campus Road.

Daniel was thinking of food, of the wonderful smell of fried bologna, as he came into the trailer park. He did not hear Daisy Saye calling his name until she was almost screaming it. He turned and saw her and took his hat off, just as he had been taught at Greenvale.

"Evening, Miss Saye," he called out.

"Son, you are getting as deaf as I am," said Daisy, leaning against the doorway of her trailer. She was a shapeless woman in her late sixties with liquid blue eyes and a huge nose. Randi Ambrose had once told Daniel that Daisy was a witch, but he had just laughed. "Come up here and get some magazines. They're about to break my table down."

"Okay."

He walked to the trailer and went up its sagging wooden steps and then inside, where everything smelled of old age, long-cooked food and starched doilies. A game show was on television.

"Are you all right?" Daisy asked. "You smell like gasoline."

"Minimum spirits," Daniel said proudly. "Cleaning it off the stones. Somebody sprayed paint on the stones, and I cleaned it off."

Daisy stood up and looked painfully out the window past Daniel. She said, "Imagine such a thing. Why would anybody do such a thing?" Daniel looked slightly confused and hurt.

"Frank told me to do it," he said. Daisy shook her head. Her tight gray hair, which rose to a clenched bun, did not move.

"Not cleaning up," she said. "I mean painting. Why in God's name would anybody do that?"

"I do not know," said Daniel. He had not really thought about it before, but now he did: Was it an act of anger? He could not say.

"Well, anyway, here are some magazines," she said. She bent over and lifted a stack of *Ladies' Home Journal* issues and handed them to Daniel. "They're for women, but they're something to read."

"Thank you, Miss Saye," said Daniel.

He came back outside and walked down the dirt road between the rows of trailers, the stack of magazines under his left arm, his hat still in his right hand. Joe Dell Bailey was standing in his yard, watering a circular patch of yellow flowers. Daniel had tried growing flowers once, but the seeds he planted had never come up, though he had watched the patch for months, even deep into winter, hoping that somehow the flowers would burst through the ground. Now Toggle whimpered happily when he saw Daniel approaching. Daniel put the magazines on the steps, leaned down to pet the dog, and then he waved at Joe Dell.

"Evening, Daniel," called Joe Dell. "Why don't you come over and eat with me and Irene this evening? She cooking up some pork chops and frying some potatoes."

"I will," said Daniel, still holding his hat. "I will wash my face first, Joe Dell, and change my shirt." Joe Dell nodded, and the smoke from his pipe curled, unmoving, around his thick features as he walked along the row of orange marigolds that Irene had planted in front of their trailer. Daniel let Toggle off his chain, and the dog leaped high to him, yelping with joy as they disappeared inside.

Daniel put the magazines with the others on the coffee table, hung up his hat and went into the bathroom. He stripped off his shirt and washed his face and chest and shoulders with a soapy washcloth and then put deodorant on. He put Rapid Shave on his fingers, slathered his face with foam and shaved it off. Then he splashed his face with Old Spice.

His bedroom was cramped, the bed nearly touching the walls. He tried to keep it neat, but everything was slightly askew as if made up by someone with crossed eyes. Once each week, usually on Thursday night, he put all his clothes in a plastic hamper and lugged them to the laundry at Oconee-By-The-River. He took a nice blue plaid shirt that he had brought from Greenvale and buttoned it on his lean chest and shoulders. All his clothes had come from Greenvale, and they were starting to look shabby, but Daniel did not care because they reminded him of his childhood home. He had not been back since he'd come to Athens, and often the mere thought of Greenvale choked him with emotion. He sat on the bed and picked up a picture frame on which was taped a photograph of a farm house that he had cut out of a magazine. Daniel did not understand how to take the glass out, so he had taped the picture outside, to the glass, and each night he held it and thought about the house before he went to sleep. Hadn't Mr. Wilkins told him that once he'd been on a farm? Why can't I remember living there? Daniel wondered.

"You came to us when you were two," Mrs. Wilkins had said. "You lived on a farm. And when your father died, we took you in at Greenvale because you had no other relatives."

Daniel never asked questions about the farm, even though he could barely remember it or his real parents. Instead, he had been slowly creating his childhood in his mind each evening when he and Toggle went for a walk, building his mother into A GODLY MOTHER AND DEVOTED WIFE, and imagining a father about whom he could say, THE STEPS OF A GOOD MAN ARE ORDAINED BY THE LORD. He set the frame gently on the small table beside his bed and walked from the bedroom.

Toggle was lying on the sofa, head between his paws, tail thumping lazily. "I am going to eat with Joe Dell and Irene," said Daniel. "I will let you out, and when I am through we will take our walk. Do not run off, okay?"

He opened the door, and Toggle bounded down the steps, clinging to Daniel's legs as he walked across the dusty road to Joe Dell and Irene's trailer. He knocked, and Irene opened the door.

"Evening, Daniel," she said. "Hey, Toggle, you stay outside now." Daniel came inside, where it was very cool, and sat on the couch. The trailer had wonderful smells, and a small record player was turning. A man was singing "How Great Thou Art," and Daniel thought the music was pretty.

Joe Dell came from the bedroom and sat down next to Daniel.

"Son, you feelin' okay?" he asked. "Irene thinks we ain't been being too good a neighbors to you lately, and I reckon she's right."

"I washed off all the stones with minute spirits," said Daniel.

"Mineral spirits?" asked Joe Dell.

"I never can remember that," said Daniel, blushing deeply. "Things just fly out of my head and never come back."

Irene put the food on the table, fried pork chops and black-eyed peas, steaming cornbread and sweating glasses of iced tea. They joined hands and Joe Dell prayed for their health and happiness, but Daniel was thinking of something else, of the farm, and he suddenly saw not an ordered white clapboard house with thick shade trees but a sagging mass of planks and a man with a fearful scowl grimly clenching a cigarette in the corner of his mouth. Daniel opened his eyes before the blessing was over and tried to think who the man might be, but he did not know.

"Amen," said Joe Dell, and they dropped their hands and began to eat.

"Why were you cleaning those headstones with mineral spirits?" asked Irene.

"Somebody painted things on the stones," Daniel said. "Spray paint. They painted twisted crosses and names of people and words."

"Like what?" asked Joe Dell.

"Oh, like 'Howard sucks,'" said Daniel. "Could I have some more cornbread, please?"

Joe Dell glanced at Irene, and she was trying hard not to laugh, and he grinned and shook his head while Daniel ate, nodding as if to confirm what he had seen.

"Thank you. I like this cornbread. I walked up town and bought the mineral spirits by myself."

"That's good, son," said Joe Dell. He started to laugh and, knowing he could not stop it, got up and walked to the bathroom and shut the door. Irene's eyes smiled, but she stayed with Daniel until Joe Dell came back, finally composed. Daniel ate slower and slower until, his plate not quite empty, he stopped altogether and simply stared out the window at the trees and the late afternoon sun.

"Daniel, what is it?" Irene said finally.

He turned to her and shook his head. He seemed confused.

"How do you know when you are happy?" he asked. "I feel like I am in the wrong place sometimes."

"We all feel that way," said Irene soothingly. She rested her pudgy hand on Daniel's arm. "If you do your best and trust in the Lord, you will find peace. You are a fine young man. You will find your peace."

Daniel looked at Irene, and his eyes filled with tears that did not fall. "I do not know who my mother was," he said. "Does your mother live in Athens, Irene?"

"Child, my mother went to her reward years ago," said Irene.

"Reward?" asked Daniel. "Did she win something?"

"It means she's passed on," said Joe Dell. "That she's died, Daniel."

"Oh," said Daniel. "Is your mother...?"

"She's passed on, too," said Joe Dell. "That's nothing to be sad about. Everything dies. It's how God shows us he wants us to be good. If nothing ever died, why would anybody be good?"

"Oh," said Daniel, trying to understand.

After dinner, Daniel sat on the sofa with Joe Dell, who dozed, feet on the coffee table, before heading to work at DuPont. Irene washed the dishes and sang along with a record of hymns sung by Eddy Arnold. Daniel looked around the room at the pieces of their life, things Irene collected, tiny porcelain farm animals, cows, goats and chickens. On top of the television was a clock enclosed in a glass dome, within which a dancing girl twirled each time it struck the hour. Joe Dell had given it to Irene when they were married.

The sun eased westward, and shadows angled around the trailer's walls. Irene finished in the kitchen and sat down in her easy chair, picked up something that she was knitting and hummed with the music. Daniel sometimes got single words in his head and turned them over and over. Now he was thinking of "love." He knew that Jesus loved the little children. He knew that Joe Dell and Irene loved each other. On the television, men and women fell in love, and sometimes it was terrible.

Joe Dell finally stirred and got up to get ready for work. Daniel thanked the Baileys for having him over and then went outside into the lightning-bug flecked night. He walked through the park, thinking about Greenvale and the farm and love.

"Toggle!" he cried. Each night just at dusk, he went to check his mail, his dog alongside, and now Toggle came bolting from beneath the trailer, snapping at bugs drawn by the lights of the park. "Good boy. Good boy."

Daniel did not see the boys or hear their frantic whispering or laughter. At the entrance to the trailer park was a row of mailboxes, and Daniel's was the third. He came around near Oconee Street and reached for the box, and just as he opened it, a deafening explosion tore the air. Daniel screamed, a high-pitched girlish shriek, and fell to the still-hot earth, holding his ears and squirming. Toggle turned and ran back toward his Cabbage Patch Kids swimming pool.

At the edge of a stand of bamboo that separated the trailer park from some single-family houses nearby, three teen-aged boys fell on the ground, laughing and pointing at Daniel. Gradually, he let go of his ears and got to his knees and looked around. He saw the boys and felt his face grow hot; this was the third time it had happened, a cherry bomb in his mailbox, and he knew who was behind it all— Wade Rucker, the tall blond boy who was walking toward him now, followed by the others. Daniel stood and waved the smoke away from the box and reached inside and pulled out the tattered, smoking remains of a circular from a variety store not far away. He loved to read the circulars, but this one was useless, and flakes of it fell at his feet.

"Hey, Dummy," said Wade, swaggering up close. "You better report that mailbox. I think it's got a loose screw or something." The boys behind Wade howled with laughter. "Lots of things around here have loose screws. Am I right, or what?"

Daniel folded what was left of the circular and held it tightly. He started to walk past the boys, but Wade Rucker stepped in front of him.

"I asked you a question, shithead," Wade said.

"Let me go," said Daniel.

"Hey, Dummy," Wade said, holding up his hands, "I wouldn't hurt a fly." Daniel walked quickly past the boys, whose laughter finally faded. When he got inside the trailer, Toggle right behind him, he was breathing hard and no longer thinking of love.

FIVE

DANIEL STOOD IN THE CENTRAL PART of Oconee Hill Cemetery, pulling weeds from around one of his favorite graves. No matter how hard Frank tried to make Daniel understand that all the graves needed attention, Daniel had a few favorites he kept immaculate, and Frank only sighed and shook his head when he saw the inevitable perfection of those plots. On this day, just past the elegance of the Billups-Phinizy stones, Daniel was reading out loud as he worked.

"OUR CHILDREN," he said, "WILLIAM MOORE AND RICHARD ARNOLD ARE GONE HOME." Sometimes he carried a small pad and pencil in his hip pocket to figure how old the inhabitants of the tombs had been at death, and the graves of children always moved him the most. The cemetery was dotted with lambs whose marble wool seemed wondrous to him. In the new part of the cemetery there were pictures of the dead people on some of the graves, a few of them children who had died in accidents or from some disease.

Mrs. Wilkins had said life and death were in God's hands, that the world was like a clock wound up by God, and that everything that happened was part of God's plan. For a while after he left

Greenvale, Daniel had tried to make plans, but confused by his new freedom, could not; after a few weeks, he merely worked and went home, having established this comfortable ritual.

Rebecca stood near the lichen-crusted trunk of a live oak only thirty yards from Daniel and watched him talk quietly to himself as he worked. She had not been able to stop thinking of him, of the way he told her about the cleaning of stone. Was it possible there was something pure about him, as pure as the poetry of Keats, tragic and simple as sunrise? You're a romantic fool, Rebecca had thought at first, but then she had dreamed about Daniel the night before. Both of them were drifting through Oconee Hill, at night, as if they were spirits in waving gowns, and Daniel was smiling and telling her that death was something wonderful, that when the gap between life and the eternal sleep was made, every corner of the world exploded with a glorious light, an unending comfort, something dazzling and triumphant. And in that dream, she had felt it, more powerful than childhood, enduring—the loving arms of some pulsing and enfolding warmth.

She had awakened, breathing hard, remembering the dream whole cloth, knowing that the light was not God because there was no God. Milton's believing in God was one thing, but not now, when science was beyond such fallow superstition. But what was the light? And more, who was Daniel? She ate pastry at The Mayflower Restaurant on Broad Street where she was a regular, bought a newspaper and read about a thousand stupidities. She had planned to visit her office, but instead she walked straight to Oconee Hill.

The day, like most late June days in north Georgia, was sunny and humid, the heat dripping down her chest in rivulets, down her back and along the waistband of her underwear. She wore light-weight khaki pants and a white cotton blouse, and the heat did not bother her too much. When she came into the cemetery, she did not see the blaze of whiteness, though she half expected it, but some indefinable feeling did wash over her, and she did not walk far before she saw Daniel weeding around a stone and whispering in secret phrases to the dead.

As emotions began to crowd into her throat, Rebecca brushed the hair behind her ears and tried to reason. She thought of Swedenborg, of Kant and Thomas Gray. She even thought of a poem by Lorca, but when she looked at Daniel, standing there in his drab clothes, looking as if he had just been named winner of some school prize, she thought, effortlessly and unexpectedly, of Lawrence Dale. She found herself walking toward Daniel in the dappled light.

He saw a flash of white and turned and smiled brightly when he saw her. The morning had not been pleasant for Daniel, because after he had tied up Toggle and said goodbye to his neighbors, Mike and Pam Gassner, who were arguing again about something outside their trailer as he passed by on his way to work, Wade Rucker had driven right up to him in his souped-up '57 Chevrolet. He had leaned out and leered at Daniel.

"Hey Dummy, checked your mail?" Wade had asked. Then he had scratched off, howling in derision, covering Daniel in a whirl of dust. Daniel had felt his rage rise and then subside, knowing there was nothing he could do, that he could not fight back because he did not know how. At Greenvale, everyone was taught to be passive and yielding, not to fight the way of the world. Many of those who lived there would never fit in, Mr. Wilkins said. So Daniel, covered with dirt after having carefully showered and dressed this morning, had walked to work, past the Salvation Army Thrift Store, over the Oconee River Bridge and then south past O'Malley's, which was quiet now early in the morning. By the time he had passed the North Campus dormitories, the anger had leached from his bones, and already he was thinking of what he would do that day, and how good the bologna sandwich would taste in the heavy shade of his favorite old tree at noon.

Daniel stepped back to look at the stone and wiped his nose, turning when he caught a glimpse of Rebecca's white blouse. She was smiling at him as she approached, walking with her hands behind her back, and he smiled, too.

"OUR CHILDREN ARE GONE HOME," Daniel said shyly. When he

saw that she did not understand, he pointed at the stone. "OUR CHILDREN ARE GONE HOME."

Rebecca saw his eyes beneath the snug canopy of his baseball cap, saw that they were alive with a whisper of peace.

"Children," she said. She moved nearer and read the stone with him, feeling the wonder of lost children swell over her. Daniel could smell her this close, a mixture of soap and shampoo and cologne, and he looked at her hands.

"You do not have your flowers," Daniel said. "You could give flowers to Our Children."

Rebecca was shocked. She looked up at Daniel with a stricken expression, the phrase "our children" suddenly swollen with meaning, and she thought of Charlie Dominic, who wanted kids. Rebecca did not have time for children; her career was, she was convinced, a tough one that allowed few distractions.

"I forgot to pick any," said Rebecca. "I guess I shouldn't be picking them, anyway."

"I do not remember your name."

"Rebecca."

He stared at her, and she felt awkward. "Gentry," she added, as if it explained everything.

Daniel took off his cap and held it tightly in his hand, bowing gently from the waist like an old-world suitor. "I am Daniel Mitchell," he said. "I saw you when it was raining, and I was cleaning paint from the stones."

"Yes," said Rebecca. "You asked me if I loved the people down there." She motioned to the earth, toward the chambers there beneath them, and Daniel nodded and smiled again. "Did you get all the paint off?"

"I will show you, Rebecca," he said, his eyes bright. He grabbed his rags and the weed clippers he kept in his hip pocket and started up the street toward the hill, the oldest part of the cemetery. She did not move, and after ten steps, he turned and saw her standing there. The morning sunlight was soft and soaked through the shade, curling around Rebecca's hair and shoulders. He saw her hesitation and wondered if she were really a person or, perhaps, just a wandering spirit returning to see her name upon a stone. Daniel did believe in spirits, but in a benevolent way, thinking that on special days they returned to earth if only for a brief moment. "Come. I will show you."

Rebecca was afraid of something. She felt her legs moving as though she were trying to run in a stream of molasses, but she finally began to follow him. This was no dream, she thought; everything about Daniel was a mirror that magnified the defects of her heart, and yet she could not turn away.

"Okay," she said. She caught up to Daniel, who had put his cap back on and was walking slowly. He moved oddly, she thought, not exactly a limp, but as if his legs were not quite sure where to go, as if his heels might sprout wings at any minute and he would rise from the earth.

"Frank said that I did a fine job," said Daniel.

"Who's Frank?" asked Rebecca. She lit a cigarette as they walked.

"Frank is the caretaker," said Daniel. "He is my boss."

They walked in silence for perhaps twenty paces.

"I have a boss," she said simply.

Daniel smiled broadly then, and Rebecca wanted to ask him personal questions: What was his favorite color? What was his mother like? Had he ever been in love? But she said nothing as they walked up the hill. Suddenly she felt hot and weak, and she dropped the cigarette and ground it out. When they got to the crest of the hill, she tried to remember which stones had been vandalized, but none showed any marks, not of paint or of cleaning, and she stared at them more in awe than approval.

"Jesus Christ, I can't even tell which ones were painted," she said.

"Jesus Christ you sure cannot!" said Daniel. "I cleaned them with the mineral spirits, and then I washed my hands with Lava. Only one thing gets these hands clean, mister— Lava!" He held up his hands and laughed, and so did Rebecca.

"I teach literature at the University," she blurted.

Daniel slowly lowered his hands, trying to understand.

"It's over there," she pointed a finger, gesturing. " The University. You know the University?"

"Yes," he said. "I have never been over there past the football place. I sit out here in the fall when they play football and listen to the sounds of the people. When something good happens, it sounds like wind."

"Wind," said Rebecca.

"In the trees," said Daniel. "You are a teacher."

"Yes," she said. "I teach twentieth century literature. Stories, novels, poetry—like that."

"Stories," said Daniel. He took off his hat and pulled a clean white handkerchief from his pocket and wiped the sweat from his brow, then folded it neatly and stuffed it back into his pants. "I like 'The Old Man of the Mountain'."

"Hawthorne," smiled Rebecca. "He's a little before what I do."

"Third," said Daniel.

"What?"

"Third. It was in our third reading book at Greenvale."

"Greenvale?" she asked cautiously. "What is that?"

"Home," he said. "Where I came from. It is my home." His eyes grew clouded, and he looked away from her at one of the stones for a long time. "Not really my home. But my home. I have never been to my home. I have never been to my farm." He looked at Rebecca and saw that she was confused, and he smiled again. "I like stories. Mrs. Wilkins said that anybody could be a story."

"Who is Mrs. Wilkins?" Rebecca asked. They sat on the two-foot-high stone wall that surrounded the very top of the hill, where former Georgia Governor Wilson Lumpkin was buried in late December of 1870.

"She was my teacher at Greenvale," Daniel nodded. "She told us stories from the books. And she told us stories about her life. She said anybody could be a story."

"What story did Mrs. Wilkins tell you?" asked Rebecca.

Daniel's eyes narrowed. Nearby, a brown thrasher landed on the wall, its tail bobbing in greeting to some invisible mate or companion.

"The farm story," said Daniel. "That was the story about me." He laughed too loud, and Rebecca was startled to see that he was blushing beneath the long bill of his baseball cap.

"Tell it to me," she said.

"Lordy mercy," said Daniel. "It was not true. I did not know where I came from before Greenvale, and Mrs. Wilkins made up this story about me."

"Why didn't she just tell you the truth?" asked Rebecca. "I think you have a right to know how you got there, don't you?"

Daniel turned on the stone wall and stared at her, cocking his head. "A right? I don't know what...."

"They should have told you where you really came from," she said. "They didn't have the right to make up stories about that."

"I love the farm story," Daniel said, embarrassed.

"Oh God, I'm sorry," said Rebecca. She reached out and touched his arm, and when she did, he felt a chill of pleasure, the way he felt when he saw Toggle in the afternoon each day. He looked up at her with eyes beginning to fill with tears, and Rebecca pulled back, her chest thumping wildly at the passion of his response to her touch. "Please tell me the farm story, Daniel."

"That is George Jordan Newton," he said, pointing to a large shaft on the east side of Oconee Hill, toward the stadium. "FIRST TROOP ARTILLERY, COBB'S LEGION. Frank told me that was in the War. That man died in this war."

"The Civil War," said Rebecca. "That was a long time ago."

"Everything was a long time ago," said Daniel. He had choked back the tears and was smiling again. Then he stuck his tongue into the corner of his mouth, the way he often did when he felt awkward, until he could think of something else to say. "Joe Dell and Irene are my best friends. They live near me. I have my own trailer. It is in Oconee-By-The-River."

Rebecca knew the place, having once gone before the Planning

Commission with a group from the local Preservation Council, trying to prevent it from being put there. The group had visited it six months after the Planning Commission had approved the project despite their objection and found it was already a scar on East Athens, a case history for unmanaged development and spot zoning.

"I know where that is," Rebecca said.

"And I have a dog named Toggle," said Daniel. "He is a brown dog."

Rebecca laughed at the odd name, and Daniel laughed, too, though he wasn't sure why.

"And Mrs. Daisy Saye gives me magazines. She is not a witch. Randi Ambrose told me she was a witch. Daisy is just a lady. Randi has green hair sometimes."

Rebecca laughed again, and when she did, Daniel took off his cap and laughed again, too. She studied his face briefly: a shock of dark blond hair, the brown eyes, the smooth, tanned cheeks and, with the laughter, the slightest hint of dimples.

"Tell me something about you," Daniel said shyly.

"Well," said Rebecca, still trying to stifle a giggle, "like I said, I teach...stories...at the University, and I live uptown in Campus North. You know, the ten-story building downtown." She waited for a flash of recognition, but it did not come. "Have you been downtown, Daniel?"

"I went to the hardware for mineral spirits," he said.

"Okay," she said. "Anyway, I live there by myself. My best friend is named Annie, and I used to be married to a man named Charlie, but we got divorced."

"I am so sorry," said Daniel.

"It wasn't anybody's fault," she said. "Oh. And I'm a poet."

"Poet," he repeated carefully.

"I write...poems," she said, her voice trailing off. She felt ridiculous. "Did you study poems at Greenvale?"

Daniel looked stern for a moment and then brightened. "Under the spreading chestnut tree!" he said, exultant.

"Yes!" cried Rebecca.

"Tell me one of your poems," said Daniel.

Rebecca felt her skin tingle with shock; through years of publishing in little magazines, through two books from major publishers, nobody had ever asked her to recite one of her poems from memory. She saw his eyebrows arch in anticipation, so she nodded and immediately remembered a short lyric, one she had written when her mother had died. It had been published in *Prairie Schooner*.

"Okay," she said, finally. "This is a short one called 'A Perfect Distance.'" She stood and faced Daniel, her hands behind her in the declamation pose she had learned in the eighth grade. She spoke softly:

"At the whispered edge of this life,
My heart fails to dream your face.
Were you the darkness of my dreams,
The primal brine of my tears as they
Laid you among the aroma of daisies?
No. You were the echo of my hands
And the shadow of my witness to love;
You were the perfect distance between
My childish waking into the night
And the rush of love, ever, ever, ever."

Daniel thought it was the most beautiful thing he had ever heard in his life, and before he could stop, his face was twisted with tears.

Rebecca was surprised to have remembered it at all, much less to have spoken it with such obvious passion. When she looked at Daniel, she saw that he was looking away from her, crying, and she felt her throat becoming choked with her own unspilled tears. But when she took a step toward him, he jumped up and put the cap back on his head in one motion and ran off down the hill, heavy-footed, back toward the graves of Our Children.

"Daniel!" she cried. "Daniel!"

She watched him run away, watched him lumbering down the hill. She thought he said something, but she could not make out the words. Finally, she did not cry; instead, she lit a cigarette and sat down on the wall. What in her poem had made him run away? She sighed and walked down the street and through the stone-clasped iron gates of Oconee Hill and headed back across campus toward Park Hall. Some unexpected emotion was growing in her, and she did not know quite what to think. She had never before met anyone like Daniel Mitchell, and she knew that she had to talk to him again.

THAT NIGHT, REBECCA DROVE TO ANNIE PHILLIPS' house in a subdivision called Forest Heights. Rebecca had bought a blue MGB the year before, but now she felt almost ridiculous driving it around Athens. The summer air was full of water, and Rebecca could almost imagine piloting a submarine in caves of water as she drove. She passed summer lawns of children lost in endless games of tag, summer lawns running over with sprinklers whose spray turned into rainbows in the shafts of sun. She saw fat women emerging from cars in the parking lot of the Forest Heights Baptist Church, laden with food for a social. She had come by Bishop Park, the city's softball and swimming pool complex, and saw men too old for glory dressed in uniforms beneath the canopy of field lights. She saw an elderly man moving slowly down a shaded sidewalk, clinging to a walker and speaking to himself. What had she lost and when had she started to lose it?

Brad and Annie lived in a ranch-style brick house on a shady side street where everything was perfectly ordered. Brad, a tall handsome man who owned a tire dealership, was pleasant enough, though Rebecca had never once heard him give an opinion about anything that mattered to her. When Rebecca pulled into the driveway, Brad was kneeling in the front yard furiously pulling weeds from his neat zoysia lawn. When he saw Rebecca, he waved and rocked back on his heels.

"Attack of the chickweed!" he shouted as Rebecca got out of the car. He threw a handful of green leaves into the air. When he stood, Rebecca was startled, as she always was, at what a good-looking man Annie had married, how in his mid-thirties he was still muscular and desirable. Once, a year before, Rebecca had thought she was in love with Brad, but of course she had never told Annie or anyone else, and the infatuation had finally died.

"How's it going, Brad?" Rebecca asked. She walked across the lawn toward him, and he admired her legs, deeply tanned in the white shorts and tank top she habitually wore on many summer days. Although she knew it was adolescent and foolish, Rebecca had never given up her summer suntan, and she began each March lying out in the sharp light.

"I'm better than you'd ever imagine," he grinned. They always played games of sexual allusion in a way that neither took seriously and that Annie seemed to find funny.

"That's not what I hear at the YWCA," Rebecca said.

"Those sluts," he said, feigning dismay. "They told on me again. How are things with you?"

"Okay," she said. "Is Whatshername here?"

"Inside, where it's cool, watching something on Public Television," he said. "I think it's dating problems of the pygmies or something. You know how those shows are."

"Good luck with the chickweed," Rebecca said, walking toward the carport and the side door into the kitchen.

"It doesn't have a prayer," he said.

Rebecca opened the door and immediately saw Freud, Annie's black cat, looking forlornly at his water dish on a mat by the trashcan.

"Freud," she said, "is the water fountain dry?" The cat arched its back, rubbed against her legs and gave a deep, mournful cry as she filled the dish. Rebecca knelt and caressed Freud, making sounds of affection.

"Be careful, Freud," Annie's voice said. "She's the famous cat burglar, Rebecca Gentry. She'll take you off and make you listen to the collected works of Anne Sexton."

"Hey," she said, standing, "how's it going?"

"Grrr," Annie said. "This is my turf. You're lucky I didn't piss on you and kill your young."

"Are you watching one of those animal shows again?" asked Rebecca. "Brad said you were watching Dating Problems of the Pygmies."

Annie laughed, the deep, resounding laugh that Rebecca liked so well. "It's *Wild America*," she said. "Marty Stouffer was just telling me how life is like a wild boar in rut or something. I may have dozed off. You want a beer?"

They both took an icy bottle of Coors Light from the refrigerator and went into the sunken den. The lights were all off and the television droned. They sat next to each other on the sofa in the darkening room and sipped their beer for a while.

Rebecca lit a cigarette. "I've met an extraordinary man," she said.

Annie turned toward her, pulling her feet beneath her hips. "You have not." She smiled. "There aren't any extraordinary men any more."

"Brad?"

"Oh, him," Annie nodded. "Not in the English Department? Is it that writer-in-residence, what's his name?"

"Tift Bronson? That creep?"

"Well, live and learn."

"No, this is somebody who's completely different," Rebecca said.

"He's sounding like somebody from Monty Python," said Annie.

"Please," Rebecca said, affecting distaste. Then she grinned. "He works in the big cemetery over there on the other side of campus, you know, Oconee Hill?"

"My God, Gentry, you've taken up with a gravedigger?" said Annie. "Freud, come here and talk to this woman." The cat sauntered into the room and jumped into Annie's lap and rubbed against her chest happily.

"He's just somebody who cuts grass and pulls weeds and stuff," said Rebecca. "He's slow—or slightly retarded—or something. He grew up in Greenvale. I heard it is a home for handicapped kids near Augusta? He's been up here for three years, and he talks about all the people in the cemetery as if they were his friends. I think they *are* his friends in some way. I know, it sounds odd as hell, but he has some quality that makes me feel something...I don't know."

"When did you meet him?"

"I've been walking around in the cemetery a lot lately, trying to get my bearings," said Rebecca. "You know how I feel, I told you that. I met him there, but I didn't really talk to him until this morning. He asked me to tell him one of my poems after I told him I was a poet, and I recited the one I wrote after my mother died. It was published in *Prairie Schooner*. And when I did, he started crying and ran off down the hill. It really shook me up. I haven't been able to think of anything but Daniel all day."

"Daniel," said Annie. "What does he look like?"

"Oh, I don't know," said Rebecca. "He's in his late twenties, I guess. He's blond, brown eyes, wears a Braves cap. He walks like each step is something entirely new to him. I can't think of anything but him crying and running off. That's really hilarious, isn't it?"

Annie stared quietly at her friend and shook her head. "You know you don't have to fake your feelings with me," she said. "He sounds a little different from the guys in academia."

"Oh, God."

"You know what I mean," said Annie. "Just be careful. Don't get carried away. What am I saying? *You* get carried away? You're the most reserved and rational person in all history who also wrote poetry."

"Reserved and rational lost me a husband," Rebecca said. She laughed, but it was unconvincing, and Annie looked at her tenderly, arching her eyebrows as if to underscore her point. "Anyway, I just wanted to tell somebody."

"Are you going back to see him again?" asked Annie.

"I don't know what I'm going to do," Rebecca admitted. "Are you and Brad going to Kent Ziegler's party Friday night?"

"I don't know," said Annie, making a face. "Brad hates those parties, and I do, too. But it's an obligation, I guess."

"Did you talk to your folks this week?" asked Rebecca.

"Mother just keeps saying, 'Your father's fine,'" said Annie. "When I think of him, I feel like I'm falling very slowly and I think I want to hit bottom, and sometimes I just close my eyes and drift."

"That's the way I feel," said Rebecca.

When she got home, Rebecca turned on the radio and listened to part of a symphony by Bruckner before deciding, after three more beers, to call Charlie in Charleston, where he had moved the year before. She was feeling more vulnerable now than she wanted to admit.

"Hi, Baby," she said when Charlie's familiar voice came on the phone after three rings.

"Becky?" he said groggily. "You know what time it is?"

She hadn't thought of the time. Now she glanced at the glowing clock on her microwave in the kitchen and saw that it was well after midnight.

"I'm sorry," she said. "I didn't."

"Is something wrong?"

She lit a cigarette and wondered why she had called him at all.

"No, no," she said. "I was just sitting here looking out over the streetlights and I...I'm sorry, I don't know."

"You had some drinks?"

"I'm sorry, Hon," she said. "It's nothing. I'll let you go back to sleep."

Rebecca wondered if another woman was snuggled beside him in the bed, drowsy, feeling the warmth of his body.

"You sure nothing's wrong?"

"Nothing. You all right?"

"Yes," said Charlie.

"Goodbye," said Rebecca. She hung up without waiting for the sound of his voice and walked unsteadily into her study, wondering if perhaps she should quit her job and leave Athens. No, she thought, I could never do anything that rash. She felt the tide of Oconee Hill pulling her back into some past she had never dreamed and into the eyes of a man who had wept at the beauty of her words.

SIX

HE KNELT IN THE SAND ON THE WEST BANK OF THE OCONEE and looked into the river, watching his face wave in uneven threads of water and, reflected beyond that image, the undulating dark green of the trees. Mr. Wilkins had taken the children at Greenvale to the Richmond County Fair one year, and Daniel could never forget the rushing laughing of the Scrambler ride. But his favorite was the mirror house. Long after all the other children were back on the bus, Daniel was missing, and Mrs. Wilkins had found him in the mirror house staring at his own reshaped image. Daniel was only nine then, but he still remembered the mirror house, and on Saturdays, like today, he would climb down past the iron bridge that separated the halves of Oconee Hill Cemetery and stare, dreaming, into the turgid waters of the river.

"Don't you fall into that river," a voice far to his right said. Daniel rocked back on his heels and saw Woodrow Faust.

"I will not, Woodrow," said Daniel. "Have you caught anything?"

"Hell, no," Woodrow said, shrugging and smiling pleasantly. He was very fat, and his skin was dark walnut, a color Daniel could never remember having seen. Today, as he did most Saturdays, Woodrow was fishing from the river bank for catfish, sitting in the strap-and-aluminum lawn chair he always brought. Pinching a lead sinker eighteen inches or so from the bait and letting it sink to the bottom, he wrapped the index finger of his right hand just past where the string was secured to the base of the cane pole. When he got a fish, the line would tighten around his finger, sometimes waking him up, for he often dozed in his chair.

"Tell me something."

Daniel walked slowly toward Woodrow, feeling the humid, still air of the river floor.

"Yes, Woodrow?"

"How come you always come back here on your day off? How come a young man like you ain't out kicking up your heels?"

"Kicking up your heels?" Daniel was puzzled.

"You know, out with the ladies, going dancing, maybe even taking a little drink once in a while," said Woodrow. "Don't you never want to kick up your heels?"

"I do not know how." Daniel laughed, blushing a bright red.

"Aw, Daniel, it ain't nothing to it," said Woodrow. "It's just living. Ain't no man a saint but them in the Bible, and they ain't no reason to be living like one. You oughtn't to be here with old colored men fishing when you could be whispering in some fancy thing's ear."

"I know of the saints," Daniel said. "Saint Paul, Saint John, Saint Matthew...."

"Whoa, looky here!" cried Woodrow. "Catfish, come up in my arms!" He lifted the slender pole, and the tip bent down to the stirring water, trembling as the fish rose to the surface, breaking the water in a waving arc. Woodrow lifted the fish out of the river, and it flopped from side to side, croaking and dripping silvered drops of the Oconee river.

"Catfish!" cried Daniel, clapping his hands in delight. When Daniel had first come to Greenvale, he could not express happiness, and so Mrs. Wilkins had taught him to clap. During his last two years there, however, she had tried to stop him, telling him a grown man should not do such things. Even so, Daniel still clapped when he felt a sudden rush of happiness. Woodrow took the fish off the hook, slid it onto his stringer and slung it back into the water.

"I'm gone have me some supper tonight," he said, rebaiting the hook, when someone called Daniel's name. It was a woman's voice. Daniel looked at Woodrow, who had turned to look up on the metal bridge, squinting his eyes. "She calling you name, Daniel."

"My name," Daniel said.

"Up there, boy," said Woodrow, nodding up toward the bridge. Daniel turned and saw Rebecca standing there in a white sundress. She waved cheerfully at him, and he felt his arm rise, unknowing, and wave back at her. He took off his hat and stood there looking at her.

"It is the flower lady," he said, turning back to look at Woodrow.

"The flower lady?" asked Woodrow, casting the bait back into the water. "She mighty nice, Daniel. You know each other?"

"Daniel!" Rebecca repeated. She looked down and saw the light enter his eyes, his clear delight in seeing her. She felt herself swell into the warm summer morning as he returned her look of pleasure.

"She makes beautiful things," said Daniel.

Rebecca felt better now that she had seen him. The night before, at Kent Ziegler's party, she had wondered if she could ever again feel *so . . .* What? So . . . *easy, this* easy, this directed.

THE PARTY, LIKE ALL ACADEMIC PARTIES, was like riding down a grocery store aisle in a cart with a flat wheel.

Kent's house was on the east side in a subdivision called Idle Acres, a fashionable cluster of taste and money, populated by BMWs and Perrier fanciers. Rebecca had arrived late and found that Annie was occupied, deep into a conversation on *The World as Will and Idea* by Schopenhauer. Rebecca got a beer from a huge iced tub on the deck and looked around. The house was all wood and angles, glass and light. The front yard was manicured with neatly trimmed Bermuda grass, while the pebbled path which led around back opened into a lush tangle of tropical plants and tiki torches. A curved walkway made of rich, lustrous lumber snaked into the yard from the deck for some thirty yards before expanding into yet another deck; this one held a hot tub covered with a palm-leaf roof and a long-haired young man playing a guitar and singing quietly.

Beer in hand, Rebecca wandered out along the board walkway, stopping to say hello to friends and colleagues from the department but not staying anywhere long. When she came to the deck, the young man was singing the old James Taylor song, "You've Got a Friend." She moved to one side, feeling unhappy and foolish.

"Hello, lovely lady," a male voice said, right behind her, and Rebecca jumped, spilling part of her beer. She turned and saw Tift Bronson, writer-in-residence and owner of a painful imitation English accent, swinging up onto the edge of the torchlit deck from somewhere in the darkness. Tift Bronson was one of those Literary Figures who had written one critically acclaimed book and then kept on acclaiming it himself until he was able to spend time moving from school to school as Writer-in-Residence.

"You out playing Tarzan or something, Tift?" She did not know him very well, just well enough to have developed a vague loathing for him. Tonight he was obviously drunk, something he took as an obligation as writer-in-residence. He also took pawing every woman within reach as part of his duty.

"I've got something wonderful to tell you," Tift smiled. He was about forty, just under six feet, with a mane of silver hair and a salt-and-pepper beard he cultivated more carefully than an old woman does her garden.

"I've been waiting all my life," said Rebecca. She set her beer down on a nearby table and lit a cigarette. The singer had launched into "Leaving on a Jet Plane."

"But on the contrary, you will be astounded by this," said Tift. He wore white pants made of a fabric not much heavier than mosquito netting and a Hawaiian-print shirt that was open nearly to the waist, exposing a chestful of dark hair and a gold necklace from which dangled a small medallion with the face of Walt Whitman, Tift's hero, raised in bas-relief.

"So?"

"Ah, but my dear," he said grandly. "You told me about your hillbilly writer. The one you are writing that book about?"

"He *wasn't* a hillbilly," said Rebecca, feeling her anger rise.

"Oh, whatever," said Tift, waving her objection away like a bug. "Anyway, he died the day before Jack Kennedy, and nobody knew he died, right?"

"Jack Kennedy?" said Rebecca. "You and Kennedy were buddies?"

"I'll ignore that," Tift said. Rebecca looked at him with mounting disgust, but she was somehow fascinated that he would bring up Lawrence Dale, a genuine talent and unspoiled writer, here among the glow of tiki torches. "Now then, are you aware that the great Soviet composer Sergei Prokofiev died just fifty minutes before Stalin, for God's sake? Nobody knew Prokofiev had died for simply days and days. You might want to include that somewhere in your manuscript."

"Is that true?" asked Rebecca suspiciously.

"Cross my heart," said Tift. "I can't lie to a lovely lady like you."

Rebecca cringed when he said "cahn't" and stiffened when he stepped closer, touched her shoulder and looked meaningfully into her eyes.

"Why don't we go back to my apartment? I can tell you wonderful things, Rebecca. I'm a writer. I see how things connect, how the world is put together," he crooned.

"Tift," Rebecca said sweetly, "you don't know your arse from a hole in the ground. But thanks for the story about Stalin."

"Well," he said, offended. "Is that all I get? I worked hard for this. I spent a lot time finding that out."

Rebecca turned and began walking away, but she soon sensed

that Tift was close behind her. He was moving unsteadily across the boards, past the singing guitar player, who had slipped into "Peaceful Easy Feeling." Two feet from the hot tub, she stopped and turned to face him.

"Come on now, lovely lady."

"Get away from me," Rebecca said.

"One kiss and you'll change your mind," said Tift.

Just as he grabbed for her, Rebecca stepped to one side, planted her feet firmy and, as he lunged past her, gave him a tremendous shove. Tift Bronson took two lurching, ungainly steps forward and fell headlong into the hot tub with Sydney Norman, a fiftyish professor of comparative literature who was obviously delighted. The singer stopped and stared openly, as did almost everyone else in the backyard, and Sydney, who had spent a great deal of money on a facelift and hair coloring, seemed to take Tift's dive as a gift.

He came up from the water, spluttering, "Fine, then, you addled bitch." He pointed his finger at Rebecca. She turned and walked back toward the house, thinking she would look for Annie. Instead, just before she got to the house, she stepped off the walkway and walked straight around the house, got into her car and drove off, feeling as if she needed a shower.

She drove back into Athens on College Station Road, passing research buildings and a few barns, some with adjacent fenced pastures that in the daytime held strong, swift horses. She turned north on River Road. Parties were underway at several of the fraternity houses, but these were subdued, as they always were in summer; in the fall, she knew, such parties were often riotous. She came out on East Campus Road under a railroad trestle, and a hundred yards past that was the entrance to Oconee Hill Cemetery. The gates were closed tightly. Rebecca pulled up next to them and looked inside at the unreal light from street lamps that played upon the stones closest to the road.

"Daniel," she said out loud.

Now, SHE WATCHED HIM STRUGGLE UP THE RIVER BANK, saw the black man clasping a cane pole that at this height looked like a reed. Daniel came up and around to her right and walked toward her, face beaming. *What is it I feel?*

"Hello, Rebecca," he called out. "I have remembered your name."

"Yes, you have, Daniel," said Rebecca. "Did your friend catch anything?"

He met her in the middle of the bridge. "That is Woodrow," he called out. "He has caught many fish in the river."

"I didn't know if you would be here or not," she said. "Do you work on Saturday?"

"I have this day off, and Sunday," said Daniel.

"Then what are you doing here?" she asked, smiling. Daniel thought she must be the loveliest woman who ever lived. Yesterday, after she had told him the beautiful words, he had thought about her for hours, saying her name over and over so he would not forget it. And now, like one of his dreams, she was here, her long brown hair soft on her shoulders. He stared at her with delight and did not speak.

"Daniel? Did you hear me?"

"What?" he said, jolted. "I am sorry."

"If this is your day off, why did you come to Oconee Hill?"

"The river," he said. He pointed down at the water, and even though it was a sluggish, muddy body of water, sun played off the surface, scattering jewels of light. "I come to watch the river and talk to Woodrow. He is my friend."

"I'm glad you are here," she said. "Would you like to go for a ride with me?"

"You have a car?" he asked.

"There," she said, and Daniel turned and saw the blue MGB parked at the edge of the bridge.

"Oh, Rebecca," he said, "it is beautiful!"

And in the middle of the bridge, Daniel Mitchell clapped his hands. Rebecca felt strange, wondered if his odd behavior extended to other things, but she really did not care.

"Thank you very much," she said, and she bowed like a courtier.

On the wet spit of sand in the river, Woodrow Faust watched the scene with bewilderment. The world was a strange place sometimes.

"Will you go for a ride with me?"

"Where are you going?" he asked.

"Anywhere you want," she said. "I just wanted to see you again." She was surprised she had said it, more so when she realized that Daniel was biting his lip and smiling.

"I wanted to see you again, Rebecca," he whispered. "You make things around you beautiful."

She felt a knot growing in her throat, felt something so unreal and unexpected that instead of replying, she inclined her head toward the car and started walking toward it. Daniel fell into step beside her.

"It's a warm day," she said stupidly. They climbed into the car, and Daniel made small sounds of admiration as he ran his thick, roughened fingers over the instrument panel. She felt as if words were somehow pointless, but the silence was even more awkward. "It was made in England."

"England," he said.

She could see him struggling with a thought, taking off his Braves cap and staring at the trees up toward the Gerdine-Cobb column, could see him come into silence without motion. Then his eyes flickered and he turned toward her, exultant.

"The country with a queen," he said very slowly, struggling to get the words out.

"Yes," she nodded. "That's right."

"I wish Mrs. Wilkins could see me remember that," he said. He put his cap back on, as if the effort of thinking, now over, would not allow his skull to be covered. "She always said that things went out of my head like rain through my fingers. She was right about that, Rebecca."

"Where do you want to go?" Rebecca asked.

"I don't know where to go," Daniel said. Then his eyes brightened. "Would you like to see Toggle?"

"Toggle?"

"My dog," Daniel said. "I live in Oconee-By-The-River. You could see my dog, Toggle."

"That's it," she said, and she started the car.

Daniel had not been in a car in nearly two years, and the motion startled him, so he grabbed the door and cried out loud, as delighted as a child on his first ride at the carnival. He watched the graves flow past as they drove back toward the gates of Oconee Hill, watched for and then recognized OUR CHILDREN ARE GONE HOME, saw the scattered iron markers of Civil War veterans, saw trees, shade, sun. The river of images flowed past him. He could smell gardenias, too, the rich and pungent gardenias that grew wild around the cemetery.

Rebecca saw the look on his face and wondered where Daniel had come from, back before Greenvale, and what Greenvale was like. Maybe it was just a warehouse for the helpless, but she doubted it. Daniel seemed to have done rather well there, and now that he sat near her, she could sense, intuitively, some kind of essential simplicity, grace.

"This way," he said, pointing the way when they got to the gates, and they drove north on East Campus Road, went under the railroad trestle, curved around by O'Malley's and came to Oconee Street. As she drove up the hill, Rebecca tried to remember a man she had seen a couple of times after she and Charlie had divorced; he lived off this street somewhere. *Andy, that was his name.* But he had moved to New York, and she could not even place his last name.

"Here we are!"

She saw the sign and turned into the trailer park, saw that it was poor and ill-kept. She stopped in front of Daisy Saye's trailer.

"Which one's yours?" she asked.

Daniel counted down on the left and pointed. "Four," he said. "This is Daisy Saye, who gives me magazines to look through, and that is Mike and Pam, they have a baby named Scottie, and somebody is always screaming there."

Rebecca drove slowly toward his trailer, listening to dogs bark, to children shouting, to the morning sounds of summer in a small trailer park. Just before they got to Number Four, not far ahead, she saw a slender woman in a halter top hanging out clothes in the sun along a line.

"That is Kelly," said Daniel. "Rob is her friend, and they go to the University. They are students."

"Is that Toggle?" she asked. A small brown dog was straining at its leash on the corner of trailer Number Four, crying and barking.

"He is a good dog," Daniel said.

Across the dirt road, Randi Ambrose sat in a recliner under a deck umbrella, drinking a cold beer and listening to the Dead Kennedys. She smoked a long brown cigarette and had, just that morning, changed her hair from pink to orange. When she saw the MG, she stood and walked across the dusty path.

"Dr. Gentry," Randi said, the cigarette dangling from her lips. She wore cat-eye sunglasses and a tight halter top that clearly outlined her breasts. "You a friend of Dan's?"

"Oh, oh," said Daniel jumping out of the car. "Rebecca, this is Randi. She is my friend."

"I know her," Randi said.

Rebecca shaded her eyes with her hand and squinted at Randi, not recognizing her at all.

"I had you for 121," Randi said, the cigarette bobbing with each word. "You'd just had that book published, uh, *Dead Curtains*, something like that?"

"*Dead Lace*," said Rebecca quietly.

"Yeah, right," said Randi. "You famous now, or what?"

"No," Rebecca said. "I'm not famous. Love the hair." She said it with a flat, sarcastic monotone that Randi completely missed.

"I've had green for four months," shrugged Randi. "Dan, you got a pink slip again. You better take care of that, pal." Randi nodded toward his trailer, where a small slip of paper fluttered on the door.

Rebecca felt her heart go out to Daniel, for the poverty of the place, for the limits on his life. His life would be a journey toward some ill-lit goal, down a narrow lane with nowhere else to go.

"I paid them," said Daniel. "I do not understand this." He looked down, obviously embarrassed. Randi started walking back across the street, and Daniel turned and looked at Rebecca. Then he trotted quickly to the door, ripped the paper off and thrust it into his pocket.

"What's wrong?" said Rebecca.

"Nothing," said Daniel. "This is Toggle." He let the dog loose from its mooring, tail wagging as it bounded in front of them. Rebecca knelt and gentled the dog, which stood, neck up, looking at her happily and enjoying the affection.

"Strange name," said Rebecca.

"He already had it when the students gave him to me," Daniel said. "He belonged to Harry."

Daniel unlocked the door, and they went inside. She ached with pity for the few belongings he owned and saw that the coffee table was neatly lined with old copies of *Ladies' Home Journal* and *Redbook,* much like a doctor's office.

"This is really nice," said Rebecca.

Daniel nodded happily. "The best home a boy ever had," he said. Mrs. Wilkins had said that when they had first brought Daniel to Athens. He had not said it since then, or thought of it, and now, as he thought of that day, of the frosty winter day when he had left Greenvale, he felt hot and choked, and tears spilled out of his eyes and rolled down his smooth cheeks.

"Oh God, what's wrong?" asked Rebecca. "Are you okay?"

Daniel wiped the tears away and tried to smile. "It is all right, Rebecca," he said. "I am not much of a man. I have a thought, and I cry."

"What were you thinking of just now?" asked Rebecca. "Please tell me." The trailer suddenly seemed very hot, and Rebecca wanted to ask: Who are you, Daniel? Where did you come from and why do you weep on this summer day?

He sat on the sofa and took off his cap, and Rebecca sat in the chair near him.

"Mr. and Mrs. Wilkins brought me here," he said very slowly. "And she said it is the best home a boy ever had. I thought of her." He looked up at Rebecca, smiling now, the tears still rimming his eyes but no longer falling. "Is that it?"

Rebecca felt as if her life were falling apart, as if the threads that had held things together had ripped and she were at the mercy of wonder. She wanted to cry, to take Daniel in her arms, to mother him, to undress him and make love to him; she wanted to possess the simple affection that made him cry.

"I guess that's it," Rebecca said, feeling choked. She stood and nervously lit a cigarette. "Why don't I drive you around town. Have you really seen the whole town?"

"Okay," he said. "I have not seen much of anything, Rebecca."

She took one more look around the trailer, opened the front door and went out to the car, and Toggle dashed past her and jumped into the Cabbage Patch Kids swimming pool. Daniel put the dog on the chain and climbed into the MG with Rebecca.

The mail came early on Saturdays, and Irene Bailey was coming back toward her trailer from the row of mailboxes on the road. She saw Daniel and Rebecca and stopped, open-mouthed.

"Hey, Daniel," she said. Rebecca could see the look of confusion on her face.

"Hello, Irene!" cried Daniel. "I am going to see Athens with my friend Rebecca."

"That's nice," said Irene. Rebecca tried to smile at Irene and wave at her. She mumbled a few words of greeting and Irene returned them, adding, "Daniel, did you see the pink slip?"

"I have it," said Daniel. He dug it from his pocket, held it up into the bright sunlight and then put it back, almost as if he were proud of it.

"You let me know if you need help," said Irene.

Rebecca started the car, and Daniel shouted in assent as Irene walked on by toward her trailer.

"What is this slip?" asked Rebecca.

"It means I have not paid the rent," said Daniel. He looked at the dashboard, studied it intently, leaning close. "England. You could be the queen, Rebecca."

"I'm no queen," she said. "Why haven't you paid the rent, Daniel?"

"I cannot always find my money," he said. He held the pink slip up and looked at it with pride and amazement. "They bring me these pieces of paper to tell me that."

Rebecca stared at him in disbelief. "What happens to your money, Daniel?" she asked.

He stuffed the slip into the breast pocket of his shirt and looked straight ahead, the cap snugged down over his eyes. He could not tell her. He could not say how he gave money to Wade Rucker so he and his friends would not beat him up again; hadn't Wade told him he'd kill him if he told? He sat there, feeling the sweat dripping down his temples, smiling grimly.

"Never mind," said Rebecca, "I don't want to know."

She put the MG in gear and drove out of the park. On the way, they passed Gene Leach, the trailer park manager. He was skulking around, wearing the perpetual scowl that had become his trademark. Even Daisy Saye had once called him "that old asshole," and Daniel had waved cheerily and yelled, "Hi, asshole!" the next time he'd seen him across the yard, but Gene hadn't heard him.

Rebecca drove uptown on Broad Street past streams of students wandering along hot sidewalks under shapely Bradford pear trees, past Strickland's and Harry Bisset's and Gus Garcia's and Helen's, past the second-hand clothing stores the university crowd liked so much. She showed Daniel where she lived, and he looked up with a huge grin, holding his cap down with his right hand. She drove out Broad Street and turned up Finley, the last cobblestoned street in town, and showed him the Tree That Owns Itself. Years before, an eccentric landowner had deeded his land to the tree itself, so that the city was obliged to keep it up and even bend the street around

it. Rebecca drove Daniel through Cobbham, the in-town neighborhood where university professors spent time and money restoring
Victorian cottages and mansions, then she cut back out to Broad.

She watched Daniel as he took it all in, saw that his mouth was
wide with delight and awe, heard him point and shout when he saw
a forty-foot-high inflated beer can in a promotional display outside a
gas station. As they crossed back over Milledge Avenue, she saw
that Daniel was watching a young woman who was jogging along,
wearing almost nothing, and she wanted to ask, Daniel, have you
ever loved a woman? When they passed an old woman struggling
down the shady sidewalk with a walker, Daniel cocked his head, and
his face seemed as mobile as wind, changeable as the summer clouds
that swelled over Athens.

To Daniel, Athens seemed like some magnificent river, a
flowing thing, its images almost too grand to comprehend. When
he noticed that a clown was driving a truck which pulled up next to
them at the intersection of Baxter and Rocksprings, he pointed,
gave an inarticulate shout and began to clap. Rebecca laughed, and
the clown looked over at them and made a face, leaned toward them
and made the flower on his lapel squirt a stream of water out the
window. Daniel laughed, too loud, and clapped again, and suddenly
the clown was gone, speeding down Baxter, past fast-food places
that seemed to go on forever.

Daniel looked at Rebecca. He wanted to reach out to her, to
tell her he was glad that she was his friend, that he had never felt
anything like this in his life. But he only laughed and bit his lower
lip, swimming in the river of images that filled each sense: the rich
aroma of steaks coming from Sizzlin', clouds dipping almost to the
top of St. Mary's Hospital up on the hill beyond them, the feel of
wind licking at his ears as the MG moved down the street, traffic
sounds, bird sounds, a smell of Mexican food from Manuel's, the feel
of the leather seat, all sweeping him along until he felt weak and
breathless, overwhelmed.

Rebecca glanced at him and could see him swelling with it all,
see this man feeling things for the first time, as unsure of his

emotions as a child would be of his first steps. She was deeply moved. She thought of all the men she had known, of all the guile and stupidity, of her own manipulative nature and how crass the world, her world, had become, how it all was wrapped in artificial goals: publish or perish, bear children or suffer in old age, happiness or misery, all the extremes we invent so we can convince ourselves we are safely between them.

They drove out to Alps Road, and at the sprawl of Beechwood Shopping Center, Daniel saw a busy gas station where a matron was looking on worriedly as men changed her tire, a fat man driving a pickup truck and cursing something roundly. He saw a bowling alley and a plastic sign with a turtle on it. They drove back to Broad Street and went east back toward downtown, and Daniel saw a Waffle House and a church bus with singing children hanging out from the windows; he saw piñatas hanging from the ceiling of the Mexicali Grille, saw a bright yellow-and-black Midas Muffler shop and a Po' Folks restaurant.

To Rebecca, Daniel's unabashed joy seemed like that of a pilgrim having reached the end of his holy mission. She took him back to Oconee Hill, and it seemed to shimmer in the midday heat as she drove through the gates and up to the top of the hill near the grave of Governor Wilson Lumpkin, not far from Baby. She stopped the car in the shade and cut the engine off. For a long time, she did not say anything, and neither did Daniel.

"Did you have fun?" she asked.

Daniel began to smile, a little at first, then more, and he looked at her and took his hat off like a gentleman from another century, as if he were the same age as the men and women beneath them on Oconee Hill.

"Oh, Rebecca," he said. "I feel like a bird that flies in the clouds."

"Daniel," she said. She reached out and touched his arm, her heart beating so hard she thought her breath would simply fade away.

He did not move but looked at her hand and bit his lower lip.

After a moment or two, he reached down and traced the large vein on the back of her hand with his thick index finger, traced it slowly back and forth until it seemed almost like a caress. Then he sighed and opened the door but didn't get out right away. Finally, he climbed out and looked down at her, holding his hat tightly, squeezing it as if he were milking a cow.

"Woodrow will be catching many fish now," he said apologetically.

"Yes," Rebecca said.

"Will you bring flowers again?" Daniel asked.

"Yes, I will," said Rebecca. And then he was gone, like a hummingbird appearing suddenly from nowhere and disappearing as fast. Rebecca got out and saw him almost dancing down the slope toward the river, waving his arms with joy in the summer light.

SEVEN

REBECCA DREAMED OF LAWRENCE DALE. She stood back from the rocky edge of Black Rock Mountain and saw him standing there, pensive, staring at the valley far below. His face, which had always seemed veiled in fog, was now distinct, the ragged thin face of cancer. At arm's length he held a pistol. A cool wind had come up, and the moon spread orange light along the pines. What was he thinking? Now she was somewhere in front of Lawrence Dale, hovering impossibly out over the edge of mountain air.

Those eyes! The dark circles of sight that seemed to take in everything, to understand it, to pity it, then forgive it. In his eyes was the genuine poetry of an elemental anguish, the knowledge that the world into which he had been born was irrevocably gone. He looked down and shook his head briefly and then, looking up, took a deep breath and raised the gun to his temple. Rebecca was back behind him again and saw only his dark silhouette. *No!* she cried. *You have so much to live for!* He seemed to stand there forever with the barrel pressed against his temple, and Rebecca heard the hammering of a woodpecker and thought nothing was ever quite so lovely or so terrible.

She awoke in the darkness and heard the hammering again, heard herself breathing hard and saying *No! no!* For nearly a minute she sat in the dark, on the side of her bed, watching the icons of her life stir from the gloom: the clock radio's familiar numbers, the bureau with the mirror, the wicker rocking chair that had been her mother's favorite possession. Rebecca was alive and in Athens, and Lawrence Dale had long been dead, but she somehow felt closer to him than ever before, close enough, perhaps, to see his face as she wrote, to begin once more on the book.

Then the hammering came again, and she realized someone was knocking on her door. She looked at the clock radio, saw that it was nearly 2 a.m. and felt the sudden surge of fear that cradles everything unexpected in the night. She stood up on her shaky nighttime legs and threw on a light summer robe.

"Just a minute," she called. She went into the den and turned on the ceiling light and got a cigarette from the pack on the coffee table and lit it. *Who in the hell could be here this time of night, and how did they get into the building?* She knew only one thing: it was either a mistake or bad news.

"Who is it?"

"Annie," a voice called, but it did not really sound like her friend. Rebecca unlocked the door and opened it back to the end of the security chain. Annie stood in the hallway, her face white as parchment, clutching her purse and trying not to cry.

"Annie?" Rebecca said, her voice still hoarse from sleep. "What's wrong?"

"I'm sorry," she said. "Can I come in, please?"

"Sure," said Rebecca.

She closed the door and slid the night latch off and let the door swing back. Annie, wearing dark slacks and a shapeless old blouse, came into the room and went straight to a window overlooking Broad Street. Rebecca closed the door, locked it and inhaled the cigarette, feeling worried and sick.

"Is it your father?"

"No," said Annie, still holding the purse and not looking back.

"It's Brad." She turned and tried to smile, her eyes full of tears.

"My God," said Rebecca, "is he...."

"...he's leaving me," said Annie, trying to control herself but failing. Her mouth began to wobble, and she sat on the couch and sniffed once, then she crumbled and put her face in her hands and wept.

"My God," Rebecca repeated.

She left the cigarette in an ashtray on the counter that separated the kitchen and the den and went to Annie and sat next to her and pulled her close. Annie buried her face in the soft space where Rebecca's neck and shoulder met and sobbed. Annie sat back, her face red and swelling.

"It was just out of the blue," said Annie. "He said he'd met this woman and...." She began to sob again and clung to Rebecca, who could feel the collar of her robe begin to grow warm and damp with tears.

"You need a drink," said Rebecca. Thinking of Charlie Dominic, she went into the kitchen and got a bottle of bourbon from the counter and two small, clear glasses from the cabinet. She came back into the den and poured them each a drink, neat, and they gulped them in silence.

"I'm here. Talk to me."

"We'd just been sitting on the patio talking about things, and I was telling him that I really was thinking again about having a baby," said Annie, finally getting her voice under control. "I mean, I won't be able to have babies forever."

"Oh, Annie," said Rebecca.

"And then, right in the middle of it, when I was thinking maybe we'd go to bed and try to, you know, do it," Annie said, "he says he has to tell me something, and the next thing I know, he's talking about somebody named Simone and telling me he's in love with her."

"When did this all happen?" asked Rebecca.

"She's the new secretary at the store," said Annie. "So what's wrong with me? Tell me that, what's wrong with me?"

"Nothing's wrong with you," said Rebecca. "People change. Sometimes they change without knowing it until something like this happens. There's nothing wrong with you."

"Except now I'm going to be alone," she cried.

"What is he going to do?" asked Rebecca.

"He's moving out tomorrow," said Annie. "I can't believe this is happening. I'm still in love with him and...."

Rebecca held her, weeping, against the back of the couch and stroked her hair. Annie trembled and clung to Rebecca like a child, feeling as if it were an evil dream from which she must surely awaken. Rebecca could feel her friend shaking, and she felt a deep pity for her, a resonance that focused her own feelings.

"I'm alone," Rebecca said. "And I'm *alive*. There are worse things than being alone for a time. And things may change. Brad might come back to you all by himself. Don't give up on things so easily."

Annie sat back and rubbed the tears from her cheeks, looking childlike and vulnerable. She took a drink from her glass, and so did Rebecca. The room seemed crowded and hot.

"So, how was your day?" asked Annie.

They both laughed, and then they both cried, and by four, Annie had slumped drowsily on the sofa, and Rebecca covered her with an extra quilt, one her grandmother had made in the mountains of North Carolina.

Rebecca could not sleep. She went into the study and turned on her computer and stared for only a minute at the blinking cursor, then she began to write.

All his life, Lawrence Dale was in love. First, he loved the mountains of north Georgia, the soaring hemlocks and the broken streams that rush proudly toward the flatlands. He loved the way sunrise breaks along the spine of the hills and comes into every room. He loved his mother and father, simple hard-working farmers who brought corn from the poor land with prayer and sweat, and he loved his sisters and brothers. Later, he loved a beautiful woman named Mary Wagner, but she died young of some fever or another, and for the rest of his days, Lawrence Dale turned his passion to the written word, until finally, worn out with time and disease, he watched his beloved hills stretch below him at Black Rock Mountain and ended his life with one swift gesture of defiance. And in that final blow, even then he was in love, easing into the arms of a comforting death that would be his consolation when life had left him only with longing and unfulfilled dreams. He often loved without demand, set off walking without a destination, sought answers without really knowing the right questions. And yet he somehow went beyond the poor soil and his history. He rose above the cynicism of the day and loved simply, loved his God and his poetry and left on those who knew him an indelible whisper of common decency and beauty.

Rebecca stared at the words, read them again and knew they were good. She walked to the window that looked out over North Campus. Annie's deep, even breathing filled the room, and the first few strands of sunlight were swelling up from the east. For a long time, she stood in the window, thinking of Daniel and of how small his world really was, how little he knew about the generation before him. Who were his parents? Why had they taken him to Greenvale in the first place?

She went back to the computer and saved the paragraph to disk, feeling calm and happy. Later, Annie awoke and cursed that she would be late to teach her class, that she had to get home and dress.

"Call me," Rebecca said. "I'll come over, or you can come over here and stay."

"I'll be okay," she said. "Thanks for last night. I'll let you know, okay? I don't know how you do it." Rebecca was startled and stared, uncomprehending, at her friend.

"Do what?" she asked.

"Live alone," said Annie.

"Oh, you know me, all head and no heart," said Rebecca. They hugged, and Annie was gone, leaving only the patchwork quilt that still lay on the couch with the cave of Annie's form under it.

Rebecca got dressed and went down to The Mayflower Restaurant, bought a paper and ordered bacon and eggs and black coffee. Then she read the paper. When the food came, she ate in silence, watching people drag in, students bleary from studying or dissipation, an old man in overalls and struggling for every step, a middle-aged woman in a blue uniform that had her name, Ila, stitched over the left breast. She could not remember ever paying such attention to the details of a room, its aromas, the way light came through the broad front windows and spread along the floor.

After she ate, she walked slowly along the sidewalks of North Campus under the ancient shade of the oaks, past Terrell Hall and then the Georgia Museum of Art, past the President's office and the Rusk Institute, then alongside Peabody Hall. She cut between the library and Peabody Hall to Baldwin and then over to East Campus Road. The warm morning promised that the day was going to be very hot, for even before she got to Oconee Hill, she could already feel the sweat gathering between her breasts under her pale green T-shirt, moistening the waistband of her white poplin pants.

When she came through the gates, she could see that two police cars were parked not far from the white frame caretaker's house. A man in civilian clothes, red-faced and gesturing, was talking to four uniformed policemen. Rebecca looked up the hill and did not see Daniel, and so she walked warily up the long stretch of asphalt until she reached the crest of the hill. There, she could smell the rich pungence of gardenias, but she could not see Daniel anywhere. She let her weight carry her back down the hill until she stood not far from the policemen, and then she heard the other man saying, over and over, "No, no, I don't have any idea."

Rebecca felt suddenly sick, full of a spreading imbalance, and the gravestones seemed to reflect all the fury of the summer sun toward her. She realized she was soaked with sweat, that both back and front of her T-shirt were soggy and that her thick hair was beginning to mat against her neck.

She edged closer. The policemen appeared to have run out of questions and were looking at each other now, hats tilted back at an angle that might have been rakish if they hadn't seemed so glum. The other man—he must be the caretaker, she thought, probably Daniel's supervisor.

When Frank Sutton saw Rebecca, he recognized her immediately as the woman he'd seen lately in the cemetery talking to Daniel. "Daniel," Frank said over the policeman's shoulder to Rebecca. "Have you seen Daniel, the young guy who works around here?"

Rebecca stared at Frank almost uncomprehendingly as the policemen turned and looked at her. One of them was perhaps forty and had the look of authority about him, graying at the temples, lean as a playing card, while the other was chubby, not more than thirty, and stared openly at Rebecca's sweat-soaked chest, her bra clearly visible under the now-transparent T-shirt.

"Do you know him, ma'am?" asked the man with the gray temples.

She nodded numbly. "What's happened to him?" she asked.

"We don't know," Frank said sadly. "They found his trailer burned completely up this morning. He wasn't in it, but nobody over there in that trailer park up the road knows where he is."

"Oh God," said Rebecca. Her shoulders sagged, and she tried to think where he might have gone. "Was his dog there?"

"It wasn't there," said the older policeman. "We talked to this woman across the road, the one who called the fire department...." He looked at the notes he had made on a small pad. "...Irene Bailey. The fire department was there six minutes after the alarm was called, but it was too late. It was already completely involved by the time they got there."

"How do you know him?" the chubby one asked.

The question struck Rebecca as absurdly personal, and she

immediately disliked the way he looked at her and held his mouth open slightly around heavy, purple lips.

"He's my friend," she said icily. "I come over here sometimes to walk. It's a public cemetery. I talk to him while he works. I teach over at the university."

"Could you tell me your name, please?" the chubby cop asked, ready now with a pencil on his own pad. *Jeez, would you look at that? She don't even know she looks damn near naked.*

"Gentry," she said. "Rebecca Gentry. I live in 912 Campus North, uptown. I'm in the Department of English." She turned to Frank. "Did he say anything about going anywhere?"

"Not to me, not at all," he said.

Rebecca remembered Daniel holding up the pink slip proudly and waving it as they got ready to drive around town. "Lord," was all she said.

"If you hear anything, let us know?" said Gray Temples.

"I will," she said. She looked at the chubby policeman, who was now staring at her breasts from behind his sunglasses.

She turned and hurried out of the cemetery, not thinking clearly, only feeling that something must be done. She began to jog up the hill and soon realized that her breath was gone and that her chest was aching from the exertion. She leaned against a tree and wheezed. She had brought a pack of cigarettes and a lighter, and now, gasping for air, she dropped them both without ceremony into a trash can and then walked up North Campus toward town.

She had to stop and rest briefly three times before she got to her car, and when she finally got in, she cursed and drove toward east Athens, crossed the Oconee River and turned right at the Salvation Army Thrift Store and then went up the street toward Oconee-By-The-River. Even before she turned into the road through the trailer park, she could smell the stench of fire. Smoke still curled around the ruins of Daniel's trailer as she pulled up. The concrete steps now went up to nothing but smoldering debris, indicating how hot and completely devastating the blaze had been.

Wearing very short shorts and a tube top, Randi Ambrose was

standing flat-footed nearby, her face reddening from the heat. Rebecca got out and walked over to her, never taking her eyes off the charred remains. Fire had always terrified Rebecca since the time her grandmother's house had burned when she was a little girl. She had been staying there for the summer, and she had awakened in her grandfather's arms as he hustled her outside into a night filled with millions of stars, and she had stood with them as her grandmother had cried, watching the keepsakes of fifty years disappear in flames. She remembered even now how it had smelled, although she had not thought about that night in years.

"Dr. Gentry," Randi said sadly, "This is some crap, ain't it? Thank God Dan wasn't in the damn thing."

"Are they sure?" Rebecca asked. She was shivering.

"Oh yeah," she nodded, her spiked hair moving only slightly. "Even the dog was gone. They know how to tell things like that. But he's on foot—can't drive, you know. Maybe he's out for a long walk."

"He didn't go to work this morning," said Rebecca, puzzled. "It doesn't seem like him to miss work. I can't figure this out. Where could he have gone?"

"Beats the hell out of me," Randi said. "You got any idea what's wrong with him? I mean, like in the medical sense?"

"No, do you?" Rebecca asked with barely subdued hostility. "I don't think there's anything wrong with him except he's different. He doesn't know where he came from. He can't remember things sometimes."

"I thought he came from that home for dummies down in Augusta," Randi said, her voice as strident as a file on metal. "Nice guy, though."

Rebecca got back into her car and sat there, trying to think, as Randi walked over.

"I didn't mean nothing by that."

"Right," said Rebecca.

She started the car and backed up next to the trailer where the university students, Kelly Cassidy and Rob Jarrett, lived. She drove out of the trailer park, and when she got to the street, next to the row of mailboxes, she saw for the first time that Daniel had painted on his box, in crude, inch-high letters, MR. DANIEL MITCHELL.

Tears streamed unchecked down her cheeks as she drove out into the flow of Athens' summer morning traffic. Why had everything in her life come to this place? Why was Brad leaving Annie, and why was Annie's father so nobly dying of cancer? Why had she met Daniel, anyway, and was this some crossroads, an epiphany she was destined to experience?

She crossed the Oconee River and looked down at its thick flow and suddenly felt that Daniel was there, that he was down there walking, looking for something. The idea was so strong that after she crossed the bridge, she pulled into an empty lot on which a sign proclaimed that some developer was promising more condominiums and stopped the car. She turned the motor off and got out, and from the mud-red bluff, she could see the river below. Until the year before, old mill buildings had stood on this spot for decades. For a time, a small club had been located in one of the mill buildings, heatless yet cheerful, but all the old buildings had been razed and now more condominiums were going up, and Rebecca wondered if city life was important at all.

The bank was crossed with timeless trails, and she chose one and walked along it to the river. A narrow trail choked with weeds ran on a ledge alongside the Oconee, and she tramped along through plantains and goosegrass, going north, feeling her Reeboks quickly grow wet. She looked back and saw the bridge above her and was delighted with its arches; although she had crossed the bridge hundreds of times, she had never seen it from this point.

She thought she heard a dog barking. She stopped and listened, aware suddenly of other sounds that enveloped her, the quiet swish of the flowing water, the brief change in wind, the traffic on the bridge. *Yes, a dog up there ahead.* She formed Daniel's name in her mouth but could not call it. The trail was now flat and broader, its weeds beaten down by old black men who came to fish. Once, in the winter, she remembered, this whole bottom had been flooded, and the usually meandering, muddy river had become a swollen menace that had driven two dozen families from their homes before it subsided. Now, it was just the Oconee, the source of Athens' drinking water and the river that had etched the banks along which the town had been built.

The sound of barking hurried her onward. There was a bend in the river, and she was almost running by the time she got there, and she was saying it out loud now, "Daniel, Daniel." Her breath was ragged, and her feet seemed to find every stone, her ankles turning over painfully two or three times before she came to the river's curve.

"Daniel!" she shouted.

She came out around the bend, and saw the barking dog, now far away from her. It was not Toggle, after all, but a white cur of no distinction, and it seemed to be barking at the middle of the river. Rebecca had seen dogs bark at airplanes, even at the wind or at thunder, but she had never seen a dog bark at a river. She looked across the water, which broke over shoals here, and saw twenty or thirty men and women standing reverently on the opposite shore, watching a gray-haired man standing with a woman in a white robe out waist-deep in the water of the river. All at once, every word they spoke stood out, clear and clean, and the man was asking God to bring Sister Hallie Anita into the new life, into the world that knows no sorrow or death, into the life eternal. The white dog saw Rebecca and bounded off into the weeds.

"Daniel," she said softly.

The woman in the white robe had folded her hands and was looking prayerfully into the humid air, up above the crown of tree branches that hung out over the water, casting a dark reflection upon it. Her face was suffused with power and fear and love, and her dark cheeks were wet with tears. She was not a young girl, but nearly into middle age, and if she had ever had a figure, it was long gone to rich food and worry.

"Sister Hallie Anita, I baptize you in the name of the Father, the Son and the Holy Ghost," the preacher said, and she took his arm as he put his other hand behind her neck. As he lowered her into the river, she tightly closed her eyes, and Rebecca could hear women sobbing, all the way from the other shore. When the woman came up, the water washed off her, and her thick dark hair lay flat against her face, and the preacher tenderly brushed it back and whispered something to her, and she smiled broadly. She tented her fingers again, and the preacher began to sing "Amazing Grace" in a loud, high voice. The others joined in, singing in many keys, and soon the crowded river bottom was alive with the old hymn of grace.

Rebecca was deeply moved, choked, and she felt as if she were a voyeur, a privileged witness to something rare and beautiful. She had given up simple faith years before, refusing to believe that the universe is ordered or that life has a purpose higher than man himself. Still, the song filled her with a longing, a wish that in her academic life everything made such sense, that she still believed what she had as a child, that God has made us a little lower than the angels and had crowned us with glory and honor.

Rebecca walked back down the river bank toward the bridge. Why had she come down here at all, and where was Daniel? And what did she feel for him? Was it the motherhood she could not give, or was it love, the kind of love that makes no sense and fills you each day no matter how much you fight it or ignore it? She struggled back up the bank, her shoes and pants wet with dew, and when she got to the top, she was gasping again for breath. She sat in the dirt, her chest heaving. Beside her was a cluster of passion flowers, fragile blue and yellow crowns that grew wild.

EIGHT

DANIEL AWAKENED TO THE MUSIC OF BELLS. He lay in the soft bed trying to clear his confusion. After a while, he sat up, and his mouth was dry, and he groaned at the ache deep in his bones and saw that someone had bandaged his hands. He swung his feet over the bed and looked around, filled at once with joy and confusion, for he knew this room as well as his own reflection in the mirror on the bureau. He stood and felt his muscles ache and realized he was in the blue cotton pajamas, the uniform of the night at Greenvale. The bells rang at nine each day to take the students to their classrooms.

The polished wooden floor felt cool. He went to the window and looked out and saw that it was morning and that the deep green campus looked as it always had and that he was back in his top-floor room of the boys' dormitory. He could see the girls' dormitory across the quadrangle and to its left the classroom building and the lunch hall. Back to the right, out of sight was the administration office. Greenvale had been built by the Baptist Church in 1926, and since then the first oaks had grown massive and shady. Succeeding administrations, buoyed by contributions of churches all over the South, had planted overflowing gardens of begonias, caladiums, coleus and, lining all the shady parts, magnificent blue hostas. Each year, Mrs. Wilkins would supervise the planting of annuals for color, and she loved impatiens, daisies, and marigolds. The grounds were crossed with brick walkways that all seemed to lead to the loveliest building, the small chapel that had been added just after World War II from funds donated by a couple in Alabama whose only son had been killed in Italy.

Daniel rubbed his eyes and felt calm and happy. Then he felt a chill of fear, the disorientation brought on by having missed some vital fact which would explain even the most common things. Where was Oconee Hill?

"Oh, no, I will be late for work," Daniel said. He opened the closet door, but no clothes were hung inside, and so he opened the door to the hall and went out. "Hello?" He called loudly, but the hall was silent. The doors to all the rooms stood open. He hobbled down the hall, glancing into rooms, seeing the beds neatly made, everything at right angles on dressers, and he remembered: each morning the rooms were made beautiful. They had all said it together: *in order there is beauty*. All the boys would be in the classroom and then go to chapel before lunch.

Daniel went to the end of the hall and came down the stairs, and he thought the sunlight that poured into the window on each landing was brighter than sunlight, that his eyes could not hold all this brightness; everything seemed to have soft edges. He rubbed his eyes and came down past the second floor and then down to the first, opened the outside door and stepped into his childhood.

They had never told Daniel much about his life before Greenvale, and though he had tried to remember, he could see only a few vague images, recall a couple of words. Mostly he remembered this place, playing with friends, learning the mystery of numbers and letters, learning that Jesus Loved the Little Children. But now, Daniel knew, he was no longer a little child, and he wondered if this were a dream. He walked out along the brick pathway until he was in the middle of the buildings. He looked around without understanding, and then his face began to furrow and his lips quivered.

He wept.

"Frank!" he called. "Frank! Frank!"

He fell to his knees and screamed Frank's name, over and over, and stopped only when he saw a young man running from the administration building toward him, trailed by two others. The young man was wearing a Greenvale T-shirt, jeans and sneakers, and he got to Daniel in less than twenty seconds.

"It's okay now," the man said.

"I am at Greenvale," said Daniel. He fell backwards on his hips and looked around, eyes wild with confusion.

"Yes, you are," the man said. "My name is Chris. I'm a counselor here this summer." He turned and looked behind him, and Daniel saw Mr. Wilkins standing there, leaning on a cane and seeming very old, next to another man he had never seen. "You remember Mr. Wilkins?"

Daniel stood up and brushed his tears away and thrust his hand out. "Hello, Mr. Wilkins," he said. "I need to tell Frank. I do not know what I am doing here."

"Oh, Daniel, what will we do with you?" asked Mr. Wilkins. "I am so glad to see you, but why did you come here, son? Chris, why don't you take Daniel up and get him dressed and bring him to the dining hall. Let's get him some food and then we'll see if we can figure this out."

"Frank will not know I am here, and he will give my job to someone else," Daniel wailed, almost crying again. Mr. Wilkins looked at the other man, who was wearing a black suit, looked at him knowingly with an obvious message that Daniel could not understand. "Why did you come and get me, Mr. Wilkins? Did I do bad on my job? I ... I cleaned the stones with ghost rocks, and...and...I pulled the vines off Baby and Our Children ... and ..."

"Sshhhhh," said Mr. Wilkins, going to Daniel and hugging him close. Daniel clung to him for a moment and then walked with Chris in the hot sunlight across the quadrangle toward the dormitory. The other man, whose name was Baldwin, stared away from them.

"I hoped this would never happen," said Mr. Wilkins, shading his eyes with his hand. "He may start to remember things."

"How in the world did he make his way back here?" asked Baldwin, who had been at a meeting in Atlanta and had just returned that morning. They began to walk toward the administration building, Baldwin moving slowly to accommodate Wilkins, who hobbled along on the cane.

"Nobody has a clue," Wilkins said, smoothing his thin white hair. He was nearly seventy now, and his face looked as if its skin might some day simply slide off the bone. He had been at Greenvale for almost twenty years, and he knew that his function there now was only that of a resident sage, that Norman Baldwin was in charge. "They found him out on the Interstate—in the median, all cut up—saying, 'Greenvale,' so the police brought him here. He'd been gone from up there two days, had everybody who knew him scared silly."

"You know he can't stay," said Baldwin gently. He was tall, not yet forty, and had pliable features and sharp eyes.

"I know that," Wilkins said, almost irritably. "But his world is getting small, Norm. It's such a terrible thing. Terrible." Baldwin took Wilkins' elbow and helped him up the stairs of the administration building and through its heavy doors inside.

Georgia summers are full of days that begin with heavy clouds, break briefly into sun and then settle again into darkness and the threat of rain. The sun was gone now, and the shadows disappeared under the oaks. The summer before, it had not rained for months, but this year, everything was emerald and soggy, and Christopher Spencer merely stared at the darkening sky as Daniel dressed into jeans and a purple-and-gold Greenvale T-shirt in the room behind him. Chris was from Madison, a town halfway between Augusta and Atlanta. A junior at the University of Georgia, he was majoring in art. Soon, it got so dark outside that he could see his own face in the glass. He did not like how he looked, almost too refined, a weak chin and sallow skin. For years, he had tried to work out, to do situps and lift weights, but nothing seemed to work, and his splayed feet and soft hands made him feel awkward. Chris turned, and Daniel had snapped the jeans and tucked in the shirt.

"That's better," said Chris. "Get your shoes back on, and we'll go get something to eat. You getting hungry?"

"I think I am," said Daniel. He sat on the bed and slid into his still-damp, soiled shoes and then stared at the wall, unmoving.

After more than thirty seconds, this began to unnerve Chris.

"What's wrong, Daniel?" he asked.

Daniel jumped as if someone had poked him.

"Am I really here?" Daniel asked.

Chris went over to the bed and looked down on him with great pity.

"Of course you're here," Chris smiled. "Don't you remember anything about how you got here?"

"I live in Athens now," said Daniel.

"I know," said Chris. "They told me. I go to school there, at the University."

"You are one of the students," said Daniel.

"Yes," said Chris. "You work in the Oconee Hill Cemetery. Don't worry, we'll get you back. Your boss is Frank."

"I've got to call Frank," Daniel said nervously. He stood up and began to wring his hands. "He will give my job to somebody else, and then I will not be able to keep my trailer."

Chris knew that Daniel's trailer had been burned and decided someone else could tell him about that. "Frank knows," he said gently. "Mr. Baldwin called Frank and told him you were here. Frank is coming to get you, or he's sending somebody, he wasn't sure which, to take you back to Athens."

"I was falling," Daniel said, eyes wide and hands working over each other.

"Falling?"

"I was falling, and I cried for Rebecca," said Daniel, "and I could not stop falling."

"Who is Rebecca?"

"She is the woman who brings flowers and pretty words," said Daniel.

Chris had no idea what Daniel meant, but he was used to it; working at Greenvale, you saw all kinds of problems, from the terrible child paraplegics to a dwindling few who were severely retarded and whose parents thought a Christian camp was best. Since Mr. Baldwin had taken over, the camp had been taking fewer and fewer cases of mental disability, preferring to concentrate on those with physical problems. But this was Chris' third summer at Greenvale, and he had seen worse.

"Rebecca," said Chris. "Let's go get something to eat."

"Okay, Chris," said Daniel. And then, as if they had just been introduced, he shook hands with Chris, pumping his arm three times as he always did with anyone he met for the first time. They walked back down the three flights of stairs, and before they got to the dining hall, thick drops of rain had begun to fall across what once was Daniel Mitchell's only world.

THE FIRST NIGHT AFTER DANIEL HAD DISAPPEARED was terrible for both Rebecca and Annie. Annie had gathered two suitcases full of clothes, toilet articles and professional papers and moved into Campus North with Rebecca. There had been a terrible scene with Brad, in which he blamed Annie for their breakup. He accused Annie of caring too little and then callously enumerated Simone's good qualities, repeatedly referring to her "unselfish love." Annie felt dazed, not wanting to believe it had happened.

"It's like somebody died," Annie said. They sat in Harry Bisset's, a small, pleasant seafood restaurant just down the street from Rebecca's apartment. "I start to get my bearings, and then I feel like I've been cut loose from my moorings."

"It's the same thing with Daniel," said Rebecca, dragging on a cigarette.

After her fruitless trek along the river, the rest of her day had crept by, and her worry had intensified by the hour. She did not know what to do, and had dropped by Oconee Hill three times and talked to Frank, who was just as baffled. *The Athens Banner-Herald* had run a story on page three about Daniel, saying he was missing following a fire at his trailer. Police were not speculating on the cause. Frank was upset, and on the third visit was abrupt with Rebecca, reiterating what he had said each time she came, that he would call her if anything came up.

She finished her glass of Chablis, and Annie turned up her beer. A waitress came and asked if they wanted another drink, and they did.

"I feel just sick inside, like I've lost my pivot."

"We're poor little lambs who have lost our way," said Annie, a little woozy from the alcohol.

"Don't say that," Rebecca said.

"Sorry," said Annie, furrowing her brow. "But I think Daniel will show up. Didn't you say he was—what? Innocent or something? He'll come back. Which is more than I can say for Brad. You know what he told me? He said that Simone made him feel alive again."

"I don't feel like this, after all," Rebecca said as the waitress brought a tray heavy with stuffed flounder for each of them.

"You always feel better when you eat," said Annie. "That's what my daddy always told me." Rebecca could see Annie's face change as she thought of her father, a change that was almost unbearable.

"He's right," said Rebecca putting out the cigarette. She had been smoking less for the past few days, and now the smell of cigarettes made her feel almost sick, but she could not stop smoking, not now. "Let's eat."

"To hell with Simone, and to hell with Brad, and to hell with love," said Annie. She raised her second glass of wine, which the waitress had just delivered, in a toast.

"To hell with Simone and Brad," said Rebecca.

A couple in a nearby booth leaned intimately toward each other over a candle flame, whispering and giggling, looking into each other's eyes as only new lovers can. Annie could see the mask descend over their eyes; each love had a built-in period of blindness that kept love from withering. Truth meant nothing when you were in love.

That night, they watched a British play on the Arts and Entertainment Network. All kind of things happened, deceptions, adultery, even murder, and yet everyone kept a sober profile and a stiff upper lip. Annie slept on the couch, and early the next morning, she showered, slipped into a robe and made coffee as Rebecca struggled out of bed. Rebecca could not remember the last time her bathroom had been steamy when she had gotten out of bed. It was probably the night she'd spent with a graduate student from her department, but that had been several months before, and she had been depressed over Charlie leaving. The boy was nothing to her and had since graduated. Rebecca showered, sick at having heard nothing of Daniel, wondering if she should call Frank or the police. Her thick hair took nearly twenty minutes to dry, and she stood there, looking at her body in the mirror. Her breasts had always been just too large, swelling out on the sides so they seemed fat, and now they hung lower than ever, the areolas starting to point down. Her hair dried, and she dressed, wondering if she could ever really get to work on the life of Lawrence Dale or if she should give it up, devote her life to poetry.

All morning, Rebecca made notes and tried to add to the paragraph she had written a few days before on Lawrence Dale. Annie said she'd be back after class, that after a few days she'd decide what to do.

"I don't want to be trouble," Annie said. She looked frightened, and Rebecca was touched by her bravery. Rebecca hugged her as she stood by the door with her briefcase like a small child ready for the first grade.

"Oh, Annie," Rebecca said. "I love you. Don't you know that?"

"I'm glad somebody does," said Annie, her face taut with unspilled tears.

"Things'll work out," said Rebecca. "Don't you give up. With Brad or someone else. Things will work out." Annie almost smiled. She and Rebecca were standing very close. "What?"

"That's what I told you when Charlie left," Annie said. "I told you everything would be all right. Why do people always say that?"

"Okay, so it's a lie," shrugged Rebecca. "But it's one of the good lies."

"One of the good lies," Annie repeated, trying to smile again.

"The world's full of good lies and bad ones," said Rebecca. "'Things will work out' is one of the best lies around. It was my mother's favorite lie."

"Keep telling me that one, Gentry," Annie said. "I could use some good lies now."

"Things will work out," said Rebecca. They both laughed and hugged, and Rebecca concluded, soon after Annie left, that friendship was possibly the only worthwhile thing in this miserable world.

Rebecca could not bring herself to leave the apartment, to call Frank or the police or go to Oconee Hill. She made more notes, trying to find the interconnections in Dale's life. The year before, she had talked to his brother, John, who still lived at the family's homeplace in the mountains of north Georgia. In the first few years after Dale had died on Black Rock Mountain, John had shown all the family icons to visiting strangers and admirers. The local Chamber of Commerce had tried to make money off Dale's fleeting fame, but by the mid-Sixties his books were out of print, and soon no one came to his grave in the Bethel Baptist Church cemetery just east of Newfield.

John had been a small, bent man with gray hair and skin, living among the lost images of his once-famous brother by the time Rebecca had come by. He was still married to Joanna Fulford, the woman he had wed in 1937, but when Rebecca had visited, Joanna had terminal cancer and lay motionless in a rented hospital bed, shrunken in the dim light of their bedroom. The house had smelled of antiseptics and death and the bare boards of poverty. The day was deep in winter, and Rebecca was startled to see a robin briefly land on the window sill and stare into the room as John was holding up childhood pictures of his brother. Rebecca had studied the photographs and seen something almost beatific about Lawrence's face in the pictures taken in the Thirties.

Was there a mark on a person at birth that made him different from others? What conspired to reveal the world's secrets to great artists? Was it some hidden planetary alignment or merely the first sounds the child heard upon entering the world?

Rebecca wanted to answer some of those questions as well as tell the life of Lawrence Dale, and maybe, she thought, this was why she could never really get started. She wanted to know too much. She was not satisfied with the simple facts of his life—or of any life, for that matter. The ideas mattered, not the feelings. That was what her poetry was about, especially *Dead Lace*, which the *The New York Times* had called "as brilliant, hard and emotionless a body of work as we have seen in years." At the time, Rebecca was elated, but lately she had begun to see a hint of disapproval in the review.

Late that afternoon, Rebecca was thinking again of the robin on the window sill when the phone rang. She fought the urge to light a cigarette and pick the receiver up as if it were something strange and terrible.

"Yes?" she said through clenched teeth.

"Miz Gentry?" a man's voice asked. Oh God, thought Rebecca, he's dead, they found him dead.

"Yes," she whispered.

"This is Frank Sutton over at Oconee Hill," he said. "Daniel's okay."

"Thank God," she said. She felt as if something in her had weakened and let go and was now sailing down the hot streets of Athens.

"Found him back down near Augusta at Greenvale, the place he grew up," Frank said. His voice was raspy and hard, but it was also kind. "Nobody seems to have any idea how in the hell he got there. He was banged up a little, but all right. He doesn't remember how he got there."

"How in the world," Rebecca said.

"Don't have a clue, Miz Gentry," Frank said. "Look, I don't have a right to ask this, but somebody's got to go down there and get him, bring him back up here."

"Does he know about his trailer?"

"Not as I know," Frank said. He turned away from the phone and coughed terribly.

"This evening okay?" asked Rebecca.

"Sure," said Frank. "They don't know what to do with him. You know how he is."

He gave Rebecca directions, and she hung up, burning with excitement and fear. What in the world had he been doing on the road? Rebecca showered and waited until nearly five o'clock when the door opened and Annie, looking haggard and pale, came in carrying her briefcase.

"You look like Willy Loman," said Rebecca.

"*Wilma* Loman," corrected Annie. She threw the briefcase on the dining room table and with it a handful of pink phone call slips. "Brad called me five times, but I didn't call him back, the son of a bitch."

"Are you late with your alimony check?" asked Rebecca.

"Really funny," Annie said, grinning. She saw the look on Rebecca's face, the transfigured glow of peace. "He's all right. Daniel's all right, isn't he?"

"You classics scholars see right into the human heart," Rebecca said. "Come on, we're going to Augusta to get him."

"What in the world is he doing in Augusta?" asked Annie.

"It's a long story," said Rebecca. "Why don't you get a shower. We'll have to take your car. I'll leave if you want to call Brad."

"He can suffer," Annie said coldly. "Give me thirty minutes." When she came out, she was biting her lip and staring down at the floor. "Rebecca, do you mind if we spend the night?"

"What for?" Rebecca asked. "I'm already tired."

"Not in Augusta, in Statesboro," she said. "I want to see my daddy."

Rebecca smiled and hugged her, and they each got a small suitcase and packed a change of clothes and personal items.

The sky was clear and hot, the sun high this time of year at 6 p.m. They stopped at a sandwich shop and bought food for the road, and as they ate, Annie driving, Rebecca watched the nearly liquid ribbon of asphalt unwind before them, watched the small towns suddenly appear like beads on a chain: Crawford, Lexington, Rayle and then Washington. They talked of small things and listened to a jazz tape Rebecca had made which featured Tom Grose, Jeff Lorber, Bob James, Michael Franks, Angela Bofill and Greg Phillinganes. Just out of Washington, a lovely town strung with antebellum mansions, U.S. 78 turns south toward Thomson as a long stretch of country road, and for a time, they fell silent, watching the fields of Holsteins and Herefords. The cattle gnawed the deep-green grass.

"How do you think he got lost?" asked Annie.

"Who knows?" said Rebecca. "And more, where is he going to stay? Is there room at your folks tonight? I didn't even ask."

"Room for the Green Bay Packers," said Annie.

"It's so sad. He must have hitchhiked or something, but what made him want to leave in the first place?"

"That's a question I keep asking myself," said Annie, and she burst into tears, her hands visibly trembling on the wheel.

"Let me drive," Rebecca said, touching her gently on the arm.

"I'm okay," Annie said, wiping her face. "Get me a Kleenex out of the glove compartment." Rebecca did, and Annie blew her nose and carefully set the tissue in her lap. "Well, we're certainly a pair, Gentry."

"A pair of what?" asked Rebecca.

Annie laughed, and so did Rebecca, but they soon fell silent, and in their silence each felt the other's pain and didn't know how to ease it. Rebecca thought of Daniel and his gentle smile, the way his words never seemed to make real sentences. His flight from Athens seemed providential, mystical, and in some ways almost perfect. Then she thought of Charlie Dominic and how much she still loved him even though she had driven him away. Charlie was not an achiever; he was happy to sit for days doing nothing at all, talking about the small pleasures of life. She felt love for Annie and knew that Brad's leaving was merely the world swaying away for a brief moment. In the long distances of one person's world, one such leaving could be only a small disaster, or color all her remaining days with regret.

They drove through Thomson, darkness now beginning to gather. They traveled east along I-20 for seven miles, turned back north and went through a small town called Appling, then east again until they found the signs that led them to the twin brick pillars over which arched the sign with a single word, "Greenvale."

"Where do we go now?" asked Annie, slowing and looking at the neatly manicured lawns and the cluster of buildings. Lightning bugs danced close to the ground and as high as the tops of the oaks.

"I ask myself that every day," said Rebecca, and Annie spluttered into laughter.

They both laughed as they drove up to the administration building and parked. They got out and looked around, glad to be standing up, stretching. Rebecca turned in time to see an elderly man leaning on a cane thumping out on the porch, and beside him, arms down in defeat, was Daniel. Rebecca felt the chill spread down her arms, down her chest, down her legs. She began to walk toward the steps, and Annie came behind her. Daniel blinked, and when he saw her, his face rose, his mouth fell open and he made a small sound of delight.

"Rebecca!" he cried. In the quiet porchlight, Daniel clapped and clapped and clapped.

NINE

DANIEL HELD REBECCA IN HIS ARMS and felt as if he would rise with joy from this world into the everlasting hands of God. He backed away and looked at her in the porchlight, his eyes brimming with tears.

Rebecca felt a bittersweet mixture of pity and happiness. She kept the choked delight in her throat, and each clutched the other's arms as they stared in brief silence. Annie stood at the bottom of the wooden steps, her hand over her own chest, and watched in sympathy and surprise. She had not expected Daniel, a man who made the gestures of a boy, his smooth face scratched badly. He was good-looking, with his dark blond hair and long, ropy muscles, and yet he chewed the side of his mouth and could barely stand still on his heavy-soled shoes. My God, Annie thought, he is a handsome man.

"Daniel, what in the world happened to you?" asked Rebecca, she and Daniel still holding each other's arms.

"We don't know," said Mr. Wilkins, shuffling over to them with his cane. "A deputy sheriff from McDuffie County found him wandering out on the Interstate calling out repeatedly for Greenvale. Have you remembered anything, son?"

He put his trembling hand on Daniel's shoulder, and Rebecca liked the old man instantly and could see his genuine affection in every gesture and word.

"I was falling," Daniel said, looking suddenly at nothing outside his own body, "and then I went to hell, and then I was floating in the air, and I came down, and I was lost." He looked at Rebecca as if he had not seen her before. "I was lost, Rebecca. Please do not let me get lost again."

"Ssshhhh," Rebecca said, and she held him in her arms. *Oh God, I think I love him.* "I have you now, Daniel. Everything's going to be all right."

"Daniel, why don't you talk to this other nice lady and let me talk to Rebecca," said Mr. Wilkins. "You *are* Rebecca, aren't you? Daniel has been talking about you."

"That's me," she smiled. She let go of Daniel's arms and turned him to face Annie, who was out in the lilt of lightning bugs. "Daniel, this is my friend, Annie."

She looked down at Annie with urgency, and Annie knew what to do instantly.

"Daniel, come walk me around the grounds," Annie said. "I've never been here before."

"You cannot go out on the grounds after dark," said Daniel, looking warily at Mr. Wilkins.

"It's okay, son," said Mr. Wilkins, nodding. "You're a man now." Daniel walked down the steps and started talking to Annie, too loud, about where he used to live, and as their voices began to fade and the silence was left, Mr. Wilkins turned to Rebecca.

"Would you come inside?"

"Of course," she said. They went through the screen door into a hall with shiny wooden floorboards and then left into a formal Victorian parlor with heavy overstuffed furniture that had obviously been there a long time. Rebecca sat in one of the chairs, and Mr. Wilkins struggled down into one nearby. A radio somewhere in the house played old-time gospel tunes, and Rebecca remembered Lawrence Dale's second novel, *Gospel,* an impassioned criticism of empty religion that brought him little in his mountains but harsh criticism and even threats.

"Daniel has told me so much about this place, about your wife," said Rebecca. "Has he seen her?"

"She passed away last spring, I'm afraid," he said, his voice hoarse with emotion.

"I'm so sorry," Rebecca said.

"It was a release," he said. "I live on in the hope that I will join her in the grace of God. Let me ask you something, Rebecca. I don't want to know what your relationship with Daniel is, but do you know much about his life here and before?"

"Mr. Wilkins, I only met him a few weeks ago, and we're just friends," she said, aware she might be telling a small lie. "He's told me a lot about Greenvale, what he remembers, but he doesn't really know anything about his life before. Do I need to know something?"

Mr. Wilkins sighed and looked down into his lap and then up at her. "He was just a boy when he came to us," he said. "I have never seen anything more heart-rending in my life. What I'm going to tell you is confidential, and I could probably be fired for releasing it, but if you are really his friend, you need to know."

"I am his friend," she said.

"Daniel was almost three years old when his aunt brought him over here," he said. "She had gotten temporary custody from his mother, and he just never left us. It was a special case, and he grew up here."

He sighed heavily and looked down at the frayed rug. "His father and mother were both alcoholics. Folks heard them screaming and fighting all along, and I often wondered how they quit long enough to make that boy. The father worked in a sawmill, drank up most of what he made. The mother was just a poor ignorant girl. I guess she drank because he did—or her daddy did, I don't know. Anyway, I recall hearing about what happened. She'd taken the boy and walked all the way to her mama's house, about nine miles away, and when they got home, she found her husband in bed with some slut hereabouts. She got this double-barreled shotgun he kept, and with Daniel right by her side, she killed them both in bed where they lay."

"My God," said Rebecca. Her eyes filled with tears.

"After that, the mother just went crazy," Wilkins said. "A neighbor heard the shots and called the sheriff, and the woman in the bed lived long enough to tell them what happened. Daniel was sitting in the corner, and his mother had painted her face like an Indian with the blood from all over the sheets. They buried Adger Mitchell over in Thomson, and the girl was laid to rest up in Calhoun Falls, South Carolina. That was when they brought Daniel here."

"What happened to his mother?" asked Rebecca.

Mr. Wilkins pulled himself up with his cane and hobbled to the window and looked out on the soft night. "She was judged not fit to stand trial, and after ten years or so, nobody wanted to have a trial anymore anyway," he said. "What it did to that boy was criminal, though. I suspect you thought he was retarded or something, didn't you?"

"I don't know," Rebecca said.

"He's bright enough," he said. "We had every psychiatrist in east central Georgia work with him, and at first he almost let it go and faced what happened, but then he developed this aura of innocence."

He looked down and turned back to her. "And I saw in it the hope of the world, Miss Gentry. Call it Paradise Regained or something. The boy learned to block the world, and when he did, he lost hatred and guile and a hundred other stupidities that wreck our lives each day. He willed himself back beyond his life into a love that never even existed at his home. We have visiting therapists, doctors, psychiatrists. Homes like this are strictly regulated by the state, and we have to keep records. But..." He came over and sat in a chair facing Rebecca and looked at her. "I want your promise, not for me but for Daniel, a promise you won't reveal one word of this conversation."

"I promise," she choked.

"All right," he said. "But not even the new administrator knows this. For over ten years, I made up all of Daniel's records. I came to Greenvale when he was four. I said he saw psychiatrists when he didn't, I said he took certain prescription drugs when he didn't. I sheltered him because I saw in his mask the comfort of my own life. In some ways, he became my own son, Miss Gentry."

"Then why did you send him up to Athens to work in a cemetery?" she asked.

"Because my wife had become terminally ill, and I was getting old," he said, "and I knew that if he stayed here, he would have to take new tests, and they would find out what I had been doing all those years."

"But you saved him," Rebecca said. "You saved him from a terrible life."

"That's true, every word," he said, "but did I have the right to deny him the treatment? I don't know. Sometimes that burden hangs upon me very heavily. When he showed up here, I nearly died of joy and grief. So I would please ask you to take him back to Athens and to help him however you can. Sooner or later, the world is going to catch up with him. I don't know how he got here or why. And no one has told him about his trailer burning up. I've done about all I can."

"Whatever happened to his mother?" asked Rebecca.

Mr. Wilkins sighed and almost smiled. "That's something else I haven't told you about why I sent Daniel to Athens," he said. "They were about to let her out. She's been at the state mental hospital over in Milledgeville. So rather than let her know about her son, I just decided to get him out of town. I decided that if she ever came over, I'd say he'd moved to Augusta, just lie about it."

"Did she ever come?" asked Rebecca.

"Not yet," he said. "But I've heard stories, just rumors really, that she's hired a lawyer, stuff like that. That's why you have to get him out of here tonight."

Rebecca could hear someone walking down the hall, toward them, as Mr. Wilkins implored. "Just do it!"

She looked up, and a gray-haired woman in a long dress was in the doorway.

"Mr. Wilkins, what are you doing?" she asked. "You come with me right now for bed."

"Mrs. Gilbert, my warden," he said. "This is a visitor to Greenvale, Miss Gentry."

He pulled himself up on his cane and looked meaningfully at Rebecca, who felt afraid and uncertain about just what she should do.

"Nice to meet you, Miss Gentry," the woman said, "but Mr. Wilkins needs to rest now. I'm sure you understand."

"I'm sure she understands," he said.

He left the room, and Rebecca walked out the front door and on to the porch, realizing for the first time that she did not know who Daniel was or what he meant to her—or why.

Annie and Daniel came toward her across the blaze of green that was turning dark with the coming of night. When they got to her, Rebecca wanted to scream, to rush for joy with him into the hidden world of darkness—to scream for the sanctified pleasures of innocence.

"Let's get out of here," Rebecca said.

"Doesn't he have to, uh, check out or something?" asked Annie.

"He already has," said Rebecca.

"When I was little," Daniel said, ignoring them both, "I would come out here just when dark comes. I would listen for this secret bird. It would tell me words and sing secret songs."

"Tell me about it in the car," Rebecca said, and so he did, as Annie drove out from beneath the old oaks of Greenvale. Rebecca also explained that they would be spending the night in Statesboro with Annie's parents, not much more than an hour away, but she did not mention the fire at his trailer or the fact that his dog was gone. After a few minutes, they all went silent, Annie and Rebecca in the front seat, Daniel in the back, humming along with a country tune on the radio.

Near Statesboro, Rebecca watched Annie's face and saw it change. The muscles of her jaws were hard and set, and she seemed to be concentrating not on the road but on her problems. Rebecca was going to say something, but then they came to the edge of town with its passing lights, the guttural rumbling of old cars.

"Where do your folks live?" asked Rebecca.

"Just out of town on the west side," Annie said. "It's not really in the country and not really in town." Statesboro is not large, but since it has Georgia Southern College, the streets were busy on a hot summer night. Just as soon as they passed through the downtown area, however, the cars disappeared, and Rebecca was just starting to catalog the features of the land when Annie turned in at a brick house with a brightly burning Williamsburg lamp by the door. When the car engine stopped, Annie stared at the house.

"It'll all be different when he's gone," she said.

"Don't do this this to yourself," Rebecca said. "He'll always be here."

They got out, Daniel hanging back, walking silently behind Rebecca. He did not know why they were here, but nothing had made sense to him the past two days. He could only remember facing the fires of hell and then falling, falling as if the bottom of the pit would never come up and hit him.

The front door opened, and a small, gray woman was standing there, waving and smiling at them. Rebecca had met Annie's parents, the Calhouns, once two years earlier when they had come to the Georgia-Clemson game in Athens. They were, she remembered, decent, easy people who wanted to please and seemed to have no pretensions.

"Hi, Mom," Annie said. They hugged, and Annie began to cry and her mother, whose name was Sue, shushed her and smiled at Rebecca over her daughter's shoulder. "I guess it's like the old days again. I'm all alone now."

"Oh, come now," Sue said. "You have friends. You're not all alone."

She pushed her daughter away and smiled, and a comfort and

strength filled Rebecca just as it did Annie.

"You remember Rebecca," said Annie.

"Of course," Sue said. They hugged, barely touching, in the old southern gesture of welcome.

"And this is Daniel," Annie said.

He was biting the inside of his mouth and hanging back in the shadows, so Rebecca grabbed his arm and pulled him into the porchlight.

"Hello, Daniel," said Sue, aware of who he was from her daughter's phone call. "We're so glad to have you visit."

She extended her hand, and Daniel pumped it twice.

"I have a job," he said, "but I got lost, and then Rebecca found me." He seemed confused, but then he smiled.

"You're lucky that she found you," Sue said. "She's a fine lady."

"How's Daddy?" Annie whispered.

Sue turned and opened the screen door. "Why, he's fine," she said. "Come ask him for yourself."

They came into a small foyer that opened into a formal living room where a clock with a glass dome ticked audibly, the gears and works turning. Rebecca saw the old sofa with doilies on the arms, saw the family upright piano and a coffee table loaded with copies of *Southern Living* and *National Geographic*. The house was close and friendly and smelled of freshly cooked food. They walked through the living room and into a sunken den that was cheerfully decorated with University of Georgia Bulldog memorabilia. Annie's father's name was Oscar, and he was sitting in his recliner watching the Braves.

"Hon, look who's here," Sue called out.

"Lord have mercy," Oscar said. He pushed forward and stood slowly, and Annie could see that he was moving more deliberately than before and that his color seemed the barest bit off.

"Hello, Rebecca."

"Hi, Mr. Calhoun," she said. "We sure do appreciate your letting us camp out here tonight."

"Hell," he said, "spend a month."

He and Annie were looking at each other, and Rebecca knew they had not talked about Brad, knew that Annie was feeling loss in a deep, personal way, but Sue saved her before Rebecca had to say anything.

"Come on, Rebecca," she said. "I'll show you and Daniel where you'll be staying."

Rebecca followed her back into the kitchen, but Daniel trailed behind, staring at a large stuffed Georgia Bulldog that squatted on the television set.

Sue saw him lagging behind and whispered, "Will you and Daniel be in the same room?"

The question struck Rebecca as so odd that she laughed, and then stopped, realizing she was blushing. She lifted the heavy hair off her right shoulder and tried to stop the heat in her face, without much luck. "No," she said. "We're just ... uh, we're friends, sort of."

"Oh heavens, I'm sorry," Sue whispered. "I always get these things wrong. You never know how to act any more." Rebecca felt the love and intimacy in Sue's kitchen, where food had been prepared and left to warm.

"It's okay," she said. "Daniel?"

Her words jolted him from his study of the Bulldog, and he clomped into the kitchen, grinning and inhaling the rich aroma of food. From the corner of her eye, Rebecca could see Annie walking slowly toward her father without a word.

"You have these Bulldogs all over your house," Daniel said.

"Oscar's the biggest Bulldog fan that ever lived," she said. "We've been to every home game since God invented leather."

Thirty minutes later, they all sat at the table, ready to eat, as Sue shuttled in and out of the kitchen, finally bringing each of them a tall crystal glass of iced tea. She sat, and Rebecca looked at Oscar and saw him staring at the food with something like regret. They were starting to eat when Sue noticed that Daniel had his hands folded over his food, like a child, silently mouthing some prayer he must have learned years before. The gesture shook Rebecca, who had not prayed before a meal in years, but Sue and Oscar merely bowed and said their own prayers while Annie and Rebecca stared at each other, unsmiling.

After supper, Daniel and Rebecca walked out into the back yard under a comforting blanket of stars and sat in Sue and Oscar's metal lawn chairs.

"It's a pretty night," said Rebecca.

"Yes, Rebecca," Daniel said. They were silent for a minute. "I do not know why I was back at Greenvale. I was having a dream. I have a dream, and then I am alive in the dream and do not know where I have been."

"Has this always happened to you, Daniel?" she asked.

"I have dreams," he said. "At night, everything is different for me, Rebecca. I look out and cannot see where I am and so I think..."

"...what?"

"I think that if I cannot see where I am, then I will die," he said. "If I die, Frank will put me under the ground with Henry May Long and Delphina Almeda Brown."

"Oh, Daniel," Rebecca said, turning to him. "Everything dies."

"Why?" he asked. His voice was not sad or unhappy, just soft and full of questions.

"Because we're just animals," she said. "We are flesh and all flesh is like the grass. It withers and dies." She was surprised to be quoting scripture, but she knew it from the Brahms' *Requiem*, not from a childhood in love with the saints. "Sooner or later, we all will pass from this world."

"I do not want to leave this world," Daniel said. "I do not want to leave you, Rebecca." She reached out and took his hand and held it in hers, feeling his rough, work-torn palm rest gently upon her skin.

"What made you start worrying about this?" she said. "I thought you were happy working there in Oconee Hill, Daniel."

"I was sitting down near the river," he said, "and I heard words

114

in my head."

She could feel him trembling slightly, so she held his hand more tightly.

"I was watching Woodrow catch catfish, and this voice came into my head, and it was a man, and he was telling me he was going to kill me, too." Daniel stood, feeling a growing panic, and he walked a few feet away and turned.

Alarmed, Rebecca rose from her chair and stood poised, ready to go toward him. "He was going to kill me, too. And then, and then, I would have to lie with Louisa Adelaide Brown. HERS WAS A BEAUTIFUL LIFE MARKED BY UNSELFISH KINDNESS, LOVING SERVICE AND DEVOTION TO COUNTRY." He spat out the inscription while clutching at his throat, even though his collar was loose and open.

Rebecca took a step toward him. "Daniel, don't," she said.

"He's going to kill me, too," Daniel said. "Oh Lordy, Wallace, don't kill me! Oh Lordy, don't kill us now!"

Rebecca felt a deep darkness, and she was aware that she was perspiring heavily. "Annie!" she cried.

"Annie!" Daniel screamed.

"Daniel, don't," Rebecca said. "Annie! Mr. Calhoun! I need some help out here!"

Daniel was stumbling backward, breathing heavily. "SHE OPENETH HER MOUTH WITH WISDOM AND IN HER TONGUE IS THE LAW OF KINDNESS," he mumbled.

Rebecca moved slowly toward him, and when she heard the door open, she turned and saw Annie and her father, who was leaning on his cane, and then Sue Calhoun came out, too. Rebecca looked helplessly at them, not knowing what to say.

"Daniel's upset," Rebecca said.

He was standing next to a bird feeder that rested at the top of an eight-foot-tall metal pole. He grasped the pole and held on, but when Rebecca started to come near, he pulled it from the ground in one swift swiveling motion and swung it toward her. Birdseed sprayed over her in an arc. Now Daniel was swinging the feeder like a censer.

"Oscar, go call the EMS," said Sue.

"Wait," said Rebecca, stepping back out of the way. "He's just confused right now. Something's happening to him."

"Oh Lordy, Wallace, don't kill me," he moaned, letting the bird feeder drop to the ground. He put his hand over his forehead and wept openly, but when he heard Rebecca coming toward him on the dampening grass, he shouted—one agonized, unintelligible word. He waved at her as if she were a phantom from the world of dreams, and then he turned and ran toward the back of the yard and into the darkness of the central Georgia woods.

"No," Rebecca whispered. She felt herself starting to run faster, gathering speed like a locomotive, but when she got to the back of the lot, she stopped, listening to Daniel, who was shouting now and stumbling down into the woods and out of her keeping. Suddenly, Annie and Sue were right behind her, and Oscar was coming across the damp grass, slowly, on his cane. Rebecca was crying, and her chest hurt terribly from the run across the yard.

"How deep are the woods?" she gasped.

"They go on forever," Annie said. "Just forever."

"We should call the EMS—or the police," said Sue. "He could get hurt in there."

"Not yet," Rebecca said. "Please. Annie, could you get some flashlights? We could go see if we could find him."

"Would he hurt you?" asked Oscar, who had finally caught up with them.

"No," Rebecca said. "Daniel will not hurt me."

In that moment, when the silence enfolded them in the darkness, Rebecca heard a voice herself—but it was Daniel's, and he was saying, *I do not want to leave this world.*

TEN

WIDE FLASHLIGHT BEAMS BRUSHED BACK AND FORTH over the carpet
of needles. Rebecca and Annie were not ten feet apart, and enough
moonlight filtered through the pines so they could see each other's
silhouette crunching through the forest.

"Daniel! Daniel!" their voices cried, Rebecca's deeper and
stronger. She heard Annie's soprano shout and recalled her own
teen-age years, when her voice began to deepen like a boy's and the
hair grew so thick under her arms and on her legs that she had to
shave all the time.

"Stop," Rebecca said, and Annie took two more steps before
she stood still. "Listen." The faint strains of music seemed to be
rising from the earth.

"There's a road back here, some houses where black folks live,"
said Annie. "Music."

"Yeah," Rebecca said. "Where in the world did he go?"

"Daniel!" cried Annie.

"Daniel!" shouted Rebecca.

She began to walk slowly forward again, and Annie matched
her steps through the trees, and soon they were close to the back of a

house from which a yellow light spilled. The light seemed unreal to Rebecca, as indecisive as a yawn. Was it because they couldn't afford stronger lights, or was this a whorehouse? The music was very clear now, somebody like Barry White, and both women stopped.

"Who lives here now?" Rebecca wondered aloud.

"I don't know, now," said Annie. "When I was a girl, a woman everybody called Aunt Bama lived here by herself. She dipped snuff and wore ankle hose and told me wonderful stories, but I was terrified of her. Mother said she died years ago, though. The first year Brad and I were married, I brought him..." Her voice trailed off.

"How'd they take it?" asked Rebecca.

"Let's talk about something else," Annie said.

Rebecca turned to look at Annie, and her eye caught a flicker not twenty feet away that at first seemed like an enormous lightning bug—or the mad eye of an alligator. She inhaled sharply when she realized it was the solitary glow of a cigarette.

"Annie," Rebecca said, pointing. They both saw the man at the same time, rising from a ladder-back chair, heard his deep voice just as a dog began to howl pitifully.

"What you women doing out in the woods around my house?"

Rebecca backed up two steps, fell over a log and felt herself in a cool, damp patch of mushrooms. Annie walked boldly toward the man's silhouette.

"I'm Annie...was Annie Calhoun. My folks live back through there," she said, "and a friend of ours, well, got upset and came off down this way. You seen anybody come by here?"

"You Mr. Oscar Calhoun's girl?" The man's voice was suddenly higher-pitched; he was curious.

"That's right, Mr. Oscar and Miss Sue," Annie said.

Rebecca stood, brushed her pants off and picked her way in the dark toward the voices.

"Lord have mercy," he said. "It's Maurice Carmack, Miss Annie."

Annie tried to see his face in the darkness, but it remained

118

unclear, though she was aware for the first time that a woman was sitting in another chair next to his. The name was not familiar, though she tried to place it.

"Junebug—you remember my name—Junebug. I come visit Auntie Bama in the summer from Bainbridge."

"Junebug?" said Annie. The sudden memory of childhood chilled her skin, pushed her backward into an earlier innocence. "My God. We used to pick blackberries together."

"You said you was going to be somebody important when you growed up," said Maurice.

"You were going to be a captain in the Army," Annie remembered.

They both laughed, and Rebecca heard in their voices the genuine edge of emotion recalled in tranquility.

"You do that, Junebug?"

"I pick up trash over to the college," he said, still laughing. "You somebody, Miss Annie?"

"Yeah, I'm the president of the United States," she said.

They laughed again, and then they grew silent. The woman in the chair was smoking. She did not stand or say anything, and Rebecca could see she was wearing white shorts and a halter top. Barry White was groaning on the stereo inside the small, frame house. The hulk of a pickup truck squatted beneath the low, trailing branches of a weeping willow. "Our friend. You heard anybody come by here?"

"Thought we did, 'bout ten minute ago," the woman said. Her voice seemed disembodied, too deep for a woman, and Annie thought immediately of Aunt Bama and her stories. "Crashing up that way." Her finger pointed behind them up the dirt road.

"Oh yeah," Maurice said. "We thought it was a deer or like that. Thrashing around up yonder."

"We appreciate it," Annie said.

"He drunk or like that?" asked Maurice. "I come help you if you need it."

"No," Rebecca said, surprising herself by speaking. "Thanks

anyway. He's just upset. We'll find him."

"Good to see you, Junebug," Annie said. Yes, she remembered. That last summer, he had been thirteen, two years older than she, and they had shown each other their genitals, though neither had been bold enough to touch. She remembered him standing in the woods, a sparkling yellow fountain of urine arching from his black penis.

"You, too," he said.

"Your Aunt Bama died, I hear," Annie said as they started to walk off.

"Uh huh," Maurice said. "Old age. Get all of us sooner or later."

Annie could not think of anything else to say, so she and Rebecca came through the yard to the rhythmic barking of a dog and the low singing of Barry White. They stepped onto the dirt road, and for more than twenty paces, Annie barely recognized that the sound she heard was her best friend calling Daniel's name.

THE MOON WAS LOW AMONG THE PINES, and Daniel saw that it was filled with blood. Red moons brought wolves into your heart. Why had he always thought of that? Perhaps it was a story he had heard at Greenvale, or maybe it was the story of his own heart. Daniel believed that each part of a body had its own history, its particular legend: this hand is the one that handles a fork, this eyebrow the one cut when he walked into a doorframe at the age of eight. He did not understand the history of his heart or what he was doing here, tangled in blackberry bushes near the quiet bubbling of a creek.

He could see wonderful things: the red moon floating on the surface of the water, hairy vines from the trees trailing like spiders' legs, stones at the water's edge that were red-gold and silver. He saw a night bird settle on a pine limb and did not know that it was a mourning dove. He could see the woods open briefly into a gentle needled floor and then close again into thick brambles. He saw a gnarled tree stump that followed Toggle's curves exactly, and Daniel thought of his dog and called its name out loud, a talisman against the night. He saw a raccoon waddling toward the water.

The sounds were the history of his ears. The mourning dove made languid notes, fluted and long. The water sounds sparkled over rocks. An occasional gust of wind made the trees whisper, made the entire forest speak to Daniel. Small creatures cracked the underbrush.

Daniel inhaled and could smell the exotic, rotting compost of the forest floor. He smelled the dirt and the mossy glade and the water, above all the water. He could remember Mr. Wilkins saying water is an odorless, colorless liquid, but that was not true. It had the odor and color of water.

He struggled against the thorny bonds of blackberry vines and fell heavily to the ground, long gashes torn in his arms and legs. He tried to stand, but his legs were entwined, and he fell a second time, thorns puncturing his hands. He rolled a little, and then he was finally free and got to his feet near the bank of the merry creek. Daniel knew he was lost again and did not understand how this had happened. Perhaps if he just came over the next slope, he would find Oconee Hill, find Frank there cutting grass and waving to him with his red-faced smile. He jumped halfway across the shallow creek and splashed on a slick stone, bounding out of the water and into a clearing, up a slope and then through a clot of thick weeds. He closed his eyes. *If you dream a path through the woods, you can walk it.* He ran headlong into a tree, knocked himself flat on the ground, a painful lump swelling above his right eye. *Why did I think I could dream a path through the woods? That was not true. So many things were not true.* He stood again. The red moon filled the woods with fire. He turned left and walked in a straight line until the woods abruptly opened and Daniel found himself at the edge of a field of corn.

The wind was steady but slow. It made the corn silk whisper against green, dark husks.

"Frank!" Daniel shouted. "Frank!" He stepped into a row and

was soon running crazily through the field, breaking the young stalks down, calling Frank's name, running forty feet or so and then veering sharply left or right. His right eye hurt very much and he stopped and held his hand over it. "Baby!" he cried and sat down in the corn, quiet now, breathing hard. Then he said softly, "THE STEPS OF A GOOD MAN ARE ORDAINED BY THE LORD." He was motionless for a long time.

The steps were coming for him, but it was not Frank. Daniel knew how steps sounded, and this was not Frank but Toggle, and he felt a swelling in his heart; this would be the history of his heart, how Toggle had found him lost in this field and come to him. The corn parted slightly, and Daniel saw in the strong moonlight the face of a grazing doe.

The deer and Daniel were so startled that neither moved for nearly a minute. He saw its smooth hairy jaw and the watery kindness of its eyes. Deer, he remembered. At Greenvale he would stand by his window at night and watch them come across the lawn, looking for food, and they had always made him think of the pictures of Santa Claus and his reindeer, made him feel wonderful and strong. Where, he wondered, were all the deer cemeteries? Did they have stones with big antlers sticking out of the top and did they have stones of the babies who died, the spotted fawns carved in marble? Daniel still had not moved when he realized the deer was gone, that it had simply vanished, and he was not sure it had ever been there at all.

The stalks lay before him, dappled in the moonlight, stretching far down the slope to the creek. A cloud blew past the moon, and everything changed colors briefly. The cloud reminded Daniel of the God of Death who killed all the first-born children of the Egyptians. How many times had Mrs. Wilkins told that story? They had watched *The Ten Commandments* on TV, and what had impressed Daniel most was not the Parting of the Red Sea or the Turning of the Waters into Blood. It had been the death that came in the night. *Unless you smeared lamb's blood above your door, God killed your oldest child.* The cloud kept moving, and the red moon swelled back out, heavy and still low in the sky.

"Daniel!" a voice suddenly called. It was very close, and he stood and wondered if it were God calling his name. "Daniel!"

"Daniel!" another voice cried. All at once, he knew that it was Rebecca, and that he was found. He listened, and when the voice came again, he started to clap. But then he stopped and looked at his hands and wondered why he did that; suddenly it seemed something only a child would do.

"Rebecca!" he began to shout, holding the last syllable of the word long. "Re-bec-caaaaa! Re-bec-caaaaa!" He stood in the rustling cornstalks and shouted it over and over.

AT THE MOONLIT CREEK'S FIERY EDGE, Rebecca and Annie followed their flashlight beams.

"Thank God," said Rebecca when she heard his voice.

"He's up there," Annie said. She took the lead, far more accustomed to the night woods than Rebecca, and they splashed across the creek and headed through the soft carpet of pine needles in the clearing and up the slope toward Daniel's shouting. Annie had not felt this strong in days. Once again she was a young girl, strong and lithe, wondering what lay ahead in life, feeling that I-can-do-anything strength. She remembered the first time she had stolen away to the woods with the Robert Graves translation of *The Odyssey*. How old had she been then? Perhaps fourteen.

"Daniel!" yelled Rebecca. She felt her heart beating crazily, throwing itself back and forth against the cage of her ribs. They came up the hill and they both saw him at once, standing in the field, arms dangling at his side, shouting. A dog somewhere nearby heard the commotion and began to bay with a series of coughs and then a long hooting howl. "Daniel!"

Annie slowed down and let Rebecca pass her. Was she in love with Daniel? Pretty weird, Annie thought, except I don't understand shit about love—or death, for that matter. She stood at the edge of the field and thought about her father.

Rebecca opened her arms and took Daniel inside. He clung to her, sobbing and shivering, and she talked quietly to him, mothering and nurturing. She pushed him back to look at his face, and she could see more scratches, including a long one almost parallel to the one he'd gotten on his journey to Greenvale. He wept without shame, and tears came down his cheeks and dripped onto his cotton shirt. Rebecca held her own tears.

"Are you all right?" she whispered.

"What is wrong with me, Rebecca?" he said, still sobbing. "Things keep coming into my head."

"It's okay, sweetheart," she said, and the term of endearment startled her; she had not meant to say it, but it seemed right. "It's okay." She wanted to hold him. She pulled him to her and felt his tears on her shoulder. She whispered, "It's okay, honey. It's okay. Let's go back to the house."

She turned, without letting go of him, and together they walked toward Annie, who was watching, feeling transfigured and heartbroken, recalling a long string of classical allusions.

"Hello, Annie," Daniel said as they reached the edge of the woods.

"Are you okay?" she asked.

"Fine," he said amiably, "how are you?"

It sounded so oddly out of context that Annie and Rebecca both burst out laughing, and then so did Daniel. They began to walk toward the creek, close together. Daniel was on Rebecca's right, and she held his hand. They walked for a time and had just crossed the creek when Daniel said, "Do they have cemeteries for deers?" and Rebecca and Annie started laughing again.

"No, Daniel," Rebecca said.

"Then where do they die?" he asked.

"I don't know," said Rebecca. "Maybe they find a special place and just lie down. A secret place no other deer knows about."

"I saw a deer," Daniel said.

Rebecca reached out and took Annie's free hand, and they

walked the rest of the way through the woods, three abreast, holding hands.

In less than twenty minutes they were back in Oscar and Sue's house. Both were relieved to see that Annie and Rebecca had found Daniel, and Sue was solicitous of Daniel, helping them put him to bed. By then it was nearly midnight, and Oscar and Sue went to bed, leaving Annie and Rebecca in the air-conditioned den, sipping cold beer and talking quietly.

"How do you think Daddy looks?" Annie asked.

"He looks fine to me," Rebecca said.

"He looks so old to me," Annie said. "He was always so strong and in control of everything. I don't think I can stand to watch him go downhill."

"At least you had a father," Rebecca said. She sipped her Coors. "I'm sorry. That sounded petty and self-pitying."

"You're right," Annie said. "I can't imagine not having Daddy around. He's always been the strong force in my life. Until Brad. Looks like I'm losing all my support systems all at once." The thought made tears well up in her eyes.

"No, you're not," Rebecca said, getting up from her chair. She went to the couch and took Annie's hand. They sat there like high school friends and held hands.

"I feel like I'm the last person left in the whole world," Annie said. "How can you ever get it back once you lose it, that innocence?"

"You can't ever get it back," Rebecca said. "But you keep on looking, anyway. Sometimes, you get a glimpse of what the world was like when it was young and green and you believed in Santa Claus and that nothing you loved ever died or went away."

"Everybody keeps telling us to grow up," Annie said, "when the only thing any of us really wants to do is remain a child."

"I've only just started realizing that the brain is the most useless thing in a human body," Rebecca said.

Annie laughed brightly. "You're the best friend I ever had," she said to Rebecca, and they sat holding hands.

The room was suddenly close, and each of them was lost in the lamplit silence of their own hearts. Annie turned to Rebecca in tears.

"I don't want my father to die," she said. "I don't know what would become of me if it weren't for you."

"Looks like we're stuck with each other," Rebecca said.

"Here's to us," said Annie, holding up the sweating bottle of beer. Rebecca touched her bottle to it.

"Here's to love."

That night, Rebecca dreamed of a forest where all the animals lived together happily, a peaceable kingdom. She dreamed of a place where nothing ever died, and the air was filled with a strong, unending light.

ELEVEN

DANIEL AND REBECCA STOOD IN FRONT OF THE RUINS of his trailer and saw that grass was not yet growing back through the burned places. She had told him about it on the trip back to Athens the next morning, but only now did the enormity of the fire strike them both. Walking with his hands in his pockets, Daniel went straight to the tether chain that was melted now to the trailer's charred axle.

Joe Dell and Irene Bailey had seen the MGB pull up, and when they saw Daniel get out they came across the dirt road. Rebecca saw them and nodded. The air was cloudless and brutally hot as July settled into Georgia. Randi Ambrose, her hair a light pink now, came swaying out of her trailer holding a large bag of M&Ms. The two students next door, Kelley Cassidy and Rob Jarrett, were looking out their side window, and when Rebecca caught sight of them, they both seemed to be naked, with only the curtain pulled across their chests.

"Where is Toggle?" Daniel asked.

"He's run off, child," said Irene.

Daniel saw Joe Dell and Irene and Randi, and he smiled broadly and walked to them. Irene took three steps toward him and enfolded him in her heavy black arms.

"Dan, where you been?" asked Randi, munching on a handful of candy. She offered Rebecca some M&Ms, but Rebecca waved the offer away in horror. "You scared the fool out of everybody here, not to mention cops been crawling around here. I had to take my plants in where they don't get enough sun."

"Hello, Randi," Daniel said over Irene's broad shoulder. "Hello, Joe Dell. I was lost but Rebecca found me and brought me home."

Irene let go of him for a moment, but she had tears in her eyes, and she grabbed him back and hugged him tight again.

"I'm glad, son," Joe Dell said.

To Rebecca, he looked like some sort of sage, with his white hair, careless clothes and intense gaze, but this seeming apparition vanished abruptly when Randi Ambrose had a coughing fit and ended it by saying "shit!" very loudly and squatting in the scorched grass.

"My house is all burned down," Daniel said, turning to look at it again.

Rebecca thought briefly of Annie, who had dropped them off at Campus North, so they could get Rebecca's car, before heading home to deal with Brad. Rebecca almost hoped that Annie would move in with her; it was wonderful having company for a change.

"How did it burn down?" Daniel looked around at Joe Dell.

"Police are saying now it looks to be something burning on the stove, son," said Joe Dell. "We all saw it about the same time. Fire was coming out of the windows, and we called the fire department. Lord, we thought you was in there for the longest time."

"Did Toggle burn up?" Daniel asked.

The answer followed the crunch of hard shoes on the few stones in the dirt road.

"I let him loose," said Gene Leach, the manager of the trailer park. He was tall and humorless, with blank brown eyes that seemed suspicious of everything while understanding nothing. "He run off, and I ain't seem him back."

128

He walked to Rebecca and stood close to her, too close to her, and she could smell him, sweat and old clothes, the smell that comes with poverty and too much work.

"You gone be responsible for Daniel, ma'am?"

His dispassionate gaze unnerved Rebecca, who had not yet thought of herself in that role, but she said "Yes," in a small voice, anyway.

"Then I need to talk with you," he said and turned and strode away on his long legs, sure that Rebecca would follow.

He was twenty feet away when Randi Ambrose, recovered from her coughing fit, suddenly popped up. "He's a real jerk," she said.

"Who is he?" asked Rebecca.

"Leach," said Irene, all but spitting out the word.

"The manager," said Joe Dell. "He's a piss-poor excuse for a man."

They had walked back out into the road, and Rebecca glanced up in time to see Kelley and Rob staring at them from another window, this one at the front of their trailer. They were holding a different curtain in front of them, and Rob was standing behind Kelley. Rebecca wanted to shout something like "Enjoy it while you can," but she only turned back to Daniel, who was still standing in awe before his trailer's ashes.

"I'm going to talk to Mr. Leach," Rebecca said. "You stay here with your friends."

"Okay, Rebecca," Daniel chirped. "Toggle is alive somewhere. We will need to find him."

"Yes," Rebecca said, and she pivoted away just as Irene was accepting proffered M&Ms from Randi Ambrose.

Oconee-By-The-River was organized on terraces that descended down the hill toward the river, and now Rebecca saw Gene Leach walking toward a small concrete-block building on the next level down. He seemed to move inside his clothes without bones, legs and arms as fluid as a rubber garden hose. She walked faster and caught up with him just as he went down a series of steep steps cut from the hard, red mud. He went inside, never looking back, and Rebecca followed him in. The office was a single room with a desk, two chairs and a filing cabinet. On the wall was a calendar from Jones Hardware that had a hunter aiming point-blank at a deer with a look of placid acceptance on its face.

Leach motioned for Rebecca to sit. She did and lit a cigarette. He pulled the desk drawer back on its unoiled runners, and it made a painful shriek. He took a cigar from the drawer and when he lit it, a foul-smelling cloud of blue smoke overwhelmed the white drift from Rebecca's cigarette.

"I knew I was taking a chance when I let them folks talk me into keeping that boy here," Leach said in a soft monotone. "And now he's done burned one of my goddamned trailers to the ground. I don't have time for babysitting, whether it's an old woman or a retard. And I cain't afford it. I'm gone have one hell of a time with the insurance comp'ny trying to get a penny out of this."

Rebecca felt her anger rising, but she held it in check. "What, exactly, do you think happened?" she said icily.

"Something burning on the stove," Leach said around the cigar. "Hell, who knows, when you're dealing with a retard?"

Rebecca got up and crushed her cigarette out in a huge ashtray on which a hula girl stood frozen in mid-dance at one corner.

"I'll take Daniel with me," she said. "I'll find him a place to live in town. But I want you to know one thing, you son of a bitch...."

She pointed at him like God, her hand trembling. Already Leach was shocked; he was a virtual pharaoh in the trailer park, and no one ever contradicted him.

"...Daniel is *not* retarded. He's probably a damn sight smarter than you are, in fact. And where do you get off acting like a martyr for that heap of trash you call a trailer? That was his *home*. He would never have burned it down on purpose. It was all in this world he had. All the friends he has are here, too." She turned and stormed out of the office, trembling with rage, not really hearing what he shouted after her, knowing they were words of anger but not listening.

130

She walked back up the steps and with deliberate speed toward Daniel and her car. Randi and Joe Dell must have gone back inside against the heat, she thought, for only Irene was still there with Daniel, and she seemed to be telling him goodbye. Before Rebecca got there, Irene had already slipped up the steps and into the air conditioning of her own trailer.

"Come on, Daniel," Rebecca said.

"Take me by to see Frank," he said. "I want to have my job. He will not be angry if he knows I just got lost."

Rebecca had called Frank from Statesboro the night before and told him that Daniel would be back, and Frank had seemed relieved and uncertain what he might do next. Rebecca understood. No one really seemed to know what to do with Daniel Mitchell.

"Okay," she said. "But we have to find you a place to live."

"Will they put another trailer here for me?" he asked with wide eyes. He almost seemed to be smiling now.

"No," she said. "We have to find you a place to live. I'll help you. Don't worry. We'll get you some clothes and things. Everything will be okay."

"I will have to come and hunt for Toggle," said Daniel. "He will be looking for me somewhere."

Rebecca felt as if her heart were being crushed. "We'll do that later," she said. "Get in, and I'll take you by to see Frank."

"Okay, Rebecca," said Daniel.

They had almost reached the entrance of the trailer park when Daniel started shouting for her to stop, and she did. He hopped out, ran up to Daisy Saye's trailer, lurched up to the door and banged on it. A woman came to the door, and Rebecca could not hear what they said, but she saw the woman hug Daniel and then go inside. She came back out in a moment and gave him a magazine. Daniel climbed back into the car and held up an old, dog-eared copy of *Redbook* as if it was the Silver Chalice. "Daisy gives me wonderful things to read," he said.

"Wonderful things," said Rebecca. She drove down Oconee Street and then across the river, turning left and coming around by

O'Malley's and under the railroad bridge. She turned left on East Campus Road, and just before the stadium, she swung through the open gates of Oconee Hill Cemetery.

"REST, HUSBAND, IN THE SILENT TOMB," said Daniel, "REST, FOR THE SHADOW AND THE GLOOM OF DEATH IS PASSED." He smiled happily. "That is for C.D. Barrett, June 13, 1852 to June 10, 1884."

"I guess this is really where you live," said Rebecca, but Daniel did not hear her. He saw Frank, standing near the old stone horse-watering trough with a Weedeater.

Frank leaned on the Weedeater as if it were an Old Testament staff as the car stopped and Daniel jumped out. He stared briefly at Rebecca, and then he turned back to greet Daniel. He set the Weedeater on the ground and hugged Daniel. Rebecca was touched. She could see Frank's genuine pleasure at Daniel's return.

"Boy, you scared the fool out of me," Frank said.

"I am sorry, Frank," said Daniel. "I was lost, and Rebecca found me, but my house burned down, and Toggle has gone away from me. I will start to work now if you will tell me what to do."

"Where are you going to stay?" Frank asked.

"I'm going to get him a place," Rebecca interjected from the car. Frank looked at her, then down at his feet.

"I could help pay for it at first," he said. "Daniel doesn't get his check until the end of the month."

"What check?" asked Rebecca.

"From that place where he grew up, down near Augusta," he said. "They send him the money for his housing. I reckon it's part of the program."

Rebecca was confused. Mr. Wilkins had said nothing about sending Daniel money. Why would a place like Greenvale be sending money to someone who was no longer a resident? Didn't the state make them account for every penny spent?

"I didn't know about that," she said. "But I'll get him a place to stay. I'll help out."

"You run on," Frank said. "Come back tomorrow, Daniel. Ma'am?" He motioned for Rebecca to step aside, and she followed him, while Daniel got back into the car and picked up his *Redbook*. "I think an awful lot of Daniel, but I can't keep him working here if he does this again. I need him to help with a lot of things around here, and if he can't do it, I'll have to hire somebody else."

"Why are you telling me this?" she asked.

"I just thought somebody ought to know," Frank said.

Rebecca nodded and, without another word, climbed in beside Daniel and drove to a nearby shopping center. Rebecca bought him pants, shirts, socks and underwear. She even bought a pair of Nikes for $49. They went by the Drug Emporium at Alps Shopping Center and bought him a toothbrush and toothpaste, shaving cream and a razor, deodorant and a small bottle of Chaps aftershave. Everything fascinated Daniel, and he kept running from one display to another, amazed at some tawdry product. Then they went to the grocery store, where they bought steaks, potatoes, corn on the cob, milk, bread and more, three other bags full, in fact. Daniel held two bags on his lap as they drove under the brutal July sun toward her apartment.

Once inside, Rebecca turned on the television for Daniel to watch while she put the groceries away. He sat on the couch with his hands folded in his lap, staring at the screen, obediently. It was time, she thought, to call around and find him a place to live, but the long, hot day had caught up with her, and she felt bone-tired. She took a shower instead and stood for a long time in the warm drench, feeling better, wondering what in the hell she would do next. She dressed and came out and poured herself a glass of wine.

"Wine?" she asked Daniel.

"Okay, Rebecca," he said.

"You ever drink, Daniel?" she asked.

"I was watching a show about this woman who is very sad," he said, looking back at the screen. "Her husband has gone away with another woman, and she is very sad."

"Don't watch that stuff," she said. "It's just soap operas." She poured him a glass of wine and sat down beside him on the couch. She was wearing a loose-fitting yellow blouse and jeans. Her hair was only towel-dried, and she was aware for the first time how nice it felt to have a man in her apartment again. Daniel took his glass and drank it all in one gulp.

"That's bitter," he said.

"You sip it," she said. "Like this." She sipped from her glass. Daniel looked at her glass.

"It is the blood of Jesus," he said. "Mrs. Wilkins said it is the blood of Jesus." Rebecca laughed.

"Only in church," she said. "Here, it's just Gallo Hearty Burgundy."

He laughed, though he wasn't sure why. Then he winced and touched the scratches on his face, which were looking red and rough.

"I've got some cream for that," said Rebecca. "Prescription stuff. Hang on." She set her drink on the coffee table and got up, switched off the TV as she passed it, stopping to put on a tape of Jazz Flavors, Sade, Bob James and Jeff Lorber. Then she went into the bathroom for the cream. When she came back, Daniel was taking off his shirt, revealing a strong, lean-muscled frame that somehow surprised her. She stared at his thick chest in admiration.

"I have these scratches all over me," he said, and it was true. A deep gash ran along his right side and up near his right nipple, and a few smaller ones strayed over his chest like secondary roads on a map. His hands had many small puncture wounds.

"My God," she said. "You got cut up pretty bad." She sat next to him again and uncapped the tube of cream, and Daniel could smell her, sweet and soapy; he had never seen anyone more beautiful than Rebecca.

"Here. Raise up your arms," she said.

He did as he was told, and she began to smear the cream on his chest and under his arm, leaning so close he could have enfolded her in his strong arms. She felt the stirrings of her body. She could smell him, sweat but almost animal and fiercely attractive. She felt his deep muscles and rubbed the cream up his chest and then put it gently on his face. As she did, he looked directly into her eyes, unblinking, with a gaze of admiration that amounted to awe. *If this had been any other man alive, he would be grabbing me now,* she thought, *and if he did, I would love him. God, Daniel needs a woman to love him.* She finished and leaned back, and Daniel smiled at her and blinked.

"That is very nice," he said.

She felt her sexuality blossom in her, no place at first, then tight and warm in her very center.

"I thought I was going to die," Daniel told her. "I was swimming in the vines of the blackberry. I fell into them and was swimming, but they cut me. I guess they did not want me in there."

"Blackberries don't think," Rebecca said, laughing, and watched Daniel stand up and put his shirt back on and begin to button it up. *Please,* she thought, the wine beginning to warm her up. *Please.*

"Everything thinks," said Daniel. His heart was beating so fast he could barely breathe, and the wine had flushed his face. He wanted to hold Rebecca worse than anything, but he was afraid he might scare her. "Everything thinks and breathes and dies. Mr. Wilkins read us about the Indians. They said only the rocks live forever. Everything is alive." He tucked in his shirt and went over to the picture window that looked out over Broad Street and the University of Georgia campus.

"Sometimes I don't think *I'm* even alive," Rebecca said. She came up beside him, and they watched the traffic nine stories below.

"I wish that I could fly," said Daniel.

Rebecca looked up at him and saw that the afternoon sun caught his profile and brought out all its full character, an easy grace, the untroubled freedom of childhood. She saw something else, too, something she had never seen before: the desire to hold a new world in his hands. "That's an old dream," she said. "People have always wanted to fly."

He did not seem to be listening to her. Then he turned, and the sun caught his face full.

"I want to go find my dog," he said, and he started crying,

huge sobs, and he hunched over and put his face in his hands. Rebecca pulled him to her and held him, led him to the couch and held him. His tears on her shoulder were warm and wet, and she felt more alive than she had in years at the exact moment that she kissed Daniel gently on the ear.

"Okay," she whispered in his ear. "We'll go find Toggle. It's okay."

Daniel clung to her.

"Come on. I'm dressed. We'll go down to the river right now. Maybe he's just lost down there somewhere."

"Okay," Daniel said, looking up. They held each other, and he looked ashamed. "What's wrong with me, Rebecca?"

His words were unexpected and hit her viscerally.

"Nothing is wrong with you," she whispered. She leaned forward and kissed him gently on the lips, and he kissed her back easily and without urgency. "Nothing is wrong with you."

They drove across the Oconee River Bridge and parked near the sign that promised new condos soon. Daniel had put his baseball cap back on and seemed happy once again, while Rebecca, behind her sunglasses, wondered what in the hell she was getting into. A few more minutes and she might have had his clothes off. And yet she knew that could be a terrible mistake. For who was Daniel anyway? Where did his drive, his emotions come from? Who was Wallace? There were so many things to find out, so many worlds within him to explore.

"Toggle!" Daniel cried from the bank.

"Let's wait until we're up the river a bit," she said. She had called Animal Control before they left and described the dog, but they had not picked up one like that.

"Okay, Rebecca," Daniel agreed, smiling. They walked down the bank through the tall weeds and came to the path along the ledge at the river bank. Cars roared by on the bridge above and behind them. The last time Rebecca had been here, she was looking for Daniel and had stumbled upon the baptism in the river. Now, he walked along with an easy lope in front her.

"Toggle!" he screamed suddenly. His voice sounded strange, thick and booming. He looked all around but they did not see the dog.

"Toggle!" she called, aware of the futility of their search. As they walked, an idea began to stitch itself together, a drive up to the mountains to see again some of the places where Lawrence Dale had lived. Perhaps having Daniel near would kick off her enthusiasm if she could only see the lost icons of the poet's life. They walked along the bank until they came to the opening where the baptism had taken place. Instead, they saw an old black person sitting on the bank, face covered by a wide-brimmed straw hat, fishing.

"Woodrow," Daniel said, then, much louder, "Woodrow!" He ran toward the figure crying his name over and over, and Rebecca saw the figure unfold and cringe with fear. It was an old woman, her lined face pulled back in terror. Daniel skidded to a stop and stood there wordlessly as Rebecca caught up.

"Don' you hurt me!" the woman screamed. "Don' you hurt me!"

"It's okay," said Rebecca. "He thought you were somebody else." The woman stared at both of them and backed away.

"You are not Woodrow," Daniel said.

"It's okay," Rebecca said. "He's just a...." But what was he?

"I ain't no Woodrow," she said angrily. "Don' you never run up on a old lady like that."

"I am so ashamed," Daniel said. He looked around them. The sun glinted off the unchanging river and birds sang. To Daniel Mitchell, everything seemed suddenly very close.

TWELVE

REBECCA FOUND HIM AN APARTMENT IN A RUN-DOWN HOUSE on Hancock Street, not far from the county health clinic. The rooms were clean, though, and Daniel loved everything about it, the cool, high ceilings, the dark wood and the front porch where some of the residents gathered late in the hot July afternoons to catch the merest hint of a breeze. Daniel's apartment was on the second floor in a corner, and from it he could see a new brick apartment complex across Hancock Street and, past that, a water tower and many trees.

Daniel did not mind Georgia's late July heat because Oconee Hill was snugged in deep shade most of the day. He did not run away again or look for Toggle, but on weekends he still came to watch Woodrow Faust fish in the slow waters of the river. Each morning, when Daniel got up, he could hear the radio in the next apartment, where an old man named Julio Gomez lived. Julio claimed to have fought with Pancho Villa, but no one believed him. Most of the morning, he sat on the porch reading Spanish magazines, and by early afternoon, he was drinking cheap wine. Daniel liked him immediately, liked all his colorful stories and the deep lines on his face. The other upstairs apartment was occupied by Mae Walters and Olga Salinger, two old women who worked at the University of Georgia Library and baked pies for the other residents. They often invited Daniel over at night for pie, and Miss Mae believed that Daniel was gay, though Miss Olga had so far reserved judgment. Miss Olga was writing an endless novel about a lesbian heroine in the American Civil War. Miss Mae told her it was ahead of its time, but Miss Olga just smiled sweetly and plunged ahead.

By the end of the month, Rebecca had not written another word about Lawrence Dale, and her feelings about Daniel were showing signs of changing from concerned interest to an obsession. Two or three times a week, she would come by his house in the early evening when Athens had moved a bit from its sluggish summer routine. She took him places, and Daniel loved these rides more than any part of his week. Miss Olga pointed out this friendship as proof that Daniel wasn't gay, but Miss Mae asked if she had noticed they never hugged or kissed. "What does that tell you?" she asked.

Sometimes, Rebecca and Daniel would drive to Annie's house. Brad had moved out in the middle of the month, leaving her alone and depressed, though nothing was certain. On some days, Annie would be bright and funny; on others, she would come to Rebecca's office, close the door and cry until her eyes were red. The news from Statesboro was not encouraging. Her father was weaker and now could get around only with a walker.

Rebecca took Daniel to an art opening. She took him to a summer concert by a string quartet at the Fine Arts Auditorium on campus. She took him to the library and showed him the richness of its volumes, hundreds of thousands, even millions, of books. She took him to the 40 Watt Club, where they heard a band called Nigger Jesus play one song that lasted for ninety minutes. When they came out, Daniel was shuddering, and did not speak until she dropped him off at home. She took him to the movies to see *Snow White,* and he was so delighted he began to clap when the Dwarfs sang "Heigh-Ho!" Rebecca giggled like a schoolgirl and grabbed his hand and held it for the rest of the movie. She had not felt this way since she had held hands with her boyfriend in the fifth grade when they saw *Gone with the Wind*.

They ate eggs at midnight at the Waffle House at Five Points and overheard a woman saying that every house in America had aliens in its attic and that soon they would come out and eat the country. The man with her had tried to calm her down, and then he got up and left while she fumed over a cigarette.

One afternoon, Rebecca bought an iced watermelon, and she and Daniel and Annie went to Bishop Park and ate it beneath the lights and watched a women's softball game. Halfway through the game, the women got into a fight, and Rebecca saw Daniel begin to get upset, so they drove out in the country. That night was the first time Daniel told her about his dream: to live in the country with chickens and cows and rows of corn. They sat on the trunk of Annie's Volvo off Jefferson River Road in the edge of a pasture. A few hazy stars drifted above them.

"You never told me that," said Rebecca.

"I think I lived in the country," Daniel said, wiping his mouth on his sleeve. "When I was a little boy, I mean. I remember a little red calf that had great big eyes. Sometimes, things come to me—and either I was there or I was not there."

"You never talk much about that," Rebecca said.

"I cannot remember much about what happened before Green-vale," he said.

Rebecca looked at Annie. They had talked about it, about his crazed mother and the horrors Daniel had seen. "In the winter you can see a lot more stars," she said. "We should come out here in the winter."

"The winter," Daniel said softly. "In the winter there is not much work for the dead."

"What?" asked Annie, who had been thinking about Brad. "That was beautiful, Daniel. Is that from a poem, Rebecca?"

Rebecca giggled. "He's talking about the cemetery."

"Oh," Annie said. "I thought it was Byron or something."

"Bowleg Byron," said Daniel, nodding his head. "He was at Greenvale while I was learning to add numbers."

Annie and Rebecca exchanged smiles. Later, after taking Daniel home, they went back to Annie's silent house. Rebecca had left her car there. Inside, they got two cold bottles of Coors from the refrigerator and sat in the deep chairs in the darkened den. Annie put on a Johnny Mathis record and pulled her knees up and hugged them, rocking slightly back and forth.

"She's small and dark and has big boobs," Annie said. Only the light filtering into the den from the kitchen lit the room, so that Rebecca could just see half of Annie's face as she spoke.

"You don't have to talk about this," she said.

"I want to," Annie said in a voice that seemed detached, nearly inhuman. "He called me at the office this afternoon, and I came down to see you, but you weren't there."

"I was at home trying to make another go of this book," Rebecca said. "I told myself I would really get it started, maybe even finish a first draft this summer—and I haven't done shit on it. I didn't do anything again today."

"Some of my best friends never get anything done," Annie sighed. "He said that he didn't know what he was going to do and that he was confused. He said he didn't feel like I needed him."

"That's what Charlie always said," Rebecca whispered, and then she drank half her beer in one gulp.

"Men are such babies," said Annie. "If you don't tell them how wonderful they are every damn minute, they think you don't care anymore."

"I don't know," Rebecca said. "I used to think that. Hell, I've probably said those exact same words."

"You did," said Annie. "Right after Charlie left. You are the source of nearly all of my speeches."

"Oh great," Rebecca said. "Did it ever occur to you that I didn't know what I was talking about?"

"Don't you still believe that about men?" asked Annie.

Rebecca took out a cigarette and lit it and walked to the French doors that looked out over the patio. Waves of heat lightning drifted through the deep green back yard.

"It's Daniel," said Rebecca. "I don't know what I believe anymore. He's changing, Annie. You know what he said to me Monday night? I picked him up and I asked him where he wanted to go eat and he said, 'It don't matter a flying fuck to me.' "

Annie choked with laughter and spouted a stream of beer halfway across the room then put her hand over her mouth and was barely able to control herself.

Rebecca laughed, too, but soon regained her composure. "I'm serious. I feel like I'm playing God with him. I mean he is a man and yet he's not a man, either. I have this sick feeling that I'm using him for therapy."

"Everybody uses everybody for therapy," said Annie. "And anyway, Brad's right. Shit. Brad's right. I probably have taken him for granted sometimes, but it's just that ... it's just that ...."

"Don't start hating yourself," Rebecca said. "That won't do you any good. You can't sit over here and hide."

Annie suddenly went icy and rocked back in her chair and stared at Rebecca. "What?" she said. "I never said I was going to hide."

"Okay," said Rebecca. "You're not going to hide." The record ended and the room was silent.

"Anywhere, where do you come off lecturing me, Gentry?" Annie said. She looked down at the floor and then hurled her beer bottle into the stone fireplace where it shattered.

One flying shard barely missed Rebecca's face, and so without speaking she set her beer down on the coffee table and got her purse and slipped out through the kitchen, never turning around even when she heard Annie faintly calling her name.

When she got to Campus North, Rebecca parked her car in the lot adjacent to her building and walked slowly toward the door where Bud, the night watchman, stood. He always wore khakis and a white, short-sleeved shirt and kept a .38 in a holster clipped to his wide belt. Rebecca hated guns, but his presence comforted her.

"Hi, Bud," she said.

"Miss Gentry," Bud nodded. "Woman was here looking for you

tonight. Tried like hell to get me to let her upstairs to wait, but I wouldn't."

"Who was it?" Rebecca asked.

"She wouldn't leave her name," he said. "I never seen her before. Lady maybe in her fifties, gray haired, kind of thin."

"What did she say?" asked Rebecca, feeling her heartbeat quicken.

"That she needed to talk to you," Bud said, chewing on a toothpick. Bud always chewed on a toothpick. "I asked her to leave a number or a message, but she said she'd call you later."

"Meaning tonight?" asked Rebecca.

"Didn't say," Bud answered. "That was it. She looked sort of ... well, prob'ly my imagination."

"Sort of what, Bud?" Rebecca asked.

"Scared," Bud said. "Upset about something. Might have been my imagination."

Rebecca went inside and rode the elevator to the ninth floor, her mouth dry. Once inside, she put the nightlatch on the door and poured herself a glass of Gallo Hearty Burgundy and slipped off her shoes. She was standing in the kitchen holding the bottle in one hand and the glass in the other when the phone rang, too loud, unreal. The bottle slipped from her hand and hit the floor but it did not shatter. Wine snaked from it in a river across the white tile floor of the kitchen. She lifted the phone from the wall.

"Yes," she said in a flat voice.

"Hi, stranger," a man's voice said.

Charlie.

She knew that voice so well, and remembered that was how he always greeted her in college up in Chapel Hill. God, they had been young and in love in those days.

"Charlie," she said. "What ... uh, sorry, I wasn't expecting ... is something wrong?"

"Nothing's wrong," he said. "I was just sitting here thinking about you. I don't know. I wanted to talk to you. How are you, Cricket?"

She hadn't heard his pet name for her in nearly two years, and she was surprised how it moved and upset her.

"You want the sanitized public version or the private angst version?" she asked.

He could hear her voice tighten as she said 'angst version,' then heard her inhale and exhale sharply.

"How about the life-is-difficult-but-I-am-coping version you give your acquaintances?" he asked. He laughed. "Angst? I warned you about using words like that on the phone. The phone company keeps records and they could revoke your doctorate for things like that."

He could always make her laugh, she thought. The first class they'd had together, he had made her laugh out loud so much that she had nearly been kicked out. Was it American history? She couldn't remember anymore. She knelt and cleaned up the wine with a towel while they talked.

"Oh, I'm all right," she said. "Maybe it's just summer. Everything goes crazy in the summer. I can't write this book, and Annie broke a beer bottle in the fireplace during a conversation we had tonight."

"Maybe you should have your personality registered with the police," he said.

"Charlie, what are you calling about?" she sighed.

"I'm going to be in Athens for the Virginia game," he said. "I just wondered if you wanted to go with me."

She smiled and thought about it. They had once had season tickets, and though she did not care much for sports, the spectacle of eighty thousand screaming fans was awesome.

"You have tickets?" she asked, almost coyly.

"Sure do, Toots," he said. "And boy, am I a good date."

"I don't know if I want a date with a divorced man," she said.

He was silent for a long time.

"It's never been the same without you, Cricket," he said finally. "Charleston's a nice town. But it ain't almost like being in love."

"And are you in love, Charlie?" she asked dreamily.

"I thought I was, once," he said. "But it turned out to be either an empty infatuation or indigestion. I'm not sure which. Are you in love, Cricket?"

She had not thought of Daniel since she and Annie had been talking earlier, but she thought of him now and wondered what he meant to her, what she meant to him.

"No, Charles, I'm not in love," she said.

"How about in lust?" he asked playfully. She could see his Italian good looks, the thick dark hair and the black eyes.

"You are the ex-husband and not entitled to that information," she said. She threw the wine-soaked towel into the sink.

"That's true," he said. "So how about the Virginia game? We can have a tailgate party and wear Bulldog-red clothes, eat fried chicken and drink gin fizzes, and then afterward puke in the hedges. How about it?"

God, it felt good to be courted, she thought. "You turn a girl's head," she said, giggling.

"I'll call you in two or three weeks to set up the details," he said.

"What does this mean?" Rebecca asked.

Charlie didn't speak for a time. Then she said, "That always was your worst quality, Cricket—trying to see what everything meant. Lots of things don't mean anything, Babe. Things just happen to people, and they react. Most of the world runs on physics, not poetry. Action and reaction."

"You haven't changed," she said.

"Yes, I have," he said. "Have you?"

"I don't know," she said. She thought for a moment of telling Charlie about Daniel, but there was no need; Daniel was not her lover, he was her friend. "Maybe," she said, and let it go at that.

After she hung up, Rebecca wondered if some kind of fundamental change was beginning to take shape in her heart. She slipped out of her clothes and lay naked on her bed and thought of Charlie, of his large, heavy hands as they brushed across her body, of the wonderful crush of his body against hers, of the terrible, urgent taste of morning kisses when he awoke needing her so badly that she was barely awake before they were loving. She had closed her eyes and was languidly rubbing the space between her breasts when the phone rang again.

Don't answer it.

She held her hand on her chest and could feel her heart suddenly beating furiously against her rib cage. She hated being afraid. She rolled over and picked up the bedroom phone from beside the clock radio, which was quietly playing jazz. It was 11:56 p.m.

"Yes," she said. Maybe it was Charlie again. She hoped so. Once, they had made love over the phone when he was away in Chicago, back when they had been married.

"Miss Gentry?"

The voice was a woman's, scratchy and perhaps elderly. It trembled slightly. Rebecca looked around for a pack of cigarettes but the nearest was on the bureau. She sat up on the edge of the bed.

"Who is this?" she asked.

"You don't know me," the woman said. "But ... I need to, uh, talk to you, Miss Gentry. You are the one who is writing the book on Lawrence Dale, aren't you?" Her voice was precise, the kind of elocution-trained speech some older women still have in the South. Rebecca could hardly make sense of the question. She sat, staring at a print of Van Gogh flowers on the wall. "I ... I came by to see you earlier, but you weren't home, so, I .... Miss Gentry, are you there?"

"Yes, yes," she said. "Just a minute." Rebecca set the phone on the edge of the bed and slipped into some shorts and a halter top and got a cigarette. She was sitting on the bed again when she realized she didn't have to put clothes on for a phone call. "Who is this, please?"

"This is hard to explain," said the woman. "You are the one writing the book about—"

"Lawrence Dale, yes, yes," said Rebecca. "Are you a colleague, or—"

"You have never met me," the woman said. "It's just, well,

there are some things you ought to know if you are going to write that book." The woman's tone betrayed her indecisiveness and fear.

"Well, like what?" asked Rebecca. She lit the cigarette. "Did you know him?"

The woman's voice became very small.

"Yes," she whispered. "I knew him very well. Could we meet?"

"Tonight?" Rebecca asked.

"Tomorrow is all right," the woman said. "I just don't know if I will have the courage to talk about this if I don't do it now. It's just that—"

"What?" asked Rebecca. She felt her skin tingle and come alive.

"Well," the woman said. "He didn't die like people thought."

Holy shit, Rebecca thought.

"Who *are* you?" she asked. "I mean, you said you knew him well? How do you know about his death?"

"I can't, on the phone," the woman pleaded. "It's just that he was ... betrayed."

Rebecca stood up. The hair on the back of her neck bristled.

"Betrayed?" Rebecca said weakly. "Uh, let's meet tonight and talk about this."

"No, no," the woman sniffed. "I know it's late. It's just that I needed to say it tonight, that's all."

"Do you know where Helen's Restaurant is on Broad Street downtown?" asked Rebecca.

"I can find it," the woman said. "How about for breakfast at eight?"

"Fine," said Rebecca.

The woman sighed deeply. "You should know what happened to him," she said.

Before Rebecca could answer, before she could ask the woman where she was staying, there was a click and in a few seconds a dial tone came on.

"All right!" Rebecca said. She clapped her hands and squealed with delight and went into the kitchen and poured another glass of wine. She kept turning the word "betrayed" over and over in her mind, considering its melodramatic sound. How could Lawrence Dale have been betrayed and who would have betrayed him? She drained the glass.

After the wine, she slept heavily and awoke to find that it was already after seven. She cursed and took a quick shower, put on a light yellow cotton dress and sandals, and walked down Broad Street toward Helen's. The sky had closed in over Athens in the night, and thick clouds and a cool wind threatened rain soon.

Helen's is a small restaurant where a pleasing mix of blue-collar workers and students eat, an easy port among the vogue eateries of a college town. Rebecca came inside, and the pleasing aroma of coffee and eggs was strong. She sat in a corner booth up front from where she could see the slow traffic on the street and across it, the tall oaks of North Campus. A man in overalls sat not far from her. He read that morning's *Atlanta Constitution*. Rebecca saw that he had only three fingers on his right hand. Carpenter, she thought automatically.

She ordered coffee and looked at her watch. It was just before eight, and she had spent the brief walk down the street trying to plan her questions, to understand what "betrayal" meant. Just before she left her apartment, she had almost called Annie, to check on her, but there wasn't time. Rebecca watched the people drift past on the street. Why were so many work uniforms blue? Three girls with red hair came by, smoking and talking. Red, Rebecca thought—the red from the Crayola box, teased up asymmetrically in punker fashion. One of them seemed familiar, and it wasn't until they had long gone that Rebecca realized it was Randi Ambrose from Daniel's old trailer park.

By eight-twenty, Rebecca started to wonder if it had been a dream; after all, she had dreamed often of Lawrence Dale. She passed the time by listening to the sounds: chinks of silverware on the heavy white plates, crushed ice being swished in sweating glasses, idle, hoarse morning chatter, the squeaking steps of the waitresses' rubber-soled shoes on the tiles. Breakfast came for the three-fingered man, and he ate heartily, but Rebecca did not feel hungry. She smoked her first cigarette of the morning, and it nearly made her sick. *I'm going to have to quit these damned things.* She ordered another cup of coffee.

Just after eight-forty, Rebecca realized the woman wasn't coming. *Shit,* she thought, *now what?* She stood up, took two dollars from her purse and was walking toward the cash register when three drunks stumbled down Broad Street past the window, talking too loud, obviously, at this early hour, having made a night of it. One she recognized immediately: Harry Carlson, a town character who claimed to be an artist and spent most of his time cadging drinks at the small clubs. He was nearing fifty and still only worked part time in the university's library. The second man was a tall, thin guy who seemed familiar. The third man was Daniel Mitchell. It seemed so unbelievable, even ridiculous, that for a moment, she stood at the register with her money, stunned.

"Oh my God," she said finally.

"What's wrong?" asked the pleasant-faced woman at the register. Rebecca thrust her check and two dollars toward her and started for the door.

"It's somebody I know," she said. "He's...uh..." Rebecca pivoted and went out the heavy glass door and onto the sidewalk. Thick drops of rain were beginning to splatter against the pavement. She ran up Broad Street to the next corner, at College Avenue, and saw them heading north, past Foreign Affairs and Gorin's Ice Cream Shop, up toward the Chocolate Shoppe. She began to run, and when she got close enough, she heard Harry Carlson talking in his loud, snobby drawl about someone around town who had cheated him. Harry thought everyone was out to cheat him.

"Daniel!" she shouted.

He stopped and turned slowly around, and when Rebecca saw his face, she wanted to die. His eyes had the unfocused, uncaring glare of the drunk, just as Harry Carlson's did. Now she remembered who the other man was—a former newspaperman named Black, who ran a record shop around the corner on Wall Street. She had bought a used copy of a Brahms' symphony in there in the early spring.

"It is my friend Rebecca," Daniel said. He was holding a bottle of gin by its neck. He left the others, and as they disappeared around the corner by the Chocolate Shoppe, he stumbled back toward her. "Hell of a morning, ain't it?"

"Daniel, you're drunk," said Rebecca in disbelief. When he got closer, she could see that his clothes were soiled and he needed a bath. "What happened? What are you doing?"

"I am learning to drink," he said, looking affectionately at the bottle. She took it away from him and walked ten steps and threw it in a trash can. He watched her, cocking his head from side to side like a puppy.

"Why aren't you at work?" Rebecca said angrily.

"Harry said I must be some kind of saint," said Daniel. She took his arm and led him up the street toward her apartment, wondering what to do now. They had crossed College Avenue when the rain came down harder, and Daniel stopped and stood there, weaving slightly and looking puzzled.

"Rebecca?"

"What is it now?" Rebecca asked irritably.

"What is a saint?"

THIRTEEN

SHE WATCHED HIM SLEEP ON THE COUCH. The only sounds were his deep breathing, the steady rain on the window and the throbbing of Wagner on her stereo. Rebecca had called Frank and told him Daniel was sick, and she hated herself for the lie, but he seemed as fragile as an eggshell. She kept hoping the woman with information on Lawrence Dale would call her, but the phone rang only once, and that was from a Kiwanian who wanted her to buy tickets to the Ice Follies for a group of poor kids.

Daniel began to stir late that morning, and as he moved, Rebecca became aware again that he was a good-looking man, that his long muscles, toned from hard work in Oconee Hill, held an energy and masculinity she could hardly believe. He sat up and swung his legs over the edge of the couch and suddenly cried out and held his head.

"I have a very bad headache," he muttered.

Rebecca laughed at him. "It's called a hangover," she said.

He looked at her and smiled through the pain.

"Hello, Rebecca," he said. He looked out the window and saw the rain and had a mild, happy look on his face for a moment.

Then, as if choked with panic, he jumped up and ran to the broad pane and looked down on the dark, wet street. "I must get to my job."

"I called Frank and told him you were sick," she said. "Where did you meet those two characters you were drinking with?"

"What?"

She could see him trying to remember. Were there signs when he was about to disappear inside himself?

"I was in the darkness and this fountain was spraying water, and they put a crown on me. I was, I was...." He smiled but could not remember.

"Come on," she said. "I want you to go back to your place and take a shower and come help me. We need to do a little snooping around at the motels in town."

"Snooping at motels?" he said.

She gave him three Excedrins, and they stopped at Dunkin' Donuts and got coffee. He sipped it slowly as the windshield wipers swung in tempo to the Beethoven symphony on Rebecca's tape player. With the top up, the MGB seemed cramped, but it stayed dry, and the spattering of rain on the roof was somehow comforting. They stopped at a traffic light near the Georgia Power building and its perfect lawn. A heavy-set woman wearing a trash bag against the rain waddled across the street in front of them. Daniel watched her in amazement, mouth open. She was obviously in no hurry, and her slow rhythm was as weary as the season. They turned left and saw a black man standing on the corner banging away at an old flat-top guitar, making chords no one ever used, screeching in high, painful syllables. You could always find him along here, in the rain or the heat or the bitter cold of winter, singing and banging on the guitar.

When they got to Daniel's house, the old lesbians were on the porch. Miss Olga was reading the morning paper to Miss Mae. They sat in creaky old rocking chairs and smiled at Daniel and Rebecca as they went past them and up the stairs. He went into the bathroom to shower, and Rebecca looked at the poor furnishings of his room. How did you ever stop being the friend of someone like Daniel? She lit a cigarette and thought of Annie and wondered what it must feel like for her. She thought of Charlie Dominic and how his call had thrilled her, how much fun it would be to go to the Virginia game. And she thought of the word "betrayed" and knew that more than anything, she had to find out what had happened to Lawrence Dale, and why.

"Saint Daniel," a voice said. "That was what they called me, Saint Daniel." She looked up and saw him smiling, naked, water pouring off his broad shoulders. He stood in the doorway, and perhaps he looked like a saint, but she felt only a carnal shock and stared with open admiration at his long, thick, uncircumcised penis. He looked less like a saint than a statue in a museum.

"Daniel, get back in the shower," she said, and he looked suddenly horror-stricken and reached down and put his hand over his genitals as if he had forgotten they hung there.

"I am naked."

"Yes, you are naked," Rebecca said, her voice cool and her blood pounding. She wanted him at that moment and felt herself boiling for his lust, for his hard body against hers, but she could not move, and she could see him blush deeply. "Get back in the shower. I want to go out for a while after you get dressed."

"I am so ashamed," he said.

He turned and went back into the bathroom, and Rebecca exhaled smoke and passion and saw, in the puddle on the floor, his image again and knew that soon she would have to be with a man. Fifteen minutes later, he came out, pale and sweating, wearing a pair of his old blue jeans and an unpressed cotton work shirt.

"You look pretty disheveled," she said, trying to imagine his body through the clothes.

"Thank you," he said with bewilderment, and Rebecca laughed all the way down the steps.

"Tell me how you met those guys," she said. "Daniel, they're just town characters. You don't want to be a town character. They get people to buy them drinks and then talk about themselves all night."

Miss Olga was reading Miss Mae's horoscope, and Miss Mae seemed amused. Daniel and Rebecca dashed through the rain to the car and climbed inside.

"I was walking home from Oconee Hill," he said, eyes focused on the dash, remembering. As always, for Daniel, memory was an act of will, not a state of mind. "And I saw them in this place and they were having a good time. So I went in and took out my money, and they brought us a pitcher full of beer."

"Stay away from that life," Rebecca pleaded. "Honey, they'll eat you alive."

Daniel smiled and rocked back into the tiny seat.

"What?"

"Honey," he said. "Mrs. Wilkins always called me that."

They drove to the Ramada Inn and then the Holiday Inn and the Downtowner and History Village, but none of the desk clerks recalled an older woman who had left that morning or in the middle of the night. They went to the Days Inn, too, and then to the Old South Motel, but their luck was the same. They ate lunch at Steverino's, a comfortable sandwich shop on Lumpkin Street, and then Rebecca drove slowly through campus and stopped in her usual place behind Park Hall. "Come on," she told Daniel. "I want to show you where I work."

Daniel felt his head throbbing, and he was dazed by the rising brick all around. This, he thought, was where the students go. When he saw them walk through the cemetery, he imagined their lives, and in his daydreams all of them studied very hard and learned all the books ever written. He thought each student had to read all the books in the library, and that was when they graduated.

Rebecca led Daniel into the lobby of Park Hall, and they went up in the elevator to the third floor. She opened her office door, and they went inside. She opened the window so they could listen to the rain, and they sat.

"Where in the world have you been?" Kent Ziegler was at the door. "I haven't seen you since you baptized Tift Bronson at the alfresco soiree at my place." He leaned in the doorway and looked down at Daniel, who had folded his hands in his lap and seemed to be trying very hard to disappear. "Sorry. Kent Ziegler."

He reached down, and Daniel stood up at once, most formally, and pumped his hand twice. Then he sank back into the chair without saying a word.

"This is my friend, Daniel Mitchell," said Rebecca.

Kent's eyes suddenly flashed with recognition, and he looked down at Daniel again.

"From the cemetery?" Kent asked.

"That's right," said Rebecca. "He's a little hung over today."

"Who isn't?" asked Kent.

Daniel seemed bewildered.

"Kent, listen, you won't believe this," said Rebecca. "A woman called me up late last night and said she had some information on Lawrence Dale, that he didn't die like people thought, that he was *betrayed*." She spoke the last word with appropriate melodrama.

"Betrayed?" Kent said. "What was she talking about?"

"I don't know," said Rebecca. "She was supposed to meet me for breakfast at Helen's, but she never showed up or called all morning. We've been going around to motels trying to find out if anybody remembers her, but no luck, so far. She said she knew him."

"Wow," Kent said.

"I know," Rebecca said.

Daniel pulled a copy of the *Complete Works of John Milton* from the tall bookcase next to Rebecca's desk and flipped through the pages.

"I mean, this could really be the hook I'm looking for to organize this thing. It's still so fuzzy that I can't see it. I can't see who Lawrence Dale was, Kent. I've been to all his places and talked to his family and friends, the ones still around, but it's all like an old movie."

"Good luck," he said. He looked at his watch. "I've got to meet a girl who wants to kill me for giving her the D she richly deserved." Another man's head suddenly poked into the doorway around

Kent's, and Rebecca saw Tift Bronson, ascot and all, looking very smug and glad to see her.

Kent looked down at Daniel's book. "Speaking of *Paradise Lost*, I'll leave Tift with you now, Rebecca." Kent patted him on the shoulder and walked off down the hall whistling.

Rebecca looked at Tift with amusement. Today he was wearing a shirt with billowed sleeves like Keats, heavily pleated brown trousers and a watch that hung from his pocket in a long arc of golden chain. He ignored Daniel completely.

"Hello, Beatrice," Tift said. "I alone am left to tell thee of the truths of the world. What are you doing Friday night?"

"Mixing your allusions pretty badly these days, Tift," Rebecca said. "This is my friend Daniel Mitchell."

Daniel set the book carefully on the edge of her desk and stood and bowed stiffly and reached out, took Tift's smooth, pink hand and pumped it twice then sat back down.

"Mitchell," Tift nodded. "What's your discipline?"

"I am Saint Daniel," he said, distracted. He realized immediately it was the wrong thing to say, but he did not know how to correct it, so he looked down at his heavy black shoes.

"I've always just adored the saints," said Tift. He dismissed Daniel with a look and continued to chatter about Friday night.

Tift left finally, and Rebecca locked her office, and she and Daniel walked down the cool, dark hall to Annie's office, but her door was closed and locked.

They checked out three more motels before they came to the Topnotch Inn several miles out on the Colbert Highway. The rain had stopped, and the day had turned steamy and unpleasant. Rebecca went into the office, leaving Daniel in the car. By now, he had run completely out of energy and seemed to be in a trance.

The lobby was crowded with old furniture, and behind the desk, a black-and-white television droned with a rerun of *Gilligan's Island*. The counter itself was almost sagging with old maps and brochures for tourist attractions, but it also had an odd mixture of toothpick furniture, souvenir car tags and bric-a-brac for sale.

Rebecca smelled the acrid smoke of a cigarette, and something else, the eternal stale smell of small motels. A fat woman wearing a shapeless cotton dress stood up wearily, a just-lit Benson and Hedges hanging from her thick lower lip. She was in her fifties, but the years had obviously been hard on her, and she squinted at Rebecca through the haze. She must have had a permanent earlier in the day, for her hair was still kinked in tight ringlets, exposing too much of her scalp. Her hair might have been brown or gray, but it seemed colorless to Rebecca. The woman's one redeeming feature was a pair of lake-blue eyes, but they were masked by thick glasses that seemed not to have been cleaned for years. She took the cigarette from her mouth and a long ash spilled on the front of her dress and then fell to the floor.

"You want a room?" she asked.

"No, no, just some information maybe," Rebecca smiled.

"'Bout what?"

"I'm trying to find a woman who was in town last night but may have left early this morning or in the night," Rebecca said.

"Why?"

"She has some information I need," Rebecca said. The woman shrugged. Behind her, the Skipper was bopping Gilligan on the head with a palm frond. "She was elderly, I think."

"What does she look like?" the woman asked.

"I don't know," Rebecca admitted.

"Where's she from?"

"I'm afraid I don't know that, either."

"You're just eat up with information, ain't you?" the woman said.

She lifted a heavy old register from under the desk and set it next to a toothpick outhouse that had a small tag on its door saying "Readin' room" and, under that, its price, $6.95. She licked her finger and turned the page back and had a coughing fit, doubled over for nearly a minute. When she stood back up, her face had lost whatever character it might have had, and it was purple, shapeless. "Damn. This crud's gone kill me." She suddenly threw her hands in the air. "Oh, hell, yeah. She come in yesterday afternoon late and left—must have been just after midnight—last night."

Rebecca strained to look at the name in the book. "Who was it?" she asked.

She took a small notebook from her purse and clicked a ball point pen. The woman turned the book around and pointed at the name distractedly, looking back over her shoulder as Mary Ann and Ginger were trying to rescue Gilligan from the Skipper. Rebecca leaned down and stared at the spidery script. It seemed something from another age, the penmanship perfect, nearly too perfect. It said Rachel Benjamin, and in the column for "town" she had written in her flowing hand, "Mountain City." Black Rock Mountain is in Mountain City, Rebecca remembered. She wrote it down and stared at the name for a moment, feeling an almost trembling excitement. "I got it. Thanks so much."

"You know what I don't understand?" the woman said, sliding the book back under the counter. "I don't understand why, with all them good-looking women, didn't none of the men on *Gilligan's Island* never even seem to get horny. Why you reckon that was?"

"I don't know," said Rebecca.

"Hell if I do, either," the woman said. Rebecca thanked her again, but she was already settling back down in her chair. Rebecca came outside into the steamy air of late July and saw that Daniel had gotten out of the car. *No*, she groaned to herself. She looked around, and saw him up a red mud hill to the right of the motel. Only two cars were outside the single-story motel's row of rooms. What in the world was he doing up there? She walked toward him and looked up the slope and could see then that he was standing in an old family cemetery which came right up to the motel grounds.

"What are you doing?" she called.

He waved and smiled broadly at her. "I am visiting with OUR DARLING BOY, JIMMY DEAN BARLOW," he shouted back. "December 15, 1927 to December 31, 1927." He looked down and his head moved side to side very slowly. "RESTING IN THE BOSOM OF HIS LOVING GOD."

He looked around once more and came down to Rebecca and, frowning slightly, walked back toward the car.

"What's wrong?" Rebecca asked when they got in the car.

"I did not know God had bosoms," Daniel said with a shrug, and when Rebecca laughed, so did he.

VERY EARLY THAT EVENING, Daniel slept in his hot room, dreaming again of some lost place in his life. He was in a small room and suddenly something was leaking down the walls, and a man said, "Look, hit's raining in," and they looked, but it was blood. Then the walls were running red, cascades like a waterfall, like a bubbling drink machine. A woman was screaming. Blood came pouring up from a pitcher on a bureau.

Daniel sat up straight and cried "No!" softly and looked around. Night had come, and the only sounds were traffic and the radio in the apartment of Julio Gomez. The old white curtains with their brown water stains hung limply against the window frames. He could start to identify shapes. He swung his legs over the side of the bed. *Was it going to happen again?* Daniel always knew when it was going to happen: his head hurt, and he did not think he could get enough breath.

He walked into the hall. Julio was cooking on the hot plate in his room, and the smell of canned spaghetti filled Daniel's nostrils. Miss Olga and Miss Mae had retired to their room. He came down the stairs and walked out into the steamy night. The streetlights were on, and crickets began to chirp drowsily in the clumps of tall grass next door. Miss Mae had told him about the grand old house that was there once. It had been demolished to make way for an office building, but then the money for the office building had gone soft, and now the lot was empty except for Johnson grass, crickets and the litter from the old house. *Ghosts live on that spot, Miss Mae had said. Every old house and place where an old house lay has ghosts.* Daniel stared at the lot as he walked down the sidewalk and tried to see the ghosts, but nothing came to him except the blood.

He was hungry, but he did not want to eat. He wanted to walk. He thought about Joe Dell and Irene and Randi Ambrose, and he cried for a while. He walked down Hancock Street past a row of run-down houses in a black neighborhood. Men and women sat on their porches, holding cold drinks and talking. At one house, three red eyes glowed angrily at Daniel, but he saw they were cigarettes, and their smoke barely moved in the still air, making filmy halos over the heads of the smokers. A cat carrying a large rat in its mouth trotted across the sidewalk and disappeared into a fragrant clump of gardenias.

Daniel stopped and inhaled the aroma of gardenias, but instead of Oconee Hill, he thought of Van Gogh. Rebecca had told him of art and how Van Gogh loved life too hard, how he had gone into the fields to paint the flowers. *I could paint this flower,* Daniel thought. He saw three children sitting on a porch step eating Fudgsicles, the brown confection dripping down their hands. They did not speak as he passed or seem to look at him. A mourning dove cried from a large oak tree that hung into the street light, and a new Lincoln Continental roared past in the street, its radio playing deafening funk. Daniel thought of the string quartet he had seen in the Fine Arts Auditorium. That was the music his heart heard. Rebecca told him each heart hears its own music, that inside everyone is a story, a music, an art. *You just have to find yours, Daniel,* she had said. He did not know what his story might be.

A dog loped past looking frightened, its tail down. Daniel was startled.

"Toggle!" he cried. He ran after the dog, which had cut between two tar-paper-sided houses. A woman stood nearby, watching from her porch as he ran for the dog, calling out "Toggle!" all the time, but Daniel barely noticed her. He ran through two yards, but the dog was gone, and other dogs had begun to howl and bark at his intrusion. He was breathing hard.

Fantastic outlines began to appear. A huge frog, a deer, a flock of chickens. They were lawn ornaments, forever unmoving, but

162

Daniel could not understand this now. He walked backwards away from them for twenty feet or so until he fell over a lawnmower and landed heavily on the ground, which was still damp from the rain that afternoon. He got up and began to run, and when he came back out on the sidewalk, nothing seemed familiar. He did not mind. He walked down the concrete. Inside one house, a man and a woman were screaming at the top of their lungs in the glow of yellow light, and their shouts lingered until Daniel got to the corner. The sounds carried a long way when the air was this heavy with unspilled rain.

The sound of singing came next. It seemed off-key, but somehow beautiful to Daniel. He stopped and listened. A streetlight had burned out, and the sidewalk here was dark except for the light from the houses. He saw an old woman sitting on a porch fanning herself. The odor of frying meat hung in the air, and a loud feminine giggle broke the silence once, then faded away. Daniel walked down the street until the houses began to dissolve and the singing was louder. He did not realize that he was nearing town, that he had walked this way a hundred times since he had moved.

The First Baptist Church of Athens, on the corner of Hancock and Pulaski, is a stately building, with its columns of stone, and the music was coming from inside. A few cars huddled around the building like dogs seeking warmth on a winter night. It was Wednesday evening, and the prayer service was under way, only this night it was all singing. Daniel walked up the smooth steps. He could see two more churches from the top step. When he was at Greenvale, Daniel had loved church, the maternal feelings of comfort and protection, and he always felt an almost unbearable pity for Jesus on the cross. Mr. Wilkins had told Daniel that Jesus died for him, for Daniel—and for days Daniel had begged Jesus to come back alive and die for someone else.

He went into the foyer, but no one was there, so he opened the door and eased into the sanctuary. The pipe organ was playing, and small clots of people sat in the air-conditioned vault and sang praises to God. In one place, three old women warbled happily. One of them wore a black dress, and the others kept reaching over and touching her arm as they sang. Daniel could see tears stream down her furrowed cheeks. He stared, open-mouthed at the woman, and her cheeks became plowed fields, and her tears became rain. The room grew green and thick with harvest. He looked to the other side of the aisle and saw thirty or forty more people, many of them old. One young woman was not singing but looking balefully at the pipes of the organ. She was not pretty. She was very thin and wore heavy glasses and shapeless clothes. Her chin was weak, and from time to time she gulped, as if trying to swallow the comfort of religion whole. A trembling old man held the hymn book with grim determination not to drop it. A young couple sang "Just As I Am" very earnestly, and their shoulders touched as they sat, and sometimes they would glance lovingly at each other and smile broadly.

He stood at the back of the sanctuary. It was cool, and he did not feel the urge to leave. Daniel loved hymns. Often, at funerals in Oconee Hill, the people would sing a hymn before it was time for everyone to leave and cover the grave. Daniel was never in a hurry to talk with the newly dead. Souls lived forever—wasn't that what Mrs. Wilkins had said? New souls needed time to learn about their special homes in Oconee Hill. There was no death in his life; everything at Oconee Hill was alive and enduring, as green as the carpet of grass that grew from the rich earth along the river.

The congregation sang old hymns, "Shall We Gather at the River," "Jesus Saves," and "O For a Thousand Tongues to Sing." The song leader was young and waved his arm in time to the music, and Daniel remembered how they had taken turns leading at Greenvale, and so he waved his arm, too, until the trembling old man turned and saw him, looked at him with what seemed to be fear. Daniel walked back outside into the steaming air, feeling his soul throb with the music of God. *What was wrong with him?*

Everything seemed to be changing around him. Athens might have been heaven or hell, and he felt always as if he had stumbled into a foreign land. His favorite book had been a primer he had read when he was nearly eighteen called *Our Foreign Friends*, and he had loved the pictures of a little Dutch girl with blond pigtails. He thought everyone in Holland wore wooden shoes and had blond pigtails and always smiled. Athens was as foreign to him as Holland.

He walked along Hancock Street and turned in front of the First United Methodist Church. The lights were on, but he did not hear any singing. He did hear a throbbing, but this time the music came from a small nightclub on Washington Street just ahead. Athens had its share of honky-tonks. This one was hardly more than a large room with a cramped stage for local bands. Daniel walked to the door and stared for a moment at the sign: The Music Box. Its paint was flaking off, and it hung over the door like an old-fashioned shingle.

He went inside. The room was thick with smoke and the yeasty aroma of beer, but there was something else: sweat, old clothes.

The tables were not very full, and a country band on the tiny stage was singing "Luckenback, Texas" but nobody seemed to be listening. Daniel sat at an empty table and looked around at the women, most of whom were hanging onto men with huge bellies that spilled from gaping shirts. The band started on a version of the old Patsy Cline hit, "Sweet Dreams."

"What can I get you?" asked a young woman with thick purple eye shadow. She wore jeans and a checked shirt and seemed bored. She scratched her head and stared at Daniel.

"What?" he asked. He seemed confused.

"What can I get you?" she repeated tensely.

"Get me?"

"Yeah," she said. "We got Bud, Pabst, Stroh, Stroh Light, Miller, Miller Light and Heineken. What'll it be?" Daniel reached in his pocket and pulled out three dollar bills. Bud was the name of the man who cut the grass at Greenvale.

"Bud," he said, looking at the band.

"Yeah," the woman said. She walked away. Daniel sat for a while, and just as the woman was returning, he got up and headed for the door. He was thinking of Oconee Hill suddenly.

"Hey, you ordered this!"

"Thank you very much," Daniel said, smiling, and he walked out the door, not listening to her curses at his back.

He walked across town, his feet sure now, heading for the cemetery, and when he got to the gate, he deftly climbed up and over it and walked up the hill in the streetlight toward the crest of the hill behind the football stadium. The air was full of cicadas and crickets. He got to the top of the hill and lay down beside Louisa Adelaide Brown.

"HERS WAS A BEAUTIFUL LIFE MARKED BY UNSELFISH KINDNESS, LOVING SERVICE AND A DEVOTION TO DUTY," Daniel said from memory. He looked up at the trees that had begun to sway over him in a dark arch. A breeze stirred the hedges and the grass.

Daniel could feel the wind, and he wondered where it came from and where it was going. He felt his heart beating.

FOURTEEN

SUMMER DEEPENED, AND EACH DAY WAS HUNG WITH THE SOUND of dry leaves blowing high in the ancient trees of Athens. Each morning, the rich smell of fresh bread drifted over the downtown area from Benson's Bakery, and shop owners struggled to open for the day. Rob Marchette would stand in front of his bookshop with a mug of coffee and survey the morning, just as Hiram Douglas would across the street. He had run a stylish men's clothing shop for thirty years, and he would stand in the still-cool morning and slap his ample belly and wonder if he would cover his overhead that day.

By eight-thirty, most of Athens was awake and at work, moving sluggishly in the rising heat. Even at night, the temperature would only go down to seventy-five, and by day, it came close to one hundred for days on end. The A&A Bakery's doors were swung open, and, for the fourth day in a row, the cook began making a wedding cake. A clot of downtown characters struggled for a drink to get a hold on themselves, and a tall, slender black man brushed off a row of brightly colored shoes in a display window with a feather duster. The chocolate shop began the day by cooking an aromatic batch of walnut brownies, the unmistakable scent of warm chocolate wafting over all of College Square, near the center of town. Women who worked for the city and wore orange vests stood yawning as they watered the trees and flowers that graced the sidewalks.

Around the block, Helen's Restaurant was open, and a few men and women ate in silence as they read the morning paper, while down the street at Johnson Hardware, a clerk was commiserating with another about the difficulty of locating timing chains for old cars.

The University languishes between the end of summer quarter and the beginning of the fall, a month in which much of the faculty leaves town and Athens shrinks back to its size of thirty years before. Merchants expect to do little business, and everyone huddles inside to escape the staggering heat. Even those who continue to work sometimes find themselves staring idly at nothing in particular, wondering if five o'clock will ever arrive.

Annie Phillips' Volvo came through downtown Athens. Rebecca Gentry was in the passenger seat, and they were heading out U.S. 441, driving north toward the Georgia mountains. Already the car was very cool, and on the tape deck was the sweet sound of Patsy Cline singing "Crazy." Rebecca watched Athens, looked at City Hall, where they had recently cut down all the trees to build something called a "bus plaza," saw the Southern Mutual building, the tallest in town. She stared at the County Courthouse, a square structure that had become run-down and was now being repaired. Across the street from the Courthouse was Benson's Bakery, and from habit, Rebecca rolled down the window and inhaled the rich air.

"God, that's wonderful," said Annie.

Rebecca didn't answer but only nodded. They had not seen each other for three weeks, since Annie had shattered the beer bottle on her stone fireplace, but when Rebecca had asked her to drive to Mountain City to help her look for Rachel Benjamin, Annie happily said "yes."

In those three weeks, Rebecca had felt herself begin to shed the skin of her cold intellectualism. She did not read T.S. Eliot anymore. Instead, she read Keats and Shelley and Byron and Wordsworth, and she began a series of poems about her father, though she was really writing them about Annie's father, because she saw his face, even in her dreams now. They were lyrical and completely different from the poems in *Dead Lace*, reflective and gentle. Sometimes at night she would feel emotion sweeping over her, and she would sit in her apartment and cry, holding a glass of red wine and watching the sun set over the old buildings of North Campus.

She thought of Charlie Dominic, too. She had called him twice more to talk about the Virginia game, and their talk had been tranquil, soothing. She even got her wedding pictures from the closet and stared at the buoyant purity of her gown, the way she seemed to drift down the carpeted aisle toward Charlie, the man of her dreams. But dreams never last a lifetime, she thought, and perhaps only the issues of the mind finally matter. And as her poems became more clear, Lawrence Dale, once almost in focus for her, began to recede until he was barely more than chartless features in fog upon the sea.

Then there was Daniel. She had been seeing him less and less, and she had lately begun to feel like a psychiatric social worker who, on a summer sabbatical, had been studying Daniel's particular disorder and sorrow. No, she did not feel love for him. How could she ever hope to understand such innocence? And how could she watch as he became a part of the world that was often so brutal and painful? Still, she could not make the break cleanly, and so for the past two weeks she had been seeing him once a week, taking him driving in the country. He always gazed with honest admiration at the animals and the fields. He would cry out when he saw a hawk banking below the heavy cumulus clouds to pick a mouse from the hayfields. When he saw a dog lope across the road in front of them, he would whisper "Toggle" and stare with hope until he knew that it was not his lost dog.

Annie and Brad had met once or twice, but Brad refused to be pushed into a decision, which infuriated Annie. And yet she felt a tenderness for Brad she felt for no other man, and she knew that if he came back to her, begging forgiveness and understanding, she would probably give in. She did not know if she ever again could be vulnerable.

Daniel talked less and less to the people buried in the cemetery, and often he took long walks at night around Athens, wondering who lived in all the houses. He began stopping at the Dunkin' Donuts at the corner of Milledge and Prince for a coffee and a cinnamon roll near midnight, then he would stroll lazily down Milledge past the Greek Revival houses that fraternities and sororities occupied. When he looked at flowers banked along the sidewalks, he wondered if Van Gogh had ever painted them, not realizing he had been dead for nearly a century. One night, he walked all the way to Oconee-by-the-River, and he spent the evening talking with Joe Dell and Irene Bailey. They were glad to see him, but when he left, he felt such an overwhelming sadness that he spent the night on the ground near Randi Ambrose's trailer and was awakened the next morning by Mike and Pam screaming at each other while their baby, Scottie, cried terribly. Miss Olga and Miss Mae were delighted that he had not come home at all and babbled about it at breakfast, but Julio Gomez didn't think it was of much import and said so.

On another night, Daniel felt himself going crazy, and he screamed "Wallace, don't!" over and over until Julio banged on the door and shook him from his trance. Daniel had walked downtown then, toward Campus North, trembling in a hot rain shower. Lightning snapped at him as the streams of water drenched him. When he got to Campus North, he stood near the entrance, looked up and screamed "Rebecca!" until he saw a police car, lights flashing, coming toward him. Julio had told him about the police, about being arrested by Los Federales, but Miss Olga had just said "Come, now," and Julio had dropped it. Daniel had run around the corner, past the A&A Bakery, past the Georgia Carafe and Draft Theatre then down the sidewalk past the office of *The Athens Observer*. He stopped and stared through the large plate glass window. A solitary man stood inside smoking a cigarette and staring at a ledger.

170

Daniel had forgotten about Wallace by the time he got home, but as he walked to work the next morning, he realized for the first time since he left Greenvale that he was not happy. He wanted to see Rebecca, and she did not come to Oconee Hill much anymore. He did not work as hard, and sometimes Frank had to shout at him as he sat in the vines like a statue.

"You all right?" Annie asked. They had driven under the towering railroad bridge on North Avenue and turned left on Water Street. A few blacks lived here now, not far from the site where, up the street, a famous whorehouse named Effie's had stood for years until it was destroyed by urban renewal. At the time, an enterprising University of Georgia graduate sold bricks from the honored brothel as souvenirs and did very well. They headed out U.S. 441 north.

"I'm sorry," Rebecca said. "I think I'm losing my mind."

Annie looked at her and started laughing, and then so did Rebecca.

"You're just the therapy I need, Annie," she said. "I reveal to you my innermost secrets and you find them hilarious."

Annie giggled again. "I'm sorry," she said. "It just hit me funny. Everything in my life has gone all to hell, too, you know. Brad, Daddy."

"How's your daddy?" They passed the motel where Rachel Benjamin had stayed and the cemetery where Daniel had climbed the red mud bank.

"He won't say much," she said. "Mother says he's weaker. I can't stand the thought of it. I can't stand the thought of anything much."

"I'm going to the Virginia game with Charlie," Rebecca said. She smiled and bit her lip and arched her eyebrows hopefully.

"You are not," said Annie. "When did this all happen?"

"In the past couple of weeks," she said. "I didn't tell you because I thought you might throw a beer bottle at me or something."

"Okay, I'm sorry," Annie said. "I told you I was losing my

mind, too."

"Just don't lose it in my direction," Rebecca said.

They both felt better, and the miles unwound behind them, the small neat towns and their crumbled old factories, the fields with grazing Holsteins. They talked about the news, about the fact that neither had a sex life, about pride and hope. They talked about Dante and Euripides and Wordsworth and Solzhenitsyn. The day was mild for August, and the sun spangled the ground beneath the huge trees of Piedmont College in Demorest, a tiny place that seemed the ideal college town.

And yet both noticed the bleached-out colors of the landscape begin to change north of Demorest. They stopped at Tallulah Gorge, a marvel of scenery that dips some eight hundred feet from the road down to the Tallulah River. In the early Seventies, Karl Wallenda had walked across the gorge on a cable, but Rebecca most remembered the pictures of him falling to his death in San Juan. Rebecca and Annie bought cider and stared for a long time at the majesty of the gorge from an observation platform.

They drove across the dam that clogged the Tallulah River into a scenic lake and headed north into Rabun County, the farthest northeast in the state of Georgia. They saw towering hemlocks and the humps of mountains shrouded in a blue fog. Just before they came into Clayton, the county seat, they could see Black Rock Mountain huddled in the mist, its bare rock face clear of the fog.

"That's the place he shot himself," Rebecca said, pointing. The town had grown in the past few years, and a real estate office in a chalet ushered them into the city limits. "What a tragic waste that was."

"And this woman says he was betrayed?" asked Annie.

They both stared at the mountain that rose behind the town.

"That's what she said," said Rebecca. She hugged her chest, feeling an infinite sadness, even a hint of desperation as she looked at the evergreen-clad slopes of Black Rock Mountain. She had been there only twice, both after she first began researching her life of Lawrence Dale two years before, back when she thought her life would turn a different way. She was still an assistant professor, and her major work was receding every day. Still, as they drove through the outskirts of Clayton, she could not take her eyes off the mountain, and she could not stop thinking of the despair that had driven Lawrence Dale to his death on that cliff.

"I still think 'betrayed' sounds awfully dramatic and old-fashioned," Rebecca said.

"Happens every day," said Annie.

The route of U.S. 441 takes it around the town of Clayton proper and past a few dilapidated bars and houses with goats gnawing in the yards. Then, within two miles, it comes into Mountain City, a tiny burg that is not much more than a cluster of houses and a post office, on the other side of Black Rock Mountain from Clayton.

"Turn here," said Rebecca. "Let's go up to the top before we try to find this woman."

"All right," said Annie. They turned on a small paved road near a sign that said "Black Rock Mountain State Park." Years before, the State of Georgia had turned the area into a park with dramatic and delightful results. Rangers proudly touted it as the highest state park in Georgia. At the base of the mountain, a rocky field held a few poor cows and another cluster of goats. The road was smooth and good, but soon the air pressure began to change, and Annie and Rebecca noticed it at the same time.

"Shit, I hate it when your ears stop up," said Annie.

"They're unstopping, actually," said Rebecca.

"Whatever," said Annie, and their car rose into the mist, higher, around the road's cutbacks and curves, until they came to a long straight stretch that dipped down and then rose suddenly straight up toward the summit. The road was choked in fog. They rolled the windows down, and everything seemed muffled. A hawk screeched, and the sound filled their ears.

The road wound again, and the curious effect of soundlessness intensified with every turn. Rebecca could scarcely hear the car engine or the tires on the damp pavement. At the last turn, they were suddenly on top of the earth, higher than anything except the clouds and the treetops. Only one car was there, a Buick from Indiana.

Annie wasn't surprised; everywhere she went, she saw cars from Indiana. She had once told Brad she thought the entire state was escaping. She parked the Volvo next to the Buick, and they got out. A snack bar and gift shop in the park ranger station at the summit was open, but no one seemed to be inside. Annie and Rebecca both noticed that the air had a certain chill, one that made them cross their arms over their breasts to stay warm. An elderly couple walked slowly back from the observation area along the edge of the cliff face toward their car and nodded kindly. Rebecca watched as the old man held his hand out for his wife and helped her up the slippery slats of stone that angled down toward a telescope.

Rebecca and Annie walked down to the bare stone and saw the valley far below them. Rebecca moved a short distance to her left and looked down at the spot in awe, as if she were examining a holy relic for the first time.

"Here," she said, and Annie walked over to her.

"Here, what?" asked Annie. "This is really something. It's like what God saw when he made this whole place."

"I didn't know you believed in God," said Rebecca.

Annie just shrugged and looked forlornly at Clayton, which seemed like an alpine village nestled in the valley below.

"Well, here it is." Rebecca looked down at the stone.

"This is where he killed himself?" asked Annie.

"Right here," said Rebecca. "It just breaks my heart. He wrote all that marvelous stuff, and then when he couldn't face life anymore, he came to the most beautiful place he knew and killed himself. I guess there's some justice in dying in the most beautiful place you know."

Annie nodded and stared at the spot, and when she looked up, her eyes were full of tears. "I'm so miserable," she said, her voice shaking.

Rebecca hugged her, and Annie let go, a flood of tears dampening her friend's shoulder. They stood in the wind along the ridge for nearly five minutes until Annie could compose herself.

"God, I told you I was losing my mind," Annie apologized as they walked toward the car.

"You don't have to explain anything to me," Rebecca said.

They drove slowly down the mountain, pausing at a scenic overlook to gaze northward where the mountains were much larger, heading up into North Carolina and Cherokee country. When they got back down, Annie drove to the main highway and stopped.

"Where to now?" she asked.

"Post Office," said Rebecca. "Over there."

A small brick structure sat on the edge of the road just north, and Annie drove into its small paved parking lot and stopped the car. They got out and walked inside, where a gray-haired man who seemed almost dainty stood behind the counter sorting mail. He smiled when he saw them and nodded deferentially.

"Morning, ladies, what can I do for you?" he asked.

"I'm looking for someone who lives in Mountain City," Rebecca said, pushing her sunglasses up on her black hair.

"That shouldn't be a hard question," he said. "Not that big of a place." He leaned his elbows on the counter.

Rebecca could see the smile lines around his eyes. "Let me tell you who I am," she said. "I'm writing a book, and I need to interview this person. I work down at the University in Athens."

"I got a girl down there," the man said. "Name's Julie Hall. Majoring in horticulture. It's crazy how somebody always asks you if you know them when you live in Athens or work at the University, like there wasn't twenty thousand other students."

"Horticulture," said Rebecca, feigning admiration.

"I know you don't know her," the man said, smiling again. "She's a junior."

"I really don't," said Rebecca. "Anyway, I'm in the English Department, and I'm writing a book on Lawrence Dale, the poet and novelist?"

"I heard of him, I think," he said. "Feller who shot himself up on Black Rock."

"That's right," Rebecca nodded.

"Nasty business," he said. "Happened before I came here. Moved here from Atlanta in sixty-eight. People around here hated that. Said it hurt the tourist trade for a long time." Rebecca stared at him.

"Right," she said. "Anyway, I'm looking for a woman named Rachel Benjamin."

"Rachel?" the man said. "Well, sure, I know Rachel. She lives back over there, just off the road up the mountain. Nice lady. Never married, you know. Lives by herself. Never worked. Guess she has family money or something." He looked past them, out the window of the post office, toward the mountain. "Just before you start going up the mountain, little road shoots off to the left. Go to the end of that. Dead ends at her house. Pretty place."

"I really do appreciate that," Rebecca said.

"What's she know about that feller?" asked the man.

"Oh, I don't know," shrugged Rebecca. "I just heard she might have known him."

"Something of a recluse," he said.

They turned to walk out and thanked him again.

"Name's Julie Hall, in horticulture, if you ever run into her down there."

"Okay," Rebecca said. "Julie Hall. Got it."

They turned off the road at the Black Rock Mountain State Park sign and drove three or four hundred yards until the asphalt began to rise steeply. Annie turned left onto a poorly paved road. A few trailers were propped up in the pasture. A small house on the right with a tin roof gleamed in the sunlight that tried to break through the overcast. A stately white pine swayed in the breeze.

The road curved sharply and ended in a graveled parking area. Just beyond it was a broad expanse of green lawn, then an area of landscaped perfection in front of a large brick house. The liriope was everywhere, and brightly colored impatiens grew in merry clumps throughout a sea of green perennials, hostas and ferns, and, in the sun, begonias. They stopped the car and got out, walking up a flagstone path that led toward the front door. When they got twenty steps up the path, a figure suddenly stood up from one of the perennial beds, a woman in old trousers and a sun hat. She was not young and wore gloves caked with dirt and held a small trowel.

"Hello," Rebecca said. Her voice sounded too loud. "Miss Benjamin?"

The woman's shoulders sagged and she looked left and right, as if plotting an escape.

"Yes?" she asked in a small voice.

"I'm Rebecca Gentry."

Annie and Rebecca stopped ten feet from the woman, who had closed her eyes and kept scraping at the trowel blade long after the last clump of soil was gone.

"How did you find me?" Rachel asked.

"Drove around looking at motel registers until I found somebody who'd left in the night," Rebecca said, trying to smile politely. "It was you, wasn't it?"

Rachel sighed heavily and set the trowel down on a small garden table and removed her gloves and her hat. Rebecca could see that she had once been pretty, and even now, probably near sixty, she had retained the grace of loveliness that few can bear in their later years.

"I know you are probably thirsty after driving all the way up here from Athens," she said. "Come on inside, and I'll make some lemonade."

Rebecca looked over at Annie triumphantly, and then, as they followed Rachel up the flagstone path onto the porch of her home and then inside, she felt Lawrence Dale suddenly clear, saw his lean features and remembered his poetry. She recalled his lyric impulse that was too painful to bear at times, perhaps reminiscent of the best songs of Hank Williams—painfully honest and yet as skillful as anyone writing in America in the Fifties.

The inside of Rachel Benjamin's house was simple and orderly. They turned right into the living room, which was prickling with potted cacti, some of which bloomed gloriously in the thin mountain light. A heavy sofa ran the length of one wall and over it hung an original oil painting of Lawrence Dale. Rebecca gasped and gently touched Annie's sleeve and nodded at the picture. They sat on the sofa and from there could see out a picture window overlooking the plantings of violets and roses in Rachel Benjamin's front yard. On the other side of the room were two chairs and between them a table on which rested several thick copies of *Southern Living*.

"Get comfortable," Rachel said, "and I'll be back in a minute with some lemonade. I'm sorry I'm such a mess."

"My God, we did just drop in on you," said Rebecca, trying to be friendly. When Rachel had left the room, she turned around and looked up at the portrait. It must have been painted, she guessed, when Dale was probably not yet thirty.

"That's Lawrence Dale?" asked Annie.

"Completely unknown portrait," said Rebecca with awe. "I've got goosebumps. What a damn perfect dustjacket. Look at my arms." She got on her knees and turned around to inspect it more closely, and saw, in the bottom right-hand corner, the name "Benjamin" in a tiny, spidery script. "She painted it. My God, this is unbelievable!" She sat back down.

Annie slowly formed a grin, and said, "Wow, you may get full professor out of this."

"Jealous?" Rebecca smiled.

Rachel Benjamin came into the living room carrying a silver tray which held a crystal pitcher and three goblets filled with ice. Rebecca thought the ice looked diamond-like through the fogged glass. Rachel set the tray on the coffee table in front of Annie and Rebecca, poured the glasses full, and offered one to each of them. Then she took the third glass, walked across the room and sat down heavily in one of the chairs. A window at one end of the house was open, and through it the wild song of a mockingbird trilled and fluted.

"I'm by nature a coward, you see," Rachel said grimly, holding her chin high.

178

Rebecca did not know what to say. Annie sipped her lemonade and felt some speechless pain in the pit of her stomach.

"I thought I could come to see you, but I stayed up late thinking about it and drove back home in the middle of the night. I suppose I didn't try to hide my identity very well. Perhaps it was the urge to be caught, to be forced to tell my story." She smiled wanly. "Anyway, I heard you were writing the book. There was a small piece about it in *Atlanta* magazine, you remember?"

"I remember," said Rebecca. "It was their section on who's writing what." She stared at Rachel and noticed that dark circles had settled under her eyes, which had once been beautiful. "I'm sorry. I've just been so surprised by everything. This is my friend Annie Phillips. She teaches classics at the University."

"*Morituri te salutamus*," said Rachel with an ironic nod.

"Yeah," nodded Annie in appreciation.

"You said Lawrence Dale had been betrayed," said Rebecca.

Rachel set her lemonade on the stack of magazines on the table and leaned back in the chair and closed her eyes. She brought her hands up to her lips in a prayerlike gesture.

"Yes," she said softly. "And I am the one who betrayed him."

Again, Rebecca felt gooseflesh rise on her arms, and she glanced at Annie, who seemed entranced by the woman's obvious sincerity.

"What do you mean?" asked Rebecca.

Rachel sat up and leaned forward. "Not many people knew Larry very well, you know," she said. "He was a bitterly unhappy man. And he was a genius, too. Have you read his books, Rebecca?"

"Everything," she said. "And I thought I'd interviewed everybody who knew him. Nobody ever mentioned you at all."

"That's because nobody knew about me at all," she said. "Larry and I were lovers for more than ten years. And nobody knew about us. Strange, isn't it? But his fame never was much outside Atlanta and in the North, you know. Nobody ever recognized him on the street, and he wanted it that way. He was terrified of crowds and speaking in public, you know, even though he taught over there at

Mount Russell College for some years before his death."

"You were lovers?" said Rebecca, her voice barely a squeak.

"Oh yes," Rachel said. "I presume you've inspected the painting behind you. I painted that back before I quit painting, back before I quit everything. Until about five years ago, I just hid up here in my house and swelled with my guilt. You see, I never had to work. My father was William Benjamin. He was one of the founders of Allied Steel in Pittsburgh. I've always had money. I got a degree in English Literature from Penn State and came South to teach at Mount Russell, but I only stayed there one year before my father died, and I was suddenly very wealthy. I came up here.

"Larry and I were friends at Mount Russell, and I was awed by his talent, but it wasn't until I moved here that he started coming to see me on weekends and that we slowly became lovers." She stood and walked to the window and looked out over her garden. "You know, he was an incredibly handsome man, not in the way Clark Gable was handsome, but in his eyes and his hands. His eyes seemed to take in the entire world. I never saw that in another human's eyes.

"Six months ago, I found out that I have pancreatic cancer, and that I probably now have less than a year. I wanted to tell the truth, but I was afraid." She turned and walked toward Rebecca and sat on the deep carpet, her knees under her. She looked up at Rebecca, and her eyes filled with tears.

The mockingbird was reaching dizzy heights of melody in the yard. Rebecca wanted to reach out to her, but she couldn't move. "I'm so sorry," she whispered.

Annie felt her hands trembling slightly, so she held them in her lap.

"It's all right," Rachel said. "Anyway, I'm going to tell it all to you. I want you to come back next weekend and bring a tape recorder, and we'll talk. But there's something I want to tell you now. This has been building in me for nearly twenty-five years, and I can't hold it back any longer."

The room suddenly seemed close and airless. Rebecca felt beads of sweat collecting at her hairline. Annie leaned forward and stared at the woman seated in the plush carpet.

"Yes?" whispered Rebecca.

"He wasn't alone on the mountain the night he died," said Rachel Benjamin.

FIFTEEN

DANIEL SAT IN THE GRASS NEAR A MARBLE LAMB and stared at the grave of Lucy, Aged 21. He read the stone very slowly out loud: BLESSED ARE THE PURE IN HEART, FOR THEY SHALL SEE GOD. He idly pulled weeds from the markers, ignoring the thin drizzle that had fallen all morning at Oconee hill.

He did not feel well. More and more he spent his small amount of money on drinks and movies, things he had never done before. But if he had begun to enjoy the limits of flesh, he was also struggling with something inside, that thing Mrs. Wilkins had told him was a soul. He knew that when you died, your soul flew out of you like a magician jerking a handkerchief from a pocket, but he still thought the bodies in Oconee Hill were in some filmy way alive, perhaps a tissue of memories, at least. So far, he had stumbled down the aisle in four churches in Athens to take the preacher's hand, not understanding what that meant except that his cheeks were damp, and each time the preacher called out his name and said he was saved. He was saved at the First Baptist Church and then at the First United Methodist Church. He was saved at the Prince Avenue Baptist Church, where there was a lot of praying, and finally he tried to be saved at a New Age fellowship, but he was told he couldn't be saved there. He walked down the aisle at mass in the chapel of St. Joseph's Catholic School and simply stood there, to the wonder of the worshippers, who politely watched as he stood, thinking this, too, was salvation.

Daniel did not understand how much to drink. Just last night, he got so drunk that he had passed out in an alley and had not awakened until some time after midnight. He sat up and felt half-numb and a little sick. A pigeon was waddling down the alley, cooing, and the light from a streetlamp cast deep shadows on its purple wings as it walked nonchalantly past Daniel and went into the street. He thought it was a dove and a sign from God. Sometimes, Mr. Shub, an old man who whistled between his teeth while he directed the choir at Greenvale, would sing that song, "On the Wings of a Dove," and Daniel knew as he watched the pigeon that this was a sign from above.

But of what was it a sign? So many things did not make sense to Daniel. He would see a jet come over Oconee Hill but would not be able to hear it until it was gone. Once they buried a baby in the new part of the cemetery across the river, and the next day, a dog had sprawled on the grave with its great head between its paws. Rebecca had come to him, would be with him, and then she was slipping away back into some strange world of books and secret words. The only book that Daniel had ever really studied was the Bible. He remembered one verse from Second Timothy: "I have fought the good fight, I have finished the course, I have kept the faith."

He had said the words over and over as he stumbled from the alley and looked up at the earnest face of a chiropractor seeming jaundiced in the yellow glare of the billboard's lights. When he had come back out on the street, the pigeon had risen in an explosion of wings. Shivering though the night was hot and damp, he had tried to find a church to join. He saw the lighted cross on top of the First Christian Church, but it was locked. He had walked down Prince Avenue and tried all the doors, but none would open, so he turned and walked the empty streets of Athens back toward his rooming house.

Sometimes, on other nights, he would sit on a wall along the sidewalk and smell the damp earth that was swelling with mushrooms and mold from recent rains. He would smell a flowering bush. Once, a dog ran out and barked at him, and Daniel ran thumping down the street with his heavy soles. When he stopped, he turned and saw a man and a woman embracing through a window in the soft light of their bedroom, and felt so tender that he started to clap, and then he wept.

Where was Rebecca?

He had stopped on a strange streetcorner, then; he would often walk for hours at night until something seemed familiar and he could find his way home. When he had lived on the other side of the river with Joe Dell and Irene and Randi Ambrose, he had rarely gone out at night, but now he could not stop. He stayed home one night and played Parchesi with Miss Mae and Miss Olga, but he was restless and did not understand the game very well and always lost.

And last night, on his way home, he had stopped under a street lamp and shouted "Rebecca!" very loud and then "Toggle!" but he was afraid after that and ran for half a block so no one would see who spoke. He had not gotten home until the house was still and quiet and his shoes sounded like cannon fire on the hollow old stairs.

Today, though, he felt better, and he worked steadily at the weeds and talked to Lucy Aged 21. Earlier, he had cleaned around the grave of William Tate. Daniel stared at the inscription chiseled into the stone and remembered with a warm satisfaction that it was his quotation from Second Timothy. He was talking to Lucy and gently rubbing the marble lamb and did not see the car slow to a stop on the road that winds through the middle of Oconee Hill.

He sat up and looked around the grave and saw that he had cleaned it very well. That was when he saw the woman walking toward him. She was gray-haired and wore glasses and seemed to be worried. She wore pants that were a strange green, not any color really, and she walked as if the joints in her knees no longer worked properly. People came to the cemetery all the time, relatives of the dead, loved ones. That morning, Frank had told Daniel that after lunch an old man would be buried in the new section across the river, but everyone here had been dead for many years. Daniel stood and removed his baseball cap and tried to smile because the woman was coming straight for him. People often asked him questions, and he hated it because he never knew quite what to say. He thought things in his head and answered those questions. Once a man had asked him how old the cemetery was, and Daniel, on hearing the word "old," had thought of "gold" and had said with a broad smile, "It is yellow and shines very much." The man had seemed disappointed; it was the wrong answer. But Daniel had always been giving wrong answers, and he hated talking to strangers on days when his heart was far away.

The woman walked up to Daniel and saw him remove the baseball cap. She shook her head and tears filled her eyes.

"Daniel?" she whispered.

"Hello," he said, "and welcome to Oconee Hill Cemetery. I would tell you what you need to know of anybody who lives here." He smiled and then looked confused; no one actually lived here, no one but Frank. "I mean about anybody who died here." But that wasn't right, either. Nobody actually died here; they died somewhere else and were brought here. Why would they do that, Daniel wondered? And suddenly he wondered where they all did die and thought, with a glazed stare, that everyone dies in one place and is buried in another. The world was hard to understand. "I mean, about anybody who is under the dirt, here." That was right, and he fingered his cap nervously and smiled.

"You are Daniel," she said.

He nodded.

"Let me look at you. My God, let me look at you."

She walked around him, and he turned and stumbled through the emerald pile of weeds that he had pulled. When he pulled stray weeds and clipped grass, Daniel always kept everything in a neat pile until he was through. Daniel wondered how she knew his name, but that was no great mystery in a world where you had to be saved to die.

"What is your name?" Daniel asked. "I have cleaned this little lamb."

He motioned down, and she looked through a gauze of unspilled tears.

"Hazel Agnes," the woman said.

"Hazel Agnes," Daniel repeated. "Well." They looked at each other in the light drizzle. "It is not very hot today, Hazel Agnes. This is a good day for you to visit Oconee Hill. If you come on Saturday, you can watch Woodrow go down into the river and catch catfish. He is my friend."

"You have a lot of friends, Daniel?" she asked.

"I have lots of friends," he smiled. "I have Joe Dell and Irene and Randi and Mike and Pam and Kelly and Rob, and Daisy Saye lives down the street and she gives me magazines, except I do not live there anymore." He wondered if that was clear; it would have to do. "And Rebecca. I think I am in love with Rebecca." The words nearly stunned him. He had been staring at the mirror every morning, saying them over and over, "I love you, Rebecca," wanting desperately to tell her, wondering if she would understand. But to say them out loud now to this stranger seemed unforgivable, and he fell into silence.

"I'm so glad," she said. "They said you were like this. Do you remember who I am?"

Daniel bit his cheek and squinted at her. She could be the woman behind the counter at the liquor store near the chiropractor's sign, or she could be the woman who got hugged and loved in the house not far from his; maybe she was related to Miss Mae or Miss Olga, or maybe she had been to Mexico and knew the people that Julio Gomez was always talking about.

"No, I do not think I do," he said.

She clutched a black purse, and she tremblingly opened it and reached inside and took out a crumpled tissue and dabbed her smooth cheeks.

Daniel saw that though she was not young, she was still quite pretty, and her eyes were the blue of the sky in the fall when the cool weather came.

"Who are you?" he asked.

She put the tissue carefully back in her purse and snapped the clasp.

"I'm a friend of your family's," she said. "I knew your...mother and your father."

He felt his skin grow gooseflesh. A car horn blew. Birds trilled in the trees down along the river, and Daniel felt as if all the dead had eyes and were watching him and waiting for his next words.

"My mother and my father," he repeated.

"Yes," she said. "That was a long, long time ago. So very long ago. You don't know how much trouble it was for me to find you here. I thought you'd gone right off the edge of the earth."

"The edge of the earth," Daniel repeated, and he thought about it, remembering for the first time the map that Mr. Wilkins had shown them at Greenvale, the old map of the edge of the earth and the warning, "Beyond this place, there be dragons."

"You look happy, Daniel," she said. "You look so very happy." She stepped close to him, and he could smell her, a light flowery perfume that was pleasant but fading, like the aroma of the gardenias back up at the top of the hill when they were in bloom and the wind was blowing.

"Sometimes I am very happy," he said. "I remember the farm, Hazel Agnes. Do you remember our farm out there in the country and the little red calf that would lie in the sun and lick my face?" Daniel looked away at nothing in particular and smiled. "And I think there were chickens and when it rained, water leaked into pans around our house." That was right. "Did you know my parents then, Hazel Agnes?"

"Yes," she said weakly.

"But then I lived at Greenvale, and I cannot see their faces, I mean my parents," he said, "and they faded away, but they come back in dreams and...."

He thought for a moment that he was going to have the black fear that often swelled in him, and for a moment, the words "Wallace, don't!" came to him, but then he was looking at her as if it were her turn to say something.

"Were you happy at Greenvale?" she asked. She looked around nervously.

"Happy?" he asked. "Mrs. Wilkins said happiness is not for this world."

The woman reached out and touched Daniel on the shoulder very lightly. "She was wrong, honey," Hazel Agnes said. "It's the only thing we got in this world. Were you happy? Are you happy now?"

"I was happy before Rebecca came," Daniel said. "Then she told me about things I had never seen and I wanted them. Then I loved her, and she did not come to see me as much. But I am saved, and so that part of me is happy, but then I am drunk and that part of me is not happy. All of me is never happy all the time. Some of me is happy most of the time." He struggled with the words and sweated heavily.

"Is it okay if I hug you now?" she asked.

"Okay," said Daniel. And she enfolded his hard body in her arms, and they were soft and insistent to Daniel, who hugged her back and felt some kind of new season in his blood. She broke away and he could see that her cheeks were shining with tears. The rain began to fall a little harder.

"Can I come back to see you again, Daniel?" she asked.

"Yes, Hazel Agnes, you can," he said. "Students walk through Oconee Hill and old people and boys and girls who love each other."

"It seems so peaceful here," she said.

"Peaceful," he nodded.

She hugged him again and then was gone, and he wondered why she had come to him and if it was a sign. She climbed into the car and drove away, and Daniel stood there for a long time until he felt a gentle tug on his sleeve.

"Best be getting back to work," Frank Sutton said. Daniel did not jump.

"Hello, Frank," Daniel said. "I was talking to Hazel Agnes, and she knew me when I had the little red calf."

Frank looked at Daniel and shook his large head; his face was always flushed, but this summer it had been burned until it seemed ready to break into flame.

"Hello, Hazel Agnes," Frank said, looking toward the river and acting as if he saw somebody.

"She is not here now," said Daniel, smiling at Frank.

"Back to work then," said Frank quietly.

Frank walked back up the narrow street toward the hill and turned and saw that Daniel was pulling weeds, and he wondered what a man like that saw in his head, and how much it hurt to be so different. But Daniel was almost like a son to Frank, and he forgave him nearly anything, though it was getting harder to keep him employed. Frank walked away in the rain.

Late that afternoon, Daniel finished work and did not feel like going home, so he walked to the University of Georgia's Main Library. Rebecca had taken him there several times and showed him the cemetery from the seventh-floor windows. She loved books, and so maybe she was there. He pictured her standing in that window with her hair folded over her shoulders. He thought of Annie, too, and he liked her very much, but Annie was sad because her husband had gone away. Rebecca had told Daniel that nothing hurt worse than for someone you love to go away.

He walked up three flights of stairs and wandered in the stacks of books. Summer quarter was over, and only a few people stood before the rows of books, turning their heads sideways to read the titles on the spines. The library was cool and silent. Daniel pulled a book out of a shelf. It was *A Death in the Family* by James Agee. He read the title over and over. Then he set the book back and tried to think who Hazel Agnes might be, but it was too much work. He thought of Rebecca and whispered her name, then said it out loud, but no one answered, so he walked around and looked for her, walked all over the building for nearly two hours, but she was not there. He climbed the stairs to the seventh floor because he did not want to ride the elevator. He walked back to the corner and looked out the window toward Oconee Hill and saw the shining shafts of marble and granite, saw the yawning mouth of Sanford Stadium and Memorial Hall, saw the rising edifice of buildings on South Campus. A stream of sunlight cut through the rainclouds and came across the stadium like a finger moving under a line in a book.

He left the library and walked under the oaks toward town. He came to the University's arch and walked through it onto the hot sidewalk that bordered Broad Street. He could see Campus North towering nine stories to his left, and he wondered if Rebecca were up there in her apartment. He thought for the first time that other people lived there, too. Maybe they loved someone just like he loved Rebecca Gentry.

Daniel stood across the street from Campus North and looked up to Rebecca's apartment, hoping to catch a glimpse of her at the window. He sat on the shady park bench not far from the bus stop and looked up. Fingers of vapor from a passing jet scratched the hazy sky above Athens. Cars grumbled past, struggling like everyone else against the heat. A car passed, its loud radio amplifying the strains of a string quartet, and Daniel sat up and stared at the car, remembering the concert in the Fine Arts Building where Rebecca had taken him. He had nothing else to do now; he could sit and look at this building and the sky and the cars. He could smell the aroma of freshly baked brownies from the A&A Bakery.

NIGHT CAME, AND DANIEL DID NOT MOVE until he saw the full moon swelling over Campus North and noticed that no lights had come on in Rebecca's apartment. *She is not here,* he thought. *Where in the world is Rebecca?*

He thought of being saved again. He didn't want to be saved tonight, but he didn't want to drink beer or liquor, either. That made him sick and he wanted to be well and to think about things.

He decided to walk back through the campus, and so he came slowly under the oaks, past Moore College and the Law School and then the old Commerce-Journalism Building.

Lights burned in many offices. Rebecca had told him that people were learning things in all those rooms, and Daniel tried to understand how much there was to learn in this world, and he saw the string quartet playing in his memory, and then the paintings from the art museum and the book in the library, and he had never even read a whole book, and you had to read all the books in that library to graduate. Daniel had graduated from Greenvale. He had worn a long black gown, and it was hot outside, and Mr. Wilkins spoke, but Daniel remembered only that a bird had sung from a nearby tree, and Bobby Josephs had laughed very loud all the time, but Bobby laughed like that all the time and nobody minded. Everyone had their families come to graduation, except no one came for Daniel because there was nobody. Afterwards, when they were all taking pictures, Daniel had stood around for a long time and then wandered back up to his room. He stood in the window in his gown and cap and saw them all spread below him. Although he knew that he was not leaving Greenvale, he did not know gradua-tion there was merely an exercise in confidence building—and a good one. He had stood in the window and felt as if the arch of stars overhead were collapsing into his heart.

There were many lights on the campus, and so Daniel could not see the stars tonight. He walked down the hill past Park Hall. This was where Rebecca worked, he remembered. He crept around the parking lot and found her blue MG, and when he knew that she was there, he stood trembling just outside the corona of a sidewalk lamp and clapped softly.

The end door was buried in a riot of privet bushes, and Daniel found that it was still open. He went inside. The hall's dark tile floor had been waxed that day and shone brilliantly, even though only a few lights were on. His footsteps were the only sound in the building as he walked down the hall. When he got to the middle of the hall, he saw a short walkway that led to the front porch, which was supported by marble columns. He had never stood there, and so he walked to the front door, opened it and came on to the stone porch, surprising Tift Bronson, who was standing at the balcony and looking dreamily out over the campus that sloped away down toward Sanford Stadium and the Tate Student Center.

"You've destroyed my reverie," Tift said. He squinted at Daniel.

"I am very sorry," Daniel said. He looked down at his feet as if he had stepped on something. "Can it be fixed back?"

Tift laughed and straightened himself up. He wore a pleated white shirt, loose white trousers, white shoes and a royal purple ascot. Daniel wondered if he had a cold. He noticed that Tift was holding a notebook and a pen.

"Now I know what Coleridge felt on awakening from his dream of Kubla Khan," Tift said in a deep, grand voice.

"I have dreams," stammered Daniel.

"Really," said Tift. "And what are your dreams?"

"I dream that I am a hawk and that I am flying over the world," Daniel said.

"Charming," Tift said. "I know you from somewhere. Night janitor?"

"Good night," said Daniel, and he turned and walked back inside. He thought the man seemed familiar, but he wanted to see Rebecca, and he was afraid she might leave. But how did he find her office? He came to the end of the hall and went through a door and saw an elevator. He hated elevators, did not really understand them, but the door was open on one, so he walked in and stood there for nearly five minutes before he realized it was not going to take him anywhere. He walked back down the silent hall and found a staircase and walked up it to the second floor, but no one seemed to be there, either, and once he called out her name, but it was only a hoarse whisper that slid down the dark hall. He walked up another flight of stairs and went through a heavy door and looked to his left. At the end of the hall, he saw her sitting in her office with the light from a lamp shining on her face. She was talking on the phone and laughing. She was happy.

Daniel felt his heart rise within him. Maybe he was a hawk because when he felt this way he almost knew he could rise above Oconee Hill, above the campus and Rebecca and soar among the clouds. He wanted to surprise her, so he did not clap very loud. He walked softly down the left side of the hall where she could not see him coming. "I love you, Rebecca," he said very softly. "I love you, Rebecca."

I love you, I love you, I love you, I love you, I love you, I love you.

SIXTEEN

"OH, HONEY, IT'S THE CRAZIEST THING YOU EVER HEARD OF," Rebecca Gentry said. She held the phone between her ear and shoulder, and a cigarette bobbed gently in her mouth as she spoke. She squinted from the rising smoke that seemed to fill the small office. "Yeah, yeah. That was hard enough to believe, but I went back last weekend and got her on tape, five damn hours of it, Charlie. I mean it's just changed everything. I've already transcribed all the tapes, and I'm so excited I'm just shaking when I wake up. Nobody knew a thing about him. He had this whole other life up there with her."

Daniel stood outside her office in the silent shadows. He held his cap in his hands and listened to her laughing voice. Who could she be calling "Honey"? The hall to his right faded into darkness, and the only sound was Rebecca's voice. Daniel felt his heart beating against his sweat-stained shirt.

"His death represented the ultimate Romantic act, Charlie," Rebecca said. "It's just beyond belief that something like this would happen. And on the day before Kennedy got killed. Think of it: the ultimate Romantic act just before the ultimate act of anarchy. Two worlds in fatal collision. How's that for a title, Charlie? 'Fatal Collision' by Rebecca Gentry."

She grabbed a yellow pad from the mound of papers on her desk and made a note of it. She laughed at something he said and smiled. "You're so bad. You always were bad, Charlie."

She giggled, and Daniel wondered why Rebecca seemed happy if Charlie was bad.

"Well, anyway, I had to tell somebody. I'm looking forward to the Virginia game." She stubbed the cigarette out and the room began to clear. "Yeah, I know." Her voice was soft, almost coy. "Well, let's just take it slow and see what happens. I guess I've learned a lot, too. Me, too. Okay, Honey. Yeah. Well, take care. Bye."

She hung up the phone and looked at her reflection in the window that looked south toward the stadium. She was still young. She needed to quit smoking, but even with cigarettes, her color seemed to be returning, and her eyes sparkled for the first time in months. Everything seemed to be finding a focus in her life. She smiled at herself and then made a face, sticking out her tongue and crossing her eyes.

When she was a little girl, Rebecca and her father would make faces each night before bedtime, but then her father had left, and she had not made faces anymore. This was the first time she had done it in years. She was in the middle of a buck-toothed grin when she realized there was another reflection in the glass, a sharp, but ghostly image of a man standing in the doorway. She cried and turned, knocking a stack of papers in swaying drift to the floor.

"Daniel!" she shouted. She stood halfway up, and then sat back down when she saw who it was.

Daniel, who had been smiling and making faces along with her, looked suddenly very sad, as if he would cry, and he stepped back into the darkness of the hall.

"No, no. Come on back inside." Rebecca stood, feeling her body trembling as if her bones were made of gelatin. "I'm sorry I yelled at you. What are you doing here, Daniel?"

"I was coming to see you, Rebecca," he said.

When she got near him, she could smell his dirty clothes, and she felt a thrill of repulsion swell in her.

"I did not know I would scare you." He looked at her.

"Well, come on in and sit down," she said.

Daniel came into her office and sat in her guest chair. To him, the room stank of cigarettes. She eased back down behind her desk, still trembling.

"What are you doing over here this time of the evening?"

"I looked for you in the books because I thought you would be there," Daniel said. "But then I thought you would be here, and so I came inside, but I got lost and then I found you, Rebecca."

"Oh Daniel," she sighed. What now? I should have known better, should have realized how much trouble I would bring myself by looking away from what was so obvious. "You need to be finding some friends other than me. I'm not the only person in the world, you know?"

"I know," he said simply. "But we are special friends and..." He smiled, but then his voice trailed off, and he looked up at her hopefully.

"Daniel," she said, "listen to me. The world is full of special friends. You just have to look for them and be a special friend yourself. Like Annie is my special friend, too."

He looked down at the floor and chewed on his lower lip.

"Oh, don't do that, Daniel. Please." She slid her chair near his and took his hands in hers and looked into his dark eyes. "Don't you have other friends?"

"I have Hazel Agnes," he said, his voice trembling. He felt terrified.

"You do have another girl!" Rebecca said exultantly. "Tell me about Hazel Agnes."

"She is not a girl," he said. "She is an old woman, and she came to me today, and she knew me when I had the little red calf and lived in the country."

Rebecca had been picking the papers up from the floor, but

now she pushed them in her lap and stared at Daniel. *Knew him when he lived on the farm?* She saw Daniel's fear and confusion.

"What do you mean?" she asked. Her voice sounded empty and cold in the cramped office.

"Hazel Agnes came, and she knew my parents from the farm, and I showed her Lucy Aged 21," said Daniel.

"No," Rebecca said. "Daniel, it's just your imagination. Please listen to me. You have to stop living in this world you've created and come alive. This world is the only one we have, not the one underground over there. Can't you see that?"

"I guess I cannot," he said bewildered.

"There's no Hazel Agnes, is there, Daniel," said Rebecca hopefully.

"Yes, Rebecca," he said.

"Daniel, stop it," Rebecca said softly.

"She came to me," Daniel said.

"She was someone in your heart," said Rebecca. "Please live here and now. Stop *doing* this." Her voice had become strident and harsh. "Just *stop* it."

Daniel stood up then, and chewed on his lip again, and looked around the office. Rebecca's eyes betrayed her disgust.

"At the whispered edge of this life
My heart fails to dream your face."

Daniel whispered the lines of her poem, then said, "I do not know how I remembered that," and held his shaking hands together.

Rebecca felt a visceral jolt. He did not seem to know what it meant, and she could not speak as he backed into the hall and in a moment disappeared into his heavy footsteps down the silent hall. She sat at her desk for nearly a minute before she ran after him. She ran down the long hall, calling his name, ran outside where the drizzle had turned into a steady rain. She called his name and cursed herself.

Daniel ran down Baldwin Street and under the railroad bridge then past O'Malley's. He wheezed and wept and barely listened to the thick drumming from the band in the nightclub. He ran across the Oconee River Bridge and went up Oconee Street and turned right into the trailer park and sat down finally in the wet dirt road not far from Daisy Saye's trailer. He sat and repeated *I love you*. When his breath came back, he walked to his trailer, but it was not there anymore, only a dark greasy place in the earth. He called Toggle, but the dog did not come, and everyone was tucked inside because of the late summer rains. He stumbled back a few steps and turned and ran right into Wade Rucker, who was staggering around with a bottle of Jack Daniel's.

"Dummy?" said Wade. He wore a Hawaiian print shirt and his face was unshaved and soaking in the glow from the park's two streetlights. "What in the hell are you doing here?"

Daniel backed up, confused, still thinking of Rebecca. "I love you," he choked.

Wade howled with laughter and put his arm around Daniel, and they walked toward Oconee Street, where the trailer park started.

"You stupid as shit, you know that, Dummy?" Wade said. "You know what I did today? I got goddamned fired from my job, Dummy. You got a job don't you, Dummy?" He handed the bottle to Daniel, elbowed him hard in the ribs and told him to drink.

Daniel turned the bottle up and felt the fire in his throat. He was ready to drink the whole bottle, until Wade snatched it back.

"You greedy son of a bitch!"

Wade hit Daniel hard in the face and knocked him into the mud and then helped him back up. Daniel coughed from the whiskey and his nose bled. He could barely see Wade in the dark rain. Wade hit him in the face again and knocked him down.

God, that felt good, Wade thought. Then he helped Daniel get up again.

"BLESSED ARE THE PURE IN HEART, FOR THEY SHALL SEE GOD," Daniel sputtered.

Wade Rucker laughed, howled.

Daniel spit blood all over his shirt, and Wade hit him in the shoulder, and Daniel staggered backwards and fell over a row of concrete blocks and rolled ten feet down the terrace to the next row of trailers. He felt dizzy as he sat up. "Toggle!" he cried.

"Damn, you clumsy," said Wade, feeling much better now. He walked down the terrace and helped Daniel back up.

"THE STEPS OF A GOOD MAN ARE ORDAINED BY THE LORD," said Daniel.

"What?" said Wade. "You making fun of me?"

"SHE OPENETH HER MOUTH WITH WISDOM!" Daniel cried out.

"I'll open your mouth, you shithead," growled Wade, and he swung wildly, missing, and fell into the mud. Enraged, he charged Daniel and pulled his feet from under him and struck him in the mouth.

Wade hit him in the chin. He elbowed him in the stomach. Daniel tried to run, but Wade tackled him. He struggled nearly free and then kicked Wade in the face with his heavy shoes, and Wade lay motionless in the mud. Daniel staggered away, holding his head and feeling the liquor now. The world reeled in swirling colors around him, and he watched as it revolved, like the drawings of the planets that Mrs. Wilkins had shown him at Greenvale. He saw planets. He stumbled out to the street and down it and then across the Oconee River Bridge and up the street toward town. He fell down on the sidewalk and got sick. When he stood up again, he felt a little better, but the stomach-churning stench of liquor was all over him. He grabbed a tree and got sick again, and then the nausea subsided and only his face and shoulder hurt where Wade Rucker had beaten him.

Why had he done it?

Daniel walked past the Hardware and remembered something. What was it? *Ghost rocks.* He remembered Frank and the ghost rocks.

Why had so much changed since then?

Daniel wandered across town, crying, his nose bleeding a little and his eyes pouring salty tears into his mouth. He tasted tears and blood.

"Hazel Agnes!" he cried.

A car came past and soaked him in the spray from its wheels. He heard people in the car laughing as they passed. The wind came up and made the trees dance, and Daniel thought of music that Rebecca had played for him, the *Fantastic Symphony* and its "Dream of A Witches' Sabbath." He could hear the drum thudding against the darkness. He stumbled down the sidewalk, now dripping rain, ran until he forgot the music, and there seemed no reason to be running. He wanted to be snug in his bed at Greenvale, but that was no longer the only world in his dreams; it had begun to fade, like a whispered promise of heaven.

REBECCA DID NOT GO HOME AFTER SHE HAD STOOD IN THE DRIZZLE shouting Daniel's name. She went back inside Park Hall and sat at her desk, trembling with anger and regret. What would become of Daniel? She didn't know, but she almost hoped he would dissolve into memory.

And yet, that would not happen; he was out there in the night. She had become entangled in his life, and wasn't that the way all relationships start, good and bad, you simply stumble into the path of another heart? She looked at her reflection in the window and tried to think of Charlie. She picked up the transcription of her conversations with Rachel Benjamin and looked at the words and remembered how it had been the weekend before when she and Annie had gone back to Mountain City to interview Rachel.

On the drive up, she had talked about her father with Annie, something she hadn't done in many years. The day had been hot and cloudless, and they both sat behind sunglasses as they drove up U.S. 441 north from Athens toward the mountains. Annie had said her father was getting weak more quickly than they had expected, that he might have had a slight stroke.

"Mother said his speech got slurred for a minute Saturday, and he seemed confused," Annie had said. "She called his doctor, and he said there wasn't much he could do if he seemed all right by then. To which I said, 'Shit,' and she got real upset with me."

"I wish I knew where my father is," Rebecca said. "When I was a little girl, he would come into my room and sit on the edge of the bed and tell me stories. He was a wonderful storyteller. We lived in North Carolina then, and he would make up stories about the Indians, and it wasn't until years later that I found out his stories were all taken from movies. He just liked Westerns. I heard that was where he went, out West, when he ran away from us. I was twelve. Bad time to run away from a little girl."

"I can't picture you as a little girl," Annie said.

Rebecca laughed. "Anyway, my mother tried to tell me stories after he left," Rebecca said. "You'd think somebody twelve years old wouldn't want to hear stories, but there was nothing in this world that I loved more than those stories. So Mother tried to make up stories, but she told me dreams of princesses and princes and I never really liked any of them."

"And that's why you became an English teacher," Annie said.

"I always liked what might have happened rather than what really did," Rebecca said. "Why'd you get into Classics?"

"Too much time in the library," Annie said.

"My father loved me, and I loved him," Rebecca said.

Rachel Benjamin had looked beautiful, and they had drunk iced tea and eaten sugar cookies while they spoke into the tape recorder. Rachel had talked about the first few times Lawrence Dale came to her house in Mountain City, how their earlier friendship had not changed into anything else at first.

"He was such a sweet and troubled man," Rachel had said, looking at his portrait over her couch. "He would be talking about something like justice for the Negroes, and his hands would just start shaking, and his eyes would fill with tears. I suppose these days he would be called morbidly sensitive, but it was not an act, and my God, I loved that in him. He could catch the song of some exotic-sounding bird, and he'd hush you and close his eyes and seem to be asleep, and then he'd quote poetry. He could just quote reams of poetry from the earliest days of the written word on up. He just adored Chaucer, but he also loved Dylan Thomas and felt his death was a tragedy from which letters might never recover.

"I liked him coming up here to escape from the pressures. You know, he had a great deal of work coming out, and they would haul him down to Atlanta, to the department stores, and he just hated that. The man was a farmer. He was still plowing his fields with a mule until he started to work for Mount Russell in the mid-Fifties. People thought he was this primitive who happened to love words, but he was self-educated mostly, though he'd been to college. He just loved the written word the way an adolescent loves her first boyfriend. He'd read everything. Just everything.

"He'd been coming up here off and on for several months, and he'd drive out here, and we would go out and listen to waterfalls and stare at the foxfire. It's strange, but if the forest is completely dark you can look at the foxfire on the wall of a deep creek and think it's the night sky and the glow is the stars.

"We came in from listening to the waterfall down at Warwoman Dell one night in June, and we were sitting in my living room, sitting right here, and he started telling me things he'd never told anyone, how horribly lonely he really was, how he felt like life was slipping away from him. I held his hands, and he told me that he had once loved a woman, but she had wanted him to be something he couldn't be.

"Well, we ended up in my bed that night, and it was as close to bliss as the world will allow a mortal. He was so gentle and sad and frightened, and I never wanted to let him go that night, and he slept in my arms, but I wouldn't let myself sleep, because I had come from all this money and had never been needed, never really been happy. You see, he needed me."

Rebecca looked at the words and could see Rachel, her strong hands and the pallor on her cheeks and the tired look of advancing death in her eyes. She had seen the look in her own mother's eyes, the body beginning to shut itself down. She read on.

"I don't know that I had ever been really needed before that, you see. That next morning I awoke, and he was standing at the foot of the bed smiling at me, and I sat up and my bed was covered...with rose petals, white rose petals that he'd gathered from my garden. I didn't have my glasses on, but I could smell them, and they looked like angel wings. So I said, 'Larry, you brought me angels.' He liked that, and all that day we touched and loved and said very little. A storm came down the valley from up near Franklin, and he held me, and we listened as it got closer, and then the rain and thunder and wind came. It lasted for, oh, maybe an hour, and we never said a word during the entire thing. We simply sat and listened and smelled the earth soaking in the rain."

There was more, pages of it, but Rebecca set it back on her desk and thought instead of Daniel and his sudden appearance. She thought of him working in Oconee Hill and pretending to see a woman like his mother. Rebecca turned out the light and locked her door and went down the stairs of Park Hall and out to her car. *Hazel Agnes.* That was her name. She felt a thrill of fear settle in the pit of her stomach.

She started home, but instead drove through Athens and down the streets of the suburbs. Lawn sprinklers hissed and chugged in the light of streetlamps, and the air smelled of damp earth. She stopped at a traffic light, and across the street in a convenience store, she could see an old man buying a six-pack of beer. What would her own father look like now, she wondered? Would he be fat or thin, prosperous or destitute? Would he still be telling stories to little girls?

"I miss him so bad," she said out loud, and her eyes filled with tears. The neighborhoods seemed settled, blurred by her damp eyes. Everything was ordered here, every shrub squared with the next one, every flagstone perfectly laid in perfect lawns. Through open windows she could see families sitting around their televisions, lost in the flickering light. She pulled into Annie Phillips's driveway. When she got out, crickets scratched merrily in the darkness of the back yard. A car full of teenagers listening to loud rock music rattled past.

Rebecca wiped her eyes and walked through the carport and rang the doorbell. She looked through the glass door that led into the kitchen, and in a moment, she saw a figure coming toward her, lights coming on in the kitchen and carport. When Annie saw her, she opened the door. Annie was smiling.

"Hey, Hoss, what it is?" Annie said. She was holding a half-empty glass of red wine. "You're just in time to watch *Casablanca* with me on the tube."

Rebecca came inside.

"What's wrong? You look completely sick," said Annie.

"I don't know," Rebecca said. "You got any more of that stuff?" She pointed at the glass.

"God, are you in luck," Annie said. "I got a gallon of Gallo. Finish transcribing the tapes?"

"Yeah," said Rebecca. They came into the living room where the television droned in black and white, and Humphrey Bogart was looking world-weary and dough-faced. Annie poured a glass of wine for Rebecca, and they both settled on the couch.

"Guess what," Annie said. Her voice was a little slurred. Rebecca sipped the wine, which tasted dry and delicious.

"Brad called me tonight. He was crying." Annie cackled with laughter.

"Is that funny?" Rebecca asked.

"I think it's terrible," Annie said, then she started laughing again. "His honey dumped him for an Amway salesman." Rebecca drained her glass quickly and poured another.

"You're kidding," said Rebecca. "Are you going to take him back?"

"Sure," she said. "But not before I make him feel like hell for a few weeks."

"What did you tell him?"

"That I'd never let this happen to me again," Annie said. "I told him that I was thinking of moving to Norway."

"Norway?" asked Rebecca. "Why Norway?"

"It was the grand prize on 'Price is Right' tonight," said Annie. "Anyway, he wants to have dinner with me, and I told him I'd check my calendar and get back to him."

"Yeah," said Rebecca. They watched the movie for a time, and Ingrid Bergman seemed always to be crying. "Damn, I hate being noble."

"Yeah," said Annie. "What are you here for? You looked upset before I started getting you drunk. You and Charlie still going to the Virginia game? Maybe we can double date." Annie laughed, too loud, and Rebecca smiled but did not laugh.

"Oh hell, you know," Rebecca said. She frowned and walked to the French doors that opened onto the patio at the back of the house. "It's Daniel. I don't know what in the world I'm going to do. He came to my office while I was working alone tonight. Told me a woman came to see him today in the cemetery. I'm sure he just imagined it."

"He still probably doesn't think *you're* real," said Annie.

The idea struck Rebecca with bitter force. "I'm not sure anything's real to Daniel," she said. "Or maybe he's the only one who really understands what the world is about. One of those."

"One of those?" Annie giggled. "Then he's either crazy or God. One of those. What's the name of the woman who came to see him?"

"Hazel Agnes," grinned Rebecca. "Can you believe he'd make up a name like that? Said she knew him on the farm when he had the little red calf."

Annie froze, remembering. Ingrid Bergman was saying that Humphrey Bogart would have to do the thinking for both of them.

"Oh, Lord," said Annie.

Rebecca looked at her, saw a new light in her eyes that had been missing for days. Her short blonde hair was clean and had been brushed. Now she had her feet pulled up on the couch and she held her knees and rocked slightly in the deep fabric.

"What?" asked Rebecca.

"While you were inside talking to Mr. Wilkins, down there at Greenvale?" said Annie, "Daniel and I were waiting outside, and this older man came up, said his name was Hailey or Bailey or something. He'd worked there for years as a groundskeeper or something. I remember Daniel was climbing a magnolia tree, and this guy was shuffling along, and he stopped and told me about Daniel, how he'd first come there as a boy. He said they'd put his mother away. He called her name; I thought it was odd, then. That was her name."

"What was her name?" asked Rebecca. Gooseflesh rose on her arms.

"Hazel Agnes," said Annie. "You don't forget a name like that."

Rebecca sat up and put her glass on the table. She looked around the room.

"Oh my God," she whispered.

SEVENTEEN

DANIEL AWOKE IN THE LUXURIOUS AROMA OF HONEYSUCKLE.
Sunlight was twinkling through the high leaves of the oaks, which
huddled around him protectively on the southern slopes of Oconee
Hill. He sat up and rubbed his head; his mouth was dry and a
pleasant wind stirred the weeds and bushes. *How had he come into the
cemetery, and where had he been?* Everything was wet. A cool front
had sagged through north Georgia, rare in summer and loved by
everyone who suffered from the subtropical heat. He saw the stones
around him and felt happy and calm. He got to his knees and pulled
weeds from around a stone and saw, covered with lichens, the words
"GONE HOME TO HIS GOD," and felt a deep peace.

He felt sick, and his left eye throbbed. When he had finished
cleaning the wilderness away from the stone, he stood, and his head
hurt, and so he sat back down. He tried to remember why he was
here, and then he saw Wade Rucker coming toward him, and he
jumped up, flinched and cried "No!" sharply, but he was alone. He
looked around. His baseball cap lay on the ground, and he picked it
up and snugged it on his head. Daniel had always loved morning in
Oconee Hill, the sweet wetness of dew and the taut shafts of weeds

bursting with juice, ready for him to pluck almost as if they had been put there for his mercy alone. But now his mind was crowded with images that left him dazed: millions of books with words that spilled into his dreams, storms and sickness, a dark stain where his trailer had been, the ghost of Toggle forever coming to him in dreams.

He stood perfectly still in the damp sunlight. Yes, he had dreamed of Toggle again last night. They had been in the country, where he had always wanted to live, and Daniel was in the edge of a field tending sheep and cattle, and Toggle was out in the milkweed, cutting joyous circles, and Daniel was smiling and standing there clapping and whistling for him. But now Daniel knew that Toggle lived only in his dreams; everything he loved except Rebecca came to him in dreams. He had never dreamed of her and wondered why. He did not move. He thought of her and then saw himself in the lamplit wonder of her office and heard her voice. *What had she told him?* He tried to remember.

Frank stood at the crest of the hill and saw Daniel down the slope in the tangle of weeds. He did not know what to do. Daniel had become a decoration in Oconee Hill, another upthrust chunk of old marble. He would be working and talking to himself furiously and then fall into a trance and not move for nearly an hour. He was in another one of his trances this morning. He stood there, arms at his sides, staring into the tree branches.

Daniel remembered the little red calf. Was that some dream, too? They told him about the farm, Mr. Wilkins did, about the country, and Daniel had drifting glimpses of that other world, but where was it? The images came and often with them a kind of sweeping horror, a disease of the night, and the walls were washed in blood, and there was screaming.

"Daniel," a voice called.

"I am here," he whispered. *Was this God calling him home?* The thought calmed him, for now he only wanted to lie in the cool earth with his own stone, with his friends like Baby and Howell B. Cobb, FIRST ATHENS BOY GIVING LIFE IN THE WORLD WAR.

"Daniel," Frank said again. He came down the slope toward Daniel, who slowly turned and smiled broadly when he saw that it was Frank. "Good God, son, what happened to you?"

"There is a bird that sits on flowers," Daniel said. "It comes to me in the heat of the day, and it has a long nose, Frank. It does not know my name."

Frank felt defeated, not knowing Daniel had suddenly thought of hummingbirds.

"You look terrible," Frank said as he came alongside Daniel. "My God." He tenderly touched the purple lump over Daniel's left eye and saw his beard stubble and smelled his dirty clothes. "Did you spend the night in the cemetery last night, son?"

"I think I did, Frank," Daniel admitted. "I am having a hard time." He remembered Mrs. Wilkins talking about hard times, about something called a "Hoover buggy," cars hitched to horses because no one could even afford gasoline. "I think that I was lost again."

"Did you make your lunch?" asked Frank. "I didn't see you come to work, and your bag's not in the Frigidaire."

"I am just here," said Daniel in wonder. "There are many things I do not understand, Frank."

Frank Sutton looked at him and then around the slope, and he knew that Oconee Hill would never be completely cleaned up, that one part of it, at least, would forever be choked with wilderness. Frank hated the thought, but without a great deal more money, nothing could be done. In the winter, everything died away, and the stones that now were lost in the coils of weed would stand in the frost with eternal clarity.

"Yeah," Frank said. He sighed heavily and shook his head and then spit. "I got some extra. I'll make you a sandwich for later. You come up to the house at lunchtime, and I'll see about making you something. Okay?"

"Yes, Frank," Daniel said.

Frank touched the swollen spot over Daniel's eye, and Daniel closed his eyes happily like a kitten being groomed by its mother.

"Why in God's name would anybody want to hurt you, Daniel?"

"Wade knocked me down," Daniel remembered.

"Who's Wade?" asked Frank. He felt his fists clenching.

"Wade?" asked Daniel. He turned and stared at the stones, up the slope to an angel whose wings hung in the still cool air. Then he said, "Wings." He turned to Frank, smiling now. "In the other world, everyone wears wings."

Frank wanted to cry.

"Okay," he said. "Get back to work around this slope. The swing blade's up there. Get as much done as you can this morning, okay?"

"Yes, Frank," said Daniel.

Frank walked off muttering to himself, and Daniel knelt in the soil. Red mud caked many hills and gulleys in north Georgia, but for a century, thick leaves had fallen on Oconee Hill, and the earth was dark and rich. Daniel pulled weeds back and tried to whistle. He did not think of anything, and birds came to the ground, mourning doves, that gargled out a low song of greeting. Once he sat back and flapped his arms in greeting, but the birds flew away, flying low across the stones, wings clapping, clapping.

Daniel did not feel the passage of time. There was only sun and air and earth and the smell of uprooted weeds. By nine-thirty, he had neatly cleaned a small spot, only ten feet square, but Frank had given up on trying to get Daniel to work on a large area. Daniel stood back and admired his work. He had just cocked his head to see it at a different angle when he realized he was not alone.

"Hello, Hazel Agnes," he said happily. "I have cleaned up this place, and a bird sat with me, and we have felt this nice breeze."

She stood a few feet above him on the slope and looked at his broken face with rising horror. She wore light blue slacks, a white blouse and off-white Nikes. She had sunglasses on, and Daniel was close enough to see his own reflection in them, and he suddenly thought of Rebecca and began to make faces at his reflection.

Hazel Agnes was startled. "Daniel, what happened to you?" she said in a hoarse whisper.

212

"I can see my funny faces in your glasses," he said, laughing. He stood there smiling, not thinking of who she was, of anything but the breeze and the stones and his funny faces.

"You been in a fight?" she asked.

"I have cleaned this place," he said proudly, looking at the damp earth before him.

She felt an unspeakable horror, an urge so irresistible that she came to him, touched him on his sweat-dirtied arm. "Would you like to see where you lived when you were a boy?" she asked.

Daniel could see her mouth was weak and trembling and that she was holding a handkerchief. A sweat bee droned up near them.

"Billy, billy, billy, come, billy," Daniel chanted, and the bee briefly descended to his outthrust finger and then flew away. "If you call a billy bee, it will land on your finger."

"Daniel," she said urgently. She moved square in front of him and twisted the handkerchief into a knot. "Would you like to see where you lived when you had that red calf?"

"My little red calf?" he said.

He looked down and stared at a spot on the ground and did not move for nearly ten seconds, and then he looked up merrily at Hazel Agnes, and his mouth came open in delight and he clapped and clapped. She looked around nervously, but no one noticed. The cemetery was silent this morning.

"I sure would!"

"Come on, then," she whispered, and she took his arm, and they walked up the hill. At the crest, he suddenly knelt and put his hand tenderly on a small marble marker.

"I will see you soon, Baby," he said. He looked up at the woman. "Hazel Agnes, this is Baby, and I am the only one who loves it."

"Was it a boy or a girl?" she asked nervously.

"It was a baby," Daniel said as he touched the stone.

He stood up and they went over the hill and walked down toward her car, which was parked on the road that ran lazily through Oconee Hill. From the house, Frank saw Daniel get into the car, and he hurried outside but got there just as the woman drove, too fast, through the gates. She turned left on East Campus Road, passing the massive walls of Sanford Stadium and heading south.

Frank stood there for a while, wondering what he would do next. A hummingbird appeared near him, and he watched it when it ascended, becoming a dot against the cloudless sky before it was suddenly gone.

REBECCA HAD STAYED UP VERY LATE READING the transcriptions of her conversation with Rachel Benjamin and drinking too much wine. When she awoke, it was nearly eight-thirty, and she rolled out of bed, groggy and disoriented, thinking first of her book and next of Daniel. She felt many things, tenderness toward Lawrence Dale for his suffering, a deepening friendship and hope for Annie, and a fear that Daniel was like an endless well of darkness and light. She thought as she showered how badly she wanted to be happy and to be normal, how terrible it was to be as sensitive as Lawrence Dale. And yet wasn't the entire history of literature bound in that controlled excess? Wasn't the only hope for a new vision entrusted to those who were guardians of the word and made life new again through it?

She looked at her body in the full-length mirror as she toweled off, saw full breasts, saw her stomach trailing off into the heavy hair, her still-strong legs. The body or the soul, she wondered. She thought of Charlie and how they would stand side by side naked when they first married and looked at each other's image in the mirror, still amazed, then, at the mysteries of the other's body.

She dressed and made coffee and saw from her window that the sky was clean and high. The radio said that a cool front had sagged through from the northeast, a "back-door front," they called it. Rebecca thought of the term and smiled; perhaps she should add it to her list of oxymorons. The oak trees on the campus across the street swayed in the fresh wind, and below, on the sidewalks, the

Bradford Pear trees seemed to swirl madly, dancing in the new light. She ate a piece of cheese toast. She dressed in a pair of khaki pants and a blue cotton shirt and went down the elevator and got her car and drove out on to Broad Street. She felt strong, but she worried about Daniel, about the woman who had come to see him. But she would go there now, she thought, make some kind of peace with him and then head for Park Hall to work on the manuscript. She thought of what Rachel Benjamin had told her.

All of Athens smelled wonderful, like Benson's Bakery. Only a few people were out on the sidewalks, and many shopkeepers were opening slowly, enjoying the fresh air and the slow times before fall quarter started. She drove down Broad past the restaurants and the shops and turned right on East Campus Road. Oconee Hill was not far away, and when she got to the iron gates, she felt for the first time as if it were a place of death. Frank was standing out in the street in front of the sexton's house, and Rebecca slowed to a stop and pushed her sunglasses back up on her head.

"Good morning," Rebecca said. "Do you know where Daniel is working this morning?"

Frank rubbed his elbow. His arthritis had been bothering him all week. "Lady, I don't know a thing about that boy," he said. "He just got in the car with an old lady and left. I was up there talking to him not half an hour ago, and he was getting down to work pretty good, but then he up and leaves with this lady I've never even seen."

Rebecca felt numb, choked with anguish. "Oh no," she said weakly.

"And, poor feller, somebody just beat him to a pulp last night, but he don't even care," Frank said. "I don't think he knows how to hate or to fight back. He's just getting eat up alive."

"He was beaten?" cried Rebecca. She was stunned. She looked around, and the cemetery was the model of perfect harmony and order. "What do you mean, he was beaten?"

"I don't know," Frank admitted. "He had a black eye. And he slept here last night and looked like holy hell. I don't know what started all this. For the past two-and-a-half years, he was the happiest kid you ever saw, just come out here and sit and pull weeds, and now he's just doing all kind of crazy things. I don't know how I can keep him working here. But I wouldn't do anything to hurt him."

Frank turned away, and Rebecca could tell that he cared deeply for Daniel, hurt for him.

"If you're his friend, lady, I wish you'd talk to him if he comes back."

"What kind of car was she driving?"

"Hell, I don't know," he said. "Something fat and old. Brown? I don't know."

"You said she was older?" Rebecca asked.

"Yeah. Nothing special about her. They drove that way." He pointed past the stadium.

"South?"

"That's it," Frank said. "They went south."

Rebecca fought the urge to scream or bite her fist. When her father had left, she had taken to biting her fist whenever she thought of him, and she had had a mark from it on the back of her right hand for years.

"If you hear from him, call me," Rebecca said. She dug into her purse and took out one of her cards and handed it to him. He looked at it curiously and nodded.

"Say, you wouldn't know who that was would you, that woman?" he asked.

"No," Rebecca Gentry lied.

She drove down to the stone watering trough and turned around and drove back up to Baldwin Street and then West toward Park Hall. She parked behind it and got out. Her knees were shaking. She heard bees drone, listened to the music of leaves as they blew in the lightly trembling air. She ran inside and up the stairs, two at a time, and when she got to her floor, her wind was gone and she leaned against the glass door on the landing, gasping for breath. *Goddamn cigarettes.*

She looked up, and Tift Bronson was on the other side of the glass door, smiling at her, standing in the hall with his hands in the trousers of a white linen suit. He carried a small book as if it might explode at any minute. *Shit*, she thought. She went through the door.

"The beautiful Rebecca," he said, following her as she headed for her office. "Have you made anything out of Prokofiev dying thirty minutes before Stalin?"

"I thought it was after," Rebecca said, not breaking stride or looking at him.

"Who cares really?" he asked. "I heard from my publisher today."

He waited for a response from her, but she was silent, and walked with long strides down the tiled hall. Soon, it would be clogged with students, and Rebecca knew that she loved to teach, that she would truly be happy when fall quarter began.

"They're going to publish my novel," he went on. "Can you believe it? Aren't you excited for me?"

"Ecstatic," she said blandly.

"I'm excited for me," said breathlessly. "I'm going to become gloriously drunk and fornicate with anything on two legs. Want to join me?" They got to her office, and she turned to him and glared angrily.

"Humility, Tift," she said. "Go look it up."

"I know that word," he said, smiling at her. "It comes from the Greek for failure."

She shook her head, went into her office and slammed the door in his face. His disembodied voice came through the door: "Thank you for sharing in my happiness."

His footsteps receded down the hall, and then she felt contrite, opened the door and saw only Robbie Singletary, an assistant professor who specialized in Chaucer. He was going into his office down the hall. She waved, and he waved back and smiled.

Rebecca sat down at her desk and cursed. The stack of her tapes of Rachel Benjamin lay before her in the dismal clutter of papers, coffee cups and magazines. A copy of the *PMLA* was halfway off the desk. She called long distance information and got the number for Greenvale and dialed it. All that spring she had watched a nest of thrashers in the tree outside her window, and now the grown babies were back, plump and confused, sitting on the limb and looking, it seemed to Rebecca, with wonder at their tiny crib.

"Greenvale," the sprightly voice of a secretary trilled.

"Mr. Wilkins, please," Rebecca said. She looked frantically for a cigarette, going through three empty packs on the desk before she found a pack with one left and lit it. The smoke choked her and tasted unbelievably foul. There was a pause.

"Are you a friend of his?" the secretary asked.

"I, uh, no, I met him and wanted to…what's wrong?" Rebecca asked.

"He's in the hospital," the secretary said. "I'm sorry to tell you he had a stroke last week, and he's in Athens Regional."

"My God," Rebecca said. "I'm calling from Athens. He's here?"

"Yes ma'am," she said. "I think he has family or something up there. He's spent a lot of time in Athens."

"How is he?" Rebecca asked.

"I don't really—"

"—It's all right," Rebecca said. "I'll go over there. Thank you very much."

"Okay," she said, sprightly again. "Have a nice day."

Rebecca slowly put the phone on the receiver and lit a cigarette. Then she realized that another was burning at the edge of a heaped ashtray. *I don't even know what I'm doing.*

She locked her office, went to the car and drove through Athens and down Prince Avenue. An old black man rode past her, grimly pedaling his bike, shirt tail flying in the wake. A fat woman yawned as she pumped her gas at the Amoco station, and four police cars were lined up neatly in front of Dunkin' Donuts, which local wags had long since called the best-protected store in town. She passed church after church and the perfect lawn of the Georgia Power Building and a row of fast-food stores.

Athens Regional Hospital was on the left, an inelegant, squat structure that had been recently transformed by an atrium in the lobby, like an urban hotel, and pastel color combinations. And yet, as Rebecca walked across the asphalt parking lot toward the front doors, it was still a hospital to her, a place not of life-giving but of death. She came into the lobby and looked up, as the architect meant for her to do, and felt the vault pull her up, and she briefly wondered if anyone had ever compared the new architecture of hospitals and hotels to Renaissance churches and their ponderous authority. Look, the hospital seemed to be saying, *if we can build this vault we can surely cure your body or your mind.* The church merely said it could save your soul.

She walked up to the desk where a round, smiling, gray-haired woman sat. It was late morning, and very few people were around. The woman smiled pleasantly at Rebecca and arched her eyebrows and asked if she could help.

"Could you tell me which room a Mr. Wilkins is in?" Rebecca asked.

The woman touched a computer terminal and hummed a hymn to herself and then looked up and said he was in room 4311.

"Thanks so much."

"Well, you're just as welcome as you can be, sugar," the woman said pleasantly. Rebecca walked toward the elevators, but then, thinking that perhaps she should take flowers, she turned and came back through a set of double doors and walked down a corridor to the flower shop, which was clean and well ordered. She bought a small vase with a single red rose and then went back to the elevators.

When the door opened, Rebecca saw an older woman standing there with a young woman about her age. Both of them had been crying, and they held each other and stepped off the elevator like one person with four legs, moving stiffly across the lobby. Rebecca watched them until the door closed and she was alone in the elevator. When the door opened, she was no longer in a hotel; crepe-soled nurses silently slid down the halls as if they were borne aloft like hydrofoils.

Rebecca walked down the hall, looking at the numbers on the doors. A nurse smiled at her, and another stared as if Rebecca had no right to be there at all. She found 4311 with little trouble, and since the door was half-open, she went inside, peeking around the door as she entered.

It was a private room, and Wilkins was gray and motionless in the bed, tubes snaked into the backs of his hands. The television droned very softly. Rebecca was almost to the bed before she noticed a small woman sitting in a low chair in the corner, holding a Bible in her hands.

"Oh," said Rebecca, stopping. She pulled the rose to her chest as if someone might take it. "I didn't see you in here."

"Do you know him?" the woman asked. She did not stand or try to greet Rebecca.

"I met him at Greenvale," she said. Was this the woman from the cemetery? Perhaps Daniel was here with her. He would suddenly come in the door as if he had never left the cemetery and say hello to her.

"Yes," the woman said. "Did you have a child there? Two people who had children there have already come by this morning." The woman was grim and humorless. She wore a dark brown dress and seemed to be in her late sixties. Her speech was that of a country woman, and her eyes were lost in dark sockets. Her skin sagged. A brooch held her collar shut at the top, but her dress was far too large.

"No," Rebecca admitted. "A friend grew up there." She looked at Mr. Wilkins, whose eyes were slightly open, staring at Rebecca. He looked dead, except for the even rising and falling of his chest.

"I'm his sister, Margery," she said. "I'm from Franklin, North Carolina."

"I'm a North Carolina girl myself," Rebecca smiled at her.

Margery stared back and did not say anything.

"I brought this for him." She offered the vase to Margery. When she stood up to take the flower, Margery was not much taller standing. "I'm sure he'd appreciate it," she said. She set the vase on the window sill, sloshing some of the water from the vase. It ran down the wall beneath the window.

"How is he?" Rebecca asked.

"His condition is listed as stable," she said, and the first hint of feeling edged into her voice, "but that only means his heartbeat. The damage is uncertain."

"Oh my," Rebecca said. She looked at him, and his eyes seemed to gather a small light, to twinkle, and then to fade back into darkness. "I had no idea. I just found out about it this morning. They said it was a stroke."

"A stroke," Margery said, and Rebecca almost thought she snorted a harsh laugh.

"Well, I just needed to ask him something, but I see that's not possible," Rebecca said softly.

"What was you going to ask him?" Margery inquired. A nurse slid into the room, adjusted his pillow, talked to him as if he were a child, and then left.

"Well, it's about my friend," Rebecca said. "I just wanted to know something. Maybe you might know."

"Who?" Margery asked. She held her bony finger in the Bible.

"His name is Daniel Mitchell," said Rebecca.

Margery audibly gasped and dropped the Bible onto the floor with a resounding smack. She gathered her composure quickly and picked the Bible up and leaned back in the chair and tried to smile.

"Mitchell," she said. She looked out the window. "Never heard him mention anyone named Mitchell." The sentence was spat out like machine gun fire.

"Oh," said Rebecca. "I was just trying to find out something. It was just a chance."

"What?" Margery demanded imperially.

"His mother's name," said Rebecca. "I was just wondering if it was Hazel Agnes."

Margery's mouth trembled, and she glanced at Mr. Wilkins with what seemed almost a sneer. "Never heard of such a name," she said. "Wallace never mentioned it to me."

"Well, it's not that important," Rebecca lied. "I'm really sorry, and I hope he improves. Goodbye, now." She nodded at Margery and had just started to walk out when she stopped and turned around. "I thought his name was Lewis."

"Wallace is his first name," said Margery coldly. "Mama and I were the only ones ever called him that."

Rebecca felt confused, but she only smiled, said goodbye again and went back to the elevators and downstairs. *Where had she heard the name Wallace?*

She walked quickly to her car and headed toward Campus North. Her hands were shaking as she thought of what to pack. She did not know where she would go.

EIGHTEEN

Daniel watched in wonder as the countryside unfurled around him. He saw shafts of corn standing at attention, fuzzy rows of soybeans waving in the wind. Cotton was swelling into bolls on its green plants. Athens had disappeared quickly, and he felt the maternal pull of country.

A hawk came head down into a field and rose with a dark lump stuck in its claws. A grinning dog trotted along the roadside with its nose on the ground, head moving back and forth, as if sweeping the earth for scent. Daniel saw a field of Holsteins and thought of their jaws as they worked their cuds. He wondered why cows always ate and what they ate. Cows moved very slow and were never angry.

Daniel saw the sky and its cumulus clouds with lightly purpled edges, saw an endless cross formed by two jets' vapor trails as it began to swell and then dissolve into the clouds. He saw colors: green and yellow in the fields, the red-brown of the earth, gray tree trunks at the edges of the fields. He saw white and tints of red among the clouds. A large orange cat sat motionless on the roadside ready to jump.

But he saw more. When quail exploded from a grain field, he

thought of the artist whose paintings Rebecca had shown him. *What was his name?* Vincent. Bright yellow. He thought of the music in the Fine Arts Auditorium, the sheer beauty of the music. How the instruments loved each other, their sound a living breath. He thought of the headless angel in the Gerdine-Cobb plot, and how Rebecca had explained marble carving. He had never thought a man had carved the angel, though he did not know how else to explain it. God must have loved the creatures he made wings. He heard the named "Beethoven" in his head, a man who made music that Rebecca loved. He thought of liquor then, and he thought of women, thought of lying with them—he had often thought of lying with them—but more, he thought of Rebecca.

Rebecca. He wondered why she was taking him for a ride in the country, except when he looked at her, it was someone else.

"Who are you?" he asked. They were forty miles southeast of Athens now, not far from Washington.

"I told you," she said. "I'm a friend of your family, Daniel."

"You are Hazel Agnes," Daniel said.

"That's right," she said, smiling.

"I thought that you were Rebecca," he said. He held his hands in his lap and licked his lips repeatedly. "I am sorry, Hazel Agnes. I remember you now. Will you take me where I had the little red calf?"

"Yes, I will," she said. She drove very slowly, as if she had only recently learned how, but Daniel did not notice. There were many things he did not notice.

"I asked God to give me back the country," Daniel said. "I talk to God, and then he talks to me. Do you ever talk to God, Hazel Agnes? The people in Oconee Hill live with God, mostly, except part of them live with me. Part of them stayed in the ground and on the stones. Their names are all on the stones. Will you have a stone when you die?"

"Yes," she said.

"I will have Daniel Mitchell," he said, and he thought for the first time about what he wanted his stone to say, and Hazel Agnes did not know why he went silent and did not speak for nearly ten miles.

Then he said, "THE STEPS OF A GOOD MAN ARE ORDAINED BY THE LORD." He smiled at her, and she looked helpless, trapped. "That is what I will have, or something else. What will you have on your stone, Hazel Agnes?"

"I'm tired of talking about death," she said wearily. "You talk about death all the time, Daniel?"

"Death?" he said. "Things change from one life to another, Hazel Agnes. It does not hurt, and then you live forever in flowers, and there I will meet every friend who ever loved me. O happy day."

"Let's talk about something else," she said.

He thought about it. "There is a grasshopper in Oconee Hill that jumps up and then flies into the football park, and it is black and yellow," he said. "Would you like to talk about jumping?"

"Not really," she admitted.

She turned on the radio and found a station that played country songs, and they listened to Randy Travis and Merle Haggard and Reba McIntyre and others, and Daniel would sometimes listen to the words and feel sad, and sometimes the songs were funny. He did not seem to notice when they went through towns or when the towns dissolved back into the countryside. He could be talking and listening one moment, and by the next, he might have gone back inside himself for miles.

My God, thought Hazel Agnes. He spends his time peeking into this world and then escaping back into another. Which one, she wondered, was the more beautiful? She saw him sitting there with his baseball cap, the swollen eye, the smell of his clothes, almost foul, but nearly something else, saw his disease and hated it. Daniel invited love and devotion, and his discomfort with this life could surely be no more than hers, she thought. He whistled a melody from some song that only his heart had ever loved.

They crossed I-20, and Daniel saw it stretching east and west and wondered where all those cars were going. Hazel Agnes drove steadily south, and soon Daniel felt a jolt and realized that she had turned onto a dirt road. His skin pulsed with expectation, and he looked back and forth so he would not miss anything.

"Where are we, Hazel Agnes?" he asked.

"Not far," she answered.

They passed a small frame house, and three black children were bouncing a frayed basketball against the grassless yard and taking positions around a rim without a net that had been nailed to a board on an oak tree. Rebecca had shown Daniel a videotape of *Swan Lake*, and he decided the children were dancing, and his mind supplied the music. He turned and saw a dog standing outside their circle, tail thumping, watching them dance, and he thought of Toggle, and for a moment he felt as if he might cry. He turned around, and both sides of the road were choked with kudzu, coils and coils of it.

They passed a trailer where an elderly woman sat in a ladder-back chair beneath a shade tree shucking corn. Daniel saw the golden hair of the corn dangle from her hands. A cat sat on its haunches next to her, not moving, waiting for nothing, he thought. Cats walked at night. They could rise into trees and hang there like birds except they did not have wings.

"My God," Hazel Agnes said, and Daniel felt the car slowing.

"My God," he echoed.

The road widened slightly, and she pulled to one side and stopped, looking through the dust that swept past them from their own wake.

"There it is," she whispered. "Do you remember, Daniel? Do you remember it, son?"

He opened the door and got out. The day was hot but not unpleasant for late summer, and he stood in the middle of the road and looked back into the edge of the forest. The roof of the house had nearly collapsed, and it was obvious no one had lived there in years. The driveway that had once stretched across the ditch had been pulled away by some nameless road crew. Twin water oaks framed the front porch, and old porch posts were falling away, giving the house a gap-toothed sag. Someone had hauled the rusting hulk

226

of an old Chevrolet to one side of the house, and it swelled with kudzu. A breeze came up, and they both walked slowly across the road, and he jumped the ditch and helped Hazel Agnes across. The hard-packed dirt from generations of children still would not support much growth, and it was easy to walk almost to the front porch. An old wind chime made of flattened forks hung from the porch roof, and when the breeze picked up again, its sound sparkled briefly against the silence of the country. A pickup truck blaring out Hank Williams clattered past, but Daniel did not turn to look at it. He stopped in front of the house and blinked as he scanned it from side to side. The right side of the house was fairly open, and they walked without talking around it and saw that just past the trees behind it was a field, and in the field were many beef cattle that gently gnawed the grass. The back side of the house had caved in, and birds' nests were visible in the ruins.

"Do you remember it, Daniel?" Hazel Agnes almost cried. "I used to come out here, and you would be sitting in the dirt playing with your little soldiers. You had this whole set of little metal soldiers, I think your Daddy bought them for you, and you would be in the dirt playing with them for hours and hours, rearranging them. Do you remember that?"

Daniel trembled. He scarcely heard her or even knew what her words meant. He walked back around to the front of the house and spoke to himself under his breath, saying "Red calf, red calf, where do you roam? Go into the pasture and then come home." He tried to recall where the rhyme had come from but could not.

"Snakes," Hazel Agnes called out as he came near the house.

"Snakes?" Daniel said, turning.

"It's snaky, son, be careful," she said. "You don't want to get snakebit out here."

He nodded and climbed up onto the porch, which sagged from his weight. He had to step over the broken boards. At one point, he accidentally kicked a beer can, and it went skittering over the edge into the tall weeds. The front door was gone, and he could look into what had been the front hall of the "shotgun" house. He saw broken glass and some old blankets and newspapers, and he stepped over the gaps in the floor and hopped inside.

The windows were all broken, and the frames lay in shards on the floor. His feet crunched broken glass and dirt as he walked into the front room, and a mouse waddled from one corner to another and disappeared into a crack behind the fireplace. Daniel smiled. Mice scurried all over Oconee Hill, and he talked to mice as he talked to the people who lay there beneath the stones. He walked through the door into another room, and in this one he saw dozens of beer cans and another crusted blanket. He heard the word "Bunny" in his head, and so he said it out loud and then sang the rhyme again about his little red calf. What had happened to that calf? He whispered Toggle's name.

The kitchen adjoined this room, added on to the back of the house, and Daniel walked into it now. The ceiling had caved in, and birds lilted in secret circles around their nests. An old stove had fallen through the floor, its burners peeking above the ruined boards. The sink had fallen through the back wall and lay half outside. The bottom of the sink was full of straw, and Daniel thought of the Scarecrow in *The Wizard of Oz*, which he had seen each year at Greenvale. When he was a boy, he only nodded gravely when Mr. Wilkins said there was no such thing as witches, but he believed in them until he was perhaps fifteen, believed in thunderstorms and miracles. He walked back into the room that adjoined the kitchen and came into the hall.

He walked toward the bedroom across the hall and as he did, he saw the silhouette of Hazel Agnes in front of the house, looking in at him. He came into the bedroom. He felt his throat swelling shut. He was afraid. He whispered furiously. The room was empty except for a few newspapers and two or three wine bottles, and the sunlight spread across the floor in a puddle from the open space where the window had been.

"REST, FOR THE SHADOW AND THE GLOOM OF DEATH IS PASSED," Daniel said ... *Wallace, don't!* ... he thought. His heart was beating faster than a bird's. He walked into the front bedroom that adjoined this one, and he was cold, freezing, breathing hard and trembling. He was so cold.

The bricks had begun to fall back down the chimney and they spread across the breaking floorboards. The mantel was still in place, and on it was a gun, and Daniel stepped over the bricks and reached up and took the gun and read slowly along its heavy handle. He read it out loud: Roy Rogers. Was he the man who healed people on television? Daisy Saye watched Roy Rogers from his temple every Sunday, and he healed people.

The room was full of people. There were women, and they pulled Daniel to them, pulled him into their fragrant skirts, and someone was crying, and he remembered the night before, how he was lying in his bed holding on to … yes, a teddy bear. He stood in the room, unmoving.

Outside, Hazel Agnes felt as if she might faint. She called Daniel half-heartedly, but he did not answer. She moved halfway across the yard and saw him suspended in the room, eyes almost closed.

I am lying in my bed, he thought, *and I can hear crickets through the trees, and I can hum "Jesus Loves Me," and tomorrow I will play with the little metal soldiers. No,* he thought, *they are Robin Hood men. Yes, …, yes.*

Now I hear the twigs breaking outside. Somebody is walking, but my Daddy is not here, he is traveling. Somebody is walking. I sit up and listen, but I am not afraid because this is my house, and my mother is here, and she will protect me. My mother is…

Daniel wept.

He opened the door to the closet in the room, and the door fell off the hinges, and he held it and leaned it against the wall. *I hear the sounds of screaming!* He jumped across the broken floorboards into the closet and squatted down. He put his ear to the wall and listened and he could hear the screaming coming from his mother's bedroom; his mother was screaming. The man from outside was hurting her. *Jesus, Jesus, Jesus.* Daniel sang "Jesus Loves the Little Children" at the top of his lungs, choking and crying.

Outside, Hazel Agnes groaned in horror. She fell to her knees and began to weep.

Daniel stopped singing and listened at the wall. His mother was crying. He could hear it. She was shouting—

Wallace, don't! Wallace, don't!

Daniel came out of the closet from his crouch like a bird exploded upward.

"Wallace, don't!" he screamed. He screamed it again and again. He heard the sound of a gunshot, then another. He kept on screaming.

Hazel Agnes scrambled to her feet, praying and cursing and crying, and she ran back toward the road, stepped across the ditch and got into the car. She put her hands over her ears and tried to block out the sounds of his shouting, but he would not stop. She started the car and waited for a few seconds and then put it in drive and floored the accelerator.

Daniel lay on the floor, sobbing.

Wearily he raised himself up on toddler's legs and walked back into the other bedroom. He could see blood in the bed, blood leaking from the old sheets, and it ran across the smooth pine floorboards, coming toward him.

"Wallace, don't!" he cried.

"Wallace, don't!" The blood was a snake, and it was twisting toward him across the smooth pine floorboards. He watched it come past the dark knots, a river with a swollen, taut surface, and it was the dark red in the Crayola box.

"Mommy, don't!"

The snake got to his feet, and it began to crawl up his leg, wet and warm. Daniel danced and shook uncontrollably. The snake filled his eyes and his mouth and his ears. Someone was trembling in the bed. He walked over to see who it was, and he looked into the covers.

"Mommy!" he screamed. "Mommy!" She was breathing hard and trembling, but the blood was a fountain coming from the man who lay beside her, and he was speaking blood, and the room was

230

full of smoke and coughing, and the man sat halfway up and blood was everywhere. He slowly began to fall back while looking around in horror and pity, begging for something. He reached out for Daniel as he fell, and Daniel reached back, but blood was on the man's hand, and as he grasped Daniel, their hands slid apart like a train uncoupling, inexorable. The man fell away into the red sheets and he did not move, and the woman, his mother, screamed and screamed and screamed.

"Oh, Hazel, how could you do this to me?" a man's voice asked.

Daniel looked, and it was Hazel Agnes in the bed, and she was very young and beautiful, and she had no clothes on, and her breasts were wet with blood and tears. Daniel backed away and realized he was still holding the Roy Rogers gun, and he knew that he had killed the man next to Hazel Agnes, and he screamed and screamed, hunched over, until with all the force in his strong arms, he threw the gun against the wall. A section of plaster crashed to the floor, and when it did, Daniel slid away from the horror and found himself in a silent, sunny room. The bed was gone and so were the people. He blinked and stumbled toward the front door, feeling sick and tired. *Red calf, red calf* ... he tried to remember the rhyme but it would not come. He went out on the porch and jumped from it into the yard.

A lizard pumped past in the dirt, all elbows. Daniel looked for Hazel Agnes but he saw that she was gone, saw that the car had disappeared. The maze of confusion seemed to straighten in his mind: he almost knew who she was, why she had brought him here, even where she had gone. He fell to his knees.

"Oh, Hazel Agnes," he cried.

He curled into a fetal ball and felt the cool dirt against his cheek. He sang and rocked and hugged his knees to his cheek, and then he slept. He did not dream.

He slept for hours, and when he awoke, dusk was settling over the countryside, and he sat up and felt very happy and strong. The light had fled into the treetops, and so he walked around the house, thinking how much he wanted a glass of cold water. He came to a rusted barbed wire fence and climbed over it easily, walked around the new pines and came up the slope into the field where the cattle still stood. They ate silently.

The world was like a hymn. He could live forever or die right now. He got to the top of the hill, and the setting sun was a ball of fire in his eyes, lovely and hopeful. He saw that the hill sloped away toward a row of trees and a creek. He walked toward it in the short grass, his feet steady, kicking up small rocks and watching them tumble down the way.

He found a cowpath and walked along it. He swung his arms in huge loops and sang the red calf rhyme. He got to the creek, it was wide and full, and it said "Hushhhhh." Daniel fell to his knees and sipped the cool water, and it felt so good that he slowly stripped his clothes off and waded into the middle where it was three feet deep. There he lay among the stones and bathed in the creek.

He lay on his back and half-floated in the current and looked through the canopy of trees overhead and saw a hawk come whistling past. Woodrow Faust would love to come here and fish with his cane pole, Daniel thought. He lay on his back until he felt cold, and lightning bugs started to come out. They always flew as if they were swimming in the air, he thought; why did they do that? Did everything with wings swim in the air? A fish's wings were too small to rise into the air. He thought about a fish flying in the air, pumping its fins, and he laughed as he dressed.

Daniel walked to the top of the hill and saw that the ball of sun was half-gone. He had to be getting home. His mother would be worried half to death.

NINETEEN

RACHEL BENJAMIN MIGHT AS WELL HAVE BEEN IN THE CAR with Rebecca Gentry and Annie Phillips as they headed east toward Greenvale. Rachel's voice droned on the tape deck, weary and hopeful, and Rebecca remembered how Rachel's eyes had brightened when she spoke of Lawrence Dale.

"When I die, I don't care what happens to my body or soul, if there is such a thing," Rachel had said.

Rebecca remembered what had happened next.

"Because those first few months, when he'd call, and then, a few hours later, I'd see Larry's old car crawling into the driveway, I felt as strong as God. That sounds strange, but that is so very true. He loved me the way he loved everything he loved: transcendently and without restraint."

Rachel had blushed slightly and then smiled.

"We would sit here in this room with candles burning, and he could recite poetry for hours. My God, hardly anyone in the world can do that anymore, but he grew up so isolated over there that he had read nearly everything and memorized it for the sheer joy. All of Keats's Odes, Byron, Shakespeare, Whitman—he could go for hours and hours with me. He had the most beautiful reciting voice. And you know what? When he would get around other people he was so painfully shy that it was almost unbearable to watch.

"He loved hummingbirds and would watch them in my garden for hours at a time, and he loved everything about nature. We went down to the Chattooga one time after two days of hard rain and sat huddled next to the river and watched it rage against the rocks. It did something to him, moved him to another world. He straddled this world and an invisible one of feeling and love, and when we were in this world, I ached for him, but when we were in that other world, our love was as nothing this world has ever seen."

The tape ended and ejected itself, and Rebecca turned it off.

"It's almost unbearable to listen to," said Annie. She wore a white summery dress with blue piping around the neck, and her blonde hair was soft on her shoulders. "What if she's making all this up? As a biographer, how do you deal with the possibility that people tell you lies?"

"I don't know what I'll do. Probably jump off Black Rock Mountain head first."

"You do seem to have grown idiotically impulsive this summer," said Annie.

"I'm glad you're feeling better," said Rebecca. "I always know you're better when you get abusive again. What's happening with Brad?"

"Oh, I'm making him feel like hell," she said, "but I think he really misses me. He sent me a dozen red roses yesterday at home."

"God, you're kidding," Rebecca said.

"No," Annie grinned. She leaned back and put her hands behind her head and let the breeze blow on her arms. "I tore each petal off one by one and made a big pile in the middle of the bed and then lay in them, naked."

"You did not," said Rebecca.

"No," Annie said, "but it sounded good, didn't it? I bet old Rachel did that every day."

"Come on, don't make fun of her," Rebecca said.

"I'm sorry," Annie said. "I'm just tired of being miserable. Misery begets death. Write that down for something. I'll give it to you for nothing."

Earlier that day, Rebecca had told Annie about Daniel, and how she was driving to Augusta to see if anyone at Greenvale might know something about his family. She did not know what to think of him: would he be back at Oconee Hill that afternoon or was he lost again? Had he been kidnapped? It didn't seem likely that an old woman could harm him. But everything harmed Daniel, every part of the world, and Rebecca, too, had harmed him, and she knew it. She had been overwhelmed with an urge to know more about him, and there was only one place.

She would call Frank Sutton from Greenvale to see if Daniel had shown up. There seemed no point in calling the police until he had been gone for a day.

As she drove, Rebecca thought of the things she loved: her lost father, her dead mother, Dairy Queen ice cream cones, Beethoven, Van Gogh, autumn nights, a man's sleeping breath at night, innocence. She thought of Buddy Caskoden and how she had lost her innocence in the eleventh grade, how she had cried all night. Sometimes she still felt as if a part of her soul had been lost that night in the back seat of Buddy's Bel Air. She loved light and darkness and rain and the way sun feels the first few days of spring. She loved a good argument, and sometimes she loved to be out of control with happiness or anger or sadness. But mostly, she loved constancy, dreamed of it, prayed for it, for something unchanging as the rotation of the seasons and the days.

They listened to the radio and talked about small things, only a little about Daniel, until Rebecca's MG rolled through the gates of Greenvale and along the driveway that cut through the spacious, neatly clipped lawns. Clouds blew swiftly across the sun, and shadows dashed on the lawn, making some patches a darker green than others. Rebecca felt her heart begin to beat too quickly.

She stopped in front of the administration building. She knew from Daniel that in late summer all the children went home. Except

Daniel had always stayed because Greenvale was his home. They got out and stood in the heavy shade of the oaks and looked up at the building.

"Sick sense of déjà vú," Annie said.

"You're weird," Rebecca whispered.

They walked up the steps and stood before the dark screen door. Rebecca rang the bell, and a cool chime sounded far down the hall. For a moment the only sound was the whish of the leaves high in the oaks. Then a door opened in the back and footsteps sounded on the shiny wooden boards of the hall. A man walked slowly toward them and came out on the porch.

"Good afternoon," he said. He wore black trousers with creases sharp enough to cut paper, black shoes and an open-collared white shirt. His breast pocket drooped with an assortment of ink pens and Magic Markers. "I'm Norman Baldwin, superintendent of the school. Can I be of service to you ladies?"

He was about forty, soft and round, and his pale eyes strained from behind thick glasses. He worked his hands together as if he were wringing out a dishcloth. He looked as if he had just shaved, and the faint, repugnant odor of inexpensive aftershave hung over him. He reminded Annie of a funeral director.

"I'm Rebecca Gentry, this is my friend Annie Phillips," Rebecca said. They shook hands, and Baldwin's heavy palm was damp and very soft. "We came down earlier this summer and got Daniel Mitchell. He is a friend of ours. We, uh, help him, sort of, up in Athens."

"Lewis Wilkins told me about you," Baldwin said. "Would you like to come inside?"

"Mrs. Gilbert!" he shouted, and the woman who had waited on Mr. Wilkins shuttled down the hall. "Please get us three lemonades. Is lemonade all right with you ladies?"

"Fine," they said.

They went into the parlor on the left of the hall and the heavy Victorian furniture squatted massively. Annie and Rebecca sat on a magenta sofa, and Baldwin settled into a wing chair facing them.

236

"You know Lewis is very ill."

"I saw him," Rebecca said. "I talked to his sister. She was with him."

"Stepsister, actually," Baldwin sniffed. "Lewis never could abide the woman, but she's all he has left now that his wife is gone. Is there a problem with Daniel?"

Rebecca sighed heavily. "I don't really know," she said. "He left his work this morning with a woman, an older woman, and nobody knows where he went. This is probably crazy, but...."

Mrs. Gilbert came into the room with three sweating glasses of lemonade on silver tray. She served Baldwin first and then the two ladies, and he seemed very satisfied.

"This is the real thing," said Baldwin, taking a large sip and nodding approvingly. "I can't abide the idea of pink lemonade. What a bizarre thing, to drink something pink. You were saying?"

Mrs. Gilbert's footsteps receded down the hall.

"Mr. Wilkins told me something of Daniel's background, and I was wondering if there was any way we could be considered like his guardians or something and find out some more information that would help us deal with him. Maybe you might know something about who that woman was."

"Oh, heavens," Baldwin said, taking another sip and finding it to his liking. "I can't do that. Our records are all confidential. The State would be in here like a duck on a junebug. Don't you think you're overreacting about Daniel going for a ride with somebody? If he's your friend, you know what he's like. I've only been here a few years, so I was here only a year before he moved up to Athens. Didn't know him well myself, but Wilkins always was terrifically fond of the boy. You must understand why we can't give you any information about our clients, present, past or future. My God, the State. Lord." He chuckled deep in his throat and shook his head as if he had successfully parried a serious threat.

"So there's nothing you can tell us about him, not a thing?" asked Rebecca icily.

"Oh well, I mean he was a decent boy, not nearly so handicapped as some of the other children here, but beyond that, I don't see much of help that I could offer," Baldwin said. He drained the glass and held it gently in his fat fingers. "The State—you see, the State just won't let us release any of that information, Miss Renfroe."

"Gentry," said Rebecca.

"Miss Gentry, sorry," he said. He chuckled again and shook his head. "You have no idea how strict the regulations are these days. I really do wish I could help you."

Rebecca stared at him for a full three seconds and stood and placed her glass on the heavy coffee table between them. Annie did the same thing, and they walked into the hall and through the screen door and onto the porch.

"It's been an education," Rebecca said coldly. "I'm glad you always put the best interests of the children first, Mr. Baldman."

"Baldwin," he said, daintily.

Rebecca and Annie started down the stairs.

"By the way, I heard that Lewis is just a vegetable. What did you think of his condition, Miss Gentry?"

Rebecca did not turn around or respond, and she walked past her car and toward the beautifully manicured campus in front of the administration building. Annie heard the front door slam, and she turned and saw that Baldwin had gone back inside.

"He's gone," she said.

"That jerk," Rebecca exploded. "That stupid jerk!"

"He'll hear you," said Annie.

"The hell with him!" Rebecca shouted. "Who in the hell does he think he is?"

"He's just a bureaucratic asshole," soothed Annie. "You should have known what we'd find here."

"Wilkins would have told us the truth," said Rebecca. "He already told us the truth the last time. I don't need Baldwin's lies." She gestured angrily toward the administration building. They walked slowly toward the trees, and Rebecca was trying to breathe deeply when they both saw, at the same time, Mrs. Gilbert standing

238

behind a century-old oak, her hands on her hips, staring gloomily at them.

They stared at each other for a moment, and when she didn't move, they went over to her. She seemed to be hiding, probably from the disapproving glance of Norman Baldwin.

"I know this is childish, hiding behind a tree," Mrs. Gilbert said. "But I wanted to tell you something, since he wasn't going to tell you." She was short and stout, wore an old brown dress over which was neatly tied a blue square-cut apron.

"About what?" asked Rebecca.

"About Daniel," said Mrs. Gilbert. "I do know one thing. I heard Mr. Wilkins mention it one time when he and Baldwin were talking. He said Daniel was from Hudson County, just south of McDuffie. County seat's named Milford."

"I know where it is," Annie said. "We used to play them in football back home."

"Please don't ever let on I told you," Mrs. Gilbert drawled, and she walked back toward the Administration Building, going from tree to tree. Rebecca and Annie walked on ahead for a few paces before swinging away and back toward the car.

"She looks like a Pepe le Pew cartoon," Annie said.

"How far is Milford from here?" asked Rebecca, still angry.

"Maybe an hour or so," said Annie. "I had an aunt and uncle who lived there a few years back, in the early Sixties, and it's sort of a mill town, extremely poor, mostly black, lots of slash pines and one big paper mill that keeps everything stinking all the time. Not much of a place."

"You know how to get there?" Rebecca asked.

"It'll come to me," said Annie.

They drove beneath a cloudless sky, and it was still hot, but not so brutally hot as it had been much of the summer. The secondary roads revealed lush pastures with many Holsteins and Angus, houses that were little more than shacks and great sprawling brick ranch-style homes in the middle of treeless fields. Rebecca could never understand why so many southerners built houses where there were no trees. She and Annie talked in small bursts, about Charlie Dominic and Brad, for a moment about Daniel, then about Annie's father, who was "about the same," she said.

Rebecca turned on the tape of Rachel Benjamin once again, but she turned it off after only two or three seconds and made a gesture to say that she could not bear to listen to it just then.

Annie's description of Milford had underestimated its poverty. In the years since she had seen the town, the paper mill had closed its doors, and now the population had dwindled to only about twelve hundred, and the buildings had the look of inevitable decay. The town proper was laid in what had once been a square, but on the east side, the structures had been razed and a new parking lot, from which waves of heat rose, had been paved. A black barber in a white coat sat in a chair in front of his shop listening to the radio; nobody seemed interested in a haircut. Perhaps forty people could be seen on the sidewalks but they might have been milling, going no place in particular. The glass front of another shop had "Sew What" painted crudely, with quotation marks around the words, as if that somehow made the business more unusual. Rebecca saw a drugstore, a hardware store, and a service station that seemed almost abandoned.

She drove through town, through its single light, and in less than a minute found herself back in the country, where poor stands of corn were dying in the fields. She pulled into the first driveway and turned around and headed back toward town.

"I guess we're out of greater metropolitan Milford," Rebecca said. "Jesus."

As they came back into Milford, the barber had not moved, and a grizzled white man was walking slowly in front of the service station, holding a tire tool and staring at it. He seemed to be surprised it was there. Rebecca parked in front of the Milford Pharmacy, and a very fat boy wearing polyester trousers and a shirt that hung loose came into the heat from the pharmacy, licking a chocolate ice cream cone that was melting quickly. They got out and stood on the old sidewalk, which was laid in concrete octagons that

240

had cracked and worn over the years.

"Did y'all beat Milford in football?" Rebecca asked in disbelief. "God, this looks like the end of the world."

"How would I know?" asked Annie. "I was in the band. I didn't pay any attention to what was happening on the field."

"Great," said Rebecca. She looked at the plate glass front of the pharmacy and saw their reflection, and noticed how different they were, how obvious it was they were strangers. "You want a Coke?"

"I want a gallon of Coke," Annie said. "Classic Coke. You don't drink New Coke, do you?"

"I'd die first," said Rebecca.

They opened the front door and went in, and they saw that it had probably changed little in the past thirty years, that a heavy burnished mahogany bar ran the length of one wall, and behind it were old photos and posters tacked to a beveled-glass mirror. Display cases went to the ceiling completely around the room, which was still except for the whirring of four ceiling fans. The ceiling was metal, but painted white, and the paint was shrinking and cracking everywhere. A black woman in a black-and-white polka dot dress sat alone at the counter, wearing white gloves and sipping a Coke through a straw. An older black man wearing an open white shirt stood behind the counter, fiddling with a balky milk shake machine that seemed to have him completely baffled.

Rebecca and Annie sat at the counter, and the man set a handful of spare parts on a paper towel and turned to them.

"What can I get you?" he asked, smiling slightly. His voice was deep, resonant, reminding Annie of the Jamaican actor Geoffrey Holder.

"Two big Cokes with lots of ice," said Rebecca.

"Anything else?" he asked hopefully. There was a sound in back, and Annie turned and saw a black man holding up a pill bottle to the light in what must have been the pharmacy section of the store. "We got some good pecan pie today. My wife made it."

"It taste like God hisself cooked it," said the woman in the polka dot dress. "Miss Milly, she cook the best pie in Milford."

"Not for me," said Annie. Rebecca held up her hands; no, she said, me neither.

"Well then," the man said, and he took two glasses from a glass shelf attached to one side of the mirror, scooped ice into them and filled them with Coke from the fountain. "Here you go. That'll be one dollar."

Rebecca fished it from her purse and handed it to him.

"Where you folks from?"

"Athens," Rebecca said.

"Nice place," he said. "You all lost?"

"Actually, we're looking for somebody," Rebecca said.

"Who for?" The woman on the other stool swiveled slightly to her left so she could hear.

"A young man named Daniel Mitchell," Rebecca said. She looked at her reflection in the mirror, at the entire store backwards; then she realized she was staring at an old newspaper photo of Franklin Roosevelt that had been pasted up there probably fifty years before. "He hasn't lived here in years but he did when he was a little boy. He's a little, well, retarded, and wanders off sometimes. Oh, he's completely harmless, but I had this idea he might have come down this way."

"Mitchell, you say?" the man asked. He wiped his hands on his apron and looked down. "Were they white or black?"

"White," said Annie.

"Oh, then that'd be hard," he said. "Few white people in Milford anymore at all, haven't been since the mill shut in seventy-four. They weren't but maybe seventy here then, and family by family, they just about all left."

"This would have been before then," Rebecca said.

"Miss Hattie, you recollect any Mitchell family hereabouts?" he asked.

The woman on the stool was delighted to be asked.

"Mitchell, Mitchell," she said, "now lets me think here. No, I do not believe I knows any Mitchell family was ever in Milford for the past forty years or so."

"I've heard there was a shooting involving his family," said Rebecca.

"Ma'am, that don't narrow it down much in a place where half the folks are out of work," the man said. "Folks always find a way to buy a gun and a drink."

"They does," the woman nodded.

"Do you have a newspaper office where we could look through back issues?" asked Annie.

"Had a newspaper once," the man said. "But it closed down even before the mill left. Called the *Milford Messenger*. Man who owned it was with the Klan."

"Terrible man," whispered the woman in the polka dot dress.

"So there's nobody who might know?" asked Rebecca. The man rocked back on his heels and put his fingers to his mouth and thought as he walked back to the milk shake machine.

"Not as I know," he said.

"Miss Bella Jones work for lots of white folks," the woman said. "She be ninety years old and still clear as a bell. Miss Bella Jones might tell you something."

"Would she talk with us?" asked Rebecca.

"I go with you," the woman said, sliding her huge bottom from the stool. "I Miss Hattie Jaynes. If you give me a ride I show you."

"Oh," said Rebecca. "My car only has two seats."

"My nephew gots a car like that," Hattie said. "He haul stuff where the back seats was."

"This car doesn't even have a back seat, never did," said Rebecca.

"It's a sports car, Miss Hattie." The man grinned, pointing through the window out front.

"My word," she said. "Well, I'll be. I can walk, then. It just two blocks. You drive down that way two blocks and turn on Jefferson Street, and it be the third house on the left. She gots big bunches of geraniums all over the yard."

"Great," said Rebecca.

In fifteen minutes, they left and drove slowly down the street. A pulpwood truck rumbled past, blowing wood chips like a snow flurry. Rebecca turned on Jefferson Street and soon saw Bella Jones's house. Hattie sat on the porch, fanning herself, still wearing the white gloves. Rebecca parked on the street, and she and Annie walked on neatly laid flagstones to the shady porch with the ancient black woman.

"Miss Bella, this the ladies I told you about," said Hattie.

"Hello," Bella said in an unexpectedly high and thin voice. "Y'all come on up and sit down."

Her voice sounded like a little girl's, Annie thought. They sat in rocking chairs that had recently been recaned with strips of white oak.

"Y'all want something to drink? Some iced tea?"

"No thanks," Rebecca said. "We just wondered if you might know something about a white family that lived here years ago, a family named Mitchell."

"Mitchum?" she asked, squinting her eyes.

"Mitchell!" Hattie screamed in her ear. Bella nodded and seemed to be thinking.

"They was colored?" Bella asked.

"White folks, Miss Bella!" shouted Hattie.

"White folks," Bella nodded. She rocked and cocked her head and then stopped rocking.

"There might have been a shooting involved with the family," Rebecca said very loud.

"Shoeing?" Bella asked. "Horseshoer named Mitchum?" She turned to Hattie for a translation.

"Shooting, Miss Bella!" Hattie screamed.

Annie had her hand over her mouth to keep from giggling out loud.

"A white family named Mitchell that had a shooting."

Miss Bella started rocking again and stared at a spot in the yard. She stopped again abruptly. "I had me a horse when I was fifteen year old," she said. "Maybe Mr. Mitchum done shoed him, but I never heard he shot nobody."

Hattie grinned helplessly. "Miss Bella's a little more feeble than I thought," she shrugged. "Sorry I asked you to come down here."

Rebecca and Annie stood up. They shook hands with the old woman, who was distraught they were leaving so soon. Hattie walked with them back to the car.

"Is there a motel anywhere near here?" asked Rebecca.

"In Milford?" asked Hattie. "They's one on the interstate back up near Thomson closest, near to twenty mile."

"Thanks a lot," said Annie. They drove back north, passing farmhouses and fields, and Rebecca wondered as she saw them if Daniel and Hazel Agnes might be there. She wondered, too, if Daniel were on his knees in Oconee Hill, pulling weeds and whispering kind words to the dead.

TWENTY

AT FIRST, DANIEL HAD CRIED, BUT HE SOON FELT A POWERFUL need to escape. Night had been swelling into the fields as he walked home, and the birds of darkness were beginning to hunt. Bats banked low and then rose, wobbly and veering, as if they might crash any moment. He had climbed across the barbed-wire fence and half expected to head for the cheerful glow of his house, back into childhood and forever into his innocence. He held his breath so the idea that he was coming home might stay. But when he let the breath go, he saw the moonwashed hulk of the house, dark and silent.

He had walked slowly around the house. It was much darker in the shadows. His boot caught a trailing vine and he fell heavily in a bower of honeysuckle. He lay still. Once he had come after nightfall to Oconee Hill and had lain on a new grave in the luxury of flowers and smelled their scent and talked to the dead, an old woman named Magda. He had lain there for five minutes and thought of Magda, how he had pictured her whispering from the narrow vault.

He stood up and brushed himself off and went around to the front of the house—to the gap-toothed banister, the porch where he had played on rainy summer days as a child of two. He wanted to call out, to clap. He had climbed on the porch again and walked through the house as mourning doves cried in the trees.

He was walking now. He walked along the dirt road, hungry and exhausted, listening to the raucous buzz of cicadas, the drumming of toads and the idle cries of the owl. *Where have I been?* Something ran across the road in front of him: a possum or a sluggish dog, down the embankment and into the woods. *What am I doing here?* He thought of the possum and remembered their sharp rows of teeth, how they could snarl and rip. He thought of dogs, and he thought of Toggle. *Toggle was dead.*

He thought of Hazel Agnes and wondered where she had been, and why she had come for him and then left him out here. He thought of being alive, and he thought of being dead, and he knew that death was peace, death was a hill of flowers beneath shade trees.

He thought of many things, but he was hungry and exhausted, and when he saw a house glowing with cheerful yellow lights, he walked across its yard toward the front door. A yappy dog came from under the porch and started barking hysterically, and Daniel stopped and took off his hat as if to greet it. A man holding a shotgun came on to the porch after he had turned the light on, and he aimed it at Daniel.

"What you want?" he asked.

Daniel could see him, a heavy-set black man wearing a sleeveless undershirt and drooping brown trousers.

"I am lost," Daniel said. "I am hungry. I have had a hard time."

"You stay there or I blow you to kingdom come," the man said. "How come you wandrin' out here in the middle of the country? You excaped from prison?"

"Prison?" said Daniel.

"They another one of you out there?" the man asked. He peered into the darkness suspiciously. "You think you gone rob me, they ain't nothing here. You try it, I take two of you out dead cold."

248

"I am lost and hungry," Daniel said in a small voice. He began to push the knowing away, he found he knew how to do it. He had always been pushing the knowing away, into that secret place in his head where the hurt went. If he would push the knowing away, the hurt would drain out of him like water down the bathtub drain. He could not be hurt if he pushed the knowing away. Daniel fell to his knees and began to cry piteously. The man lowered his gun, and a woman came on to the porch, then a younger woman who was their daughter. They stood in the buggy light wondering softly who this stranger might be.

Daniel held his hands in front of his chest, clasped together, and pushed the knowing away. It did not want to go away, and he cried harder, and thought of flowers and the sun, and nothing beyond what he could reach with his thick fingers. The older woman and the man argued, and Daniel heard them as if they were at the bottom of a dry well, far away but rising. When her hand touched his shoulder, the knowing had gone away, and Daniel did not remember; he never remembered just when the knowing went away. He raised his face and felt happier than he had ever been.

"You ain't no excaped convict," the woman said.

"He cut you throat," the man muttered, still holding the shotgun at arm's length.

"Papa, be nice," the younger girl said.

The older woman helped Daniel up, and the man came and searched him for a weapon but found only a small, smooth stone that Daniel had picked up while swimming in the creek. They helped him up the porch, which sagged beneath their weight, and into the house.

The front room was happy and filled with the smell of turnip greens and fried ham. Old blankets were thrown over the furniture, and Daniel sank into a sofa, trying to smile but feeling bewildered. They brought him water in a Smurf glass, and he drank it quickly and looked at a Smurf who was saying he hated music. He sat on the sofa and held his baseball cap in his lap, looking ridiculous, almost as if he had come to call on the daughter of the family.

The man and woman were in the back of the house arguing while she scuttled to and fro carrying dishes. The daughter sat in a chair across from Daniel and looked at him curiously. She was fourteen and very beautiful, skin clear and a rich chocolate, full lips and black eyes with a sheen that was full of light. She wore an old cotton dress. She held the shotgun across her lap, finger outside the trigger guard, and watched Daniel. He tried to smile.

"I am Daniel Mitchell," he said. "I know a bird that sits on flowers."

"My name Odessa," she giggled, showing two rows of fine teeth and too much pink gum. "My Daddy tell me you come at me I blow you brain out. I do it, too."

"Hello, Odessa," he smiled as if he had heard nothing about the gun. "I am lost and very hungry. I was where the little red calf once lived, and Hazel Agnes left me, so I swam in the creek and saw a hawk."

"What you say?" She grinned.

Daniel grinned too, and mimicked her: "What you say?"

She giggled again and looked at him. His clothes stank and were filthy, and he needed a shave, and his face was cut and swollen. "You sure one big mess. How come you to get lost? You a dummy?"

Daniel considered this; Wade Rucker had said he was a dummy, too, so that was true.

"I think I am, Odessa," he said, nodding. "Wade says I am a dummy, in addition to."

That didn't sound right, but he shrugged and she giggled again. The woman came back into the room, wiping her hands on her apron. In the light, Daniel could see she had once been as beautiful as Odessa. Hard work and too much rich food had left her squat and her eyes lined. The man came around her then and took the shotgun from Odessa and held it pointing at the floor. The room was silent for a moment, and Daniel's stomach growled fearfully.

Odessa laughed. "He say he a dummy," she said.

"I am a dummy," Daniel said, mugging and making a face just like the ones he'd seen Rebecca make in her office. "I am a hungry dummy."

The woman, whose name was Iris, smiled in spite of her discomfort. The man snorted unhappily. His name was Rafe.

"It our Christian duty to give you food," Iris said. "Are you hungry, son?"

"Oh, am I hungry!" Daniel cried out. He stood up and began to clap, and Rafe leveled the shotgun at him.

"Put that down, Daddy!" Odessa shouted. "He don't mean nothing. Just leave him alone."

She took his arm and guided him through a bedroom and back into the kitchen, which ran the length of the house in back and smelled wonderful. A small wooden table was in the middle of the room, covered with a plastic red-and-white checkered tablecloth. On the table, there was a napkin holder with pictures of Jesus on the sides, flanked by shakers of salt and pepper and a jar of hot pepper sauce.

A place had been set for him, a glass of tea poured. Odessa pulled the chair out and offered him a seat. Daniel sat down and took a sip of the cold sweet tea. Iris had put a napkin beside the place setting, and Daniel took it as they had taught him at Greenvale—unfolded it and laid it carefully in his lap.

Rafe stood in the doorway holding the gun and glowering. Daniel could hear a television in another room as Iris set a plate in front of him mounded with fried potatoes, turnip greens, field peas and a single greasy pork chop. Daniel stared at the food and remembered. He folded his hands under his chin and closed his eyes.

"Baby Jesus bless this food, keep us on the way," he chanted, "show us what is right and good and give us peace today. Amen."

"Amen," said Iris.

Odessa sat across the table from him and watched in fascination as Daniel ate like a man who had been away from food for a million years. His hands trembled at first, and he ate too quickly, but then he felt better and slowed down. Rafe came sullenly into the room and set the gun in the corner. Iris sat in another chair at the table and watched Daniel eat. After a while, she asked, "Where you from, and what you doing here?"

"I am Daniel Mitchell," he said. "I am afraid I smell bad."

"You sure does." Odessa giggled. "Lord a mercy."

"But what you doing here?" Iris asked.

Rafe had worked at the sawmill all day and was exhausted, and he did not want some lost white man in his house. Still, he was curious about Daniel, too.

"Hazel Agnes brought me forth into the wilderness," Daniel said to Iris. He stopped. Was that from the Bible? It sounded like it was from the Bible.

"Who is Hazel Agnes and where she go?" Iris asked.

Rafe took a beer from the refrigerator and sat down at the table, no longer very worried about Daniel. Something in his eyes. He decided he was no threat to anybody.

"She is an old lady who took me where I had the little red calf," he said. "I was a little boy, and I had metal Robin Hood men." He was surprised to remember them, and he stopped and stared at his plate and saw himself as a child in the dusty yard.

"But where that place be, and why she leave you?" Iris asked.

Daniel stopped thinking about his Robin Hood men and cleaned his plate and shrugged, trying to think, but the knowing had gone very far away. He was happy again. "What is your name?" he asked.

"Iris Mealor," she said. "That Rafe." Rafe grunted and nodded. "This Odessa."

"I know Odessa," he said. "I am Daniel Mitchell."

"How many time you gone tell us that?" asked Rafe.

"Leave him be, Daddy," Odessa said. "Where you from, Daniel?"

"I am from Athens," he said.

"Damn, you is lost," Rafe said.

"And this Hazel Agnes carried you down here?" she asked.

"I am very full now." Daniel smiled. "I am very tired. Do you have a place for me to sleep, Iris Mealor?"

"Hell no, we don't have no place for you to sleep," Rafe said.

"You can sleep in the glider on the porch," said Iris.

Rafe started to say something, but Iris cut him off with a glance that seemed frightening to Daniel. He might have been afraid, but already he was falling asleep.

"Odessa, go get you a sheet from the bathroom and you takes that sofa cushion out there for him." She turned back to Daniel. "In the morning, I call the sheriff, and we see can we get you back home."

"Thank you, Iris," he said. "Thank you, Rafe, thank you, Odessa."

"He probly gone slit our throats," Rafe said languidly, sipping his beer. "Don't nobody gone do nobody no good come out of the night."

"He just lost," Odessa said sweetly. Something about Daniel excited her.

They walked on to the porch. Cicadas buzzed high in the stalk-straight pines, and a bird cried from the power line that ran down the side of the road. Daniel sat on the glider and took off his shoes, and his socks smelled very bad, but he merely curled up, lay down. Odessa came running out and slipped the cushion beneath his head and threw out the sheet to cover him. A gust of cool air crossed the porch, and the sheet hung, billowed, for a moment, before settling on him. Iris had pressed it flat just that day, and it smelled wonderful. Daniel felt himself going into the enfolding warmth of sleep. He was gently snoring before Rafe went inside, muttering unhappily about throat slittings. For a moment, Odessa and Iris stood close to each other and looked at him.

"What you reckon wrong with him?" asked Odessa.

"I don't have no clue," Iris said. "He seem awful down on his luck and sad."

"I don't think he sad," Odessa said. "I just wants to hug him all over." Iris made a face and shook her head at Odessa. She had been born when Iris was sixteen, and already she was changing from a shy girl to a boy-struck young woman. Soon, she would leave with some boy, get pregnant and repeat the cycle of children and hard work that never seemed to end in Georgia.

"You be glad you Daddy don't hear you say that," Iris said.

"I bet you want to hug him all over," said Odessa.

Yes, thought Iris. I ain't never seen anybody in my life who need huggin' more than that man.

"You crazy, girl," she said.

They went inside, leaving the porchlight on, and for a long time, Odessa sat in the window, dressed in her thin cotton gown, and watched Daniel's face as he slept and dreamed. After midnight, they were all asleep, Iris huddled next to Rafe's familiar snoring warmth, Odessa in her room beneath a single sheet.

Daniel woke up after having slept for four hours and did not remember where he was. He sat up in the glider and thought about it. He could walk across the road and talk to Joe Dell and Irene Bailey. They could tell him why he was here. Randi Ambrose would have pink hair, and she would laugh at him, and he would laugh at her. He stood and slipped into his shoes and laced them up, and for a moment, he looked at the house and thought of a young girl, but when he looked back at the road, he saw that all the trailers had been moved, and he remembered Hazel Agnes and his house, and he remembered Odessa. She was very pretty.

He started walking down the road. He looked once over his shoulder at the house, and it seemed small, and he sang the red calf song and wondered what he was doing here. Since the cool front had gone through Georgia the night before, the sky was brilliantly clear and choked with stars. Daniel remembered Van Gogh first, and then he remembered Rebecca Gentry. Then he thought of Oconee Hill and his new apartment. He came to a field of cattle, and they all slept.

Why do cattle sleep without completely lying down? How far was it to the moon? What was dirt made of? Why did your voice come back sometimes when you shouted?

"Toggle!" Daniel shouted, and his voice came back, but only a little. He crossed the fence and got within a few yards of the cattle and sat down. Moonlight filled his mouth, his ears, came into his eyes. There was so much to know, he thought.

He lay down in the grass.

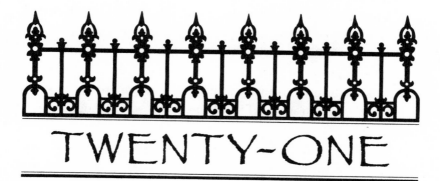

TWENTY-ONE

REBECCA AND ANNIE GOT BACK TO ATHENS ABOUT TEN, and Rebecca dropped Annie off. She called Frank Sutton from Annie's house; no one had heard from Daniel. Frank had already called the police again, but you had to wait twenty-four hours before filing a missing person's report. The police didn't seem very worried.

Rebecca could not relax, and she smoked continually, drank several glasses of wine, and listened again to the recording of her conversation with Rachel Benjamin. Everything seemed confused; who was the woman who had taken Daniel? There was no way to know. Was he in danger? He seemed like a boy at times, but he was really a strong man, and that didn't seem likely. Rebecca called the two women at Daniel's rooming house and tried to explain, and Miss Mae kept saying, "My, my."

Rachel Benjamin's words filled her apartment.

"One thing you must understand is that he was my friend first and my lover second," Rachel's tired voice said on the tape. "At least he saw it that way. If I had seen it his way, like a blood pact, I suppose I would have never betrayed Larry. That is the central fact of my life, Miss Gentry, that my life is veiled by my solitude. I could not actually believe it when I heard about it, you know." *Smiled gently here,* Rebecca scribbled in a notebook she held on her lap.

"Poets tell us death is merely a sleeping and awakening, a falling into another world. But I think death is the ultimate horror and evil, and I think at the moment of death, everything black and unfulfilled in your life rises. Then you are gone. I do not hope to see Larry in some next world. That was his great lie, you see, that we would be in groves of sweet shrubs and singing birds, that in the newer world, everything was beautiful, therefore true. He really believed Keats. You are an English professor, so you know what I mean."

"Why do you believe that about death?" Rebecca's voice asked. She had been sitting farther away from the tape recorder, and her voice sounded peculiarly lost and girl-like.

"Because Larry was brilliant and right about a great many things, but you have to understand he was raised in poverty," Rachel said. "The house where he was born is still standing down there in Newfield, and it's a shack up on the side of a mountain. It had a beautiful view but no indoor plumbing and no electricity, even long after the REA came through. On the other hand, I was born into luxury in Pittsburgh. A typical story, isn't it? Poor little rich girl or something? But it's a true story. I never wanted to die, Miss Gentry, because I never believed in some greater truth. My father believed in business, and my mother believed in my father. I studied literature because I pretended I believed in the greater truths. But I never did, not really."

"Do you now?" Rebecca's small voice asked. She shut off the tape recorder and looked out the wide glass window over Broad Street. It was silent in the glare of streetlamps. She was suddenly very tired, and she drained the last glass of burgundy and lay on the couch. Rachel had become tired not long after that and had ended the interview before she had ever explained how she actually betrayed Lawrence Dale. Come back in a couple of weeks, she had said, and I will be up to it, but not today. Rebecca had been terribly disappointed, but she had packed up the recorder, still wondering

258

what the old lady meant by betrayal. Rebecca slept, woke up troubled once, and then fell back asleep.

She awoke to the sound of bells. She sat up, her mouth dry, and she thought of sleighs; she had been dreaming of whiteness and some far northern winter, the kind of endless snows she imagined they had in Pittsburgh. The phone was ringing. Sunlight was streaming through the window, and she looked at her watch and saw that it was nearly ten. She got up and walked to the phone, wiping her eyes.

"Yes?" she asked.

"Miss Gentry?" a deep voice asked.

"Yes," she said. Her hands were shaking.

"This is Frank Sutton over at Oconee Hill," he said. "I got Daniel back."

"You do!" said Rebecca. She brushed the hair back from her face and looked, still unbelieving at the clock on the stove. "Did he just come back, or what?"

"Sheriff down in McDuffie County called me this morning about three, said he'd wandered into a little town called Milford and told them he worked up here, said he sounded confused. I drove down and got him."

"I was in Milford yesterday looking for him," said Rebecca. "Damn, I was right!"

"About what?" Frank asked wearily.

"Oh, nothing," she said. "Is he all right?"

"He's awful tired, and I tried to take him home, but we drove around, and he couldn't remember how to get there, and he said you'd know how to take him home. He's not in shape to work today, and I got a funeral at two. Any chance you could come get him and take him to his place?"

"I'll be there in twenty minutes," she said happily. "Is he talking about what happened to him?"

"He's not making sense anymore about much," sighed Frank. "He's trying to talk about the whole world all at once."

"I'll be there," she said.

"I'm mighty grateful," Frank said.

She hung up and ran for the shower and scrubbed with a bar of green soap. She dressed in jeans and a blue halter top and went out with her hair only toweled dry, shining wet in the thin sunlight. Already, clouds were building from the southeast, and a storm was swelling toward north Georgia from the coast.

When she drove through the gates she saw Daniel standing beneath the spreading water oak that shaded Frank's house. He had his hands in his pockets, and his Braves hat was too far down over his ears so they stuck out. To Rebecca he looked like a first grader waiting for the bus, uncertain, afraid. When he saw Rebecca's car, he waved and smiled, but as soon as she rolled to a stop, she could see how terrible he looked. He got in the car, and she could smell him, and his clothes were filthy, and his face was sandpapered with light red stubble.

"My God, Daniel," she said. "What are we going to do with you?"

"I do not know, Rebecca," he admitted. "You are so very beautiful. You are more beautiful than Odessa Mealor."

"Who?" asked Rebecca.

"You are not even the same color as Odessa or Iris," he said. He looked away from her straight through the windshield and snapped his head as if trying to dislodge a fly from his ear.

"Who was that woman who drove you down there, Daniel?"

"That was Hazel Agnes," he said. His eyes seemed glazed, and he was only barely pushing the knowing away now.

"Daniel, did you know her, did you remember her?"

"Oh, oh, oh," he cried, and he put his right hand over his eyes and held it tight. He was trembling all over. Rebecca reached for him, tried to pull his hand off his eyes.

"It's all right, Honey," she soothed. "It's all right, Honey. Honey, come on."

Daniel took his hands slowly from his eyes, and blinked at her, and then he reached out and traced the curve of her cheek as gently as any man who had ever loved her. He was forgetting, thinking

260

only of Rebecca now. Tears wandered down his cheeks.

"I am so very tired," he said.

"I'll get you home," she said.

She put the car in gear and drove through the gates and stopped at the edge of East Campus road to see if any traffic were coming. Daniel looked back over his shoulder at the graves of Oconee Hill and thought again how peaceful they all were, how they still spoke with each other. It was a park—like Oconee-by-the-River, a picnic, and the people beneath the soil lived forever.

"I love you," he said. He was staring at her and trying to smile, looking nearly deranged with his cap too far down on his ears and his hands neatly in his lap.

"Everybody loves *you*," Rebecca said, and she could see his face fall.

"I do not love everybody," he said. "Jesus says to love everybody, but I cannot love everybody. I only love Rebecca."

She could not speak. Her tongue was as heavy as a fist. Daniel put his hands over his ears and sang the red calf rhyme when he knew that she was not going to say she loved him, too. All summer he had loved her, had loved her eyes the color of winter skies, her hair and her voice. During all the sweltering summer he had thought of her as his girlfriend. Maybe they would get married like Joe Dell and Irene Bailey. He could lie with her and she would love him, and they would not be ashamed because they were in love.

"Daniel," she said. She tried to pull his left hand from his ear, and he let her and stopped singing about his red calf. "Oh, Daniel, please."

"I am so ashamed," he said, and he burst into tears.

Rebecca's hands were shaking on the wheel, and she pulled out onto East Campus Road, her mind barely working any longer. Poetry was supposed to come from deep feelings, from looking into the heart of experience and not blinking.

"Don't be ashamed," Rebecca begged him when they stopped at a light. She reached for his hand and took it. She felt its scratches and scabs. She looked at his hands, at his face, which was badly bruised; his neck and hands had abrasions too. "Love is the only thing worth having in this world, Daniel."

He inhaled sharply and tried to smile, to put her at ease. He did not want to make Rebecca feel bad.

"Today is my birthday," he said.

"It is?" said Rebecca. "How old are you?"

"Oh," he said, touching his lips with one finger. "I am wrong. I was born in January. Is that when Christmas comes?"

"Almost," she said. The knot in her throat would not release any more words. Mae Walters and Olga Salinger sat on the porch rocking. Miss Olga was reading from a slender volume called *Nightwood* by Djuna Barnes. As Rebecca walked up the steps with Daniel, they both stood and welcomed him back.

"Oh my word, look at you," whispered Miss Olga. She held the book against her withered breasts like a plate of armor. "What in the world happened to you, Daniel?"

"My word," echoed Miss Mae.

"He's had a bad time," said Rebecca. "But he's all right now." She took Daniel up the stairs and unlocked his door and took him inside. Since the last time she had been there, he had cut out pictures from magazines and taped them all over the walls, pictures of horses and cows and farms, a large red tractor up to its axles in mud, a rooster heralding the break of day on some farm. There were also pictures of women on one wall—Madonna, Carly Simon and Mother Teresa. On the rough table in one corner were several magazines, a pair of scissors and a roll of Scotch Magic Tape. The room was so sadly ordered that her heart nearly broke. His bed sheets were soiled and balled, and so she smoothed them out as well as she could.

"When was the last time you washed these?" she asked. She tried to say it with a jaunty air, as if she were prodding a college freshman in a disordered dorm. But as soon as she said it she knew that he was no college boy, that he was just Daniel and this was his home.

"I have forgotten to wash my sheets," he said dejectedly.

"Oh, hell, never mind," she said. She turned to him and stood close. "Why don't you get a shower and then lie down and sleep? You need rest so badly, Daniel. Will you do that for me?"

"Yes, Rebecca," he nodded, now utterly defeated. He nodded and something about his dark eyes and his suffering resounded deeply in her, left her tottering numbly. She reached out for his shoulders to steady herself and realized how tall he was and how strong. Without wanting to, she stood on her toes and kissed him on his rough cheek. He pulled back slightly and looked into her gray eyes, and she felt a choking panic, as if she were at the crest of some utter loss of control and order. She stumbled backward, pushing her hair from her eyes.

"You get that shower and some sleep," she said. "I'll...would you like to go to the mountains with me Saturday?"

His eyes brightened.

"I have never seen the mountains," he said. He stared out the window and imagined the pictures of Mt. Everest from the magazine Daisy Saye had given him. Rebecca knew he must be telling the truth.

"There is a woman there I have to talk to," she said. "I need some company. You could come with me. Would you like that?"

"Yes, Rebecca," he said. He smiled in that far-off, completely genuine way that she had grown to fear and embrace. "I will shower now, and I will sleep."

"Okay," she said, feeling better.

"Goodbye, Honey," Daniel said hopefully. His glance was filled with such obvious longing that Rebecca wanted to scream.

"Goodbye," she choked. She came down the stairs, and Miss Olga was still holding the book against her breasts and idly speculating with Miss Mae about the cause of Daniel's rather spectacular disorder.

"Is he quite all right?" she asked when Rebecca came out the door.

"He is fragile as an eggshell," Rebecca said. She did not mean to say it.

"Then he will break," said Miss Mae, stifling a yawn. "He seems pleasant, to be a man." Miss Olga smiled benignly and glanced lovingly at Miss Mae, and even Rebecca was warmed by their affection.

"Yeah, well," Rebecca said. She went out to her car and drove away. Why had this summer been so odd, so filled with images of innocence? And who in the hell was Lewis Wilkins? She should go back to the hospital and see if he could talk yet.

DANIEL SLEPT ALL DAY AND DID NOT DREAM. When he awoke, he dressed and walked to Wendy's. He ate a hamburger and felt better, then he headed downtown, not thinking. The night was hot again, and the air full of water. A few cars grumbled past, one of them full of shouting men. Daniel whistled. He was going no place. He stopped at the First Baptist Church to get saved, but the doors were locked, and so he shook the door handle of a tire dealer. He was looking in the windows after having shaken the doors when he realized you could not get saved at a tire store. Oh, he said. He walked up the street to First Methodist and it was locked, too, so he walked across Hancock Street to the Main Post Office and went into its massive stone lobby and saved himself while kneeling in front of the stamp machines. While he was there, murmuring words from any Bible chapter he could recall, a tired-looking woman wearing squeaking sneakers came inside, heading toward the machines, but when she saw Daniel she turned around and left, cursing around a cigarette that bobbed in her mouth.

Daniel could not unscramble the Bible verses he had learned at Greenvale, and he said, "Blessed are they who live by bread alone. Yea, though I walk through the valley of the heavens and the earth, and God saw that it was good. Amen."

He stood up and put his cap back on, having removed it in the presence of the Almighty. Daniel had eaten and been saved again and felt much better now, so he decided to take a walk.

He didn't know how he got in front of Olive's Tea Room, but the music inside seemed to be drumming out his name: Dan-i-el, Dan-i-el, Dan-i-el, so he went inside.

Harry Carlson was sitting at a table with Leon Kretchnik and Elaine Flye. Leon had been a student at the University since 1976, majoring principally in philosophy, zoology, pre-law and insurance. He was heavy and nearly bald and had a way of talking as if his tongue were about to fall from his mouth, gulping the words down. Elaine was married to an importer who spent most of his time overseas and who had long before given up on keeping her satisfied, and she spent most of each week wandering around bars looking for young boys and trying to stay drunk. She prided herself on sleeping with at least three different men a week, though she had never slept with Leon, which would have been silly. Leon and Harry were both sexless. Harry claimed to be painting a history of the bars in Athens, but there was no real evidence he had ever painted anything.

Olive's Tea Room was a narrow bar without character and without music, except for a jukebox which was only rarely played. Tonight, a lonely truck driver looking for a woman was keeping it going, to the dismay of the regular patrons. Elaine had already offered herself to the truck driver, who declined after looking at her coarse features and the thick mascara over her eyes. Elaine's teeth were stained from tobacco, and though she might have looked good some years before, she now looked worn out.

Daniel came inside, and Harry Carlson spotted him immediately, wearing his baseball cap and standing next to a huge stand-up cardboard poster of Spuds McKenzie.

"Saint Daniel!" Harry cried. Daniel smiled and waved when he saw Harry and the others sitting at a table in the corner. He put his hands in his pockets and walked toward them. Harry stood drunkenly and met Daniel halfway, put his arm around his shoulder and escorted him back to the others.

"This is Saint Daniel," he said. "And this is Leon and Elaine."

Daniel took off his hat and crumpled it in his hands, and they saw the cuts and bruises.

"Jesus Christ," said Elaine.

"Jesus Christ," nodded Daniel. "My soul was just saved by Jesus Christ."

Leon groaned. "Religion?" he cried. "I thought that was all over now. Is that still with us? Sectarianism? Dogmatism?"

"Toggle is lost," Daniel said engagingly. Elaine, who enjoyed disorder, grinned approvingly and patted the seat, and Daniel sat.

"What in the hell happened to you, sweetheart?" she asked. "You look like you got run over by a sleigh and twelve tiny reindeer."

"I would like to have a beer," Daniel said, and he pulled his last ten-dollar bill from his pocket. Leon and Harry all but pounced on it, screaming for the waitress, a tired woman named Doris who took the bill, brought them three pitchers and fresh frosted mugs. Leon poured the beer, and Elaine slid nearer to Daniel.

"I was lost, and Hazel Agnes took me to the place where I had the little red calf."

Elaine laughed riotously. She lit a cigarette. Daniel thought she smelled like an ashtray.

"This is great," Elaine said. "I might have to take you home, sugar."

Leon grinned cadaverously. Harry stood up and held the beer out over the filthy table. The jukebox was playing "Free Bird" for the fourth straight time. Harry cleared his throat and began to declaim in a voice he took to be like Lord Olivier:

"Little Lamb, who made thee?
Dost thou know who made thee?
Gave thee life, and bid thee feed,
By the stream and o'er the mead;
Gave thee clothing of delight,
Softest clothing, woolly, bright,
Gave thee such a tender voice,
Making all the vales rejoice?
Little Lamb, who made thee?
Dost thou know who made thee?"

Daniel knew what Harry was talking about: Oconee Hill was full of lambs, marble pets with woolly stone and peaceful eyes. Daniel stood and clapped and clapped. Elaine laughed so hard she slid into a coughing fit, and Leon kept touching his left earlobe with his index finger, a nervous habit of long standing. The truck driver, who was holding on to the jukebox listening to "Free Bird," whirled angrily at Daniel.

"How about shutting up?" he shouted.

The room was suddenly quiet, and Daniel sat down. Elaine's harsh laughter erupted again, and the truck driver swore and put in another fifty cents. Slowly the talk resumed, and Daniel drank his beer in two yeasty gulps.

"Let's get out of here," Elaine said. Neither Harry nor Leon moved or said anything. Elaine leaned to her left and kissed Daniel on the neck, and he felt his heart beating very hard; she loved him. He just knew it. "You'll come with me, won't you, sugar?"

"Yes, Elaine," Daniel said.

"Yes," she almost hissed. She drained her beer, got up and all but pulled Daniel from his seat.

"Ah, how easily our saints fall these days," mourned Harry. "Saint Daniel hath seen the darkness."

"Religion," muttered Leon. "Pablum for those who have never had a thought."

"I have a thought," said Elaine, arching her eyebrows.

Her words were slurred, and Leon only shook his head as she put her arm around Daniel and they went outside into the late August night. Elaine's husband had recently bought her a new Volvo so she would leave him alone, and it was parked between a Jeep and a Ford Ranger pickup. She walked unsteadily to her car and got inside. She never locked it, preferring to hope someone might steal it and irritate her husband beyond measure. She knew he was having an affair with a nurse, but it meant nothing to her anymore. The tenderness of their early years had dissolved in the mist of whiskey and loneliness. She and Daniel got in, and she backed out and drove down the street. She glanced at Daniel, who was staring straight ahead with his hat down too far over his ears.

"Saint Daniel," she said, barely stopping at a red light next to a new-music hangout. "Where is it you work, Sugar?"

"I work at Oconee Hill," he said. "I clean the people who live there." That was wrong, and her choked laughter made his face feel hot. "I mean, I take the plants away from their…beds…I clean off where they lie."

"You clean off graves?" she brayed.

"Yes, Elaine," he said. She lit a cigarette, and the car filled with blue smoke.

"I guess somebody's got to."

"Thank you, Elaine," he said. She lived in Five Points, a neighborhood where anybody with money lived in Athens, and as she pulled into the long driveway, she felt herself being pulled down into the night. Often, her husband found her on the lawn and had the yard man haul her inside after a night in the dew. She stopped the car not long before it would have slammed into the corner of the garage.

"Damn," she said, and put the car in reverse, jolting it back away from the garage. She turned the car off but put it in neutral instead of park, and it rolled a foot and gently thudded against the side of the garage.

She barely noticed. She leaned against the door and looked at Daniel. He could see her in the moonlight. Her face seemed suddenly hideous, and he could not believe it when she opened her blouse and waved a fat, shapeless breast at him. "You want some of this?"

"I will be loved," Daniel said. He wanted to run.

"Loved," she said. Her face became a mass of gums and laughter and her eyes flew wide. She clutched her breast in one claw and waved it in a circle at Daniel. "Love," she said and fell back against the door, belched loudly and was suddenly asleep, snoring heavily.

Daniel felt a deep horror coming upon him, and he knew it was the knowing. *Yes, it was coming up like a man rising from deep in a pool, plowing upward to break the surface with his face.* He opened the door and ran down the driveway and saw that he was in a place with large old houses. Lawn sprinklers hidden in the thick sod chugged spurts of water. He breathed very hard and wept as he ran down the street. *Had Elaine died? Had he in some way killed her?*

He stopped under a streetlamp's umbrella of light and saw a lawn party at the next house. A string of cars was parked down the street. Flambeaus lit the sculptured yard, and men and women were dressed in grass skirts. Hawaiian music thudded from somewhere. The party had spilled from the back yard around front, and small clusters of partygoers talked and laughed. A woman shook from side to side, dancing. Daniel groaned and held on to the utility pole and closed his eyes to make the knowing go away. When he opened his eyes it was still there, and more people were dancing in their grass skirts. He ran back up the street past Elaine's house, but he did not look down her driveway as he passed.

His heavy-footed gait carried him through the neighborhoods, though the smell of meat roasting on gas grills. Lights were on in the houses, and he could see people watching television. A gray-haired woman opened a front door and gently set a large yellow cat on the porch. It licked its shoulder once and lay its ears flat, annoyed. Daniel walked on until he came to the Waffle House at Five Points and recognized Milledge Avenue. He knew where he was now. *How do I know where I am? Yes, I know.* He was terrified to know. He walked down the sidewalk, knowing exactly how to get to his house on Hancock Avenue.

Milledge Avenue is lined with sororities and fraternities in antebellum mansions with white columns and spacious lawns. Rush was under way, and at each sorority, dozens of clapping and singing girls swayed and smiled. Daniel stopped, mouth open, at the first sorority house and watched for a while and then walked down the sidewalk. A woman wearing a skimpy jogging outfit came past, frightening him. He passed other houses with singing girls, and they all seemed beautiful and blonde, perfect and happy. Their singing was so beautiful he could believe it was the voice of angels. The music calmed him, and he walked more slowly down Milledge until he came to Hancock and then to his house.

Julio Gomez was sitting on the porch watching the cars go by. Daniel nodded at him, and Julio started talking rapidly about how much the weather reminded him of Juarez, but Daniel went inside and slowly up the stairs to his room. Inside, he walked into the bathroom and used it and then, as he was zipping his pants back up, saw his face in the mirror over the sink. He took the cap off and clenched it in his hands. His face was battered and stained with tears, and he touched the reflection of his face in the glass.

"I am so ugly," he cried. He took off his clothes in his room and hung them over the chair and remembered Iris and Odessa and Rebecca and Annie. He did not think of Hazel Agnes until he was nearly asleep.

TWENTY-TWO

HEAVY DARK CLOUDS SWEPT LOW ACROSS THE SOUTHERN SKY. Rebecca had raised the top on her MG before picking up Daniel at Oconee Hill. Frank didn't mind letting him go for a day. It's like therapy or something, he had told Rebecca, and she had only smiled and arched her eyebrows and wondered who needed therapy more.

From the moment he fell heavily into the seat, Rebecca sensed that something profound had changed in Daniel. He no longer seemed so defenseless and doe-eyed, and when she asked how things were going, he nearly sneered. For the first few miles, they listened to a tape of *Don Juan* by Richard Strauss, and Daniel stared out the window, chewing on his lower lip.

"You okay?" Rebecca asked. Near Clarkesville, the mountains always came into view, but today they were obscured by the cloud cover. She glanced at him and saw a brief sparkle of light in his eyes.

"I was," he said.

"What do you mean?" she asked.

"It is not important," he said.

Strange man, she thought; this doesn't sound like Daniel at all.

"It's important to me," she said.

"Why?" he said. "Do you love me?"

She was stunned by the sharpness of his words and their unexpected impact. She inhaled deeply. A field of crows exploded, and the air around them was full of wings.

"What's brought this on, Daniel?" she asked. "What's happening to you?"

"Love lifted me," he said very softly. "When nothing else could help, love lifted me."

"That old hymn," she said, trying to change the subject. "Did you know Lawrence Dale used to sit in his mother's rocking chair and sing hymns for hours when he was a little boy? I told you about him. He's the man I'm writing about. The woman we are going to see used to be his...friend."

"He still her friend?" Daniel asked.

"He died, Daniel," she said.

"Oh," he said. "Then he is happy now."

"Don't say that," Rebecca scolded. She felt sick at what was happening to Daniel, but she did not understand it. "Life is the only thing sacred in this world. We have to believe that. Life and love."

"Believe," said Daniel. He looked away from her at the heavy clouds. That morning, when he had awakened, he felt the knowing inside him, felt his old life shed as a snake sheds its worn-out skin, and he had known that every broken hinge of his life would hurt now and forever. He had gotten up very early, dressed, and walked to Oconee Hill and climbed over the fence even before Frank had unlocked the gates. He had sat high on the hill and watched the sun come up, thinking of Hazel Agnes and Rebecca and light. He sat near Baby, but he didn't pull the ravenous weeds away; soon, the grave would have disappeared to anyone but someone looking for it. No one was looking for Baby. When the sun came up, Daniel had stared dry-eyed around him and realized that God was not love as they had taught him at Greenvale, nor was the embrace of another body love. The only love that finally embraced every human soul was death, the only beauty the narrow sweetness of the grave. He had sat for a long time listening to a mockingbird, thinking that it was singing a secret song to him, but he no longer knew secret songs. If he could just push the knowing away, he might understand the bird's cry, but he could not push it away. He knew for the first time in the full light of his heart who he was, where he came from, and why he could not live in the harsh glare of such an unforgiving world.

"What's wrong?" she asked. She reached out and touched his arm, and he looked at her hand as if it were a certain talisman from a world he could never have, and he traced the veins with his rough finger and then looked up at her, and his eyes were filled with tears. "Oh, Christ, Daniel, let's talk about something else." She felt her hands trembling on the steering wheel. "Be a lamb again for me and let's talk about something else."

"Little lamb, who made thee?" he said.

Rebecca stared at him in disbelief.

"That's Blake," she said. "Where have you heard Blake? Did you read that on a tombstone? Is that where you saw that poem, Daniel?"

He turned away from her and stared wordlessly out the window. Rain had begun to fall as they crossed the Tallulah River into Rabun County. The mountains swelled around them on either side of the road, tall firs and hemlocks and pines thrust into the rain. When she came into the Clayton city limits, she looked up where Black Rock Mountain should be and saw only a cloud, the stone precipice lost up there hundreds of feet above them. She drove around town and into Mountain City, turning left at the sign that said "Black Rock Mountain State Park." Daniel said nothing as she then took another left and drove down the long road up to Rachel Benjamin's house. When she stopped, the rain began to drum on the roof of her car with a throaty roar.

"Here we are," Rebecca said. "Try to be nice, even if you aren't feeling well today, okay?"

"Okay, Rebecca," he said.

They got out. Rebecca grabbed her tape recorder and dashed to the door, then turned to see Daniel lumbering heavy-footed behind her. She had never in her life seen a more graceless man, and yet there was an honesty about his awkwardness that was endearing. Before she could ring the bell, the door opened, and Rachel was standing before them, smiling, wearing an orange pants suit. She had lost weight since Rebecca and Annie had been up weeks before, and her eyes were going dull. *She's dying,* Rebecca thought.

"Come in out of the rain," Rachel said in a sepulchral voice. "This is a wretched day." They went inside, and Rebecca took Daniel by the arm and turned him toward Rachel.

"This is my friend Daniel Mitchell," said Rebecca.

"Daniel," said Rachel, shaking his hand. He pumped it twice and nodded, pursing his lips. "I'm Rachel Benjamin. Are you a professor, too?"

"Hello, Rachel," he said. "No, I'm a dummy."

Rebecca turned sharply to him, mouth slightly open and her eyes flashing. "He's not been feeling well," she said. "He's my friend, and he works at Oconee Hill, that big cemetery in Athens. Did you ever go there?"

"Come in," Rachel said, and they walked into her comfortable living room, and she and Daniel sat on the sofa, while Rachel settled in a chair across from them. She has grown frail, Rebecca thought.

"Indeed I have been there," said Rachel. "Larry did readings in Athens several times, and once I met him there, and we took a long walk in that cemetery. It's very beautiful."

"I didn't know that," Rebecca said.

"Would you like coffee?" Rachel asked.

"Yes, we would," said Rebecca. Rachel disappeared and Rebecca sat up and touched Daniel's sleeve. "Okay, what's wrong with you? What happened? Are you mad about something?"

He looked at her with deep affection and shook his head. "I cannot tell you," he said. "You would hate me, Rebecca."

"What are you talking about?"

"It is all over."

274

"What's all over?"

"I remember too many things," he said, turning away from her and looking out the window.

Rebecca's skin felt as if it had been scrubbed in ice.

"What?"

"I have the knowing," he almost cried. He grabbed her arm and tried to pull her to him. "Please help me. Please. Please. I need for you to help me."

"Daniel, stop," she hissed. She tried to pry his fingers from her arm and felt afraid of him for the first time. His strength was terrible. "Please stop. Let go of my arm, Daniel."

"Please help me? Please?"

"Let go," she said, her voice rising. "What do you want me to do?" He finally released her, and she slid a foot away from him on the sofa, the fear now showing in her eyes. "What do you want from me?"

"I cannot stand it," he said, "I cannot hardly stand it no more."

"Get hold of yourself," she said angrily. He turned away from her and settled back on the sofa. Rachel came into the room, barely able to hold on to a large tray on which were two cups of coffee. She is still working at the civilities of life, Rebecca thought. It was painful to watch her set the tray on the coffee table and then totter breathlessly to her own chair.

"I'll let you fix it the way you want to," Rachel said, pointing at the silver cream pitcher and sugar bowl.

Rebecca fixed her coffee and plugged the tape recorder into the wall. Daniel moved forward and took his cup and cradled it in his hands and blew at the steam, which moved away like a storm over a lake and then came back.

"This is wonderful," said Rebecca as she sipped her coffee.

Rachel didn't reply directly. "I want to get this over with," she said. "I've never told what happened to a soul, and it has been killing me for nearly a quarter of a century. I lay awake all night last night thinking of Larry and that night."

"Okay," said Rebecca. Daniel stood up and walked to the window and looked out at the shrouded mountain that rose straight above them. Rebecca pushed play and record on the machine and it began to whirl silently.

"Is it working?" asked Rachel.

"Yes," said Rebecca.

Rachel inhaled and then sighed and closed her eyes for a moment and then opened them. Rebecca thought, *God don't let her die without telling it all to me.* She looked over at Daniel, who stood motionless by the window.

"All right," Rachel said. "I had seen it coming for weeks with Larry. He had periods of serious depression, and he was convinced that his career was at an end. He had a contract with Harper and Row for a novel, and he couldn't finish it, you know. It was a book about his own childhood and his mother, and his relationship with his family seemed so perfect—yet there was something dark about it. His father had died not long before that of cancer. And his mother had the disease, and then Larry found out he had it, too."

"He was confirmed with cancer?" asked Rebecca incredulously. "I never heard that."

"He never told anyone but me," Rachel said. "And that only added to his gloom. He felt as if the world of his childhood had died and that the simple times were gone forever. He kept saying over and over, 'Everybody will know everything. There will be no sense of discovery.' I didn't believe that, of course, but my God, Larry did. To him, we were losing the Garden. I told him Milton had fretted over the same thing and not to worry, but it did no good to tell him that.

"So he began to drink. He'd come up here on weekends, and I would drink with him, and I would hold him while he cried about his disease and told me how the world was decaying before his eyes. He felt like he was in a Bosch painting. Now, I recognize it as clinical depression, but then I felt Larry was the only thing I had to live for.

"He wrote dozens of poems up here then. They've never been

published, and I will give you copies before you leave. It was the best stuff he ever did, and I've loved them alone for all these years."

"My God," Rebecca said. "Dozens of unknown poems?"

"Oh yes," Rachel said. "We would go up on the mountain, and he would take a spiral notebook along and sit there and stare for hours and hours at the landscape and write poems about life and death and love. I felt as if I were in the presence of something very rare and wonderful. It's odd, you know, but I came to believe that I had been born to be the handmaiden of his works, to be Larry's muse or whatever, to inspire him and usher his works into the world. But our life together was so special and private that I could never tell anyone. And then after he died, I found that everyone considered Larry a minor sort of regional writer—you know, the hillbilly poet and novelist. I'm sure you've run across that."

"Yes," said Rebecca.

"Anyway, late that summer of 1963, Larry started to look like a ghost when he'd drive up here from Mount Russell. He'd all but quit eating, and he drank heavily. We'd both been sitting around drinking for a couple of weekends when he first decided life was too much with him."

Daniel, who was still standing by the window, now set his coffee cup carefully on the floor and walked toward the front door, opened it and went outside. Rebecca saw him go, but she didn't dare interrupt Rachel Benjamin from her narrative. Daniel could go outside into the fragrant world of Rachel's garden and inhale the beauty of the place.

He went down the steps and looked around him. The rain had stopped, and the clouds broke up over the top of the mountain. Dazzling sunlight poured down the hemlocks and pines and stroked Daniel's eyes. He blinked and looked around him at the dark green world. Above, just a little higher, were the hardwoods not yet beginning their ascent into the colors of flame. Daniel had never seen mountains, and they seemed to rise forever above him, like the pictures he had studied in the books at Greenvale. He thought of those books and his life.

Daniel walked behind Rachel's house and looked upward. The first turn in the road to the top of Black Rock Mountain was only about fifty feet above him, and he climbed up the slope easily, turning back every few steps to see the changing landscape. He could see the rain clouds drifting across the valley behind him, trailing showers. He climbed higher and came out on the road, which was very smooth and winding. The trees were wet, and when the wind blew, they rained, and he felt the water on his shirt, in his hair. He had left his cap in Rachel's living room. He walked along the road, and it wound steadily upward in the sunlight, but then the sunlight was gone, and it was dark again, and Daniel could feel the water heavy in the air.

Birds called his name. He thought of clapping, but when he raised his hands, he only looked at them for a moment and then let them fall to his sides. A family that had driven to the top went past him on the way down. He saw a golden-haired little girl in the back seat crying, and he turned and watched the car until it disappeared around a curve. Birds called his name. The wind whispered in the tallest branches of the pines and cedars.

"Amazing grace," Daniel sang, forgetting the tune, "how good the sounds that saved a wretch like me. I...." He could not remember anymore. He always remembered the wretch part, because Mr. Wilkins had always said ... Mr. Wilkins. Daniel wept.

The woods were full of stones. They lay before him, dappled in the sunfall, stretching up the mountain toward its rocky face. The aroma of earth and trees and wind and air filled his nostrils and his heart as he walked upward. This was like the country, where he had always wanted to return. He wanted to fly into some new identity, to become a stone or the dirt or rain. He remembered how rain fell and then rose again into the sky and then rained again. Mr. Wilkins had said that rain falls forever as the living gift of God, falls, rises back into the sky, comes right back down again. That would be good, Daniel thought, to fall wherever he pleased, to be part of the growing season, to be snow in the winter. He could fall anywhere, at Annie's house, over the tall building where Rebecca lived, over

Greenvale and its ancient trees, over all the places he had been lost in his life. He could fall over Oconee Hill and wash among the stones of his friends there, past Baby and C.D. Barrett and Henry May Long and Howell B. Cobb, FIRST ATHENS BOY GIVING LIFE IN THE WORLD WAR. He would go past all of them and into the river where Woodrow Faust fished for catfish, and he would go inside of the catfish and drain off its silvered skin as Woodrow pulled it from the river and laughed at his good luck. He would fall back in the river and go with the other water down the Oconee toward south Georgia, and he would flow past where Annie's father lived, past Greenvale and the other towns and then into the sea. He remembered how it worked. The sun would harvest the rain from the seas and bring him back over the land and once again he would fall on Oconee Hill. *Oh!* he thought, *that is what love means.*

He pulsed between rage and a transcended love for things he could never hold. His stride was faster on the road to the top of the mountain. Another car came down the shiny filament of asphalt, and when it passed, he saw that it had white words all over it and that a woman was sitting very close to the man who drove. He nearly ran now, higher. The road ascended in great loops, and Daniel could see where it came out higher up, and so he scrambled up the steep slope, taking a short cut off the curves. His feet became sure on the wet stones, and he came out on the last rise before the crest. He looked north.

Now, Daniel could see the real mountains, those magnificent peaks of the Blue Ridge that stretched from Mountain City up past Dillard and Rabun Gap and into North Carolina. *Oh!* he cried, stunned by the grandeur. His ears were full of birds who sang languidly, their music hanging from every shimmering tree. Clouds descended and the sky grew dark, and then a wind arose and the sun came out again, and the forest filled with jewels.

He walked up the road, swinging his arms like a child. The woods to his left were full of stones that stretched down the mountain, stones crusted with lichens. Vines enfolded the rocks in their tendrils, and Daniel felt an echo of emotion that rang in his heart, resounded like a brass bell. He came to the top. On his left was the welcome station. His ears felt full of cotton. Once at Greenvale he had had an earache, and Mrs. Wilkins had filled the ear with cotton and made him lie on that side for an entire day. He walked more slowly now. The hike had left his knees trembling and rubbery, and his hands shook, too. He knew that this was the top of the world.

TWENTY-THREE

RACHEL BENJAMIN CLOSED HER EYES AND LEANED FORWARD in the chair, her hands gripping each other so tightly her knuckles seemed to Rebecca like fine ivory. Rachel shook her head, and her voice became nearly inaudible.

"Larry and I made a pact," she whispered. "He said that he was dying and that he did not want to watch himself slide slowly into the darkness. He wanted to leap, as a deer leaps. He said that over and over. It would be like a deer leaping a creek, and he would come down in a different place. That was all death would be, to leap and come down in a different place.

"I was convinced. Oh my God, he could make me believe anything. There was a poem by Faulkner, of all people, that Larry would stand in my garden and recite for me. We would lie in the dark of my room after lovemaking, and he would recite it. He spoke it more and more as he came closer to the end. Faulkner had died only a year before, and Larry had been devastated. He was inconsolable."

"What poem?" choked Rebecca. She felt hypnotized, unable to move, and her pulse raced.

Rachel cleared her throat and sat up, eyes bright with unspilled tears.

"If there be grief, let it be but rain
And this but silver grief, for grieving's sake,
If these green woods be dreaming here to wake
Within my heart, if I should rouse again.

But I shall sleep, for where is any death
While in these blue hills slumbrous overhead
I'm rooted like a tree? Though I be dead
This earth that holds me fast will find me breath."

Rebecca got up and came to Rachel, sat at her feet and held her hands. Rachel's eyes were full of light again.

"Oh, how beautiful he could make those words," Rachel said, trying to regain her composure.

Rebecca felt as if she were dying inside.

"I'm all right. Truly. Let's finish our story." Rachel cleared her throat again. "And you're between me and the recorder."

Rebecca tried to laugh, but as she went back to the couch, she felt as if her bones had changed to flower stems, as pliable as those of early spring. She glanced up, looked out the window for Daniel, but did not see him. "I'm fine," she said, not believing it.

"Let's finish our story," Rachel repeated softly. "Larry convinced me that he was dying, and that in death all beauty came together and that we shed the horror of life like a roof sheds rain. He was going to leap into the new world, but he was afraid to go alone. Of course that sounds silly now. Everyone is afraid to die—because you always go alone."

Rebecca looked at the frail woman before her and was nearly stunned at her courage.

"So quite simply, Larry and I made a pact," said Rachel.

"A pact?" said Rebecca.

"A pact of death," said Rachel as if she was surprised Rebecca did not understand. "He said we must come to God as we were made. He didn't believe in God anymore, and neither did I, but God was the tissue that held our lie together, so we allowed him to exist briefly. We stood out in my backyard one night in early November that year, completely naked, with our arms over our heads, and we swore to go with each other into the new world. We planned it all very well. He wanted it to be a vast symbol that people would recognize immediately as love, that this earth is not a fit place for those who truly love."

"My God," said Rebecca. "What happened?"

"Larry got two pistols," she said. She leaned forward again and held her head in her hands and looked at the floor. "I don't know where he got them, but they were both .38s, for the record. We went up the mountain so often for picnics and such that he decided that we should kill ourselves on the face of the cliff up there.

"That whole night seems now like the most terrible dream of any life. He cleaned up his affairs at Mount Russell that morning, and all day I sat in this window staring at my flowers, trembling uncontrollably because I loved Larry terribly. But I did not want to die. You have to understand, I was only in my mid-thirties. When I saw his car pull up, I ran into the bathroom and threw up. So much for my bravery.

"Larry was absolutely transfigured. He came into the house, and his face shone as if it pulsed with some brilliant inner floodlight. He talked wonderfully about the entire literature of death, about the Bible and its words on it, the Koran, and his own works. He was only sorry he would not finish the novel about his family, but he couldn't have done that anyway. He paced and paced, and talked, and I grew more and more unsure that death was the release. I remember it was a glorious autumn day, and that birds sang, and the trees that had leaves left absolutely rang with color. But in Larry's presence, I felt as helpless as a matchstick in a hurricane. He was my life, you understand.

"We had a final supper together here. I cooked up steak and potatoes and a fine salad. He ate heartily, I ate nothing, and he was so upset with me. As evening came, he grew more and more transfixed, as I grew more and more anxious. You have read that he killed himself wearing a tuxedo. He'd bought it in Atlanta a few weeks before. I wore a white gown. It was all his idea, to be married by death, as if death were some great Minister who bound us eternally together. I thought it was strange and sad, but he insisted.

"We stayed here until about ten and then drove to the top in his car. On the trip up, we sang hymns, and I tried to think of my family and what they would say. I didn't want to die, but I couldn't leave or try to persuade Larry to forget it.

"No one else was up there but us. This was before it was improved very much, you understand, before it was patrolled very carefully as it is now. The night sky was filled with millions of stars, and Clayton twinkled below us. We walked out onto the rock, and Larry was quiet and happy. He gave me one of the guns, and we were to count three and pull the trigger. He would kill himself, and I would kill myself at the same time.

"I began to cry, and I begged him to kill me first and then kill himself."

Rachel still looked at the floor, and Rebecca stared in horror.

"I told him I would let him kill me, and I closed my eyes and almost shouted for him to do it, and he brought his gun up to my temple, and for one moment it was almost as if I had died. I felt an elation that I have never felt since. But he hesitated, and I understood then the enormous horror of it all, and maybe Larry did, too. He lowered the gun and said that he could not do it, that if he shot me it would be murder, which was a sin. Odd words to you, I imagine. Then he reminded me of our pact, that he expected me not to betray him now.

"And so he stepped back from me, and we turned and looked out at the valley and the stars. And he commanded me to prepare for it. He said that our love was greater than the night, greater than life or death and that it would be sealed for eternity. We would count to three and fire. He put his pistol to his right temple. I did the same."

Rachel sat up suddenly, and her face seemed twisted by the grief of memory, and Rebecca wanted to scream, to return in time and stop it all.

"All we had to do was count to three and move one finger a quarter of an inch," Rachel said. "But something strange happened. As I stood there in the moment of death, I felt as if I were being filled with light and life. I felt as if the world were more beautiful than I'd ever seen it and that I was regaining some kind of innocence, perhaps even regaining the Garden.

"Larry and I stood there with the guns to our heads, and he looked at me, and even though it was very dark I could see him smile. He said the word 'Love,' out loud, as if it were a talisman, and then he turned away from me and said 'One' very loud.

"I was completely unprepared for it. When he said 'Two,' I closed my eyes and gripped the gun. I was waiting for the word 'Three,' and I never heard it. I suppose if I had, I might have gone through with it."

Rebecca wanted to get out of the house, to run away, to forget that she had ever heard of Lawrence Dale.

"What I heard was the gunshot. It sounded like a cannon. I couldn't believe he'd pulled the trigger, and he just fell like a sack of potatoes. I was standing there looking at him, still holding the gun to my head. I couldn't do it, and I had not had the strength to stop him. Do you realize that I stood there and let him kill himself? I leaned over him and spoke his name, half expecting him to leap up laughing, but he'd already leaped into the next world. The bullet had blown half his head away, that marvelous brain that had given me so much.

"I knelt in the blood and cried and cried for him. Oh, it was gory. And then I couldn't bear it any more. I took my gun and started to walk back toward my house, and then I started to run, and I fell halfway down the mountain, stumbled and fell, broke my arm in two places, but I waited two days to get it set.

"After that, I hid in this house for about a year. I had my groceries delivered, and I lost forty pounds. I betrayed Larry, at least as far as our pact was concerned. And I felt his presence with me every day, and he kept asking the same thing: Why did you abandon me? And I didn't have an answer for a long time.

"Then it came to me. Do you know what it is? It's so simple, yet life is so hard we make excuses to believe it isn't true. Human life is God. We invented God not to dream of a great father but to sanctify human life. Larry came to believe that God was Death. And in the summer of 1964, I came out of this house because I knew Larry was wrong, and that you don't stop loving those who are wrong.

"And so I came into my garden, which had become overgrown and I resolved to make it more beautiful than any place on this earth as a memorial to a man who should have lived. I wanted it to be a memorial to the God in Lawrence Dale and the God in me."

"What happened to the gun?" asked Rebecca.

"I buried it in a secret place," said Rachel. "And that will be a secret that goes with me to my own grave."

The tape came to its end and shut off, and Rebecca turned it over.

"Have you ever had another relationship with a man?" Rebecca asked.

Rachel laughed suddenly, unexpectedly. "I've been as chaste as a nun," she admitted. "I suppose it has been half to honor Larry and half simple fear that any other man would fall so short of what Larry was. If regular men are like stars, Larry was the sun. He was the most decent, honorable, reliable, talented and tortured man I ever met, and I would not let my family push me into a marriage with some convenient mogul to satisfy their financial whims."

"What happened to your family?" she asked.

"All dead now," she said. "Would you like to see the gown I wore that night?"

"You still have it?" Rebecca gasped.

"Didn't you keep your wedding dress?" asked Rachel. "Or have you been married?"

"I did keep it," said Rebecca. She smiled at Rachel. "I'm divorced, but I still have the dress."

Rachel stood up then, and they went into her bedroom, which

286

was very simple except for a magnificent four-poster mahogany bed of antique vintage. Rachel opened the closet and reached far back and pulled a wrinkled white dress out. Dark stains matted the fabric together at knee level.

"My God," said Rebecca, "is that..."

"Yes." Rachel nodded. "That is Larry. His blood, the poetry of his life. God. That is God, Miss Gentry." She put the dress away.

"What will become of that?" asked Rebecca.

"I am giving all my materials to the Mount Russell Library," Rachel said, "but I will let you use them first for the book. The dress I will burn before I go into the hospital for the final time. That will not be very long now."

They went back into the living room, and Rebecca was weak and tired. She wanted to get home, to talk to Annie or Charlie. Lawrence Dale's life was much more than she had expected to find.

"Where has your friend gone?" asked Rachel.

Rebecca had barely thought of Daniel for more than an hour. She expected to find him sitting against the base of a tree. She saw his cap on the coffee table and knew he would not be far away. "He's probably just out there in your garden," she said.

She opened the door, and they both went out into the garden. "Daniel?" She called his name. "Daniel!" She looked back and forth and did not see him. She screamed his name very loud, and then she sighed. "Christ Almighty," she said under her breath.

"Perhaps he is around back," Rachel Benjamin said. "I'll wait inside. My strength isn't much anymore."

She tottered back up the steps, and Rebecca, annoyed, went around the house. The sun moved in and out, and the trees shimmered with water.

"Daniel!"

She saw moss-covered rocks and birds that hopped across the wet grass. She also saw sunken footprints that were filling with groundwater. She stared at the prints and followed them until they reached the edge of the mountain and began to go up. *Holy Mother of God.* She scrambled twenty feet up the steep slope and saw broken twigs and scrapes where someone had climbed higher.

She screamed his name again, and again.

She climbed high, losing her breath and clinging to small trees for support. By the time she came to the road, she was wheezing. She turned and saw the valley stretching away north, the magnificence of firs and cedars and hemlocks. Muddy footprints went up the road very clearly. *Christ Almighty.* She came back down the same way, sliding ten feet or more on her bottom before staggering into the soggy grass of Rachel's backyard.

"Daniel!" she cried. It's like calling a dog, she thought angrily. He had gone up there. She went into the house and told Rachel that Daniel had apparently climbed up the mountain, and she needed to go after him, that when she got him they would be back to say goodbye.

"What is his problem?" Rachel asked.

"He's a good man," Rebecca said, "but he's very simple. He doesn't see things normally. He's all right."

"Oh," said Rachel. She sank on the sofa and closed her eyes, exhausted.

Rebecca got her purse and went outside cursing, and looking up at the mountain. *What is wrong with him today?* She backed around and drove down the lane toward the road which winds up the mountain. She drove very slowly, and soon she had forgotten Daniel and was thinking of Lawrence Dale, of the horror of that night. It was more real now than ever, palpable. How would it be to live alone with that memory for so many years? And had Rachel really betrayed him? Maybe, Rebecca thought, the book would hint that Larry had really betrayed Rachel.

She drove to the place where Daniel had climbed up from Rachel's house and saw his footprints stretching up the road. She followed them slowly, stopping the car and checking from time to time to make sure of their direction. Before long she could tell that he was obviously climbing toward the top. *What in the world would he be doing up there?*

A JEEP WAS IN FRONT OF THE RANGER STATION, but no other cars were around. Just past the building, the sheer rock face of Black Rock Mountain opened with a powerful view of Clayton and a valley below. A telescope was there, but you needed a quarter to see through it. Daniel could not believe the world below.

As a boy, he had learned of God in His Infinite Wisdom, and he had asked Mr. Wilkins what that meant. Mr. Wilkins had said God had a plan for every life, and that no man could see this plan or understand it, but it was the glue that held the world together.

Daniel looked out over the valley. This was the world as God saw it on the day of Creation, green and blue, rain and sunshine, air and rocks; this was the sound of heaven, and when birds flew higher than this, their wings grew white and they became angels. *Yes,* Daniel thought.

He felt the joyous love of heaven. What a fellowship! he remembered. What a joy divine! Leaning on the Everlasting Arms!

Daniel walked to the low chain-link fence that warned tourists away from the edge of the precipice. He stood before it with his hands in his pockets and felt his arms beginning to grow wings. *Yes,* he thought, *God's final plan is for flight.* He looked down and saw the stone all around him, one gigantic, unending stone, and he knew that it was a tomb, the grave of all men who must rise and unfold their wings.

Daniel Mitchell stood at the edge of the world. He knew many things now.

He knew that love makes you sick inside, and the living hurts more than a wound; he knew that he had known two peaceful places, Greenvale and Oconee Hill. He knew that you could die in bed from the terrible thunder of a pistol or you could die Giving Life in the World War. You could die even if you "openeth your mouth with wisdom." And yet all he wanted was love and life, the things that hurt more than any death. Men were cursed not with death but with love, Daniel thought.

If only he could grow wings! He could spread his arms and watch them flame into feathers, fly down the valley way above the houses, the ranches, the hospital. He could come even lower over Clayton and look at the shops and the houses and the dogs on the lawns. Then he could rise again and bank south toward Athens and then smell the bakery and see the football field and just past it, Oconee Hill with its old trees and scattered marbles. He could sit in the trees around Howell Cobb's grave or watch Woodrow fish for catfish, see Frank Sutton standing by a funeral tent as the last tears fell. Then he could rise again and cross the river to the trailer park, and there is Irene and Joe Dell Bailey welcoming him into their cool living room, and Randi Ambrose has purple hair again, and she is going out to have a good time, and Rob and Kelley are there, and Daisy Saye will look into the tree and see him and wave magazines at him with a smile. And he would come screeching down and rip the living eyes from Wade Rucker and watch him squirm. Daniel felt the hatred pumping in his chest.

He raised his arms slowly from his sides. His head felt as if it might explode. He closed his eyes and then opened them, and when he looked, he saw long, curling black feathers that had grown from his arms. He could fly now. *Oh!* thought Daniel. *I can fly!*

REBECCA'S EARS WENT FUZZY, and she worked her mouth to equalize the pressure. Her car's engine sounded suddenly like a toy as she drove to the top of Black Rock Mountain. By now it had become very familiar, but she had not been up here since she found out how Rachel Benjamin betrayed Lawrence Dale. She drove very slowly, and was almost past the area of open, exposed rock when she saw Daniel standing there, far beyond the chain-link fence, flapping like a bird.

"Oh, Christ! Oh, Jesus!" she cried. She stopped the car and got out, and her legs were water. Through a window she saw a park ranger in the building, his back turned, unseeing. Her heart felt like a top losing its spin, off-axis and out of control. She walked down the dark rock, which was slippery from water oozing through its cracks. Her mouth felt dry.

"Daniel!" she shouted.

He stopped flapping but did not look back toward her. He had never been surprised when some unseen person called his name.

"Daniel, stop!"

He looked down, and only two inches of stone separated him from the trees below. His head was drumming now, his veins ready to explode; he felt as if his whole body would explode. What he needed was not stone but air. He needed the benevolence of flight.

Rebecca came to the chain-link fence and called his name again. The sun went behind heavy clouds that were rolling down from the north. She felt tears come into her eyes.

"Daniel!"

He knew this time that someone was behind him, and he turned sharply, nearly losing balance and plunging over the edge.

Rebecca put her hand over her mouth and felt sick.

When he saw her, he smiled wanly. "I cannot feel this any more," he said. He shook his head slowly.

"Daniel," she said, climbing carefully over the fence, "come up here and get away from the edge. Come on."

"I am so sad," he said. "Rebecca. Rebecca. I can fly now." He laughed, and his eyes were all pupil, black and crazy with terror.

"Come up here," she said. "Daniel, come up here." She took a few steps toward him and felt the wind rise and the slipperiness of the rock.

"Can you see my wings?" he said. He flapped his arms. "Can you see my wings!" He wept.

"Yes, I can see your wings!" Rebecca said. Her voice was weak, and she felt the strong certainty that Daniel would fall. Perhaps she would fall, too. "I can see every feather."

"Wallace, don't!" he screamed. "Mother! Wallace, don't!"

He slowly raised his arms to his head as if to contain the terror of the memory. He tottered. Rebecca was frozen with fear and could not save him or come closer. His eyes rolled up in his head, and for a moment he jerked back toward the cliff, and then he fell headlong into the rock, and his skull hit with a sickening thud. Rebecca forgot the heights and knelt and scrambled to him and tried to pull him up the slope, but he was too heavy and blood was pulsing from a wound in his skull.

Rebecca began to scream. She cradled his head in her lap, and she felt the warm wetness soak through her pants. She kept scream-ing. She barely noticed the hands on her shoulders or the first drops of rain that swept along the mountain.

TWENTY-FOUR

DANIEL AWOKE AND SAW THE WORLD SWAYING IN A GENTLE BREEZE outside his hospital window. *Oh,* he thought, *how pretty it is today!*

Five days had passed since he had collapsed. He had been transferred three days before from the hospital in Clayton, suffering from high blood pressure and a serious concussion. But his condition was good. By Monday his doctor thought he could go home and be back at work in a week.

The day before, everyone Daniel knew had paraded in to see him. Irene Bailey had cried. Randi Ambrose had brought him a teddy bear with punker hair, which he loved. Daisy Saye had come with them and had brought him a *Redbook* magazine. He had been sedated, coming and going from life to the lost world of the drugged and back again.

When Rebecca walked into the room, Daniel was sitting up in bed looking out the window. He wore a large white bandage around his head that made him look ridiculously like the old painting of the patriots with drum and fife in the Revolutionary War. She had made sure he would get a private room, and he looked out upon a large water oak that graced the lawn of Athens Regional. Summer was nearly over. Soon, Rebecca thought. Soon. Down the hall by the elevator, Charlie Dominic was waiting for her with Brad and Annie, on their way to the Georgia-Virginia game.

She stood by the foot of the bed for nearly a minute before he noticed her. He smiled. The fall had hurt the bruises he had already suffered, and his face was still slightly swollen and discolored. His lip was puffy, pulling his smile askew, but it only made his face more endearing to her. What did Daniel see that made him different from other men, and was it good or evil? Did good or evil even exist?

"Hello, Rebecca," he said. He pushed himself back up, being careful not to move the tube stuck into the back of his right hand. "I did not see you come here. There is a red bird that sits in that tree, and I watched it." His eyes were full of light.

Oh my God, Rebecca thought. *Who are you, Daniel? Why can't you live in this world?*

"You did?" she said.

She sat on the edge of the bed and took his rough hand, and he looked at her, at the thick, shiny hair and her even features, her gray eyes and he thought, Yes, God made woman to look like Rebecca.

"How are you feeling?"

"I have a head that hurts," he said. "My mouth tastes dry. I am not too bad. The doctor says things I do not know. I do not remember. I was lost again, Rebecca. I get lost all the time."

"Everybody gets lost," she whispered, her eyes shining. "There's nothing wrong with getting lost."

He brightened. "Frank came to see me this morning and brought me that flower," he said, pointing toward the window.

She had not noticed the single rose beside the large arrangement she had brought the day before. The gesture seemed odd for such a rough man. Rebecca was touched.

"How nice," she said. "I am surprised."

"Oh, Frank knows very much about flowers, Rebecca," he said.

"I guess he does," she said.

"And Frank said that the back of the hill is growing up and that he needs me to come and clear away the weeds," he said. "If someone paints the stone, I will get mineral spirits and wash the words away. I will make the stones all clean again. I will always keep the stones clean."

Rebecca choked; she could hardly bear the antiseptic stillness of the hospital room. Annie's father had gone into the hospital the week before, and they didn't know when he might get out. Annie had come to Rebecca's apartment the night before, and they had stayed up late drinking, and Annie had cried for her father. Rebecca thought of him, slowly fading away.

"The cemetery needs you, Daniel," she said.

"Yes," he said. "I will. I will see the flower lady. She comes to Oconee Hill with flowers and puts them on the people there. She is their daughter or mother or something. She brings orange flowers, and she is my friend."

Rebecca could think of nothing to say, and she was just sitting on the bed holding his hand when the door swung back and a male nurse came into the room, pushing Lewis Wilkins in a wheelchair. For a moment, Rebecca did not recognize him and thought someone had been brought to the wrong room.

"He says he wanted to visit his friend," said the nurse, who was overweight and had a high voice.

Mr. Wilkins' mouth was slightly open, and he seemed to have lost weight, but his eyes were alert. Daniel let go of Rebecca's hand, and in the drowsy stillness of the hospital room, he clapped and clapped. Rebecca was afraid he would pull the tube from his hand, and she finally grabbed his arm to stop him.

"Yes," said Rebecca. "It's fine."

"He can't stay but five minutes," the nurse squeaked. "I'll be right back." He adjusted Mr. Wilkins' shirt. "I'll be right back for you, Mister Lewis, okay?"

Mr. Wilkins looked up at him gratefully and nodded. Then he returned his eyes to Daniel.

"Hello, Daniel," Mr. Wilkins said slowly, his voice hoarse.

"Mr. Wilkins, you came to see me!" Daniel was exultant. "But why are you in your pajamas? Is this Greenvale? Are we at Greenvale?" Daniel looked out the window hopefully.

"No," Mr. Wilkins whispered. "Hello, Miss Gentry."

"Mr. Wilkins," Rebecca said softly.

"This is a hospital, Daniel," he said. The nurse had left Wilkins three feet from the bed, and he struggled with the wheels to get closer, so Rebecca pushed him up to Daniel. He reached out and took Daniel's hand.

Rebecca felt suspended above them, frozen with indecision. This moment, she knew, was private, and yet she could hardly make herself move. She took two steps toward the door and sank into a black chair. Neither Mr. Wilkins nor Daniel seemed to notice she was still there.

"I have been lost again, Mr. Wilkins," Daniel said. "I fell down and hurt my head. I have seen mountains! And Hazel Agnes took me where my little red calf lived."

"I know," Mr. Wilkins said. "She came and told me herself. She was very scared, Daniel. She shouldn't have left you there. She hasn't had an easy life, but most of it wasn't her fault."

Rebecca did not try to stop the tears.

"She meant well. Everyone who ever knew you meant well. You have been a good son."

Daniel missed his meaning, but Rebecca did not, and she stood and walked out of the room and into the hall. Two minutes later, Mr. Wilkins struggled to roll himself out next to her. She trembled as she tried to make his image clear among her tears.

"What really happened?" Rebecca asked.

"I came home and found Hazel Agnes in bed with another man," he said quietly. He was looking at another place, another life. "I shot him and killed him." He closed his eyes, and tears came down his weathered cheeks. "And she became completely deranged. I let them think she had killed him, wiped the gun, put it in her hand. She became catatonic a day later and stayed that way for four years."

"But I could not live that way, either, not with the guilt. So I took our little boy to Greenvale, and I left him there. I never

296

intended to come back. I certainly never intended to work there. But I was drawn to him because of love. I wanted to protect him.

"Hazel Agnes has forgiven me, Miss Gentry. She has forgiven me for taking my common-law wife to Greenvale and saying she was my wife, for changing my name, for everything. The only hope I have in this world is that Daniel can believe in something good. Do you understand?"

She wept and nodded. The nurse came back and rolled Wilkins away. Rebecca ran down the hall to the elevator.

"What's wrong?" Annie asked, trying to comfort her. "Is he sicker?"

"He's fine," Rebecca said. Tears came down her cheeks. "I've been so wrong about so many things. Oh, Charlie! Take me out into the sunshine."

"Are you okay?" Annie asked. They walked to the elevator. An old man carrying a rose in a vase shuffled past them.

"For the first time," Rebecca said, "I think I've walked in the Garden alone."

In the elevator on the way down, no one spoke, but Annie and Rebecca looked at each other and slowly began to smile, and Rebecca realized that if life is God, friendship is peace. She let go of Charlie just long enough to hug Annie Phillips.

DANIEL STANDS IN THE EARLY MORNING AND WATCHES the red and orange leaves drift around him. He leans on a rake and looks down at Baby and smiles. His baseball cap is snugged down over his ears protecting him from the chill. Oh ! He thinks, what a pretty day this is !

He looks at the stones that stretch away down the slope at Oconee Hill, and he inhales, but the rich odor of flowers is long gone. Now, he can smell autumn, soil and leaves and cool air. He studies the colors: gray-green stones and umbers and ochres that tumble along the ridge, the high blue of the sky.

Frank is down the hill using a Weedeater, and Daniel waves at him, and Frank doesn't look up for a long time, but when he does, he sees Daniel up there like a weed drifting in the wind, and he waves back. Frank is happy to have Daniel back. Daniel walks to the grave of C.D. Barrett and says good morning and slowly reads: "IN THE SILENT TOMB, REST FOR THE SHADOW AND GLOOM OF DEATH IS PASSED."

It is fall now, and Daniel has seen the weeds begin to curl and die, and he tries to order the pieces of his life, but he has forgotten the ruins and remembers only sensations: the thin air of mountains, mockingbirds singing at Rachel Benjamin's house, the feel of water over his body behind the red calf house, the loving glance of Odessa and her smooth skin, the sensation of falling and being lost when they had gone to that house—where was that? Was it where Rebecca's friend lived? No, a sick old man lived there. Daniel sits and tries to remember where that was and who the man was, but nothing comes back. He does not even know that the knowing has gone.

A wind arises, and he feels the ecstasy of freedom sweep over him. *Mr. Wilkins was sick in the hospital, too, and he came to see me, and that was so very nice of Mr. Wilkins. He is my friend. Hazel Agnes was my friend, but she has gone away.*

Rebecca has not come to see Daniel in weeks, but he does not mind. She is like Mr. Wilkins. Once you love someone, they are always with you, Daniel believes. Even if you never seen them again, even if you never understand them or know where they came from, they will be with you forever. Sometimes when he is cleaning a stone, he feels Rebecca inside his own heart, and speaks to her in there just as he speaks to the men and the women and the children of Oconee Hill.

Daniel watches a chickadee hopping along the ground in search of seeds. *Why do birds hop,* he wonders? The bird flies up and lands on a tall marble shaft, and Daniel watches its flight until he sees a girl down the slope sitting on a flat tombstone, staring wistfully at the blowing leaves. She is not pretty, but her hair is long and auburn, full of light, and in her lap a puppy naps. She strokes its head. Daniel stares at her for a long time and then starts walking toward her, and when he gets twenty feet away, he takes off his cap. She does not know whether to run or stay.

"Hello," he says. "My name is Daniel, and I work at this place. I am glad you are here."

She stares at him, and now he can see that her eyes are red. *This means that she is sad.*

"Hi," she says softy, warily. "Is it okay for me to be here? Am I bothering anything?"

He thinks about it for a moment.

"You may not bother anyone here," he says, "because they are all under the grass and the flowers." He smiles. *That was a good answer.*

"What do you do here?" she asks. *Yes, she thinks, this is the man.*

People on campus have talked about Daniel. He belongs to this place now—or it belongs to him.

"I work in this garden," he says. "I come to these stones and keep them clean and then look at them, and they are happy to be clean."

"Stones are happy?" she asks. The puppy stretches and groans then curls back into her lap. "How could stones be happy?"

"Oh, I do not think stones can be happy," he says. She can see his face grow red. "Or maybe they can be happy. I do not understand many things. What is your name?"

"Janie," she says. "My name is Janie." She looks down at the puppy. "This is Zip."

"Hello, Zip," Daniel says. "Hello, Janie. I am Daniel." He puts his right hand over his mouth in embarrassment. "I have already told you that. I am ashamed." She smiles now. "I had a dog named Toggle, but he ran away, Janie. Can I pet Zip?"

"Sure," she says. She shakes the dog awake, and it yawns and stretches.

"Zip!" Daniel cries. "Come here, Zip!"

An echo throbs in his memory, a picture book of a boy and a girl and a dog, and large words printed on the page, something from Greenvale, from his childhood. The puppy struggles up and falls on its face from her lap and waddles over to Daniel, body wagging, head down a little. Daniel picks the puppy up and pulls it to his chest. "Look, Zip. This is Oconee Hill. This is so pretty."

He sets the dog back down, and it scampers back to Janie, who is standing now.

"Will you come back?" Daniel asks.

"I don't know," she says. "I've got to take him home and then get to class. I came over here last Sunday, and it was beautiful. It makes me feel better. Things haven't gone too well for me."

"Okay," Daniel says. She has nothing more to say, and he watches her walk down the hill and toward the gate, the puppy hopping along after her. "Janie," he says out loud. "Janie." A nice name.

Daniel stands in the shade, but he walks to a patch of sunlight that spreads between the trees. He sees a grave that needs cleaning. It can wait for a moment. He looks up and feels the sun on his face, the warm, enfolding sun.

I could be a statue, he thinks, and stand like this forever. Can you feel the sun? he asks his friends deep in the heart of Oconee Hill's shadowed silence. Yes, he hears them whisper. We feel it, Daniel. When the leaves fall, he thinks, I will rake them away. Yes, they whisper. Daniel opens his eyes and looks at the falling leaves around him.

"I am in love!" he cries.

This is the country, he knows. Any place you love is the country. In the grace of his unknowing heart, one word rises, one incandescent word that spills into the luxury of Oconee Hill. "Home," he whispers. In the moment of his heart's autumn sky, Daniel whispers it with love.

Home.